The Irreversible Decline of Eddie Socket

"This richly romantic comitragedy recalls . . . the work of Fitzgerald. Weir may have as distinguished a career (hopefully more fortunate) ahead of him."—Ray Olson, *Booklist*

"Plenty of . . . mordant humor, but none of it masks or trivializes the awful losses. . . . Affecting."—Richard Lipez, *Washington Post Book World*

"Controlled and brilliant . . . elegantly written. The elaborate plot machinery . . . is seamless."—Raymond Sokolov, *The Wall Street Journal*

"A winner . . . rollickingly funny, tender and sad. *Eddie Socket* transcends the genre of AIDS fiction. It's a book about letting go." —Bob Thompson, *Review*

"Compulsively readable . . . fresh and surprisingly funny. Weir exhibits considerable narrative skill . . . an astonishingly mature first novel [that] . . . should not be missed."—Allen Smalling, *Washington Blade*

"Fresh, funny and eloquent."—Ken Furtado, *Arizona Community Echo*

"There's no moving away from this wrenching, beautifully told story."—Carolyn See, *The Los Angeles Times*

"[*Eddie Socket*] effectively chronicles the fate of sex and intimacy among gays in the post-AIDS era."—*Kirkus Reviews*

the irreversible decline of Eddie Socket

a novel

JOHN WEIR

HarperPerennial
A Division of HarperCollins*Publishers*

A hardcover edition of this book was published in 1989 by Harper & Row, Publishers, Inc.

First HarperPerennial edition published 1991.

The Library of Congress has catalogued the hardcover edition as follows:

Weir, John, 1959—
    The irreversible decline of Eddie Socket/John Weir.—1st ed.
        p. cm.
    ISBN 0-06-016162-0
    1. Title.
PS3573. E3974517   1989
813'.54—dc20   89-45083

ISBN 0-06-092062-9 (pbk.)
91 92 93 94 95 FG 10 9 8 7 6 5 4 3 2 1

To Suzy Kitman, Ron Hufham, Mindi Dickstein, Eric Washington, and Gordon Powell; Dorothy Barnhouse, Vicki Vinton, and Patrick Godon; for Michael Quadland; for my brother, Rob; for my friend David Williams; and in memory of Bruce and Tom

* * *

I would also like to thank everyone at Sotheby's Appraisals 1985–1988, particularly Betty Byrns and Anne O'Callaghan, and my friends Michele Cherry, Jack Nussbaum, Patricia McEntee, and Kathleen Flowers.

"Then the war came and we were swept apart."

—Bette Davis in *Deception*

Although this novel is set in New York City, none of its characters represents or is based on persons living there, or, indeed, anywhere. All events and personalities are imaginary.

PART 1

Perhaps

La Bohème

Eddie Socket had his mother's sharp, slightly prominent Anglican nose, and his father's deep set, sentimental blue eyes and pale Irish complexion—standard white American features, neatly arranged but lacking authority, he felt, because of his chin. It wasn't square enough or strong enough to carry the rest of his face, which was boyish and fine. It hadn't emerged. Neither had he. He was twenty-eight years old, but he looked, and felt, and probably acted nineteen. He was still waiting for whatever miracle he thought it would take for his real life to begin.

"I want a hero," he said, in the bathtub, which was wedged between the stove and the sink in the apartment he had shared since college with his roommate, Polly Plugg. They had two rooms in a fourth-floor walk-up on Eleventh Street, near the East River. Polly slept in the back, where she had a great cast-iron bed, a drafting table, and light in the morning through a gated window. Her room was crowded with objects. Eddie, who wasn't object-oriented (he claimed), slept on a worn red Oriental rug in the small front room, the floor of which was painted white to match the walls and ceiling. He had a bicycle and a piece of industrial waste —a splintering, white-painted trolley on big rusty wheels—and a single narrow window over the sink, which gave only a little bit of light at sunset.

The sun was just beginning to shine across the porcelain sides of the tub when Eddie, who had been soaking and dozing since noon, leaned forward into the thin stream of light, blew his long sand-colored bangs unconsciously out of his face, stared at himself in the mirror Polly had tacked to the wall, and repeated, "I want a hero."

He was having a pig attack. Mirrors always activated the pig, the punishing voice inside Eddie's head, which he had tried to neutralize by giving it a size and shape, a constant perch on his left shoulder, and a voice like Mercedes McCambridge forcing obscenities through Linda Blair's innocent mouth in *The Exorcist.*

"Who am I quoting?" he said.

"Don't be evasive," said his pig. "I caught you napping."

"I never nap."

"Guess again."

"I don't nap," he said. "I was thinking of Richard the Second. He was the king who couldn't emerge. He couldn't decide. But then it was time for him to be deposed. He had had a life, after all. He called for a mirror, and said, 'How can I have been alive so long, how can I be important enough for such an event, and still look seventeen?' I just turned twenty-eight," Eddie said, softly. "I still look like a prepubescent, towheaded, drug-free Montgomery Clift."

"Don't flatter yourself," said the pig. "Montgomery Clift at least had a job. You're too lazy."

"Laziness is just subverted rage," Eddie said. "There's no such thing as laziness."

"No, of course there isn't. There's just napping in the tub all day, instead of working, or reading, or starting your day, or your life. Doesn't it occur to you that sleeping in the middle of the afternoon is a sign of something ominous?"

"Not really," Eddie said, sliding down in the tub. "Perhaps my waking landscape is evaporating."

He was tired of spending his time with a pig, but this was part of his own performance, the quotes he had set around his life. He had his little devices to keep himself out of the world. He was afraid of the world, ironically, because of how much he felt he deserved. He was a white boy, after all, an American, and he secretly had the greatest expectations. He was trapped between an overwhelming sense of entitlement and the paralyzing suspicion that his actions, whatever they were, wouldn't reverberate. So he had learned to be aloof and sophisticated, in an East Village way, part Gertrude Stein, part Charlie Chaplin, part Jean-Paul Belmondo in *Breathless*—he was wry in his charming illogic, comically inept, and casually facing despair with a gesture (in his case, the unconscious habit of blowing his bangs). That his life was filled with despair he never questioned: the despair of loneliness or the despair of boredom, the despair of having had too much of what he nominally wanted yet nothing of what he yearned for truly in his heart of hearts, the despair of being white and guilty about it, and of being generally gifted, but not specifically motivated, just inert. He could have been earnest, he thought, if he wanted, but what was the point? He didn't believe in actions; faithful imitation of real events, the exact sequence of motion and fact carefully re-created, was the closest he felt he could come to an earnest response to the world. To give himself the illusion of having a connected emotional life, he had created his punishing pig.

"Your problem is you've never been in love," Polly had said, when he complained to her, but she was impatient with unanswered questions. She was pragmatic, though she had a sense of humor that was limitlessly campy and self-amused. She could pick a phrase, or a gesture, out of contemporary culture, and wear it, or pronounce it, with exactly the right degree of joy and disgust, putting the crowded world of instant objects in place. She knew who she was in the world. Eddie, who had taken acting classes, written poetry, and failed at a series of real jobs, told himself vaguely that he was an artist. But he walked through Soho, and nothing happened. He had worked a lot of temporary jobs, gotten by on quantities of brown rice, wrapped ties at Brooks Brothers at Christmas; he had been poor in New York, without feeling gilded, or glamorous. He had been in therapy, done affirmations, marched in rallies, voted for Jesse Jackson; he had been rolfed, by a friend of a friend, but he didn't feel centered, or a part of something larger than himself. He had come out of the closet. Waiting longingly for the love of his life, he had had sex with men he liked, or didn't like, but none of them stayed, and none of it really mattered. He had stopped having sex two years earlier; he had stopped thinking about having a real job not too long after that.

But perhaps his life had begun, after all. What if it was this, just lying naked in the tub, or mindlessly word processing for one full week a month, twenty hours a day, when the bills were overdue, or sneaking into the Plymouth Theater for the second act of *Burn*

This, in which Lou Liberatore walked onstage shirtless in a pair of alpine shorts? That was leisure, work, and love, and that was a life. He didn't want to think about it; he wanted Polly to come home, so they could go to the movies. She was on a free-lance job this week that kept her sometimes until nine, but if she got home early they could go see Montgomery Clift in *The Misfits* and *A Place in the Sun.*

Lately, Eddie had been going to a lot of double features, creating his own festivals around revival house trends. For instance, during the past two months there hadn't been a week when there wasn't a film with Montgomery Clift playing somewhere. Monty was suddenly in vogue, and who knew how long it would last? Eddie tried to see the most obscure of his films. It was easy enough, after all, to see *From Here to Eternity* or *Suddenly, Last Summer,* but *Lonely-hearts* and *Freud*? There was the challenge. Of course, *The Misfits* had to be seen, whenever, wherever it played. But the night before he had tracked down *Wild River* at last, having first had to sit through *Viva Zapata!,* which was part of another festival altogether. *Viva Zapata!* had Marlon Brando rather imaginatively cast as a Mexican revolutionary. He rode white horses and wore sombreros, and stormed into Catholic churches shouting imprecations while stalking beautiful virgin women. He painted his eyelids strangely and wore a tiny mustache, but he sounded like Nebraska when he talked, and his hips were too wide, Eddie thought, for gaucho pants. Marlon Brando got to play foreigners in the fifties much as Meryl Streep did in the eighties, but her accents were better, and she stuck to Brits and Europeans. You would never catch her, say, in *Teahouse of the August Moon.*

In the middle of his meditation on Marlon and Meryl and Monty, Eddie heard the street door slam, followed by the sound of someone walking up the stairs. He knew it was Polly because the cats, Darth and 2b, who recognized her footsteps, leapt out of hiding. They were brothers with nothing in common. Darth was black with four white bucks and white antennae over his eyes, and he liked to have a lap to curl into, slowly, luxuriously, with an arm curved protectively around his spine, while he slept; 2b, a ball-playing tabby cat, had no subtext, but was charming and funny. Though they were a shared responsibility, Darth was clearly Eddie's cat, and 2b was obviously Polly's.

"Daddy's home," Polly said as she opened the door. When Polly was working, and Eddie was tubbing, she was Daddy.

"I feel naked," Eddie said.

"You are naked," Polly said, switching on the overhead light, and dropping an armload of shopping bags onto the floor. She was a nice Jewish girl from Cleveland, and her name was actually Polly Plugg. "Maybe once it was Pflug," she had said, "or maybe Rabinowitz. I have no idea. Plugg is something my grandfather saw on the side of a milk truck in lower Manhattan when he got off the boat in 1902." Eddie had met her at the end of their last semester of college, and had instantly changed his name to go with hers. He had a rather naive, perhaps even racist faith in Jews as uniformly intellectual and self-examining, and being gay he felt an affinity for anyone who had been discriminated against, historically or personally. But Polly didn't indulge his sententious ideas; she got impatient, even irritated when Eddie got romantic about the Jews. "That's so reductionist," she had said. "A stereotype is a stereotype. It's nice that yours is so exalted, Eddie, but still."

He liked her for that. He liked her for having a midwestern plainness in spite of New York and herself, Mary Pickford lost in a part that had been written for Clara Bow. She worked in film animation, and she was pixilated sometimes like a cartoon character, her gestures delightfully broad.

"Ask me where I've been spending money that isn't my own," she said.

"Where have you been spending money that isn't your own?" Eddie said, turning around in the tub. He wanted to be especially indulgent tonight, in case she was free to go to the movies.

"Bloomingdale's," she answered.

Eddie crossed his hands over his dick. "I've never been naked in the presence of a bag from Bloomingdale's."

"Well, here's your chance to get over it," she said, unwinding a scarf from her head, which was wet with new snow. Stray wisps of hair glistened. "Now ask me why."

"Why what?"

"Why a girl with a seven-thousand-dollar debt to Visa and MasterCard would spend her afternoon in Bloomingdale's."

"I assume to plant a bomb in Men's Accessories."

She pulled off her gloves and stuffed them, with the scarf, into one of her coat pockets. Then she pulled off the coat and tossed it over the stove. She gave each of her movements a little flick of self-satisfaction, snapping the scarf, rolling the gloves, perfunctorily brushing the coat. She stamped her feet and stood, triumphantly dry, in a circle of wet. Eddie, who was mesmerized by any act of self-sufficiency, real or imagined, watched her helplessly.

"I've been to Bloomingdale's," she said, bending at last to her bags, "because of a boy I met in Brooklyn, at a straight singles-only party given by someone from Oberlin you never knew."

"That includes just about everyone at Oberlin."

She unwrapped a sweater, dropping tissue paper on the floor for the cats. "This is angora," she said, giggling. She held it up to her chest. "Touch it, it's something like the kind of little dog you want to kick, the ones that women carry on Madison Avenue?"

"A Shih Tzu," Eddie said.

"Gesundheit," Polly said. "Isn't it hairy and weird?"

She was delighted. She was at her best when she was handling fabrics, or food. She had a feeling for texture and shape, a sensual pleasure in objects, which Eddie admired. She didn't have much luck with men, but she knew how to treat herself to little rewards —outrageous sweaters, new recipes for cakes and desserts, which she prepared, Eddie thought, almost magically. Nothing small and delicious escaped her enjoyment.

"Who is this boy?" Eddie said.

"That's the fascinating part. Do you promise not to laugh?"

"John F. Kennedy, Jr."

"His name is Brag. No, really. He's a trader, and he works at the Commodities Exchange, and all of them wear name tags with these queer last names when they're on the floor. I like that, 'on the floor.' His real name is William Boleslawski, but they call him Billy Brag. I wanted to know what his forearms were like, and when he asked me out on a date, I accepted." She held up a green plaid wraparound skirt. "What do you think?"

"Is this wardrobe entirely in quotes?"

"It's entirely on credit, and it's thoroughly in earnest," she said. She kicked the bags out of her way, and started changing, putting on the skirt, and a white blouse with a Peter Pan collar and lace cuffs. "I think you should meet this guy, Eddie, he's a phenome-non."

"Will I have to dress like Sandra Dee?"

She kicked off her shoes, put on the plain brown loafers she'd just unwrapped, and reached for a small red box, from which she pulled a strand of pearls.

"We started talking," she said, "about his need to be creative, even though he's a trader, and I told him I was in film, and he was absolutely enthralled. So I told him about my acting class. 'I'm taking it just for a lark,' I said, 'to remain in touch with that part of me.' " She giggled. "I said, 'My roommate suggested it,' of course not identifying you by gender. I want to remain a little mysterious. But he said, 'Acting class. Well, that's very exciting.' And Eddie, if you want to know the truth, I hate that fucking acting class. But you know, when Brag started telling me how exciting it was, and how brave I was to be doing it, I started feeling brave and excited, too, and I invited him to see me perform. Tonight. Before we go out on our date."

"He's going to your class?"

"It starts in twenty minutes."

"So what's with the sweater? You're doing a scene from *Bye Bye Birdie?*"

"He's in finance," she said. "I don't want to frighten him off. I thought I might dress a bit conservatively."

"That sweater is not conservative, it's Dress to Get Laid."

"I sort of thought it made me look like Julie Nixon Eisenhower."

"Sleazy midwestern. Polly from Parma, Ohio."

"Shaker Heights," she corrected. "Anyway, I made the effort. It's not my fault if I have no idea how a trader really dresses. Except like him."

"We're talking Captain America, here? A shiksa?"

"A shegetz."

"A WASP."

"Actually I think he's Armenian or some kind of Slav."

"But fully assimilated."

"Well, he looks very white."

"Republican, of course."

"No, I think he's a Democrat."

"Same thing. And hung?"

"I haven't seen it yet."

"At least, metaphorically hung. But he has a beautiful ass?"

"He was wearing a suit."

"You didn't see his ass? He left his jacket on?"

"All right, I noticed his ass."

"And? It's gorgeous?"

"Perhaps."

Eddie smiled. "Alas."

"Indeed," Polly said, sitting on the edge of the tub. "I do get fooled by asses."

"It's what you always do, you know," Eddie said. "You make a beeline for the righteous, literal-minded type, as long as he's shapely, and big, the clabber-headed Marlboro man who's great in the sack but has this hidden agenda. Come on, 'Billy Brag'? Three good fucks, and suddenly he's talking about things like moral imperatives. Right?"

He nodded smugly to himself. He knew how to be discouraging. He had talked her out of men before. She was the closest he had to an intimate partner in life; they did everything but sleep together. He didn't want to lose her to a trader.

"Come to the movies," he said.

But she was not so easily swayed, not anymore. For she had emerged, in the past few years, from the lumpy raincoat and shapeless hat she used to wear all the time, even indoors, looking like Anne Baxter in the beginning of *All About Eve*. If she hadn't found her self-esteem, she had learned, at least, to act as if she had. She got up from the tub and swung her hips, satirically now, like Bette Davis in *Beyond the Forest*, piling empty boxes and bags on the stove, and checking herself in the mirror.

She said, "I'm going to class."

"You'll miss the next program in the Monty festival."

"Go without me."

Eddie sank down in the tub. "Oh, well."

"You're angry," she said, turning hesitantly.

"I'm not."

"You're sulking."

"You'd better go. You'll be late for your appointment with Banco de Buttocks."

"Try on my pearls."

"They're so pure, and I'm so bargain basement."

"They're not so pure. Hold still. They're imitation."

She clasped them around his neck.

"They look expensive," he said, rolling one around between his puckered fingers. "I feel like a Kennedy. Do you feel like you're rooming with a Kennedy? Then again, you couldn't be, could you, because Kennedys are beautiful."

"Oh, Eddie, I really have to go," she said, swaddling herself again in her coat, her scarf, and her gloves.

"Yeah, well," he said. "Far be it from me to come between you and a lay."

. "It isn't that," she said, at the door. "It's just that I'll be twenty-nine in a couple of months, and I'm thinking, I'm still living here, you know . . . "

"With a eunuch."

"I didn't say that, you did. I'm sorry if your feelings are hurt. I have to go."

And she shut the door behind her. Eddie lay in the tub, listening to the sound of her banker shoes clicking down the stairs.

Hello, Larry

My name is Montgomery Clift," he said, when he heard the street door slam, and knew that Polly was gone.

"He farted all the time," said the pig. "Monty, I mean. It's true. He spent the end of his life comatose on someone's floor in Fire Island, farting uncontrollably. They just stepped over him, and held their noses. 'There goes Monty,' they said, circling wide with their drinks. He farted and farted." The pig laughed. Eddie farted, and drained the tub. He reached for the pile of mail that Polly had brought up and left on the stove. There were bills, of course, and an underwear catalog, full of beautiful men, posed differently but all with the same set of pecs. There was also a note from Dad, one of the cautionary, epigrammatic postcards he had been sending at regular intervals for the past five years, since Eddie had told him he was gay. Eddie's father was fervently Catholic. He taught religious history at City College, and mailed postcards off to his son (Eddie was an only child) on all the major religious holidays and historical dates, such as the ascension of various popes, the excommunication of cardinals and kings, the convening of Vatican II. He had an immaculate one-bedroom apartment in an Irish Catholic and Dominican neighborhood in upper Manhattan, where he kept a remarkable library, and an altar in the dining room adorned with a hand-tooled mahogany cross which looked to Eddie like an enormous pepper grinder.

He had been living apart from Eddie's mother for eighteen years, though they had never divorced. She was not Catholic at all, but western, from Sacramento. That in itself seemed to her religion enough. His parents claimed they were still in love, despite their inability to be in a room together for more than fifteen minutes without wanting to wound each other mortally, which for Eddie's father, of course, was a sin. But five or six times a year, he went out to the family home in Flemington, New Jersey, to fix a leaky faucet or patch the roof, to attend a science fair (when Eddie was a boy) or bury a dog (Eddie's mother had eleven Yorkshire terriers), and each time he stayed longer than he intended, to "give it another try." Invariably, two weeks later, he went hopelessly back to the city in silence, though Eddie's mother, who never disguised her disappointment with him, called him Bishop Disdain, or Father Shenanigans. Then six months later, they did it all again.

This had been going on since Eddie was nine, though their current separation had lasted the longest—almost from the day that he had come out to both of them. He liked to think his candor affected them—that his parents, in response to his own honesty, had decided to be more honest with each other, and themselves. But who knew what affected them? They didn't let on to their emotions, except disappointment and rage. And Eddie's father hadn't spoken directly to him in years. Eddie always called him on his birthday, but his father was never home. Eddie felt as if he had been purged from his father's life, and so he named him Joseph Stalin. He was not a communist, of course, just Catholic, though as far as Eddie could tell they were about the same—dogmatic, antigay, hierarchical, and male. Unconsciously fingering Polly's pearls, which still hung around his neck, he read the postcard.

"The dragon is by the side of the road," it said, in crabbed handwriting, "watching those who pass. Beware lest he devour you." It was attributed to Saint Cyril of Jerusalem. Then it said, "To be continued, love, Dad."

"What do I need a pig for, when I've got a father?" Eddie said. "Or vice versa."

"You're a depressive," said the pig. "You need all the help you can get."

"I'm an artist."

13

"So was Mitzi Gaynor, baby, depending on who you ask."

"You've been watching too much television."

"I've been dating the Supreme Court. You think the world can stomach one more arty little homosexual? Faggot nonsense. I can't wait until you all gets AIDS and die."

"I have made choices," Eddie said. "I have. You think I haven't made any choices with my life, but I have."

"Yeah? Name three."

"I choose to go to the movies," he said, getting out of the tub, and dropping his father's postcard on the back of the stove, along with some of the remains of Polly's wrapping paper.

"Well, that's something, at least," said the pig. "You see, if it weren't for me, you'd never get anything done."

"I've made other choices, too, without your help," Eddie said, trying to remember what they were. What were choices? Getting dressed was a choice. He went to his closet and pulled out his worn old pair of black, button-fly jeans. Then he changed his mind. "Suspenders," he said. "There's a choice," as he searched in the back of the closet for a pair of woolen tuxedo pants with bright red-and-blue–striped suspenders. They were wrinkled and covered with cat hair, but when he shook them out and put them on, they looked all right.

He borrowed Polly's clean white Indian blouse, which opened to his breastbone and displayed his chest hair, he thought, to some advantage. He also took a pair of her socks, which he rolled down over the tops of his bright pink high-topped sneakers. Then he put on his coat, a blue warm-up jacket with mustard piping, which had the name "Bruce" embroidered on the front, and the words "Pequannock Wrestling" on the back, arranged around a yellow and blue design of two brawny men wearing spandex jumpsuits cropped at the thigh, and holding each other in intimate places. He pinned his "Reagan Youth" button to the collar.

"I've had enough of you," he said to the pig, as he stood in front of the mirror and pulled at his bangs, until they lay, sort of neatly, sort of parted, to the side. He kissed the cats, and found his keys, which were under the tub. Then he grabbed a pair of handwoven woolen Pakistani gloves, from which the fingers had been heartlessly snipped, leaving only blood-red strands of thread to dangle ghoulishly.

"Okay, people," he said, Jersey style, "I'm outta here."

He jogged to First Avenue. What were his choices, he wondered.

14

He chose to cross the street against the light. Did that count? He chose to be walking quickly down to St. Marks, his jacket open to the breeze, his shoulders hunched against the snow that was falling very lightly. He brushed his hand through his hair, flipped his collar up around his ears, and tried to think in French. When he reached the theater, he looked once over his shoulder sulkily, and swung through the door, without breaking stride.

He was early for *The Misfits,* so he waited in the lobby, ordering a hot chocolate at the concession stand, and sitting on the red carpeted steps leading up to the fire door, at the far end of the long, narrow room. He stared at a framed poster for *The Razor's Edge.* It was his mother's favorite "perfectly awful" movie, a film so bad it was great. They both loved the scene in a Paris opium den (decorated Hollywood style with overstuffed pillows, gorgeous wickerwork, and fat little men in turbans) where Anne Baxter, deeply addicted and slightly morose (but splendidly dressed), looks up to see her beloved Tyrone Power come to rescue her from despair and unflattering lighting, and rasps, narcotically, "Hello, Larry." "Hello, Sophie," he says, blandly unmoved by his glimpse down into the abyss.

It occurred to him now that what he secretly liked about the scene, apart from Anne's dress and her rasp, was what his mother liked, too: the fantasy of being brought back from the edge of despair by a dark-haired lover (though preferably someone more intriguing than Tyrone Power). He and his mother were waiting for the same man. But when that man appeared, would he be indifferent to Eddie's suffering? Heroes, after all, were normally rather arrogant, and wholly self-absorbed. They were not generous or tender, just driven. But Eddie only half acknowledged this. In his heart of hearts he knew his hero would be perfect, though he was already a little bit late. "Alas," he sighed, out loud, as if he, too, had been to hell in an Orry-Kelly gown. "Hello, Larry."

"Hello, Eddie," said Saul Isenberg. "You're wearing pearls."

Eddie put his hand to his neck. He said, "Oh God."

"That's all right, darling, they do wonders for you," Saul said.

"I think not," Eddie laughed.

"To each his own," Saul said. "I thought I'd mention it, in case you didn't realize. Shall I help you out of them, Grace?"

Saul was an art appraiser. He went around from one Fifth Avenue apartment to another with a miniature cassette recorder, fixing values on things. His tapes, which Eddie transcribed at one of his word-processing jobs, were little gems of erudition. He knew the difference between a settee and a loveseat, breche d'Alep and fleur de peche.

"No offense, honey, but if you paid more than a dollar ninety-five for these, you got swindled," he said. He was a big man with tiny gestures, contained in a very tailored suit, and wearing a bow tie. His hands were everywhere. He was only six or seven years older than Eddie, but he treated him like a son, or daughter, which Eddie alternately resented and enjoyed. He had to be in the mood for Saul, and right now he felt like being alone. But Saul's cajoling was finally irresistible. He clumsily undid the clasp at the back of Eddie's neck, and clucked in mock disdain.

"They're imitation," Eddie said.

"Imitation, nothing. They're not even a clever variation on the wrong necklace. I wouldn't even call these dreck," he said, holding them out to the light. "Where'd you get them, off your Barbie doll?"

"Actually, they belong to my roommate. She's probably wondering what happened to them. Unless she's already doing the wild thing with her trader, and no longer cares. Her trader's name is Brag. No kidding."

"I have a roommate, too," Saul said, "but he wouldn't be caught dead wearing pearls, for this Mr. Brag or anyone else. Not that I would, either, mind you. But he's absolutely paranoid. He's standing over there, you see? Holding a D'Agostino bag. Anyway, that's the back of him. You want to meet the front?"

"Oh, well, I don't know."

"Sure you do, everybody does. It's one of the wonders of the world, Merrit's front. As long as you don't try and get inside of it. I'm speaking confidentially."

"I was sort of just sitting here."

"Listen, you'd be doing us a favor. We've kind of had a night. We've just come from a viewing. As in, dead body. Not that it's such an unusual thing. Actually, it would be unusual if we had not just come from a viewing, these-days-wise. Come on. Hold on to your drink." He touched his elbow, and Eddie got to his feet reluctantly. "Listen, meeting Merrit changed my life," he said, guiding Eddie across the lobby. "It could happen to you."

They moved to the opposite corner of the room, where a classic-looking white preppie with graying temples handed Saul a D'Agostino bag and frowned. He was dressed conservatively, but with a slightly 1940s flair, in pleated woolen trousers and a cobalt-blue shirt with an ivory collar. His tie was a warmer shade of blue, with imprinted red roses. He was wearing a blue and white cardigan underneath a camel's hair coat, and black wing-tipped shoes, which looked like golfing shoes, Eddie thought, yet which Merrit wore in earnest. Nothing about him was in quotes. He dressed in antique clothes as if they had been purchased new, and simply were the way one was meant to be dressed.

"This is Eddie Socket," Saul was saying, rhythmically swinging the D'Agostino bag, "my word processor extraordinaire. He may handle other kinds of equipment with equivalent finesse," he said, lowering his voice, "but then I wouldn't really know." He touched Eddie affectionately. "I've only seen him type. Eddie, this is Merrit Mather, the man with whom I voyage through the brief period of light between the twin darknesses of the womb and the hereafter. I mean, he's my lover. Is that too direct? Whadda you know, you can take the boy out of the Grand Concourse, but you can't take the Grand Concourse—"

"Saul is working out his anxiety tonight," Merrit said, frowning at Saul as he offered Eddie his palm. But the corners of his mouth were turned up in a way that made Saul's histrionics an open mockery, to be shared as a kind of joke.

"He told me," Eddie said, nervously shoving his pearls into his jacket pocket, and switching his cup of hot chocolate from his right hand to his left. "I'm sorry."

"Don't be sorry," Saul said. "Just don't be next." He twirled the bag in circles.

"Saul, you're going to break that," Merrit said, but whispering— he was now losing patience.

"Well, that would be a scene," Saul said, loudly.

Eddie looked at the bag.

"Don't ask," Merrit said.

"Yes, don't," said Saul. "Actually, it's our baby." He took it in his arms and cradled it. "We'd like to talk about it, but our therapist is undecided. Merrit's therapist."

"We've also just had a fight," said Merrit, apologizing.

"You're supposed to be running interference," Saul said.

"I guess I can see that," said Eddie, who was suddenly busy casting Merrit in *A Place in the Sun*. He was twenty years too old for the part, and he was probably, Eddie thought, fierce and ferocious, an alligator. Oh, but the hell with it. He was lovely. He was —what?—a poem, something queer like that, dark and diminutive,

17

with a heroic nose and a delicate mouth like a rose. His lips were the definition, he thought, of a rose filled with snow. Why not gush? He was art. Art, like love, he thought, could happen in a second, and occupy a lifetime. That was how Merrit struck him. He was someone who occurred with full impact all at once, and afterward existed fully only in reverberation. He was lost in a glance. Eddie already missed him.

"Why do I feel as if I were on a date with myself?" Saul was saying now.

"Because you always are," Merrit said, without malice.

Readjusting his wraparound scarf, Saul said, "It isn't polite to cast aspersions on my character when others are present." He was handling the bag, Eddie thought, the way Bette Davis used her purse to punctuate words in *All About Eve.*

"Will you stop with the bag, please?" Merrit said.

"He likes a bit of a spin."

"He?" Eddie said.

"I'm sorry," Saul said. "I tend to personify everything."

"Maybe we'd better explain," Merritt said, clearing his throat. "It's a bit delicate."

"Oh, honestly, Merrit," Saul said, "what, were you raised in gentility? Really, Eddie, I'm sorry, sometimes I forget I'm married to Mrs. Miniver. Now we're making you uncomfortable." He set the bag on the floor, but Merrit found an excuse to cross to the concession stand. Saul watched him go, as if wondering whether he should follow. "Oh, let me deal with him in a minute," he decided. Then he lowered his voice. "Inside this," he said, picking up the bag, "is a canister containing my friend Horatio. Containing his ashes, at least. He's been sitting on a shelf for seven months unclaimed. They called me up today and said, 'Nobody wants him, he's yours.' Lucky me. And, well, I meant to take him home before the viewing, but . . . New York, you know, you run to this, you run to that, you live out of your briefcase, your knapsack, whatever. So I took him shopping and I took him for a fast slice of pizza, and then I took him to the viewing. He's really a much nicer person now that he's twelve inches high. You want to see? It isn't so bad."

"Saul," Merrit said.

"You stay right here, honey," Saul told Eddie. Then he went over to Merrit, leaving Eddie with Horatio.

Eddie finished his hot chocolate slowly. He could hear them talking, softly, heatedly, but he didn't want to know what they were saying. He looked at the bag. He couldn't believe what Saul had told him, but he wasn't about to check. Anyway, he was still considering Merrit, who, unlike himself, was three-dimensional—not really Montgomery Clift, not flat like an image on the screen, but someone whose actions reverberated in the actual world. Eddie keenly felt his own flatness in comparison, and his inadequacy, which suddenly struck him sharply, like yearning, or pain. He breathed in deeply now as if to inflate himself, to fill himself with something Merrit could want, or respond to. Then suddenly Merrit was back, but he was alone.

He said, "Saul left."

"I'm sorry?" Eddie said.

"I'm not."

"He went to the men's room?"

"He went home."

"I didn't notice his leaving."

"I know. He was discreet. A miracle."

"Oh."

"Oh."

"Indeed," Eddie said, tentatively, feeling a bit duplicitous already. This was Saul's husband, after all.

But Merrit smiled encouragingly, and said, "Indeed."

"He left his bag," Eddie said.

"Oh, shit."

"You swear."

"Yes," Merrit said, "I swear. And you came here wearing pearls. Saul told me. And I've got our friend Horatio here in a bag. I guess that means nothing's quite what it seems tonight."

"Seems, I know not seems," Eddie said, trying to be charming. "Who am I quoting?"

"As long as it isn't Saul," Merrit said, "I don't care." Then, with breathtaking self-assurance, he boldly looked Eddie up and down with an appraising sexual glance. "Come on," he said, as if deciding something, "let's get out of here. I hate these movies. I only see them for Saul. I think you're my date tonight. You're hungry?"

"I'm broke," Eddie said, embarrassed. "I just spent my last six dollars."

"Well, I'm loaded," Merrit laughed, bragging and shrugging at once. "Tell you what. If you take charge of this," he said, handing Eddie the D'Agostino bag, "I'll take care of dinner."

Eddie pulled his ticket out of his pocket.

"But I've already paid," he said.

"Then you've got nothing to lose," Merrit said, heading out of the lobby. Eddie followed him quickly. "They can't come after you if you've already paid."

Scenes from a Marriage

Oh, what can you say about a man like that?

And I mean, it isn't just that he was vaguely flirting with Eddie. He flirts with everyone in his laconic way, his gorgeous taciturnity. He can't help it—right?—if people fall in love with him, the way Eddie did. I know he did, I saw. And even if I sort of set it up myself, well, just because I want him out of my life doesn't mean that I can stand to lose him, after all. I mean, he gets offers. Let me tell you now, you have to understand, this man, this Merrit Mather, he can't leave the house without returning home stained with the slobber of a drooling admirer, and damned if it isn't always someone marginally famous, too—a member of the original cast of *A Chorus Line,* someone in the woodwind section of the New York Philharmonic. I'm telling you it happens everywhere, his slippery exchanges—at the riverside, of course, and in the park, in evening dress at concert halls, in bookstores browsing over Edmund White, movie theaters certainly, the Pines, Vermont, Monhegan Island. Honestly, there's not an acre of cruising ground from Dupont Circle to the Charles River that hasn't received the seed cast in honor of Merrit's circumspect attractiveness—not even the Harvard gym, where in his day, Merrit achingly remembers, men still swam with nothing on, and, walking naked from the pool, would pass along a tiled hallway fitted with an oversized bidet that sprayed their legs and thighs and testicles and buttocks with warm water, to his incipient (he was still married to a woman then) homosexual delight, all those men, all naked, all at once.

This week, he's feeling forty-five, and all his friends are dying, and he thinks he wants a virgin boy to make him innocent again, like in those Harvard grad school days. Eddie's not a virgin, I assume, and he isn't innocent, but he is a boy in high-topped sneakers, who's never on time. When Merrit spotted him across the lobby, I thought, perfect, they will drive each other crazy. I mean, Merrit is the sort of man who uses shoe trees. All right? And Eddie, just look at the way he dresses—his shirttail hanging out in the back, his bangs in his face, his shoes not even tied. So there's a philosophical difference between them already. And the thing that matters in love isn't apocalyptic sex, or sex at all, or even similar thoughts, the thing that matters in love is when he sends you out to the store to buy some underarm deodorant, do you instinctively know that he prefers it unscented, as you prefer it yourself? Because this is what matters to Merrit, these logistical affinities. Merrit says he wants a boy to make him feel unencumbered and young. But he's wrong. He doesn't want any kind of lover, boy or man. He wants a self-cleaning oven that washes out his underwear, balances his checkbook, takes him to Europe on vacation twice a year, and sucks his dick on alternate Tuesdays, when his psoriasis isn't too bad and he's feeling horny enough just to lie there and allow it.

No, it isn't just that he had Eddie, zipper straining, succumbing to his quiet, lethal charm, like so many others before him, and so many more to come. Better Eddie, I suppose, than a lot of people. What it is, it's this morning, hours before the viewing, or the flirting, or the movies, when we're still asleep, when we get the wake-up call.

It's six o'clock, the dog isn't even awake. We're sleeping under Merrit's flannel sheets, his country quilt on top, as if you couldn't guess he's from New England, with the sound of western Massachusetts ringing in his vowels and his asshole sealed tight. He twitches in his sleep. I think it's guilt. Me, I roll around. Maybe that's guilt, too. But in the last three hours just before the day begins, say four to seven, we are actually together quietly, perhaps even contentedly, on the mornings when Merrit doesn't wake at three and need a back rub and a cup of heated milk just to ease the tension in his shoulders.

So anyway, the phone rings, six o'clock this morning, cold Friday morning late in March. Merrit picks it up, he blinks, he looks at me and frowns. He doesn't have to say a thing. Right away I know another person died. It's the wake-up call. It always comes at six o'clock. It never means a visitor from out of town, or an obscene caller rising early, or my mother back from the grave, just checking in. It can only mean death, and I don't have to hear it to know how it goes. "Hello, Merrit? This is Tom: I just got a call from Jim who spoke to Richard, who just talked to Luis who was in the room with Peter when Claudio—" and it's the whole gay community inside your telephone receiver at dawn, rehearsing the chorus that begins, "I just got a call," and ends with a pause, a dash, the word left out, the crucial word. That's the space for you to fill in for yourself, to tell yourself the words in whatever way you prefer —he died, or he expired, or he smoked his last, or crossed the River Styx to meet Saint Peter at the pearly gate.

If I had read the Torah like my mother said, I'd understand a little of the world, and so I wouldn't continue to be surprised when someone calls before my morning blend of orange juice and yogurt and bananas, and invites me to a viewing later on tonight. But listen, everyone does not get asked to viewings twice a week, unless they're eighty-seven or living in London in the plague of 1592, or fighting in a war. Or a New York homosexual at 6:00 A.M. this Friday at the end of March, when the dog wants a walk in the snow and Merrit, getting off the phone, says, matter-of-factly, if a bit resignedly, "Claudio."

"Claudio what?" I say, a reflex, not a question.

"This morning," Merrit says. "At three. His mother was there, apparently. He called her up last night, and said that it was time. They argued in Spanish. Then he stopped breathing." He puts the receiver back in its cradle, and turns over, pulling the quilt around his shoulders. "The viewing starts at five. Open coffin. The funeral's tomorrow."

"Open coffin?"

"What's wrong with that?"

"When was the last time you saw Claudio?"

"I don't know, his birthday."

"How did he look?"

"All right,"

"Well, the last time I saw him, he didn't have a face."

"What was there instead?"

"One big lesion."

"Well," Merrit says, coolly, "he's getting a full military funeral tomorrow, out on Long Island."

"A full military funeral?"

"That's what I was told."

"He forged his papers to get out of Vietnam. A full military funeral. That queen. They should bury him in his cheerleading uniform."

Merrit mumbles something, and the dog begins pawing the bed. It is now my job to walk the dog while Merrit sleeps another twenty minutes. That is the agreement, unexpressed but strictly observed. But something goes off in my head this morning, some memory, something dimly recollected, and I turn to Merrit, who hasn't quite fallen asleep, and say, "Make love to me."

Because, let me tell you now, you have to understand, it wasn't always like this, the way we interact, like Ibsen crossed with Elie Wiesel. I remember, early on, before the wake-up calls, before he started therapy and got permission not to touch me, I remember, at his barn in Massachusetts, in a patch of pink narcissus—I think it was white, but I remember it somehow as pink—he broke flower stems in half and smeared their sticky liquid on my hips and thighs, and later, in the night, in a field up behind the barn, we lay down in the grass, and made love. Afterward, we held each other, and looked at the sky. It was a clear night in spring, the stars were bright, and I had never thought about the stars before. I'm just a city boy, the only light that I had known at night was neon, pink, the lights of Jersey on the Hudson. I held him very tight and said that we were cosmic twins, and he said, "Saul, if I get AIDS and die, will you die, too?" And this was very early on, before we knew we couldn't even take each other in our mouths, an innocent time, it's funny to think of it now as an innocent time, innocent because we still believed that if we slept only with each other, we couldn't get sick. But I said, not believing then that either one of us would ever die, I said, "Of course I will," and I think I even mentioned God. That's embarrassing, and I had never mentioned God before, and haven't since, but let me tell you now, you have to understand, the way it felt, the stars, the grass, the promises, his lovely head between my palms, between my legs, the exact sensation of his tongue, his lips—all of it, not six years ago, it's not just first love, Merrit's love, I'm losing, it's the possibility of any love at all, and

24

so I ask again, this morning, I say, "Merrit," touching his shoulder, which is warm, and brown. "Merrit."

I know he won't respond. I know it's inappropriate to want to lie in someone's arms when everyone with whom you've ever lain is dying on the phone with numbing regularity. That's what Merrit would say. He would call it "inappropriate," a word he learned from his shrink, when what he really means is that he cannot stand me anymore, my touch, my voice.

I say, pleading, "Come on, Merrit, we can still do something, hold each other, jerk each other off, it isn't going to kill us," and he answers, "I'm not having sex at all, not ever, not with you or anyone," which isn't true, but I say, anyway, "You know, that's kind of an hysterical response," to which he replies, "Well, maybe it is hysterical, but I'm comfortable with it."

So Merrit's comfortable with his hysteria, but I'm not. Though my wanting him is genuine at first, it starts to get obsessive. I'm sorry, I can't help myself, rejection makes me crazy, and I start to beg. The more rejected I feel, the less I want to make love, the more I beg. So within minutes I'm begging for something I no longer want, and maybe Merrit's therapist would have an expression for this, "approach-avoidance conflict" or something. Merrit's therapist has words for everything, but it hasn't helped us. What we need, I think, is not a single therapist. What we need is a committee.

"Merrit," I say, more aggressively, pressing on his shoulder blade.

"Saul, please," he says.

"I want to be held, at least."

He says, "We're not even going to discuss this."

"Why not?"

"Don't you know why not?"

"Right, it's inappropriate. So what's appropriate about the two of us curling separately into our pillows?"

"Your wants are absurd," he says. "I can't believe you'd even suggest having sex."

"I need reassurance."

"Well, I'm just not feeling very reassuring right now. I'm certainly not feeling sexual."

And then, by an act of self-discipline alarming to behold, he makes himself even more inert beside me, so that if I did try to stir him, it couldn't be done. He says, "I'm sick of this, I'm sick of our relationship, I'm sick of feeling trapped and sterile all the time, I'm exercising my option to look other places," which is how he talks since therapy. "Exercising my option" and "your wants are absurd" —he's picked up this pseudoscientific argot which is supposed to be a neutral expression of his emotions, but as far as I'm concerned it blocks any feelings completely, and is just another way for him to withdraw.

But then the dog gets into the bed. This is how our fights resolve themselves. The dog gets in the way. He always has to pee, or vomit on the furniture, or drool on your new linen trousers just when you're trying to tend to your own little crisis in life. He pushes his big muzzle at me now, Merrit's goddamned dog, an awful bowser named Bacillary, who has capacious jowls and an expression of profound stupidity stretching across his pushed-in face. He squeaks at me and wiggles what might have been a tail if it hadn't been cropped down to a stump, presumably to draw attention to his terminally red erection, as if it needed advertising.

This is what I get instead of Merrit, this dog, his sexual alter ego. I walk with Merrit, he gets cruised, I walk with Larry, he gets patted on the back, I walk alone, I get no attention at all. So I'm trapped between a dog and a wonderful dick, Bowser and a boyfriend, and I get out of bed this morning, singing "Every Day a Little Death," and I say, "Merrit, you walk Bowser, I'm sulking," and I have my morning juice and vitamins and walk to work, where I value the property of famous people who are recently deceased.

All right? And I mean, lately at my job we've been getting what I call the AIDS commissions, the estates of Perry Ellis, Liberace, only they don't acknowledge it's AIDS. Felled by their watermelon diets, right? I walk in the door, my supervisor hands me photographs of jewelry, brooches shaped like baby grand pianos, candelabra pendants, as if, being homosexual, I would naturally be the expert in kitsch. It's her way of showing her concern. Oh, thanks, Louise. So when I get the call to fetch Horatio, I'm staring at a picture of a diamond just about as big as Howard Johnson's, and nearly as tasteful, in the shape of a big bass clef.

Poor Horatio. His relatives in Argentina never came for his remains. They probably don't know that he's dead, not to mention gay, and who can say which would be the greater shock? I dial Merrit's office number, to see if he's free to pick up an old friend

(I mean, of course, Horatio) on the way to the viewing, but my husband isn't answering his phone.

Merrit has an office, but he doesn't really work. He's an heir, you see, to a family business, though he hasn't ever said what kind of a business it is—I assume the manufacture of some small, relatively useless household item. But Merrit won't even kid about it, it's one of his "things." He won't discuss his family, his source of income, or his sexual desires, not with me. I've never met his parents, but I've spoken to his brother on the phone, just once. I called Merrit, in Vail where they were skiing, and I dropped my voice an octave when his brother answered. His brother has a wife who has never refused him sex in twenty years of marriage (this is the only information Merrit has ever willingly given me about anyone in his family, and don't ask me how he got it), and a palatial home in a Sunbelt city to which Merrit retreats, sans husband, every Christmas. As far as the family's concerned, I don't exist. They miss Merrit's ex-wife. They don't know he's gay, and they're getting older and older and closer to death every year, and Merrit, who cries at any father-son or mother-daughter reconciliation movie—*Terms of Endearment* put him out of commission for months—claims it isn't important. "They wouldn't understand," he says. "It would only confuse them. They're hardly a part of my life."

His brother manages the family business, from which Merrit apparently is not too alienated to draw each month a check of adequate size to finance more than half of our apartment—an eight-room co-op in the Prasada, on Central Park West—his place in Massachusetts, his car, his vacations, and his penchant for expensive sweaters. Last count there were maybe seven hundred, and if he lives to a hundred and three, he'll have to wear four and a half of them a day to get even a modest return on his investment. Or something like that. But anyway, the point is that he isn't answering his phone this afternoon, so when I get to Redden's Funeral Parlor, on West Fourteenth Street, with Horatio, to see Claudio, after stopping at a nearby D'Agostino's for some aspirin, Merrit tries to check my bag in the reception area, and I say, "Hold it, that's Horatio."

"Do you think Claudio would have wanted that?" he says, skeptically.

Because, let me tell you now, you have to understand, the two of them were rivals. Horatio was from Argentinian aristocracy, a son of coffee growers, while Claudio grew up poor on West 106th Street, went to Vietnam, and put himself through school. Claudio was jealous of Horatio's birth, and angry at his wealth, and Horatio was ashamed of Claudio's early poverty, embarrassed by his accent, and disdainful of his social pretensions. They didn't get along, and what made it worse was that it couldn't matter less to any of their Anglo friends whether they came from Harlem or Honduras, because Spanish-speaking, in racist New York, is Spanish-speaking; as far as white people bother to know, they all come from just one massive country somewhere off Florida with a colony in Yonkers.

So I shrug at Merrit, holding up the bag as if to say, "At last, a context in which equality is possible," and off we go to Claudio, upstairs, where, it seems, everyone in the room has clearly been planning an outfit for this moment, somewhere in the back of his or her mind, for months. Ever so many boas and colorful sweaters. Claudio was at the center of a group of drama queens, you see, all of them in a high rage all the time. They can't cross the street without turning it into an Easter parade, so you can imagine how they might respond to this. Huge bouquets of roses are placed around the room and up behind the platform where the corpse is laid out, forming a solid panel of red, almost black, around Claudio.

The coffin is open, of course—these gruesome Catholic queens, honestly, they shouldn't be allowed to bury people. We all take turns going up to say good-bye to Claudio. He's a big man, and he looks even bigger dressed in a suit, though in life he always wore jeans. They've had his nose restored, a piece of putty spliced in where there used to be a lesion, and his eyes are closed (the left was missing), and he doesn't have any fingernails. At least, that's what I think, until Merrit notices that he's wearing flesh-toned gloves. His hands are crossed, and he's holding a rosary.

"He looks dead," I whisper.

Merrit says, "I know."

Then someone shrieks and points, and it isn't the night of the living dead, it's just his feet. One is pointing straight, and the other is drooping to the side, spoiling the impression of eternally symmetrical rest. So I set Horatio down, and we lean over Claudio, and try to fix his foot. Four of us struggle with his leg, which isn't moving, of course, because of rigor mortis. It's absolutely stiff.

Then Merrit gets the bright idea of untying Claudio's shoe, and setting it at an angle so that it looks as if his foot were pointed straight, and just as we are stepping back to admire the job, I realize that I have lost Horatio. Misplaced him, I mean, which makes me shriek, and suddenly we're all on our knees in front of a dead man searching for someone in a bag.

And I think, when they make this into a movie, people are going to leave the theater halfway through, laughing in disbelief. I want to fucking forget it. I want to abandon Horatio, turn away from Claudio, leave Merrit. I want to leave the fifty-seven mourners standing in the room in boas and sweaters, people I see only at other people's funerals, who used to be the people I saw only at other people's cocktail parties.

And now I have to ask you, is it bitterness to envy Eddie what appears to be his ignorance of this: that my marriage is to me a series of funerals, and wake-up calls, that when Merrit takes my hand after I locate Horatio and we move away from the coffin, I'm aware that it's the first time he's willingly touched me since the last viewing we attended together? For this is what love engenders. I was a boy, once, too, I fell in love with Merrit, had joy, held hands. That was six years ago. Tonight I hold hands with Merrit again, and look around the room. Standing in the corner is the first gay man I ever met in New York City, after Merrit—Mark Bloom. Merrit and I had dinner with him in his loft on lower Broadway, shortly after we met. Mark and his lover served gazpacho, and handed out paper fans. It was June. Claudio was there, in his shorts, with his lover. Afterward, when we got home to Merrit's apartment—he was living then on West Eleventh Street—we pulled the mattress onto the floor and slept before the doorway to the garden, where it was cool. Mark nods at me now, and I smile. He has AIDS, and so does his lover. Claudio is dead and his lover, diagnosed a year ago, is in the hospital tonight, too sick to come to the viewing. I squeeze Merrit's hand. I think, I'll never leave you, Merrit. There's no way I can ever leave you.

The Company She Keeps

t was Eddie who had recommended Polly's acting class, saying that the teacher was ruthlessly critical but wise, and scrupulously fair. "You'll learn a great deal about life," he insinuated. But all that Polly had learned in seven weeks, not to her surprise, was that the instructor was critical only with women, and that to the men, especially those who presented scenes in which they were required, by some set of circumstances, to strip to their Jockey shorts, he was laudatory, even kind. He may not have realized that among the men in the class this was known as "showing the requisite box," and that it was the kind of adolescent male rite of passage that they had probably all experienced already, in some midwestern junior high school from which they seemed to have only recently emerged.

They were not really men, they were boys, as Brag was just a boy, not twenty-four years old. But he carried himself like a much older man, though his hands gave him away. They were finely shaped with long, thin fingers, and he spoke sometimes with his palms, which he waved stiffly in the air around his face, making eager, yearning gestures. But he was the sort of person to whom the business of being an adult came otherwise quite naturally. That was Polly's initial sense of him, Mr. William Boleslawski, at the singles party in Brooklyn. She was impressed. For she could never wholly manage the willing suspension of disbelief that projected him and others like him credulously into the world. She was not, like Eddie, nihilistic and self-mocking, just self-conscious. She didn't perfectly trust who she was.

She was hardly aware of this, but it made her aloof sometimes, and suspicious of men. Of course, she had funny taste in men, she had to admit; she seemed to be attracted, in spite of herself, to boys like Brag, who were really in New York only for the money. As soon as he got what he wanted, he said, he fully intended to leave. He was from the prairie, too, like the men in her class, but at least he wasn't silly. If he stripped to his shorts, it wouldn't have been to garner false praise from a teacher. She imagined that he kept his weapons concealed against more serious engagements.

"All right, dear," said the acting teacher. "When you're ready."

Polly heard him through the wall, for she was standing in the hallway just outside the classroom, where she waited nervously to make her entrance, through the flimsy door, onto the makeshift set. The class was held on the fourth floor of an old townhouse on Bank Street, a building that hadn't been converted to a series of scene shops and acting studios so much as gutted, and stripped of its period moldings, its showy pilasters. Only the stairway retained a little of the building's Edith Whartony, old New York charm, with a long, elegantly curving railing supported by hand-tooled spindle-turned wooden balusters. The big, formal parlors had been broken up into barren rooms, crowded with folding metal chairs and interlocking gray-painted prop furniture on rollers, which fit together like a Chinese puzzle.

Polly had figured out easily enough why Eddie liked the class, for it took place in a room exactly like his, empty and white, with furniture gathered from the street, painted a uniform color, and used in place of real objects—wooden benches posing as beds and couches, sinks without any faucets. The asceticism, combined with staginess, must have appealed to him. Even the prop silverware was mismatched, and had clearly been collected, as Eddie's silverware had, from garbage piles and the refuse left out behind moving vans. Polly liked kitsch, but Eddie seemed almost to have no taste at all; his refusal to enjoy even tacky collectibles was sometimes unnerving.

"Objects weigh too much," he said, sententiously, though he was perfectly comfortable borrowing Polly's clothing, or eating the food she prepared. But he had an answer for this, too. "Do I contradict myself?" he said. "Very well then, I contradict myself. I am large, I contain multitudes." Then he would ask her who he was quoting.

"We are holding our collective breath," the teacher said, histrionically, and Polly remembered that she had a scene to perform, and a new boyfriend, somewhere out front, to impress. He hadn't arrived by the time the class had started, but perhaps he was there now. He would be sitting among the other midwestern boys, who gathered in the front two rows nearest the teacher. The women sat in the back, below the big red exit sign and the windows overlooking a courtyard of broken cement. It occurred to Polly now that her life had been organized around the satisfaction of various men, feminism notwithstanding, for she had taken the class to humor Eddie, had rehearsed her scene to please the teacher, and was performing it now to demonstrate her depth and creativity to Brag, who was just a trader in a nice blue suit, after all. She was in thrall to men, as her mother had been—indeed, her mother still called once a month to pry into her love life, which made Polly feel only as important as whatever man she was currently seeing. She didn't think her mother similarly questioned her brother, who had, with impunity, had seven hipless, vapid girlfriends in the past eight years, each one more passive than the one before, until they seemed so pale they almost disappeared from the page, like invisible ink.

Polly had grown up happily suburban, which sometimes made her feel ashamed. She hadn't seen any contradictions in her life, until she came to New York with Eddie. Her parents were good liberals, and they adored her. She had one boyfriend all through high school and college, a hometown honey whose name was Joe Veteri. He was wildly attractive, with black eyebrows straight across, shiny black hair, and beautiful chocolate-brown eyes. She only vaguely knew that he was boring. When he told the same stories over and over again, she nodded, not listening. He didn't seem to need her full attention, which may have been why she liked him so much. He was an easy keeper. He had a nice body, and he was a decent lover, generous, and scrupulous about birth control, for which he always took responsibility. So what if he was dull? "Not only dull, but dangerous," Eddie had said; he had fifteen vicious, damning things to say about Joe Veteri and everyone like him. She saw his point, without completely agreeing. But Eddie was uncompromising. It was all or nothing with him. Either Joe Veteri was Satanic and boring, or he was sainted and delightful.

"He's just a nice guy, with kind of a big dick," Polly had said, "which is probably the only surprising thing about him."

"Sell your soul for a dick," Eddie had said.

"I don't think that's the issue."

"No, it's okay to like dicks," Eddie said. "It's America. Everyone in America is supposed to like dicks, as long as it sells the product. Just don't take your dicks with your legs up over your head. Don't get fucked. Like dicks, but don't get fucked. That's the national double standard."

Eddie hated men and liked dicks, but he didn't see the contradiction. Polly did. She saw contradictions everywhere, from the moment they came out of the mouth of the Lincoln Tunnel into Manhattan, all the way from Ohio. They had driven thirteen hours, in pursuit of what Polly supposed was some kind of chic. For she suspected, in her heart of hearts, that she was dull, too, like Joe Veteri, and she didn't have a dick. According to Eddie, dicks were the really important thing; he had dedicated his life to wanting them, or disdaining them, which kind of left her out completely. The problem was, she kept on meeting men like Eddie. Whether they were straight or gay, they were all men; they were all more interested in dicks, she suspected, than anything else. What was a straight banker, after all, other than the flip side of Eddie Socket, played fast and turned up high, with drums?

"Five, four, three, two, one," said the teacher, like a wolf about to blow on the thatched straw hut of Polly's ego. He sat at a little table against the wall, before a sealed fireplace, in which logs must once have been stacked and burned by scullery maids in flowing dresses. Polly could picture him as she took one last breath, her hand on the door knob, before making her entrance. He would be elaborately poised, pencil in hand, over a lined yellow pad, on which he would immediately begin scrawling notes, clucking disgustedly, as soon as any of his students began their scenes. He had big square glasses and a long blue scarf which he wore all the time, like a fur. If he liked a scene, he stopped his pencil halfway to the page, and sat, "enraptured" (she had never seen anyone more effectively demonstrate in life the stage vice known as "illustrating," for he drew big circles around all his gestures and moods), and said, afterward, "I have no criticism." That was an A, a gold star. If he disliked a scene, the scribbling commenced, or, if it was just too appalling, he put down the pencil loudly, leaned back in the chair, and hissed, "I'm sorry, but I have to stop you." Polly had never finished a scene in his class. She had been stopped every time.

She went over the scene again in her head very quickly. It was called a simple-object exercise. She had to perform a simple task in five minutes' time, keeping in mind a clear objective, a "want," and dealing with whatever obstacles she had predetermined for herself as getting in the way. There was to be little, or no, dialogue. She was not to create a character, or attempt to tell a story, but merely to act exactly as she did under normal circumstances. "Try and focus on your life," the teacher exhorted, week after week. "What do you do in your life?"

Polly appreciated the simplicity of the assignment, but felt it missed the point. For the objects, the desires, and the obstacles she had in her life were hardly dramatic material. She couldn't put Joe Veteri on stage or dramatize her yearning for the span of flesh between William Boleslawski's shirt cuffs and the backs of his hands. Her life was not external, it wasn't as Eddie said once, merely a sequence of motion and fact, which she could reproduce at any moment, as if she only had to freeze the frame and show how things looked. Although she was a visual artist, she didn't live as if things had only appearances. For there was an internal logic to the arrangements of things, emotional and physical, an inner-connectedness that she felt Eddie missed. Certainly her acting teacher missed it. They both underestimated her, as if her gift, and her exertions, were to be focused entirely on manipulating objects, or failing to do so.

But the world she lived in, and the men she dated in New York, didn't believe in inner-connectedness, it seemed, and she went on explaining resonance and meaning to people who had limited themselves to sequence and fact. She had partly given it up. If Brag wanted to fuck her, if he wanted to be mounted, or paddled, or eaten and rimmed, well, she thought, if he supplied the saran wrap and the water-base gel, the condoms and creams, then, okay, she would do what he wanted. For the more she desired an internal connection to a man, the less she seemed able to choose anything but sexual acrobats who looked pretty in shorts. She could imagine that Brag looked ravishing in shorts, and of course she wondered about his dick. She liked dicks, but she wanted more than just that. She liked men, but they always disappointed her.

She stepped onto the set and started her scene. She was carrying a cup of tea in a brown paper bag, from a grocer stand on Hudson Street, and a cap she had borrowed from Eddie, a red-and-black–checked logger's hat, with tuck-under black insulated ear flaps. She had no idea what she "wanted" with these objects. She had brought them along to appease the teacher, who liked a scene to be crowded with props. She put down the bag and took off her coat and tossed it onto one of the pieces of rollaway furniture. She opened the bag and pulled out the tea, which was no longer hot. She had to remind herself now to endow it with the qualities of heat and steaminess. But she couldn't remember—how hot was a hot cup of tea, a hot paper cup? Did it burn the fingers? Or was it reassuringly warm, like a hot-water bottle? She got self-conscious, and dropped the cup on the floor, spilling tea everywhere.

"Shit," she said.

Leaning down to clean up the mess, she saw first the teacher (not even scribbling, but motionless, apparently stunned), then Brag. He was standing by the door, with his arms and legs crossed, looking furtive, and embarrassed. She understood immediately that he had come to class only to be able to observe her unobserved, and had gotten more (or less) than he wanted. He was sizing her up, and she decided instantly that she would make him wait for it, days, perhaps weeks. Granted, there was something reassuring about his posture, the broadness of his shoulders and the cock of his narrow hips; she wanted him, that much was clear. But she could make herself wait. And that was both an object and an obstacle, and she felt, after all, wiping up the tea, that her scene was complete.

So did the teacher, who just said, sharply, "Dear," as if she were causing him considerable pain. He fiddled scornfully with his scarf, grasping and twisting it as if it were an excitable blue fox as sensitive to bad performances as he. Then he asked, with devastating calm, "What is that in your hand?"

Polly looked down at Eddie's logging hat, with which she had been mindlessly wiping the tea off the floor.

"Oh," she said, surprised.

"What are you doing on the floor?" the teacher asked, presenting himself as the soul of forbearance. She could almost see the words telegraphed over his head, like a caption. She understood at once that she was to be his sacrifice tonight. She hoped he was quick about it.

"Do you have an objective?" he said.

"Yes, I do."

"Would you care to share it with us?"

"No," she said, "I don't think I would."

"I see," the teacher said, and six of the blondest boys in the front row dropped their heads and giggled.

"Now I'm going to tell you something," the teacher said, leaning forward, "that is going to feel like a cold bucket of water over your head."

Polly stood motionless with the hat. She dared not look at Brag.

"You have no life in this room," the teacher said. "Do you understand me? You haven't found your life here, or any reason to walk through the door. There's nothing real here that you want. You've come just to deliver your lines. You don't *want* anything. Do you understand?"

"I want to clean up this mess."

"Yes," the teacher conceded. "Yes, perhaps you do. But that wasn't what you rehearsed, was it? We make adjustments to accidents, of course. But we don't direct our lives around them. Is that clear?"

Polly thought maybe she should be directing her life around accidents, but she nodded and smiled, because she wanted to leave. Mercifully, the teacher let her go. She grabbed her coat, and her empty container of tea, and before the next scene began, she had taken Brag's arm and led him downstairs, holding the nineteenth-century railing on one side, and him on the other.

He was wearing one of his twelve blue suits, which he claimed were not identical; there were variations in the cut, he said, the width of the lapels, the frequency of stripes. This is what they had discussed in Brooklyn, when they met—his suits. She knew she wanted him for the wrong reasons. She even knew that he would get tired of her eventually. But she would stay with him until he told her to go. She was never the first to withdraw; she always waited for the man to tell her they were incompatible, and compiled a list of all the stupid ways in which they had done so, one by one. Afterward she would go home to Eddie, who put on torch songs from musical comedies—Bea Arthur singing, "There Goes My Heart," Michele Lee complaining, "Nobody Does It Like Me,"

Jo Stafford lamenting, "The Gentleman Is a Dope." They encouraged each other to fail with men. Eddie had given up, but Polly hadn't, not yet.

Because maybe, when he was stripped down to nothing, after his pleasure, when they lay together with nothing greater at stake than wanting, slightly, to like one another, maybe then he would turn out to be a decent man, this William Boleslawski, or maybe he would be nice to sleep with, just sleep with, at last. And maybe, she thought, she would fuck him tonight if he wanted, after all, just to find out.

Tea and Sympathy

How old are you, then, exactly?" Eddie asked, trying to make the question sound casual. Actually, he didn't care, but Merrit kept drawing attention to the difference in their ages, unsuccessfully hiding his concern behind a harsh chuckle.

"How old do you think?" Merrit said, flirtatiously. His voice had a low, reedy quality that was gentle and coaxing, and he flattened his r's like a Kennedy. Eddie stared at his plate, mopping it clean with his last delicate slice of quail. He was vegetarian, but the menu at the (very expensive) French restaurant Merrit had guided them to (in a cab) consisted entirely of different preparations of helpless dead animal. He felt bad about the bird, but Merrit offered warm encouragement, even feeding Eddie, with his own fork, a bite of his dead duck liver ground to a paste and served in plum sauce and brandy. Eddie was smart enough to know he was being seduced, and the duck was politely consumed, along with the quail. He felt instinctively that it was best, with Merrit, to suppress as many of his personal idiosyncrasies as possible, to remain tantalizingly nonconformist without being threatening.

But if it was so easy to suspend his principles (and just for a man?), then he had to wonder how seriously he took himself, after all. Was he really that desperate for male attention? Was Merrit so extraordinary? Well, he was pretty enough, though a bit vicious, perhaps. But Eddie liked arrogant men, and anyway, he felt himself suddenly, if cautiously, ready to emerge from his withdrawal. What were his so-called principles, after all, if not excuses to hide from the world? He didn't eat animals, he didn't have any furniture, he wouldn't sleep on a bed, he didn't have a television, he didn't ride the subway (he rode his bicycle, or else he walked), he wouldn't have sex anymore. He had made choices, but they kept him away from anyone other than Polly, and a few people like Saul whom he knew at word-processing jobs.

Merrit was sinuous, catlike, alternately aloof and seductive. Eddie felt like Norma Shearer batting her eyes histrionically at Chester Morris. He forgot about cause and effect, and the voice of the pig—this was MGM, and Eddie was wearing the emotional equivalent of an Adrian gown. He knew what Merrit probably was in real life, a very handsome preppie guy over forty who needed drooling boys to buttress his flagging male ego.

But he looked thirty-five except for the gray at his temples, which anyway was very sexy. Indeed, Eddie was hot, everywhere, watching Merrit; he was light in his stomach (bird or no bird), and staining his jeans very slightly with dampness (and wishing also that he had worn underwear tonight). How old did Eddie think he was? Well, did he like flattery, or honesty? And, if this was a test, or a game, what space would they proceed to after Eddie gave the right answer? To Merrit's apartment? Surely not, even if Saul wasn't there. To Eddie's apartment? That was probably worse. For suddenly Eddie felt ashamed of his naked white walls, and ceiling, and floor, his chairlessness, his red Oriental rug for sleeping (and, presumably, for making love, though he had never brought anyone home), his splintering slab of white-painted industrial waste. He forked his last bit of quail, uncertainly, into his mouth.

"You can't be more than thirty-five," he said, swallowing, "but I would guess thirty-two."

Merrit seemed genuinely pleased. He smiled and said, "I wish. But aren't you sweet."

"No, really," Eddie said, laying down his fork. This was the candlelit moment in which Norma Shearer touched her pearls, leaned across the nearly devoured duck, looked into her lover's sad, gray-green eyes, and said exactly the right thing. Sheepishly (but not at all dishonestly), Eddie said, "I think you're beautiful."

"Your sense of the world is very askew," Merrit said, laughing, "but romantic. You are a romantic dove."

Not to mention the romantic quail in my stomach, Eddie thought. For if he was aware that he had attached his self-esteem impetuously to a man he had known a few hours, and who probably wouldn't, or couldn't, remain in his life much longer than that —well, he put that information carefully off to the side, like the canister filled with Merrit's friend Horatio, which he had kept beneath the table, next to his foot.

"All right, then," he said, opting to please, after all. "You're forty-something. So what?"

"Forty-*something*," Merrit said.

"I like older men."

"*Older.* That's what I mean. You think of me as older."

"Well, you are. You're older than me. That's all I mean. Older than me could be thirty."

"Don't apologize, please," Merrit said. "It's sweet. But I know what you meant." He sipped the last of his wine, and said, "I'm forty-five."

"So is Mick Jagger, I guess," Eddie said, trying to be reassuring.

"I'm probably closer to your mother's age than to yours."

"My mother is eleven." He reached across the table boldly and touched Merrit's wrist, but Merrit hardly seemed to notice. Signaling the waiter, he asked for a package of cigarettes. "You don't smoke, do you?" he said to Eddie, who made a noncommittal sound somewhere between a yes and a no, to which Merrit again seemed oblivious. He said, "I do, once in a while. I regret it later, but . . . "

"But alas," Eddie said, helpfully.

"But alas." Merrit nodded, finally returning his attention to Eddie. "You're a funny man."

"Funny ha ha or funny strange?" Eddie asked, uncomfortably.

"Funny way too young."

"I'm twenty-eight," said Eddie, aware that he suddenly sounded eleven or twelve.

"Seventeen years between us," Merrit said.

"Oh, chronology," Eddie said a bit flippantly. "I mean, really. Anyway, my soul's eternal. Maybe we were . . . maybe we knew . . . maybe we were . . . friends, in a former life?" He shook his head. "Sorry, I'm babbling. Normally, I'm less Annie Hall."

The waiter arrived with the cigarettes, and lighting one, Merrit exhaled slowly and smiled. He smoked defiantly, like a boy sneaking drags behind the barn. *If I kissed him now,* Eddie thought, *his mouth would taste warmly of tobacco—duck and plum sauce and wine and tobacco.*

"I'm attracted to babblers," Merrit said.

"Oh, Saul," Eddie said, hunching his shoulders unthinkingly, and frowning.

"What's the matter?"

"He's sort of my boss."

"Mine, too," Merrit said.

"I like him."

"So do I."

"So this is sort of weird, is all I mean."

Merrit leaned forward, and this time it was Eddie's wrist that was enclasped. "Do you know that you blow at your bangs?" he said. "It's a little explosion from your lips, aimed at your bangs, as if to get them out of your eyes. But it doesn't work. Your hair just falls back into place."

"Oh," Eddie said.

"How close is your place?"

"We can get there by cab," Eddie said, coyly, and they did. He felt as if he were in high school, on his way to an obvious seduction. He had had plenty of sex in New York, but never an assignation in his home. It felt new, and exciting. Merrit got the check, and the cab fare, and Eddie got Horatio again, and when they were standing finally in Eddie's apartment, minutes later, Eddie wished at least that he had some throw pillows, something. But Merrit, who said he was trying not to be an adult for a change, merely sat on the floor.

"The last time I was in a cab," Eddie said, putting Horatio down on the floor by the tub, and chattering nervously, "I was eleven."

"Six years ago."

Eddie laughed, uncertain whether he was being made fun of. Merrit's being in the room was somehow terribly wrong, like Proust in the pages of *Blueboy;* Eddie wanted him out on a chrome and black enamel glass-enclosed terrace, with a view of the East Side twinkling behind them. The white room made him look smaller, more piquant, and younger, out of his element, certainly. But he took up his circle of rug decisively, and lit another cigarette, and then, in the spirit of the surroundings, he flicked it into one of his shoes, which he had removed. He wanted Eddie to know he could swing, that much was clear.

"Actually," Eddie continued, "I was eleven the year the Beatles broke up, 1969."

"I was married," Merrit said.

"To a woman?"

"She used to play a song over and over again from one of their albums. We were living in Boston. Something about a wet dream."

" 'Everybody had a hard year,' " Eddie sang. " 'Everybody had a good time. Everybody had a wet dream. Everybody saw the sunshine.' "

Merrit laughed. "That's it," he said. "When the song stopped playing, she was gone."

"What's it like to be married?"

"What's it like?"

"I mean, you know, to a woman. Conventionally married."

"I can't remember."

"Oh," Eddie said, pacing. It had occurred to him suddenly that he had nothing in the house like condoms, or lubrication. Maybe Polly did, but she had probably taken her equipment along, for the trader. Anyway, what did forty-five-year-old men in cardigan sweaters like to do? Maybe they would need champagne, and baby oil.

"So," he said, "the last time I was in a cab, I was eleven, with my father, and we had an argument about the Immaculate Conception."

"Saul told me once that I was the Immaculate Conception. Or maybe he meant that sex with me was like the Immaculate Conception."

"Oh," Eddie said, suddenly unable to respond to any comments Merrit made about himself. He had lost his sense of humor, and was vaguely aware that it made him seem rather slow. "My mother had just told me that everyone on earth was a product of two people fucking," he went on, nervously. "I mean, in so many words, and I repeated this to my father, who dealt with it, typically, by advising me to pray. As long as I live, I am never going to pray. Do you pray?"

"Come here," Merrit said, confidently. He was going to take control, after all.

"I'm sorry?"

"You're still wearing your coat. Come over here."

"You want some tea, or something?" Eddie said, going to the edge of the rug, and bending stiffly to Merrit, who undid all the buttons on his coat. Was this the big move, then? Eddie wetted his lips, just in case. "I mean, I'm the host," he added irrelevantly.

But Merrit got distracted by the button pinned to Eddie's collar. "What's Reagan Youth?" he said, no longer sounding seductive.

"It's a joke."

"You think it's funny?"

"Not a funny joke. Some other kind of a joke."

"I don't find Ronald Reagan very funny."

"Well, neither do I. Except, you know, to the extent that he's achingly funny. You know, tragically funny."

"Not even tragic," Merrit said. "He isn't interesting enough for that. Why would you wear a button like that?"

"Does it bother you?"

"I don't understand how you could joke about something like that."

"I'm sorry," Eddie said, taking off the coat. He felt vaguely attacked. Merrit's voice had dropped, and his features were hard. "It's just how I deal with, you know, reality."

"What's reality?"

"Well, that's the point. Listen, did you want tea? Otherwise I think I've got some old papaya juice. Look at me, playing host."

"I just don't think it's funny or chic to be imprecise about Reagan, or anything else," Merrit said.

Eddie lit a burner on the stove and said, "I'm sorry, I didn't want to be offensive. I mean, if I'd known I was running into you, I would have left it home, you know, and I get imprecise when I'm nervous. You make me kind of nervous," he said, turning around to fill a pan with water from the sink. He stopped with the pan in his hand, and said, "I've never had a man here before. Not any kind of a man, and certainly not a man like you. I really think you're beautiful."

He knew that he sounded like a boy, but something told him that this was what Merrit wanted.

Indeed, Merrit frowned to himself, then smiled. "No, *I'm* sorry," he said. "I can't seem to relax, sometimes."

"You like herbal tea?"

"I like whatever."

"Because all I have is Lipton."

"Just, whatever," Merrit said. "I'm sorry, sometimes I'm not very trusting."

"I'm not very trusting, either," Eddie said, putting the pan on the stove. He rinsed out a pair of old mismatched cups and left them on the edge of the sink. He said, his back to Merrit, "I trust some things, though. I trust Lou Reed, even though he's married to a woman now, and lives in New Jersey. I can trust the IRT, not to be on time, I mean, but to be completely itself, at least the Broadway line, when I was still riding trains, before they got the big new cars from Canada, or Japan, or wherever. I trust the Union Carbide Building, on Park Avenue. Same reason. I mean, it's a big ugly box. Banks can move in, they can change the facade, it's still a big ugly box. I can trust my mother to say things like 'Get your hair cut. Pay your medical insurance.' I can trust my father to send pious postcards once a month. I trust Saul, actually, when I think about him, pardon the reference. I can trust masturbation, and," he said, boldly, suddenly deciding to be a little seductive, "I trust my dick, but you can get dependent on a thing, and anyway, nothing's ever quite enough to bring about whatever miracle it is I keep expecting from my life. I trust the Hudson River. I trust you."

But when he turned around, Merrit was stroking Darth, who had come out of hiding. He was curled in Merrit's lap, and he was purring loudly. Merrit was the sort of man who couldn't hold to more than one thought at a time—though when his attention was engaged, it was engaged completely—and he stroked Darth now with all his concentration. He rubbed his head, and took the tips of his ears in his fingers. He scratched his chin. He shaped his hand around his spine, and smoothed his fur, and scooped his tail into his palm, caressing it.

Eddie walked slowly across the room, stood behind Merrit, and put his hands on his shoulders. He massaged Merrit's back, his neck and his shoulders, and Darth still purred. "That's nice," Merrit said, "that feels nice," and Eddie, his hands sliding up under Merrit's sweater, felt the tapering, slender muscles of his back through his button-down shirt. But then the stove went *whumpf,* very loudly, and Darth fled, and Merrit jumped up.

"Jesus Christ, what was that?" he said.

Eddie looked at the stove, which was fully in flame. All the burners had caught from Joseph Stalin's postcard and Polly's wrappings, which Eddie had forgotten to move off the top of the stove. Red, orange, and blue flames reached up to the mirror, and cast bright reflections on the walls. Eddie regarded it as a hopeless moment of romance, but Merrit went quickly to the stove and put out the fire. He turned off the burner, blew out the flame, sprinkled water, and finally covered it with Eddie's coat, which was slightly singed. He was not just agitated, but was no longer there in the room, for the crisis had projected him into a private world of accidents and plagues in which nothing was casual, not even laughter. He was shaken. Eddie took his shoulders again, but Merrit stepped away, and he would not be calmed until he had found a screwdriver, removed the top of the stove, and put out the pilot light, which wasn't needed anyway, he explained, for the burners to light. They could be lit singly with matches. All the pilot light did was run up the gas bill.

Merrit returned to the rug, and they had their tea, anyway, but the warmth had gone out of the room, perhaps with the flame, and the white walls looked oppressive, and their voices echoed too loudly.

Eddie said, carefully, trying to recover their moment, "If you could choose between a single night of love worth all remembering, but finally lost, and a lifelong relationship, an intimacy that lasted your life, but was filled with unhappiness—"

"I would choose to be a swan," Merrit said.

But Eddie put his hand on Merrit's face, and said, "You're lovely. Do you know that? You're really just, I don't know, lovely. I'm sorry if I'm imprecise."

"I'm not very good at not being in charge," Merrit said, softly.

"And I'm a boy."

"You are a boy," Merrit said, taking him in his arms. "You are a boy."

They sort of huddled together on the rug, just holding each other, and when after a few hours of intermittent sleep Merrit got up to leave, Eddie said, " 'When you speak of this, and you will, be kind.' Who am I quoting?"

"Is this some sort of game?" Merrit said. "I don't like games unless I can win."

"I like to lose games," Eddie said. "We're perfectly matched."

And Merrit picked up Horatio and quietly left.

The Man in the
Brooks Brothers Suit

Polly wanted to like him, though she was beginning to see that he was not especially charming (at least, not tonight), or witty, or much of a conversationalist. But as long as he was kind, she was willing to overlook a lot of things, like the tirade against Jesse Jackson he had just completed (she had an old 1984 Jesse Jackson for President button on the collar of her coat, which she had unfortunately forgotten to remove). "You, as a Jew, of all people," he said sententiously. They were at a crowded Cajun restaurant near the river, where a roomful of white bankers and lawyers in their twenties and thirties were listening to Motown's greatest hits on the jukebox—Smokey Robinson, Marvin Gaye, Martha Reeves, the Supremes. Their waitress, who was leggy, and beige, arrived with their orders, interrupting Brag's encomium to Albert Gore. Polly bit into a rubbery circle of a conch. Brag filled his mouth with gumbo, and said, "If your issue is rights for the poor, and the blacks and the gays, then I say, go for Gore, he's your man. Best record in Congress on—"

Polly, who was trying very hard not to quote Eddie on how all straight white men were exactly the same—supremacist, complacent, and controlling—changed the subject quickly. She distinctly did not like Brag on politics. But Romeo and Juliet had settled their political differences—at least, they still had sex—and Lyndon Johnson had acquiesced to John F. Kennedy. There was hope. As long as they stuck to easier topics, like movies, or fashion . . .

Trying to be delightfully irrelevant, Polly said, "What do you think of my sweater?"

Brag smiled encouragingly, whether out of politeness or approval she couldn't decide. He seemed to be able only to lecture, not to converse, and when they did attempt to banter words back and forth, he adopted a stagey game-show-host persona, projecting a hearty enthusiasm. He was like a road company Steve Martin in his business suit, always playing the nerd. This was his way of apologizing, Polly understood, for being a financier—he made fun of himself. He made fun of his conventional values and his conventional life, just to show that he could swing over to the avant garde and back again as easily as anyone. He wanted her to know that he knew how uncool he was. But the joke, he implied, was finally his, for he was making pots of money, and she was not. She could hear him saying, "pots of money." She liked him best when he dropped the pose, and spoke plainly about himself. He had a nice smile, and a warm laugh. He was sometimes very boyish, and he could be caught by surprise. But he must have been as nervous dating her, a woman with frizzy hair and a Jesse Jackson button (so little it took, these days, Polly thought, to antagonize people), as she was, contemplating even the briefest affair with a man in a Brooks Brothers suit.

"I got it at Bloomingdale's," she said, giggling. "You wouldn't believe the act of hypnosis I had to perform on myself just to get in the door. I mean, I had sworn to curb my shopping mania." She smiled, her hands going up in the air. Whenever she was nervous, it registered in her hands, which she moved expressively, waving her fingers in the air, or touching the side of her head—her thinking gesture. "But there are these arguments, six arguments in favor of shopping, and I invoked them. Do you want to know what they are?"

But Brag was eating absorbedly, with enormous self-satisfaction, and sipping a frozen margarita. If he was listening closely to Polly, she would never have guessed it. He looked up from his gumbo every other bite, and smiled, regarding her rather shyly, as if he couldn't trust his clear blue eyes to give him much useful information. His Adam's apple bobbed suggestively as he swallowed, and she thought she felt the pressure of his kneecaps against her own, under the table. They were kneecapping, Brag was eating,

Polly was babbling. If she could just keep talking till they got home to bed, she thought, she might discover she liked him. Though she could never tell how much she truly liked a man until after he rejected her.

"Well," she said, sipping her Perrier, "argument one is this: I'll learn from this mistake. Except, I never do. So that doesn't work. I'm not that self-deceiving. Argument two: You've gotten through another day in New York City. Only eight million other people in the world can make this claim. Reward yourself. Except, so what? I'm no longer impressed with myself for being a New Yorker."

"You should try San Diego," Brag said, irrelevantly. Polly spooned some fried okra into her mouth, which snapped. She wasn't certain how to weigh his interjection. But he helped her out. He said, "My sister lives there. Or she did. Now she lives in West Hollywood. This place is very West Hollywood," he said, looking around the restaurant.

Well, she thought, at least he had stopped lecturing. "Argument three," she continued, filing away the tip about Brag's sister. If she lived in West Hollywood, she was probably gay. What would Polly do with this information? She thought briefly about sharing it with Brag, but changed her mind. "Argument three is a really good one," she said, "especially if you've been brought up Catholic, or Jewish. It's: This will ruin you financially and morally, which is what you deserve. I found this one infallible for a long time. It got me into almost any store I wanted. Only problem was," she said, snapping another piece of okra, "it isn't true. I mean, I owe as much money now as my roommate, Eddie Socket, made last year. Or maybe he made twice as much—the point is all that happens is they up your interest, and if I feel sometimes like an indentured servant to Visa, well, if it weren't Visa, it'd be the IRS, right?"

"The firm got audited a couple months ago," Brag said, uncomfortably, it seemed. "Ripping off the IRS takes a lot more creative teamwork than you'd think. We had our best men on the job."

"Success?" Polly asked, satirically.

But Brag had little gift for irony, at least about some things. "Yes," he said, proudly. "We shook them off."

"Is that like ripping them off?"

He leaned forward, truly interested in the conversation for the first time all night. "We shot them through with little pellets, dipped in horseshit," he confided.

"Maybe I should give my taxes to you."

"You could do worse."

"Well, then there's argument number four," Polly said, abruptly. The pressure on her knees had intensified. She wasn't sure she enjoyed it. He had smooth, smooth skin, flawlessly smooth, as if he had taken a power sander to his face and scrubbed away even the suggestion of pores. His cheekbones pulled his skin tight, holding his jutting chin in place like a sling.

"Argument four is kind of a syllogism," she continued, testing his vocabulary. "God made us all in his image. God is perfect. Therefore, shopping must be perfect, or else he wouldn't have inspired in me the need to buy. Too bad I don't believe in God, but then there's argument number five, for the skeptics and the existentialists: Actions don't reverberate, they just occur. There's nothing here nor there about a shopping spree. It only is. That's Eddie's argument."

"Who's Eddie?"

"He's the guy I live with. My roommate, remember? I think I mentioned him."

"I was distracted by your lips," Brag said.

"Oh," Polly said, as if she had been pinched.

"I love the way you talk," he said.

"You do? I wasn't aware you were listening."

"When you talk," Brag said, "my mind races."

"Races?"

He leaned even closer.

"Everything goes very fast," he said, softly, emphatically.

"Oh, well. I guess that brings us to argument six, which is, Why the fuck not?"

"Why the fuck not," Brag said, respectfully.

She giggled. "It's the only one that always works."

"You're very pretty," Brag said, wiping his lips on his napkin.

"Am I?"

"I'd like you to feed me," he said. Then he lowered his voice, leaned forward, and said, "And then I'd like to get worked."

"Excuse me?"

"I want you to feed me."

Polly looked around the room. "In here?"

"I want you to handle my silverware." He smiled. Did he have a sense of humor, after all? He took her right hand in his palms, and lightly stroked her fingers. His eyes were clear Mediterranean blue. Polly took his spoon, and dipped it in the gumbo. He grunted, very

49

softly, never taking his eyes from her hand, which trembled slightly. She leaned forward, slipping the spoon gently into his mouth, which he held open expectantly. There was something touching, she thought, about his tongue. He closed his lips, and swallowed.

"Big piece of shrimp," he said, "Yummy."

"Yummy," Polly repeated.

"Another," he said.

"Yes, another," she agreed, filling and refilling his spoon with pieces of shrimp. They cleaned his plate. Her head felt wadded and sticky, like unpicked cotton. Her synapses hummed. Some people affected her that way, and Brag was one of them. She couldn't help it. She hardly knew what she was doing as they got the check (he let her calculate their shares) and split a cab uptown. He suggested the train, but that would have broken the spell, and Polly quickly flagged a spacious, luxurious checker.

The only time she ever rode in cabs was on her way to somebody's bed. It was what she liked the most about a date, the brief, ecstatic interlude when, for five or ten minutes, she felt fully in control of her pleasure. There was always time in a cab, after all, to change her mind, and let herself out at the next light. She never did (she always went through with the evening, always), but she liked to know that the opportunity was there if she wanted to. And there was rarely conversation in a cab, which helped. Sometimes there was hand holding, sometimes even groping, but never the distraction of talk, or the actual project of sex. And then, a cab ride was simply a treat, a nice reward for just being Polly, herself. The dinner before and the dithering after were seldom as satisfying as her ten minutes in the cab.

They rode to the Upper West Side, to the apartment on Broadway he shared with two other traders. "I wouldn't have thought to paint the walls yellow," Brag said, explaining that the fellow who owned the place, six rooms in a big prewar building near Columbia, was gay, "but I have to hand it to him, he knew exactly the shade. Of course, I've never been sure of the drapes."

Polly followed him into a narrow bedroom, which had been carved out of the parlor when the apartment was broken from four generous, high-ceilinged rooms into six cramped ones, twenty years ago. Brag's cell was opposite the bathroom. He had a narrow single bed, a window overlooking Broadway, a compact disc player, and a stack of unread magazines, *Fortune, 7 Days, New York.* The room was tidy and collegiate, carpeted wall to wall and decorated with old snapshots, from summers on the beach. There was probably a stash of pornography under the bed, Polly thought.

He had a closetful of pressed shirts and rep ties, and the twelve identical suits (eleven at the moment, of course, because he was wearing number twelve). His dresser top was crowded with creams and lotions, lubricants and gels, after-shave, skin softeners, cuff links, cologne. He obviously took a great deal of pleasure in being a male, or at least in buying products made for a male. Such attention to the way he looked and smelled Polly found alternately thrilling and rather absurd; she liked and loathed his vanity, at once. And his bed was neatly made up with a hand-dyed spread over crisp blue sheets, the corners tucked military style, the surface so unbroken by wrinkles that she could have bounced a diaphragm on it. The pillow (only one) was pleasantly plumped. There was a mother behind all this, she could tell.

Brag took off his jacket, loosened his tie, and rolled back his sleeves, exposing the all-important forearms, which didn't disappoint.

"Can I sit here?" Polly said, eyeing the bed, which looked like a still blue David Hockney pool, in which she didn't want to make the wrong kind of splash.

"Please," Brag said, selecting a compact disc.

"That's nice," Polly said, as the room filled with the sound of morbid violins. "What is it?"

"I don't know," he admitted. "I just like it. It's on a classical anthology. Somebody gave it to me."

"Maybe Mahler," she suggested.

Brag sat down beside her on the bed. "I like your knowing that."

She touched his wrists, which really were quite lovely. He said, rather awkwardly (both of them watching her stroke him), "There's something you should know before—I mean, before we get worked." He laughed, and cleared his throat. "I can't put anything inside of you."

"You mean your . . . " Polly said.

Brag nodded gravely. "There's a problem with it."

It was missing? "You're like Jake Barnes," she said. "You know, Hemingway?"

51

"I've got urethritis," he said, shaking his head apologetically. "I think I picked it up at the gym. I'm out of condoms, too. Do you mind?"

Were people ever "out of condoms," Polly wondered, the way they were out of paper towels, or soda pop? "Unless you brought—" he said.

"No, I didn't," Polly interjected quickly, but of course she had brought condoms. Did he think she was a fool? She had gotten a package of twelve, on the way home from Bloomingdale's. But she didn't want him to know this.

"Well, then," he said, reaching into her sweater and pinching her nipples. "We'll have to make do."

"I gather we will," Polly said, lifting her chin as Brag licked the length of her neck.

"I give great j/o," he said, reaching her ear.

"That's reassuring."

"With my tongue," he said, undoing her bra. It slipped down to her shoulders. He rolled her sweater and blouse up to her chin, and she wondered briefly whether he was going to strangle her. She was hating herself. She would rather have been doing anything, right now—vacuuming, even—other than this. But she didn't stop him. The more unconnected she felt with a man, the less she was able to leave. She was put in the peculiar, sleazy position of pretending to like what she didn't, as if to protect his feelings when she clearly had no regard for her own. So she disengaged. She left the room emotionally, if not physically, and watched it happen. He said, "I like doing this, too," and closed his mouth over her left nipple. He took her hand and pressed it to the gather in his trousers. "Let's get undressed," he said, perhaps trying to sound unbearably seductive.

She pulled her sweater over her head, and unbuttoned her blouse, and Brag got out of his trousers and shirt. He was wearing boxer shorts decorated all over with the insignia of Dartmouth College, an Indian head. Feather-headed Indians danced across his buttocks and climbed the rising length of his penis, which curved to the left beneath his shorts, like a line on a graph.

"You wanna jerk off?" he said, rather sweetly.

She did not. But Brag was still wearing his socks, and his shorts were stained in front and torn in the back, which she found oddly moving. She nodded uncertainly.

"Wanna see my big dick?" he said. "Wanna put your hands around my big, big dick?" Polly had the feeling he was talking dirty as if to try out that strategy. It was only a test. He wanted to see how best to reach her. The problem was, he didn't sound sincere. He sounded like an actor in a pornographic movie.

"Put your hands on me," he said, trying a more traditional approach, and dropping his shorts. Polly sat on the edge of the bed, still in her panties and shoes and her skirt.

"Wanna stand up," he said, very gently, and then you can play with my chest?"

Polly got up. Well, what else could she do? She was too embarrassed to withdraw. Brag was squatting now, stroking himself. They were standing in front of the window, and she wondered if anyone could see.

"You wanna see me come?"

"Why not?"

Suddenly he let go of himself. "You sure you're into this?" he asked, apprehensively.

"Oh, yes," Polly said, almost sincerely. It was a certain kind of intimacy, after all, sharing embarrassment.

"It's perfectly safe, this way. Is that what you're worried about?"

"No, I'm not worried."

"Because if you're worried, well, I promise not to splatter on you, anywhere," he said, kindly.

"Oh, that's all right," Polly said. "Go ahead. Splatter away."

"Yeah?"

"Yeah, sure."

"Oh, excellent," he said. He put his hand to her groin and said, "We can both get into this, if you want."

"No, you go ahead," Polly said. "I'll wait my turn."

"You like to watch?"

"That's right," she said, "I like to watch."

Brag said, "Excellent," again, and then reached to hold Polly's hand under the head of his penis, while he stroked himself, more and more rapidly. He moaned, and bent his knees, and when he talked all the words ran together.

He came in her palm. His knees jerked, and he yelped, the stuff dripping onto Polly's skin. He watched his hand proudly, not looking at Polly, and held on tightly until the last of it was out of him and onto Polly, covering her fingers. He shook his penis, once or twice, familiarly, gratefully. Finally, he sighed, and smiled. Polly stood still, and waited. She wanted to be told exactly what to do. She watched him carefully. He inhaled deeply, then exhaled. Then he straightened, moved quickly across the room, and grabbed a towel.

"So," he said, conversationally, drying himself (even though he had splattered mostly on her), "you like Hemingway?"

"Hemingway?"

"You mentioned Hemingway. Jake Barnes." He smiled, as if they were chatting casually at a cocktail party. As if Polly held, not semen, but a gin and tonic in her hand.

"Jake Barnes," Polly said.

"Personally, I prefer Joan Didion," he said, toweling his thighs, "if you like that kind of thing. Anyway, I don't have much time for reading."

Polly started crying; she couldn't help it. She tried to be quiet, but Brag saw.

"Oh, gosh," he said.

"I'm sorry," Polly said.

"No, really," Brag said.

"I'm really sorry," Polly said.

"I'm not being a very good host," he said. He dropped the towel, and pulled on his underwear. His gism was drying on her palm, tightening the skin like beauty treatment.

"Give me just a minute," he said, disappearing into the bathroom. He returned with a damp towel. "Just sit down," he said. "Your turn." He kneeled before her, and took her hand, wiping it with the wet corner of the towel. He wiped her palm, and then he wiped her fingers, individually, tugging lightly on each one. He watched her face intently as he wiped her hand. He sat in his underwear, cross-legged on the floor, and wiped her legs, and her toes. His body looked believable again.

"Oh," said Polly, slowly leaning back on the bed.

He wiped her feet, her calves, her knees. He pulled her panties down, and washed her there, too. Polly turned to face the window, and thought of Eddie. It was snowing. The snow fell up, blown by the breeze, swirling in circles. Brag put his head up under her skirt, and bathed her with his tongue.

Maybe this is what it's like, she thought, suddenly remembering her acting teacher. *Wanting, overcoming obstacles, and then having.* What was the difference between wanting and having, she wondered. She used to think they were related, logically, sensually, interconnected. She had wanted Brag, for instance . . .

But having him was not like getting what she wanted. He brought her off with his tongue. She closed her eyes and wondered how he knew that she was safe.

Duel in the Sun

'm in the kitchen, Merrit's kitchen, with Horatio, who came home with Merrit at four o'clock in the morning, from God knows where. I say "Merrit's kitchen" not just because the apartment is primarily his (I can hardly afford this kind of real estate on the salary I get appraising collectibles), but because this room particularly reminds me of him. It's the leanest, sparest room in the place, with varnished, wide-board floors that squeak comfortably underfoot, an inefficient (no thermometer) old white enamel gas stove I call Rose, painted pinewood American-primitive jelly cupboards, a grocer's table, and some chairs. It's the kind of kitchen in which men in big leather boots sit laconically next to the Franklin stove dropping their *r*'s and refusing to discuss their feelings with the women in the room, who stand erect in calico dresses and dainty aprons. Merrit and me? Well, perhaps. But listen, let me tell you now, you have to understand, it's also the kind of kitchen in which, not so long ago, Merrit would come back with the dog and the paper on a Saturday morning (my one day free from dog duty) still smelling of January cold, and stand still before me, and I would undo the buttons of his ratty old jeans and take his dick in my mouth. It was cold, and so were his hips and thighs, and his ass, which I stroked, and he played with my hair,

56

still holding the *Times*, though the dog crept away with his leash, which scuttled over the floor.

But not this morning. This morning I'm making a salad, and interrogating Horatio. "Where did you boys go last night?" I ask him, but he just sits in the canister on the counter, next to the salad bowl, into which I'm chopping all kinds of vegetables. I'm making something Indian, as in, from India. Sunlight coming in through two big windows on Central Park West illuminates the bowl, which was an anniversary present from me to Merrit, years ago. It's colorful, catching the sun, and I want a sunny, colorful salad to go in it. I'm turning and turning pages of a cookbook by Madhur Jaffrey (a birthday present from Merrit to me), looking for a recipe with the proper color combination, and I'm listening to Stephen Sondheim on the stereo, to which Merrit (he slept four hours last night, guiltlessly, for once not even twitching in his sleep, and awoke as if refreshed, with Marlboro mouth and a sickening grin) has carefully wired big invisible speakers for the kitchen, possibly to drown me out with Mozart first thing in the morning. But now he's out with the dog, and I'm singing along with Miss Alexis Smith, " 'Leave you, leave you, how could I leave you,' " and slicing a carrot.

Then Stanley Kowalski comes in the door. I mean the dog. He's nothing but a strutting couple of balls attached obtrusively to slobbering meat, leading dainty Blanche DuBois, or no, Merrit's more like Alma Winemiller, terminally virginal or rather, sporadically virginal depending on whom she's with and whether she's angry with her father at the moment, or—no, who Merrit is, he's Mary Tyrone, as long as we're doing women of the American stage, he's a nun. He's not addicted to morphine, but he is a nun. "You mustn't touch me when I'm going to be a nun." That's Merrit.

So he walks in with the dog, carrying the *Times*, and a bag with some juice.

" 'Could I wave the years away with a quick good-bye?' " I sing.

Merrit says, "Can I turn that down?"

But he isn't getting an answer from me, not till I know exactly where he was until four this a.m.

I say, "If I had a lover in my life with whom I was conversing, not to mention making love on a regular basis, I would hug him first and say, 'Good morning, darling, turn it however you like.' But I don't have that lover anymore. And thanks to retrospective rage, I'm beginning to wonder if I ever did."

"A simple yes or no will do," he says. He's looking delicious in his blue down parka and blue jeans, through which I can see the outline of his dick, but I've done conciliating, and a dick, even a beautiful dick, is never enough. Take it from me, even if he knows exactly what to do with it—and it's been so long now since I had sex with Merrit I think I've forgotten—it's never enough.

But Merrit is being "reasonable" this morning, his favorite defense. All right, I can play that game as well as anyone. I lay down my carving knife, and walk across the room, and put my arms around him.

"Morning, love," I say, "I'm making *koosmali.* Do I smell like asafetida? And you reeking of twelve-year-old-boy. I don't mean to offend."

"You're intolerable," Merrit said.

"And you're unfaithful."

"You introduced me, Saul."

"Then you admit you were with him."

"I don't admit anything. I'm only saying you introduced him to me. That's all."

Then the dog comes over to me with a nice string of drool, which he's been cooling in that reservoir mouth.

"Will you wipe the goddamned drooler?"

Merrit bends down to Larry, and takes his face in his hands, wiping away the slop with his fingers, as if to demonstrate to me that he's Mother Earth, and nothing living and warm repulses him. He says, "It's all right, Larry, he loves you."

I do not love him. I do not even remotely not mind him. He's a prop, the thing that Merrit pushes between us when we're fighting. When Merrit won't touch me, he touches Larry. When he won't kiss me, he puts his face to his jowels.

"Kick him," I say.

"He doesn't mean it," he says.

"Of course I mean it, Larry," I say.

"Look," Merrit says, getting up, "why don't we just try and have an easy morning together? I think we need more easy moments together, okay?" He starts unpacking his grocery bag. "I wanted to buy us some nice pastry, but I couldn't find any. So I got some wonderful peaches. Look at those. Yummy," he says, running his hands over his stomach and smiling stupidly. And, I mean, I used to find this attractive. I used to find a lot of things attractive about

Merrit that now strike me painfully as the shattered remains of broken promises. I have this thing about broken promises. Maybe because of my father, who was the projectionist in a Loew's Orpheum palace on the Grand Concourse. He always promised to get me into the movies for free, and never did. I waited twenty years. I guess in some respects I'm still waiting, though he's been dead a long time. Is that why I'm married to Merrit? So I can keep on waiting to be taken to the movies?

I say, "I'm waiting for an apology."

Merrit is peeling peaches, and slicing them into the blender. Too many knives at hand, in this little room, I'm thinking. He says, "You'll wait a long time, if you ask."

"Meaning what? You can't at least be bothered to explain?"

"Explanations and apologies have to be given freely, like sex," he says, slice, slice. "They can't be demanded."

"They goddamned well can too be demanded. And sometimes received. Ask Eddie."

"Saul, you're relentless," Merrit says, pouring juice into the blender, with yogurt, and turning it on. *Whoosh, whoosh, whoosh.*

"Don't patronize me."

"Some toast?" he says, plugging in the toaster.

"I want some hot green chilis," I say, turning back to my salad. "This recipe calls for hot green chilis."

"You're a hot green chili," he says.

"I fail to understand," I say, turning around with a bunch of thick carrots with long green stems (Merrit is attentive to visual stimulants), "what makes you so fucking cheerful all of a sudden. After our fight, I mean, and me walking home with not even Horatio for company, and you strolling in at dawn with plum sauce on your collar."

"Who told you I had plum sauce?"

"Dried on your collar, and cuffs."

"Did you run a forensic check on my shirt while I was out with the dog?"

"Not forensic, never forensic, Merrit darling. Forensic is fire. What we have this morning is solid blue ice, the kind that sticks to your tongue."

That is worthy at least of Margo Channing, I think, snapping off the stems of my carrots for emphasis, and dropping them in the garbage.

"You should save those greens," Merrit says, lamely.

"Where were you?" I say. "Picking fruit like Miss Carmen Miranda? With Eddie?"

"Don't get faggy with me, Saul."

"Right, butch."

"You really ought to save those carrot ends, for soup or something."

"How come you never answer me back but with critical little remarks?" I say, chopping carrots. Chop, chop, chop. "What were you and Eddie doing?"

"Shouldn't you wash those?" he says. "They could have insecticide or something."

"They're organically grown. I got them at a health food store."

"Well, they could still be coated with insecticide," says Euell Gibbons. "Never trust a label."

"They don't have labels. Mayonnaise has labels. These are carrots."

"They could still be toxic, that's all."

"So you've never had anything toxic in your mouth? A little bit of rubber, perhaps, or don't you use protection? Hey, Alma, your toast is burning."

"Thank you, I'm aware of that. It's stuck. Have you seen my knife?"

"What am I, Lady Macbeth? You put a knife in there, you'll be electrocuted."

"Compared to you, I might enjoy it."

"That was, as your shrink would probably say, hostile."

"I know."

"Unplug it first."

"No kidding," he says, pulling out smoking slices of bread that he insists, in his general inability to accept failure, on calling, "just a little black around the edges." So he's standing at the garbage pail, scraping charcoal onto the carrot tops, which should have been saved.

"I don't see why," I say, as he scrapes, "I don't see why," and I'm keeping the judgment out of my voice—the thing that Merrit hates is feeling judged, this is something he's developed in therapy, this clinging to the illusion that judgment can be eliminated from any exchange of information, like bones from a chicken, he's a new disciple of feeling, the primacy of feeling and feelings, which apparently are judgment-free, when carefully expressed—"I

60

do not see why," I say, very gently, neutrally, with feeling, "and I'm not expressing opinion, here, I'm just expressing my feelings, Merrit, all right? I respect my feelings, and I respect yours. All right? Just say all right."

"All right," he says.

"All right," I say. "But I don't see why, when you've come home at dawn, and we've just seen Claudio, and carried Horatio, and have to see Claudio again this afternoon, or bury him at least, I don't see why, when you've been dipping your prong into little Ms. Socket, or, God, whatever you were doing, playing the bongo drums and reading aloud from *Tropic of Cancer,* I do not see why you can't just hug me once you get in the door and say you're sorry, even if you're angry, you can say you're sorry, even if you have to lie a little, you can hold me once without its being sexual and say, 'I'm sorry,' which would free me, Merrit, don't you see, to say *I'm* sorry, and then both of us are sorry, even if we're lying, still we've said it, and then we can go on from there. I'm only talking from my feelings."

"You're not," he says, still scraping. "You're making demands."

"I'm not making demands!"

"You know what I asked," he says. "I said that if you wouldn't pressure me. If you would just leave me alone."

"I did leave you alone. You slept four hours this morning."

"You've been after me since yesterday," he says, "suggesting sex."

"I didn't mean sex, necessarily. I wanted to be held. So what?"

"You always want something more, something else."

"What are you, sweet sixteen? You're a cheerleader, Merrit, you know that? A cocktease and a cheerleader, and a Catholic."

"That is wholly beside the point."

"It is right to the point. And so is this: You wander in here, at dawn, I say to myself, 'I won't ask him now. I'll give him time. I'll let him explain and apologize, in his own good time.' "

"You haven't given me a chance. It may take longer than you want."

"How long?"

"Longer than it would take you."

"How long is that?"

"It could take years."

And he says this with absolute conviction. But I've been waiting years already for him, and I'm no longer patient. I remember what

I want, and I compare it to what I have, and the gap between the two is big enough to set up a discotheque. I'm a reasonable person; maybe Merrit is, too. But we're holding on to fantasies, we both believe in the love we felt at first, and projected into the future. Maybe I'm disappointing him, too. I suppose I am. But if I can't have what I want, I'll make him see what a bastard he is. Is that compensation? All right, I'm punishing my father. Maybe with me he's withdrawing from his mother. And it might be easier to get our parents in the room, and let them fight it out, but, of course, my parents are dead, and Merrit's parents might as well be since they moved to Florida.

He says, "I'm not going to deal with you when you're like this."

"You won't deal with me at all."

"This is shit," he says, finally throwing the toast in the garbage, emptying the blender into the sink. "Breakfast is ruined." This is my father, as well, I suppose, this preternatural cool maintained against an antagonism that might easily have been defused with a stroke, a smile, a squeeze, but which he aggravates instead with his withdrawal, until at last he explodes, and says stupid things, like "Breakfast is ruined." He dumped over a card table once, my father, I mean, on which my mother and I were doing a puzzle made from a photograph of a canvas by Jackson Pollock. So many pieces, all painted the same, with different shapes, one of which was missing for years after my father hurled the table across the room and shouted, "Christmas is ruined." Not Hanukkah, you ask? We weren't that religious. My mother's family, they celebrated. At home with my father, we were posing as goys. "Christmas is ruined," he said. I told this story to Merrit once. Apparently, now, he remembers. "Breakfast is ruined," he repeats. He uses all my stories against me, everything I tell the man is ammunition.

So what do I do? It's shameful, but I have to admit, and don't pretend you haven't committed similar acts, with someone, your mother, your lover, assuming there's a difference. I knock Horatio on the floor. I was aiming for the salad bowl, except my aim was never very good. I do knock some carrots off the table, but also, alas, poor Horatio. His canister shatters everywhere, and the bag he was in bursts open, spilling brittle bits of bone and powdery ash on the floor, and his remains get mixed with round bits of carrot.

Merrit says, "Oh Christ."

I say, "That's what you've done to my heart."

I'm not kidding about that.

And now everything happens very fast. Merrit's in a panic to go, and all I know is I don't want him to go.

"You make me sick," he says.

I say, "I feel so rejected, all the time."

"You really make me sick." He's getting into his coat, and rushing out of the kitchen, through the dining room, the living room, the hall. "Your anger," he says, "is outrageous."

"Where are you going? To Eddie?"

"That's perfect," he says. "That's just perfect. Your absurd paranoiac outbursts."

"I'm not paranoiac, Merrit, I'm in love with you. Maybe paranoia is how I express my love."

But he just says, "I'm getting out of here." He says, "You have to learn to act like an adult."

"I am an adult," I say. "I am. I'm just upset. This is how an adult behaves when he's upset."

He's at the door, he's going.

"Just because I handle my hysteria like this and you handle yours like that does not make you any more adult than me," I say. "You're just quieter."

"You're goddamn right I'm quieter," he says, trying to leave, but I'm blocking the door. "You don't have to tell me what you're thinking, what you're feeling, Saul, every minute of the day. Sometimes you can just hang on to it."

"Don't go."

"I want to go."

"I don't want you to go."

"I can't stand being near you, Saul. I can't stand to be near you when you're like this."

I'm clutching his jacket now, and he hits me. He swings his arm around and brings the flat of his palm against the side of my cheek. He says, "That's what you do to me," spent now, going to sit on the floor. "That's what you do to me, because you always have to be the victim."

Now we're both on the floor. I'm holding my face. He's playing with the zipper of his jacket. All his clocks are ringing out the hour. Merrit has about eleven clocks, they ring at different times, with different gongs. It lasts for minutes. Ten gongs here, ten there, like a round, each one starting at about the fifth gong of the one that started just before. Merrit says, "I want out of this. I'm clear about that. I want out." I hold my face. I'm thinking, how did I get to be the wife in this relationship? Then Larry walks into the room, with ash on his nose. He comes for a kiss, and lays a sooty slop of drool on each of our laps.

Secret Love

Eddie went to sleep with Merrit, but he rose with his mother. "This is your wake-up call," his mother said, at seven in the morning. "I'm coming into the city at ten, to do an interview for *Cat Fanciers*. Some man has Abyssinians who jump through hoops or something, I don't know, drink milk through a straw, for God's sake, short-haired skinny cats who yowl and look like drowned rats. He lives on Great Jones Street. Where's that? Wally? Do you want to meet me for lunch? The interview will only take an hour. I thought we might have tea, at the Algonquin. Then there's some new movie with Cher, where they play *La Bohème*. Have you seen it? They have seven dogs who howl at the moon. The man has twelve. Abyssinians. He sent me photographs. They climb on his head. I don't like cats. I never have. Wally, you sound like you were asleep. It seems to me that you're always asleep when I call. Is it just my timing, or are you never awake, or tell me, exactly, what?"

Eddie carried the phone from the trolley to the floor, and lay back down on the rug. The spot where Merrit had lain, with Eddie in his arms, was still imprinted warmly with his shape.

"Don't call me Wally," he said.

"High tea is fourteen dollars. A person. But if we go around noon, it's cheaper, I think. Do you know anything about Abyssinians?"

Eddie's mother wrote articles for half a dozen different dog and cat magazines, *Cat Fanciers, Yorkie Tales, Terrier Chit-Chat.* He called her Doris Day. There were reasons: She was blond and freckled. She loved dogs. When she got drunk at dinner parties, she would wrap herself in a tablecloth (preferably checkered) and sing "It's Magic." Then if there were men around she dropped the tablecloth and they would whistle and she sang "Ten Cents a Dance." She had to be seductive with someone, because Joseph Stalin never responded. He was a cold, exacting man who had restored her to virginity. She was his Immaculate Conception. "I knew Doris Day before she was a virgin," Oscar Levant said once. He meant the real Doris Day, of course, who used to be a band singer before she made all those movies with Rock Hudson, in which they were never allowed to do the wild thing. Eddie dropped his head quickly in silent tribute to Rock, who wouldn't have done the wild thing with Doris, anyway. All that chastity for nothing. But his mother, he thought, had once been passionate, before she married a man who was emotionally stingy, and probably sexually unavailable, too, although that was hard to think about. Still, she had submerged her passions too long, and now she was passing into her eccentric phase, all that energy finally loosed on *Cat Fanciers* and *Yorkie Tales* and Eddie.

"Meet me somewhere glamorous at noon," she said. "Try and wear something nice." She meant a tuxedo. She wanted a son who was romantic and solicitous, with whom she could safely flirt. He wanted a mother who was caring and affectionate. So he was tender with her, and reassuring, as much as he could manage, and she was clever and charming with him. They gave each other what they wanted for themselves. The irony, of course, was that Eddie's homosexuality made him perfectly safe, if only she would acknowledge it—for she could flirt as much as she liked, without too much attendant Oedipal weirdness.

He said, "I wish you'd show me something you're writing, sometime."

"Oh, yes, your mother the doggie journalist," she laughed. She thought acerbic self-deprecation was charming. "We're not going to talk about work. I want a lunch that's scored by George Gershwin. 'Who Cares?' "

"That's sort of my line."

"Yes, but you say it with ennui. When Fred Astaire sings 'Who Cares?' he sings it with élan. He celebrates. You lament."

"I don't think Fred Astaire sang that song."

"Whoever."

"Why don't you come here and I'll cook some oatmeal? Brown rice?"

"I'm not in the mood for a garret, and anyway, you can't cook."

"I can try," he said, doubtfully. He did not feel as incompetent as he pretended with his mother, but it made her more comfortable to see herself as someone with a degree of wisdom, and authority. Actually, she had an emotional range of about three notes, and Eddie was mostly careful to help her stay within her boundaries. But there came a point in every conversation where he got hostile. And he didn't want to fight with Mom this morning. He wanted to lie alone on the floor as long as possible, and imagine that Merrit was the sort of man with whom he was about to get involved in an intense and lasting affair. Merrit was no more that man than Doris Day was an MGM mom, Mary Astor in *Meet Me in St. Louis.* But he had to go with what he had.

"Meet me at Rockefeller Center," he said, humoring her. "I haven't seen the tree."

"The tree's long gone," his mother said. "How long have you lived here?"

"Oh, gosh. Well, we'll look at where the tree was. That'll be exciting, sensory deprivation."

"Your sense of humor escapes me," she said.

So they agreed to meet at Rockefeller Center, where, five hours later, waiting for his mother (she was always ten to fifteen minutes late, though she would have denied it), Eddie leaned over the skating rink and watched the dancing woman, who had been there as long as Eddie could remember, vaguely dressed like Sonja Henie, or Carol Burnett impersonating Sonja Henie. In a corn-yellow wig and lots of rouge, with bells threaded through her laces, she turned pirouettes in the center of the rink, her mouth pinched in self-satisfaction. Eddie did not think she was lonely, or grotesque, just self-absorbed, and rather brave. " 'Once, I had a secret love,' " Rosemary Clooney sang over the sound system, and Eddie thought about Merrit.

There were two Merrits, factual and fictional, but Eddie, who had grown up merely dreaming his sexuality, was more comfortable with the fantasy. That he could have an actual relationship

67

had never occurred to him as a possibility. Sure he had had sex, sometimes more than he wanted, but that wasn't the same thing. He thought about all the times he had stood overlooking this skating rink, watching the dancing woman, or some variation on the dancing woman—sometimes men in Lycra jumpsuits, sleek and epicene, like Conrad Veidt, sometimes teenaged girls from Queens got up like Peggy Fleming. He remembered one Christmas when, having taken the bus home from college, thirteen hours from Cleveland, Ohio, he waited here, as he waited now, to meet his mother, and watched a beautiful white man in a leather flight jacket and corduroy trousers skate circle after circle around the rink. He could have been waiting to meet his date, but no one appeared to claim him, or even to distract him. He kept his hands crossed behind his back, and, tilted forward, his dark brown hair falling in his face, he skated, alone.

Eddie had watched him a long time, wondering secretly, darkly, whether he would ever love a man himself. This had been the crisis of his teens, deciding whether he could dare to love a man. Then he had been surprised to discover in his twenties that daring wasn't enough; he had to find a man first. Had he found one? Merrit was married and forty and fastidious and rich, but Eddie wanted it to be hard. He had spent so much of his life guarding and nurturing secret obsessions, that now the prospect of loving Merrit discreetly, and with difficulty, seemed to him only natural, even preferable. This was how he was accustomed to love.

" 'At last, my heart's an open door,' " Rosie sang. Someone threw a quarter at the dancing woman. She raised her arms over her head, touched her fingers together, and bowed, but she didn't pick up the change, which would have been Eddie's immediate concern. He was always out of money. " 'And my secret love's no secret—' "

"Don't look a gift horse in the mouth," said a familiar voice at Eddie's shoulder. He turned. Indeed, it was Doris Day. "I want a pretzel," she said. He kissed her cold cheek. She said, "Turn around and look at Saks."

"How come?"

"I've got a present for you, and if you're nice, you can have it."

"What present?"

"First turn around."

"I want my present first."

"Just do as you're told."

68

Eddie turned. His mother said, "I met your father there, in 1954. I was off the train from San Francisco. Have I told you this? I came east to be with an opera singer, and I had a ring. He was a tenor, but a nice tenor. I ran through *Rigoletto* in my head, 'La donna è mobile,' all the way from the coast, and I got to Grand Central Station, and he met me, this singer, at the train and took me to the Oyster Bar—and dumped me. In the Oyster Bar. I don't think I was ever in love with him, really, but still. I was more in love with how he rode with me in cable cars at midnight, and how we drank a lot of Irish coffee at the Buena Vista Cafe until three in the morning, and how we swooned at the view from the Top of the Mark, and I thought I would feel even better about him in New York. But he told me, Wally, that a foggy season dangling over the Pacific wasn't like a lifetime in New York. Well," she laughed, "he goddamned knew what he was talking about."

"Don't call me Wally," Eddie said, but affably.

"Why not?" his mother said. "It's not your name? But anyway, Steve Grant. The singer. I had these visions of waking up in an art deco living room somewhere high above Central Park on Saturdays, and watching rehearsals at the Metropolitan Opera, from the family circle. The old Met, I mean, on Broadway, that crumbling old building. It was decadent and nice. They tore it down, of course, just like they tear everything down, Penn Station, for those awful boxes. That's too bad."

"What happened to the singer?"

"Oh, him. I think he's touring in *South Pacific*. That's a basso part, but his voice must have dropped. Serves him right," she laughed. "But as for me, I left the bar that day and slid his ring into a ticket taker's booth, and walked uptown, up Fifth, and ran into your father, there, in front of Saks. He was handing out tickets, his first job out of college (back when one *got* jobs out of college), to a game show called 'You Bet Your Boyfriend.' Ever hear of that? Jesus Christ Almighty, I haven't thought of that in thirty years. 'You Bet Your Boyfriend,' and your father, in a wrinkled suit, a skinny tie, handing out tickets, across from St. Patrick's. That should have been my first warning. The theater wasn't even in the neighborhood. It was way over on Forty-second Street, one of those theaters which is now for dirty movies but in which, at the time, they filmed game shows and early, early soap operas. 'The Secret Storm.' 'The Edge of Night.' How much are pretzels?" she said, fumbling in her pocketbook.

"Let's get some real food," Eddie said. "I'm hungry."

"I want a pretzel first," his mother said, "and then I want some lunch, and then I want to see a movie. Not just any movie, something lush, romantic, something where you don't have the director always telling you that you're watching a goddamned movie. You like that kind of stuff, don't you? I hate it. Too self-conscious. I grew up in the forties, I like big, blunt, gorgeous movies. Not these little neurasthenic things. Woody Allen! Maybe not."

"There's a pretzel vendor over there," Eddie said, pointing across the skating rink.

"Woody Allen wasn't bad, before he started imitating Bergman," Eddie's mother said, still searching in her pocketbook. "Like the Beatles. They were fine, you know, until they started taking acid. 'Love Me Do' is a very pretty song. And then 'Michelle.' But all that double tracking. Maybe it was Yoko Ono. Listen, all I've got's a dollar and a credit card."

"I've got a couple of dollars," Eddie said. "I'll spring for pretzels."

"Would you? I'm sorry, Wally, but it's just I've only got the ticket for the bus ride home. Unless the pretzel vendor takes American Express."

"On me. Just promise not to call me Wally anymore." He moved across the plaza.

"What would you prefer?" his mother said, a step behind him. "Toulouse-Lautrec? No, actually, that I might understand. At least it has a little bit of style, and you could wear berets. It makes you think of *An American in Paris*. Gene Kelly, Leslie Caron. What does Eddie Socket make you think of? General Electric."

"That's the point," said Eddie. "Besides which Waldo Jeffers is only slightly less ridiculous. What does Waldo make you think of? It makes me think of Waldron Farms, the dairy, where we used to get our milk."

"It makes me think of Clifton Webb, in *Laura*. His name in that movie, if I am not mistaken, was Waldo Lydecker."

"Oh God," Eddie said, finally beginning to giggle. He didn't like to laugh with his mother at his own expense. It felt like collusion. But it was old habit. "How can you remember things like that?"

"Well, anyway, it was your father's name."

"Past tense? *Was.*"

"That's all over with now," she said, unconvincingly. Eddie had heard this before.

"Oh," he said, stopping at the pretzel stand, "let's not get Joseph Stalin into this."

The vendor, a little man with thick black eyebrows and a watch cap, looked like Michael Dukakis. Eddie ordered two hot pretzels, and the vendor painted them with runny, acid-yellow mustard.

"Your father used to know a man who looked like him," his mother said, flicking her head at the vendor. "Some religious academic. I tell you. Catholics. It isn't bad enough that they believe in it, they have to read and talk about it, and discuss it all the time. Though I never heard this man speak, this pretzel vendor man. He was kind of . . . strange. He lisped. Like Truman Capote. Sometimes I suspected they were having an affair."

"I'm having an affair," Eddie said, suddenly.

"What?" she asked. "Don't talk with your mouth full." She had the pretzel halfway to her face. Eddie paid the vendor, pulling old, wadded bills out of his pocket.

"Do you want to hear about it?" he said, shyly.

"Hear about what?" she said, taking a huge bite out of her pretzel. Eddie handed her a napkin. Mustard dripped to the sidewalk, splattering the toes of Eddie's sneakers, yellow on pink.

"I think he's married."

"Who's married? Listen, other people have normal families. Sheepdogs, basketball courts, economy cars. I get an old-time Catholic intellectual, and then a son named Eddie Socket."

"I think I really like this guy."

"I really liked your father. For about eleven minutes."

"But you stayed with him for years," Eddie said, getting his change. "What was the secret of his appeal?"

"He didn't know anything about opera."

Eddie smiled.

"Here's your present," she said, pulling a book out of her bag, a paperback biography of Montgomery Clift. "Let's go have lunch somewhere your father would have hated, and overtip the waiters." She took another bite of pretzel, getting mustard on the tip of her nose, which now matched Eddie's shoes.

"I thought we agreed on the Algonquin," Eddie said, reaching for the book. But his mother still held on to it. This was a gift with a message attached.

She said, soberly, looking down at *Monty,* "It's very sad."

"I've never been to the Algonquin," he said, feeling needled. His life was sad, so what? He pointed to her nose. "Wipe," he said.

71

"His life was very sad," she said, still somber, but touching her nose experimentally, and finally releasing the book. She got the mustard on her fingers.

"We'll pretend," Eddie said, tucking the book under his arm, relieved, "that we're Robert Benchley and Dorothy Parker. We'll have tea and brioche. Of course, for them it would have been gin and cigarettes, but anyway, we'll fake it." He handed her a napkin. "I'll be Dorothy Parker."

"I don't need to hear about that kind of stuff," she said, wiping her face.

They sat at a small table in a room in the Algonquin which was not the famous one, though it was outfitted convincingly, Eddie thought, in weighty restaurant drag, with tacky crystal chandeliers and pewter candelabra, starchy tablecloths and fat-handled silverware, career waiters smiling obsequiously, sugar cubes, individually wrapped, and an abundance of ashtrays. The stale afternoon air was as heavy as the doughy crumpets served on thick white china, and the room was oppressively quiet. Their waiter was a small, gray man (his hair and hands and face all uniformly gray) with a slight paunch and a droll expression, and he actually had a white cloth draped deferentially over his left forearm. His mustache was a thin dry line of bristle on his upper lip.

"He looks like Clifton Webb, in *Laura*," Eddie giggled.

"Will pastry be enough?" his mother asked. "Oh, well, it'll have to be." She nodded to the waiter, who moved away so quietly, and with such awareness of his servitude, and pride in his invisibility, that it was impossible not to watch him go.

"That's how you'll end up," his mother said. "If you don't settle down."

"What do you mean, 'settle down'?"

"If you don't get a job, I mean."

"I have a job."

"I mean a job job."

"What's wrong with word processing? Or waiters, for that matter?"

"You know what I mean."

"Yeah, right, as in, waiter is a euphemism for the G-word.' "

"I don't care what you do," his mother said.

"G as in Gay."

"I told you that I don't care what you do."

He took a sugar cube, unwrapped it, popped it in his mouth. He sucked, and then he chewed, thinking of Merrit. He decided to believe he was on the verge of marriage, to a man—just to counter his mother's attacks. Why not? Merrit was already married, but if he got a divorce, then he could marry Eddie, and they could have his mother for tea at his apartment. But they hadn't even done the wild thing, not yet. What would his naked body be like? Eddie wondered, enjoying the fantasy. How soon would he get to see it? He took another sugar cube, and chewed first, then sucked. There wasn't much to suck on after chewing, he thought—a pornographic notion. His mother was still talking.

"That's insidious," she said, "and vile."

Eddie sat up straighter. "What?"

"Your button."

Eddie touched his jacket collar. He had forgotten to remove his "Reagan Youth" button, which his mother hated.

"It's in quotes," he said, appeasing.

"What's that mean, 'in quotes'?"

"It's ironic."

"Not ironic enough. Not for me, at least."

"I thought you didn't care what I did."

"What you do. Not what you wear. At least, when you're with me."

But the waiter brought tea, and two of the doughy white crumpets, speckled with blueberries, and Eddie's mother cut her crumpet silently, as if reconnoitering. The knife clattered against the plate.

"You're a generation of critics, Wally," she said finally. "You can't do. You can only undo."

Eddie sighed. This was their standard argument.

"You taught me how," he said, unable to resist his lines. "All your disenchantment with America, in 1969. You talked about it all the time. I listened."

"I want you to take that button off," she said. "Waldo Adlai Stevenson Jeffers."

"You don't respect me, do you?" Eddie said.

"Waldo is your name. It's a perfectly good name. I don't know why you want to change it. Just to make an anti statement? Why bother. You're so lethargic. What makes you so lethargic?"

"You gave me everything I ever wanted."

"Another cliché to mask your laziness."

"I got a postcard from Dad yesterday," Eddie said, changing the subject. It was a survival tactic. He wanted to neutralize his mother, or, at least, redirect her. Sometimes Joseph Stalin was good for this. "Another one. Plain white, no picture on the front, the prestamped kind you get at the post office window. On the front was my address, with the apartment number wrong. I'm amazed it even got to me. On the back, another one of his aphorisms. Like he was Polonius advising Laertes or something, sending me away to Wittenberg."

But his mother didn't respond the way he wanted.

"I'll say this about your father," she said, "he's unyielding."

"No kidding," Eddie said.

"Principled, I mean."

"Oh," Eddie said, disappointed. Whenever she praised Joseph Stalin, he knew he was in trouble.

"He's never sacrificed his principles," his mother said. "When you get to be my age, you'll understand how hard that is."

" 'Principles are something people with character can do without,' " Eddie said. "Who am I quoting?"

"That's 'reputation,' " said his mother, "not 'principles.' I don't worry about my reputation, either, but I do have principles. You take that button off right now, or I'm leaving." She bit into her crumpet. "I don't understand you," she said. "I grew up with patriotism and World War Two and kill the commies. You grew up with Watergate and Vietnam. Why are you the Reaganite?"

"I'm not anything, because it doesn't matter. I could go for Reagan, I could go for Teddy Kennedy. They're both murderers. You know? What does it matter?" This was his official pose, when Mom got aggressive—he played the hip disaffected. She was disaffected, too, perhaps even more profoundly than he was, but she never posed. Even when she was being flip, she was always deadly in earnest.

"Well, my feelings matter, and I will not be seen in public with a young man wearing a reactionary slogan on his chest. If you want to be a fascist in your own time, that's your prerogative." She chewed angrily. "I suppose you must have gotten it from one of your apathetic friends. Someone who plays feedback on a cattle prod and you write lyrics."

Eddie laughed. "You're so retro-sixties, sometimes," he said.

"I suppose they're all homosexual, your apolitical friends, and misogynistic?"

"Is that what this is about? I don't like the word 'homosexual.' "

"You tell your mother you're in love with a man. What would you call it?"

"We prefer 'gay.' " He laughed, and said, "Listen to me, I sound like I'm quoting David Leavitt. All I mean is everybody's gay to some degree. But that doesn't matter. It's just what I'm doing right now."

"Well, what I'm doing right now is telling you to take that button off."

"Take off your turtleneck," Eddie said, "I'll think about it."

He sipped his tea. His mother glared. The waiters watched them disapprovingly, for the room was slowly filling, and they were drawing some attention. His mother looked around angrily, considering the crowd. Then she seemed to make a decision. She wiped her fingers on her napkin, crossed her arms, and pulled her turtleneck over her head. It caught in her earrings, covering her face but exposing her bra. Then, in a muffled voice, she said, "Now, if I spray-painted 'McCarthy Youth' across my tits, would you be embarrassed to be seen with me in public?"

He actually wanted to laugh, but he was hurt now, and didn't want to reward her. She would always settle for laughter as a concession of her victory. And Eddie shared her sense of humor, completely. He loved her for being outrageous. They found the same things funny. Unfortunately, his life was one of those things. It was perhaps their biggest shared joke. He refused to indulge her now. He picked up his present, and said, "You ought to have a lover."

"Don't be flip."

"You ought to leave New Jersey."

"I did leave. Just this morning."

"But you're going back."

"I don't abandon my responsibilities," she said, pulling her shirt back into place.

"Maybe you should."

He looked at the pictures in *Monty*. It occurred to him now that his mother believed all gay men ended up like Montgomery Clift, dead too young, without a lover, drinking and swallowing pills. That was what her gift had been about. But if adulthood meant not being lonely, or alone, well, then, she wasn't any better at being an adult than he was. She was lonely, too, even frightened, though she would never admit it. He felt a sudden, inarticulate rush of tenderness for her that frightened him, and he thought again of

Merrit. He decided, oddly, that they would make a good pair, Merrit Mather and his mother. They had similar tastes. They both liked dogs, anyway. And she was only ten or twelve years older than Merrit.

"He's the man I think you should have married," Eddie said. "That must be it."

"You can look now," she said, tucking in her turtleneck. "I'm decent. What man?"

Eddie put down the book. "Merrit Mather." He hadn't meant to tell her his name, but now that he had said it, he was glad. If he could convince her they were lovers, maybe it would come true. "He's from Massachusetts."

"I don't like New Englanders." She finished her tea. "What does he do?"

Eddie scraped the crumbs from the tablecloth around his plate, brushing them into his palm. Their lunch was over. He signaled for the check.

"I don't know," he said, blushing. "We only met last night. He has nice eyebrows."

"Your father had a smile. What a smile. What a disappointment. Well," she said, reaching for her pocketbook. The waiter brought the check. "Well." She got into her coat. "Listen, call your father. He's got a birthday coming up."

"You care?"

"If you don't call him, he calls me, complaining. Only time I ever hear from him."

The waiter brought the check. "They overcharge here," Eddie said.

"I know."

"Don't pay."

"Don't tempt me."

She signed the receipt.

"Eddie," she said, pocketing her credit card. "You and your friend. You don't . . . hold hands . . . in public, do you? Walking down the street?"

"What?"

"You don't hold hands in public, do you, walking down the street?"

"Do we? Oh. Well. I don't know."

"What do you mean, you don't know. It's a yes or no question, either you do, or you don't. Which is it?"

"Well, I guess we don't," Eddie said. "We only met last night."

"Just don't do that," she said. "All right? I couldn't stand the thought of that."

Eddie shrugged and laughed, giving up, and said, "Perhaps" and "Alas," and he and his mother went to see the Cher movie where they played *La Bohème*. It was a movie to see with a lover, not a mother, or a son. Eddie clutched *Monty* consolingly, and he saw the movie again, the following night, with Merrit.

A Weekend in the Country

At the time of his outing with Mom, Eddie had already convinced himself that he would probably never see Merrit again, much less hold his hand, or do the wild thing. But Merrit surprised him. He had called the following day, and the week after that, and again the week after that, two or three times. Their dates were oddly nonsexual—five minutes into some kind of embrace, which Merrit initiated, he withdrew, leaving Eddie to wonder exactly what he wanted. A younger brother? But he kept pursuing, flirting, seducing. They still hadn't done the wild thing when, after almost a month, Merrit invited him to his barn in Massachusetts, where, Eddie thought, they would surely go into the wilderness together at last.

It was Friday morning at the end of April, still faintly winter, and Eddie was running late. He had agreed to meet Merrit downstairs at eight, but by the time he got outside, it was eight-fifteen, and Merrit was annoyed. He had double-parked, and his dog was panting in the backseat of his car, which was spitting exhaust. He leaned on the hood, waiting. Country Merrit: he was wearing blue jeans and canvas boating shoes, and a blue down parka. His jeans fit perfectly. He had small hips and high, rounded buttocks and a neat, square waistline; his trousers hung on him as if they had been arranged there by a photographer's assistant. The cut of the material was just exactly right for him; the way the fabric tucked and wrinkled at his crotch was sexy and exciting. *He's a Levi's commercial,* Eddie thought, crossing the street to meet him. *I'm in love with a man who is a Levi's commercial.* And the button-fly would open cleanly, simply, quickly, from the top, a pull at the waistline and the sound of metal knuckling through supple fabric.

But Merrit was tense from waiting, and his face and forehead were red with early-spring cold. His cheeks and chin were lightly creased with salt-and-pepper stubble, and he had a stern look pasted on a boy's face; a boy's face, tense and excited, peering out of a man's disconcerted expression. He could be arbitrary, and he could be punishing, but when he smiled or laughed, he was eleven. He wasn't smiling now.

"I'm late," Eddie said, apologetically, instinctively stopping an arm's length away.

"Do you worry about that kind of thing? Punctuality?"

"Oh, well," Eddie said, indifferently, surprised at Merrit's coolness. He wanted to kiss him, maybe on the cheek, and was annoyed that he felt he couldn't. "Sometimes."

"Is that all you're bringing?" Merrit pointed to Eddie's knapsack. The street was quiet, except for a group of high school–aged children, speaking Spanish and English alternately and rapidly, boasting and yelling and laughing, skipping rocks across the street.

"I've got enough."

"You'll need a couple of sweaters, probably."

"I'll wear yours."

"And warm socks."

"I brought socks," Eddie said, finally putting his hand on Merrit's shoulder. "Hi." He leaned close.

Merrit slid the knapsack from his arm. "I'll put this in the trunk," he said, slipping out of Eddie's reach.

"Don't we get to hug?" Eddie asked, following. "I mean, would you call and invite me away for the weekend if we weren't even planning on having a hug?" He laughed tentatively.

Merrit opened the trunk. Exhaust fumes sputtered out of the tail pipe in rhythmic blasts, warming their ankles. "You're not serious," he said, wedging Eddie's knapsack neatly between the spare tire and a pair of old riding boots. "It's eight o'clock in the morning."

"We'll be arrested?"

"We're out in the street."

His mother needn't have worried, Eddie thought. No chance of holding hands in public with Merrit. "Nobody's watching."

"Those kids are watching."

"Those kids are kids."

"They're speaking Spanish."

"Some of them."

"Too many of them."

"So what? You're speaking English."

"And carrying a wallet."

"Maybe they have wallets, too."

"Maybe they have knives."

"Plastic knives," said Eddie, "from McDonald's. You're more dangerous to them than they are to you."

"Can we get started?" Merrit said, impatiently, closing the trunk, glancing at his watch. "I think we can continue this debate in the car."

Eddie shrugged. He was going away for the weekend with a man who was uptight about Puerto Ricans. Merrit was a closet racist. He was impatient, patronizing, and homophobic. Not kiss in the street? Did he think he was trapped in *The Well of Loneliness*, or what? In the story of his life, he probably killed himself in the end, like something out of Gore Vidal. Eddie saw all this at once, distinctly. But he kept it to himself. It was important to him to be able to kiss Merrit in the street, but it was even more urgent to appease, which was what he did best.

"You're not happy," Merrit said, when they were in the car.

"Oh," Eddie said, dishonestly, "I don't know, not really. It's nice to be with you. It's just that you don't seem too glad to see me. Kind of cold and on the march, you know? I mean, I was ten minutes late. So what? It feels more like I'm going away to military camp than to a—I don't know, romantic?—weekend. This is supposed to be romantic, isn't it? I mean, it's about the most romantic thing I've ever done," he said, ingenuously.

Merrit leaned back in his seat, relaxing a little. He laughed stiffly. "I guess I'm pretty uptight," he said. "That's what Saul tells me. And my therapist. Eddie, you're going off to spend the weekend with a married man who has a therapist. Why aren't you uptight?"

"I think you're beautiful. Really, that sounds corny, but it's true. It's not that I'm uncritical. For instance, I don't think your dog is beautiful. But you are."

Merrit laughed. Eddie had said the right thing. He wanted a kiss, and he got it. Merrit leaned across the seat and offered the inside of his lip, which was warm, and tasted like coffee. Eddie relaxed. He was wrong; it wasn't Merrit's self-loathing homophobia, or his disapproval, that kept him so cool. He was just nervous, the way that Eddie was nervous, yet he wanted to be affectionate. Eddie hugged him, feeling the pleasing hard smallness of his upper body. "You're wonderful," he said.

"You're very sweet. Now would you mind wiping the dog?" Merrit pushed Eddie away, and buckled his seat belt. "He's sort of drooling. Make sure you get the towel way up inside his cheeks. He's a saliva factory."

He shifted into gear. The car and the dog lurched forward at once. Larry slopped a glob of drool on the back of Eddie's neck, and the glove compartment sprang open onto his lap. "Funky car," he said, giving Larry's jowls a perfunctory wipe. "Funky dog."

"Sentimental value," Merrit said.

"Which one?"

"Both."

Eddie wondered briefly what Saul would have to say about Merrit's dog. It would be cruelly accurate. For that matter, what would Saul have to say about him right now? For weeks, Eddie had been trying not to think about this.

"Listen, Merrit," he said, "can we stop and get some caffeine? I need my fix." He slammed the glove compartment door. It didn't stick.

"I was thinking we could drive straight through to Massachusetts," Merrit said. "I'd like to get there kind of early, start our day." He looked hopefully at Eddie. "Turn the knob, and really push," he said.

"I desperately need some caffeine," Eddie said, still struggling.

"You don't see eight o'clock in the morning too often, do you, my little dove?" Merrit said, leaning over. He flicked Eddie's hand out of the way, and closed the glove compartment door securely. Eddie could smell his hair.

"Oh, and I need to stop at the bank, too. The closest one is Fourth and Twelfth. You mind?"

They stopped for a light at First Avenue. Larry turned restlessly in the backseat, panting anxiously, breathing in Eddie's ear.

"Why didn't you do all of this ahead of time?"

"Are we on a schedule?"

"Of a sort."

"I thought this was a carefree weekend in the country."

"Well, but some people manage to work out all of their errands ahead of time. Then they don't have to worry. That's what carefree means."

"No, it doesn't. Carefree means the opposite. It means not caring. I don't work on an ahead-of-time agenda. I'm not that kind of person."

"How do you ever get anything done?"

"I get a lot done."

"You haven't gotten to the bank."

"I'll get there now. You'll take me."

"What if I don't?"

"Of course you will. You're not that controlling, are you?"

"Yes, I am, if you're that irresponsible."

"Oh God. Are you sure you're not my mother?" Eddie said, lightly. "I could have had this conversation with her. 'When are you getting a real job? When are you getting medical insurance?' "

"You don't have medical insurance?" Merrit said, brutally inquisitive.

"Don't you start."

"How can you be a gay man living in the city in this day and age and not have medical insurance? That's not rational."

"What's rational?"

Merrit tapped his fingers on the wheel, impatiently, waiting for the light to change. Larry pushed under his arm, and Merrit stroked his ears, slowly, woefully, and lay his face against Larry's cheek.

"Look," Eddie said, "it's not a big issue, okay?" He pulled one of Merrit's hands away from the dog. "I don't believe in health insurance. I don't believe in hospitals. I don't believe in planning ahead. That's all. You don't believe in things, too. Spanish-speaking people. Spontaneity. We're just different."

"I'm quite spontaneous," Merrit said. "Otherwise, we wouldn't be here."

"That's true," said Eddie. "I'm sorry."

"I don't mind your stopping at the bank," said Merrit. "I don't mind your having very little money. I don't mind your bringing nothing warm to wear this weekend, or your being late, or any of that. What I just can't stand is your pretending that it doesn't matter. I just can't stand it; that's a pose. If you have to stop for money, then you have to stop for money. Don't pretend it's philosophical, because it's not. All right? I just can't stand that kind of posing."

"It *is* philosophical. Sort of."

"No, it's not."

"Oh," said Eddie, sighing, "it is and it isn't."

The light changed. "Just don't pretend with me," Merrit said, shifting gear.

"The coffee shop's right there," Eddie said.

They pulled to the sidewalk.

"Here," Merrit said, reaching for his wallet, pulling out a twenty-dollar bill. "Get your 'caffeine.' Pay me later. Wait," he said, replacing the twenty, and pulling out a fifty. "That should do you for the weekend."

"Can't we just stop at my bank? I've got the money, I just need to get to it. Your money is in your wallet. Mine is in my bank. I don't like to carry money. You do. Could we just stop at my bank?"

"Take the money," Merrit said. "All right? It's easier. Pay me next week."

Eddie took the bill, reluctantly, opening the door. "Listen," he said, "do you have anything smaller? It's just I don't think they'll change a fifty."

Merrit handed him a dollar. "Why don't you get me something, too. Some coffee," he said, heavily. "Is this enough?"

"It's fine," Eddie said.

"Black."

"Okay, fine."

"But hurry up."

Eddie shut the door. When he came back with tea and coffee, the dog was in his seat, and Merrit was still sulking. He sulked all the way out of the city. Eddie was surprised, and slightly hurt, but he didn't let on, not even to himself. He believed that Merrit had the right kind of life—a house, a dog, and a car, and a beautiful body—and he didn't want to question his authority. If he was sulking, Eddie thought, and unpleasant, that must have been the best response to the situation. Merrit was supposed to be a hero, after all, and heroes were always right. And indeed, an hour later, when he finally spoke, he was gracious and apologetic. He took Eddie's hand, and said he was sorry. Eddie said, "Me, too."

"I *am* uptight, Saul's right," Merrit said. "It's my thing about sex."

Now they were getting down to business, Eddie thought. What was his "thing" about sex? "If you're worried about AIDS . . . " Eddie said.

"Well, of course I am," Merrit said, sounding more relaxed.

Eddie had made the correct response. "But only in the abstract now. I didn't tell you, Eddie, but I got the test, and yesterday they gave me the results. I tested negative."

Eddie laughed. "That's good timing." He touched his arm. But Merrit didn't seem to want to be touched, and went on talking about himself very coolly, as if what he wanted wasn't empathy, but verification. In that respect Merrit was like his father, Eddie unhappily decided. He didn't want to be loved; he only wanted to be told that he was right.

"I guess I shouldn't worry so much," Merrit said. "I've never gotten fucked. Do you mind my being so direct? But it's not really that, not AIDS, not really." He paused. "I've been scared a long time," he said, finally. "Scared about sex. I've had a difficult time."

"I'm sorry," Eddie said, immediately, sympathetically, loving him. Of course, there had been something, back in high school, grammar school, for Merrit, too. He could bear Merrit's coolness if he knew it came from his pain. And he couldn't help wondering, conceitedly, if Merrit talked this way to Saul. It was his competitive streak, which he hardly ever acknowledged. But the idea of a forty-five-year-old man confiding in him, rather than his longtime lover, was rather exciting. He said, "Difficult how?"

Merrit answered the question with a question. "Do you remember the first time you ever came?"

"The first time I came?" Eddie wasn't certain whether he should laugh, but Merrit was absolutely serious. Eddie touched his cheek. "I don't know."

"The first time I came," Merrit said, "was with an older man. It was scary. But I think I was in love with him. I wanted his attention. Though I'm not sure I wanted sex."

"How old were you?"

"I was ten."

"Gosh. How old was he?"

"He must have been—how old are you?"

"I'm twenty-eight," Eddie said.

"Well, he was twenty-nine."

"And you were ten," Eddie said. "Kids that age are far more sexual than people realize." He wanted to say the right thing, to console, or gently probe, or simply understand. Very gently, he asked, "You had sex?"

"No, he didn't touch me. He never really did, it wasn't what he

84

wanted. Sometimes he would show himself to me, I think, but mostly he would talk to me. He talked about masturbating, and things like that. I think young boys are sexual, you're right. I was sexual, but unaware. I didn't know the consequences. Perhaps that's the difference." He cleared his throat. "But I was excited. The thought of talking to this man about masturbating, which, the very word, when I was ten, in 1953—"

"Mamie Eisenhower didn't masturbate."

Merrit laughed. "I like you," he said. He squeezed his hand, quickly. "I wasn't even supposed to masturbate," he said. "I certainly wasn't supposed to be turned on by a man. But I liked his attention. He was attentive, and attractive, and attracted to me. I got all confused. I wanted him, except I also didn't. But I know I had an erection." He lowered his voice. "It hurt me, Eddie, it was so exciting, and confusing, and I didn't understand. I really wanted him. Maybe I wanted a father. But I had a father, and this was my teacher, talking seductively, and I got an erection, and came. I came in my trousers. And do you know what? In some ways I think it was the most erotic thing that ever happened to me."

Eddie was quiet a long time. He said, "Gosh." He wasn't certain why Merrit was confiding in him. It was pretty personal stuff. He wanted to feel moved, but there was something about Merrit's delivery he didn't trust. But he felt excited. For the peculiar effect of Merrit's story was that it gave him an erection. Was that what Merrit intended?

He said, "Would you like a hug?"

Merrit said, a bit patronizing, perhaps, "You're very sweet."

"Well, you're very brave," Eddie said, though Merrit didn't seem to notice. He said, "Thanks," nodding sadly. He had a very sexy way of feeling sorry for himself. Eddie undid his seat belt, and rearranged his dick in order to lean over into Merrit's lap.

Merrit stroked his hair. "Are you falling in love with me?" he said, very softly. It occurred to Eddie that he probably was.

Merrit's barn was back in the woods, far from the road, at the end of a long dirt lane. They got there at noon, stopping first at a market for breakfast supplies, then following a series of narrower and narrower roads. Larry stood on the divider between the two front seats and panted, and Merrit actually babbled. He talked about the houses they passed, mentioning all the neighbors by name. He talked about the former lovers he had brought to the barn. Eddie counted back from Saul two lovers, three affairs, an ex-wife, two girlfriends. What were they all doing now? None of them was happy, Merrit said; they still sent birthday cards.

Finally, they turned onto an overgrown path, which led to the barn, a small square building with weathered siding and a red tin roof. It was set low against the sky, back in the woods, surrounded by long, tall grass. It was very primitive, Merrit said; it had electricity, but no indoor plumbing. There was an outhouse, and they could bathe in the pond. Or for two days they could go without washing.

Inside, it was one big room, with a sleeping loft, a wood-burning stove, and a funky old couch and a couple of armchairs, spread over a big braided rug. The ceiling was high, and the windows were small and square. Larry hung around the door, sniffing and pissing. The car doors were still open; they hadn't started unloading. But Merrit ran upstairs to the sleeping loft, and pulled Eddie onto the bed, where Eddie buried his face in his neck. This time there was no hesitation. He pressed his groin against Merrit's thigh, and ran his hands over his sides, and Merrit responded. He was a good lover, an attractive one, anyway; Eddie liked his smallness, thinness. He held him and giggled, and the dog was barking, now, at the foot of the bed.

"Go away," Merrit said, chasing the dog down the stairs, and out the door. He ran back up to Eddie, pulling off his shirt, which came over his head in a single, efficient gesture. He pulled at the fly of his jeans. Eddie wanted to do it for him, but he understood instinctively that Merrit preferred to be watched, and admired, like something under glass. And after all, he had a fabulous body. His trousers came open, and his belly, flattened, tapering, was soft with hair, and his pubic hair sprang back from where the jeans had crushed it flat. He wasn't wearing underwear. He slipped his hands palms-down inside the waistline of his trousers, which he slid to the floor, took two steps, and was naked. Eddie saw him naked. And his legs were shorter than they might have been, and he had hair that grew out from the center of his chest and curled to his nipples, which were brown and ovoid, slightly pinched. There was something tidy and reassuring about his body; he was almost perfectly symmetrical. His arms were thin and he was small-waisted, and his shoulders were smooth and lightly freckled, and the muscles of his chest formed hard and flat and lean, and well defined, and his ass was smooth and his prick was wonderful, erect.

He crossed his arms over his chest and hopped, three short, ecstatic hops, to the bedside, and took Eddie up in his arms, and started pulling off his clothing. His slender body, smooth brown skin, neatly formed chest and arms, tight stomach, muscular legs, came into Eddie's awareness a bit at a time, cutting into his flesh, hitting his skin. Eddie let himself be undressed, aware that his skin was pale, his stomach round like a baby's. But his shoulders were broad and his legs were long, and he wasn't wearing underwear, either. He was sorry that his socks were three days old with wear, they probably smelled. He had forgotten about his socks this morning. But his dick was stiff, it was out in the open, and Merrit pulled him off the bed.

He followed Merrit back down the stairs, across the living room, to the door, which Merrit pushed open, going outside.

"It's cold," Eddie said, lingering at the door, unable, standing in the open now, to hide his nakedness against Merrit's.

"It's not," said Merrit.

"It's like winter."

"Early spring."

"A cold spring. I'm a city boy."

"Don't use that excuse. You're a farm boy from New Jersey."

He pulled him outside. Eddie felt the cold air slightly at his breastbone, and below his buttocks. Larry followed along, barking. He carried a stick in his mouth, swinging it dangerously around Eddie's knees, twisting his powerful neck. The grass was brown and wet as if after a rainfall, and the sun had moved brightly into the open, warming Eddie's back. Merrit was standing naked in the garden patch, among a bunch of white narcissi. His prick swung out above the flower heads. Eddie almost laughed.

"You're D. H. Lawrence," he said, crossing his hands over his chest and pressing his knees together, crouching.

And Merrit said, slyly (he was performing, but it was delightful), "Handle my stamen."

Eddie ran to him, moving carefully through the grass, avoiding rocks and stickers. Merrit had a flower in his hand. He had broken its stem in half, and a sticky, slick liquid, thick and cloying, dripped from the stem, and from his fingers. When Eddie reached him, he felt Merrit's hand around his cock, coating it with the substance from the fresh green stem of the narcissus. It was grand. If Merrit would promise always to be this outrageously seductive, Eddie thought, he could endure any degree of insensitivity. But, alas, he understood that part of Merrit's ability to be charming came from his knowing their involvement had a definite ending.

Merrit put on a brilliant performance, and the setting, Eddie thought, was so picturesque. Merrit was smiling, and the dog was nearby. He felt the sunlight, and the cold, and Merrit's hand. The flowers were pink in the sun. There was grass between his toes. It was too queer. He giggled. He said, "For God's sake let me live, and have my love!" He said, "I'm quoting John Donne." He laughed. He had no idea what a normal love affair was like, but, gosh, he looked up at the sky, and down at Merrit's dick, and he thought, *I've had a moment.* It had been two years, after all, and Merrit's dick was absolutely safe. He slid to his knees and took Merrit full in his mouth.

My Lover Is a Fish,

This Merrit Mather, scale lapping scale with spruce-cone regularity. Eddie Socket doesn't know it yet, but he'll find out, the man's a fish. I don't mean Christlike, either, I mean cold. Just look at him, his face, it's narrow, two-dimensional, his brow slopes sharply down to his nose, which ends above a pair of puckered lips. It is possible to see Merrit only in profile; from the front, he disappears. Oh, and neatly structured, fishily, with flat white bits of flesh arranged in symmetrical strips along a sharp, straight backbone and glistening ribs. In the summer, he is browned like a charbroiled bass; in winter he is haddock pale. And what about his soul?

We're standing in the doorway leading out of our apartment, and Merrit is carrying his matching vinyl luggage with leather fittings, a shoulder bag, and a small duffel bag. It's Saturday morning, and he's got the dog on his leash. He says, "Do me a favor, and call the garage, tell them I'm coming for the car." He's going away for the weekend, his great excursion to his barn in Massachusetts, and he's taking Eddie. It's their fifth date, exactly. Merrit doesn't think I keep track, but I do.

"Call your own goddamn garage," I say, "you're the one who's leaving."

"I just thought you could do this one last thing."

"I've done a lot of things for you. It hasn't gotten me what I wanted."

"That's because the only thing you want is my dick."

"It's not your dick."

"It is."

"It's not."

"Then what?"

"Oh God," I sigh. He looks determined, independent. He looks separate from me. He looks "clear." That's one of his words. Or maybe it's one of his therapist's words. Anyway, whenever Merrit feels clear about something, shortly afterward, he's leaving. Recently he's clear that he needs to think about another way of life. Which consists, apparently, of running off to Massachusetts with a twenty-one-year-old, and being worshiped for a weekend. Poor Eddie.

"Maybe I just want a hug, sometimes," I say.

"I'm going off for a liaison with a man and you want a hug?"

"Oh," I say. "Maybe not."

Merrit drops his shoulder bag, his duffel bag, the dog leash. "Come here," he says.

"What?"

He holds out his arms.

"Come here."

All right, so whose side am I on? I let him hug me. He puts his arms around my back and squeezes, briefly, and he pecks me on the cheek. It's pathetically little, but he acts like it's so much. With Merrit, a wink sometimes is as good as a fuck—you have to learn to take the intention for the act, or else you'll die of loneliness.

Merrit pulls away, saying, "Saul, I got some good news, yesterday."

I'm thinking, What, you discovered you had a soul, after all?

He says, "I got tested, Saul. It came out negative. I tested negative."

I say, "Back up, I missed a transition. You got tested?"

"Oh, yeah, sure," he says, "I thought you knew."

"I certainly did not."

"I know that we discussed it, Saul, and you decided that you didn't want to know, and I decided that I did."

"That was hypothetical," I say, "that conversation was completely hypothetical. Wasn't it?"

"But then I said that I was going to get the test."

90

"You never said that, Merrit."

"Oh, Saul," he says, patronizing now. "You do have a way of remembering selectively." He kisses me again on the cheek. "Anyway, I thought that it would make you happy."

"Happy? What, so now that I can fantasize about your plugging safely into Eddie Socket I should sing the 'Hallelujah Chorus'?"

"Oh, Saul," Merrit says. "I have to go. We'll talk this out when I get home."

Then he shuts the door. He leaves without calling the garage. Goddamn him, I think, going to the phone. Goddamn him.

No, but there's a precedent for this behavior. Let me tell you how I met him. It was in a bookstore. Not the kind you're thinking of, but a real one, on Greenwich Avenue, the Idle Hour. It's a magazine emporium, with books. I was twenty-nine years old and practically still a virgin. He was nearly forty. I was living in my mother's house. I had told the family I was gay when I was seventeen, it killed my father two years later, my brother disowned me, and my mother had made me promise that I wouldn't have sex with men until I found a man that I could marry.

Well, I kept my promise, mostly. When my mother died—and she was dying for about eleven years—it was like a second coming out for me. I had always been gay, as far as anybody knew, but now I could finally do something about it. Except for here and there, a little groping, I had never touched another man that you could call me on it. I never even looked at pornography, all right? I was repressed, I was a mama's boy, I got these letters in the mail, anonymous letters, they said, "Faggot"—misspelled, mind you, one g, "fagot"—and "cocksucker," and I said, I sadly laughed and said, "I wish."

So I was living in the Bronx, my mother died, they got the body in the ground within twenty-four hours, she wasn't even cold, and I was on the A train heading for West Fourth Street from Mount Hebron Cemetery, out in Queens. Like I had been waiting all my life, and now I knew exactly where to go. I walked into a bar, a place called Uncle Charlie's, and there were all these men, on Greenwich Avenue. And I said, very politely to anyone who was listening, white Jersey boys and rich white kids from NYU and men in blazers, and Hispanic boys with ponytails, Asian boys, Koreans, slickly dressed, and little dark Italian boys and Jewish boys with shag haircuts and rolled-up trousers, and black men, some preppie, some effeminate, I said, politely, "I'm just here to use the bathroom," and I used the bathroom, and I left. I crossed the street, I walked into the Idle Hour. Just a slightly cruisy little magazine emporium, it turns out, but otherwise respectable. I didn't go to the porno in the back, I went to the literary section, and picked up a journal, the first thing that I laid my fingers on. I think it was the *Kenyon Review.* Then I turned around slowly, safe behind the journal, and, lifting my eyes, looked around discreetly.

And there, of course, he was, this man. This man, this man, this Merrit Mather. Merrit Laconic Withholding Rowlandson Mather, circa 1943, excellent condition, teeth restored and moles removed (later coloring to the hair, to hide the gray). Of course, I didn't have this information then. All I knew was he was looking at me, with his eyebrows raised. I couldn't tell if he was my type—at this point I was thinking, Well, if he's a man, then he's my type. All I noticed were his eyebrows, waggling at me. Lovely, sad, expressive eyebrows. Gentle man. Okay? So that's enough.

And this is where I want to stop myself and scream, "Don't do it, Saul. Don't say hello. Don't let him follow you, don't follow him." I want to keep myself from making that decision, but I can't. Because in order to understand now what an asshole Merrit is, I had to have been hopelessly in love with him. Which I was, almost at once. He was gorgeous. All right? I had been waiting twenty-nine years for this one gorgeous man, it turns out he's Simon Legree, is that my fault?

So anyway, I said hello. I walked outside, I mean, and felt him following. And what the hell, I didn't know where I was going, anyway. I couldn't find a train from there. I'd never been south of Thirty-fourth Street after dark, alone. My mother was freshly planted in the ground, and I was twenty-nine years old, a long, long time to be alive, and I was thinking, Do it, Saul, just do it, and I turned around and put my hand out straight and smiled, on the street, and I said, "Hi, my name is Saul."

And he said, "I'm Merrit."

"Oh, really, aren't you?" I said.

We stood on the corner where Greenwich intersects with Seventh Avenue and West Eleventh, underneath a streetlight, which was casting shadows on our faces, and his eyes looked even deeper, more exciting.

I said, "I've just been to a cemetery."

"A cemetery."

"Yes."

"Someone . . . ?"

"You mean, 'died'? Oh no, it's just a thing I do this time of year, I visit cemeteries, I get this feeling for granite and marble and long, sad inscriptions."

He smiled. So, I think, he likes a sense of humor. Good thing. He says, "You want to take a walk?"

He asked me that. I heard it.

"What?"

"I live nearby. I thought that we could walk."

"Oh, right, instead of getting in a cab, you mean."

This time he laughed. Great laugh. One thing I've always liked about Merrit is his laugh, which is like a reward, because he's so difficult to amuse. He said, touching my arm, "I mean, let's walk."

And so we walked. We walked to his apartment, where we sat together on his godforsaken green velvet–upholstered reproduction George III–style settee (the legs restored), a piece of furniture in which it is impossible to be comfortable, or even interesting, and he took off his shoes, or rather, his shoe, just one shoe, a running shoe, and draped his ankle across my knee and told me —right?—told me that the first time he ever came was in his trousers when he was ten with an older man who was talking about masturbation. He was telling me this, and we were getting high, I don't smoke pot but then again he offered it, I was Mr. Agreeable, and all the time I was thinking, Yes, there it is, an ankle. Do I touch the ankle, do I hold the ankle, what the hell do I do with the ankle?

I mean, it happens to me all the time, people stop me on the subway and they tell me how when they were eight they were trapped in the Coca-Cola pavilion at the 1964 World's Fair for eighteen hours, and they haven't made love since, you know, it's —What? I've got an honest face? They like my looks? I'm resting Merrit's ankle on my thigh and it's because he thinks that maybe I give unrelenting head? I don't know, or I didn't know, but I know now. It's this: The ankle, it's a ruse, it isn't everything. Because when I get up and say I need some water, and he leads me to the kitchen, where I press him awkwardly against the Frigidaire, and kiss him sloppily, he takes me to the bedroom and it happens, but he comes, and I do not. That's not a minor thing. He comes, and I do not.

Which is really our relationship. And he told me later, Merrit told me later, that the walk to his apartment made the difference, between his taking me down into the basement of the building, where he took his tricks, and fucking my brains out, and inviting me in, upstairs, where he came, and I did not. The walk got me in upstairs. Eleven blocks. I often wonder what it was I could have said in those eleven blocks, or what I shouldn't have said. Should I not have offered my name, should I not have talked about the cemetery, should I just have bluntly stated, "Look, my mother died, I just threw the last handful of dirt on her grave, I'm horny as hell, it's been thirty years, take me to the basement"?

Because I'm the kind of guy you take upstairs, for long, sad confessions, and biscuits, and tea. They tell me, "Saul, sex is nothing, really, it won't sustain a love relationship," Merrit tells me this, and I say, "Merrit! Merrit! Merrit! Jesus God, how dare you tell me sex is nothing, you've had sex with seven hundred and thirty-seven people, not including women, your (low) estimate, and I've had three. Four, counting you. Four!" Well, that's how it is, he tells me I'm afraid of my sexuality. He says I wouldn't be involved with him if I were not afraid of sex. I say, "So, I should leave you and be healthy?"

But I haven't left him. Not the first year. Because that first year, any sex to me was straight from God. And not the second year, in which God died, and we were struggling to "work it out." But I had faith. And not the third year, when it went to hell. And not since then. But for a while, I would try, I would approach him, and caress him, and go down on him, and he would lie there doing absolutely nothing. Like the ankle. He made himself available, but he would not reciprocate, much less initiate. He wouldn't touch me, he wouldn't call out my name, he wouldn't stroke my hair; he did nothing but allow it, and enjoy it, even moan a little, and finish off in my mouth (which I wouldn't do now, of course, but this was then).

Afterward he pulled away and said he hadn't wanted it, but he was wrong, he liked it, I hated it. I hated all of it, the begging, the humiliation, the desire, blah blah blah. It simply stopped, I stopped pursuing and it stopped, and that was when I really started talking. Merrit hates it when I talk, he has his ways of stopping me, sometimes with a swat, sometimes with his coldness, his with-drawal. I feel like screaming, "Merrit! Merrit! Merrit! You can shut me up, you can shut me up, it would be so easy for you to shut me up." He thinks it's good enough to have me as a confidante, but listen, he's wrong. Because even us upstairs girls like to have a little time in the basement every now and again.

94

But still I haven't left him. I walk into that bookstore every day with Merrit. Every time I call him on the phone, or lie down next to him, or beg for him to hold me, and make love to me. I keep thinking, well, it changed my life the first time, Merrit's making love to me. Well, it did.

Except that lately I've been hearing voices. Optimistic voices, rabbinical voices, short, clipped, satirical, sounding like the voices of the fathers, or the received community of guilt; sounding like my uncle Shmoi when I was twelve, on Holy Days.

"Saul Isenberg, Saul Isenberg," they call.

I say, "Oh, yes? Oh, yes?"

"Saul Isenberg, so foolish."

"Who are you?" I say.

"Never mind who we are, who are you? You lie around the house, you waste your time, you pine away. Saul Isenberg, we're watching you, and we've got information."

"Information?"

"First of all, you know, you have a very tiny penis."

"Oh," I say, "it's true."

"A tiny penis, and a stomach, Saul, some stomach, you should watch the carbohydrates. And your ass."

"Oh, what about my ass?"

"It's flabby. Pear-shaped. Jiggling. Obscene."

I say, "Oh, yes. It's true. Everything you say is absolutely true."

"No wonder Merrit won't make love to you."

"Oh, you're right, I get exactly what I deserve."

And then they pause, and they are quiet. And they say, "Do you believe that stuff?"

I say, "I'm sorry?"

"We were asking if you honestly believe that stuff. You know, because this man, this Merrit Mather, Saul, you could have the economy of the state of Arizona hard between your legs, he would not notice. He would not notice. He absolutely would not notice, Saul, the man's a fish."

"I know."

"You know. He knows. We know. Everybody knows. It's in the *Daily News*. Now what are you doing, is what we would like to know. What are you doing still involved with this crustacean?"

"He's an alligator."

"Alligator doesn't do him justice. Doesn't do the alligators justice. He's a waste of time. That's it. A waste of time. You're understanding what is being said here? Or is he just a place holder? Maybe anybody else would do? It isn't him, it's you, is what we're saying, here. It isn't 'Merrit does, or doesn't,' it's 'Saul does, or never does, or never will.' "

"You've been talking to Merrit's therapist."

"Doesn't take a therapist to figure out. The man's a mess, but, Saul, you're worse. You ought to leave him."

"But I can't."

"Why not?"

"He has a great dick."

"Saul," the voices say. They cluck their tongues. Again, they are quiet. Then, finally, they ask.

"Are you trying to keep the rest of your life from happening?"

And I want to respond to that, but they are already gone.

PART 2
Alas

It Never Entered My Mind

Eddie Socket got it. AIDS.

"America is dying slowly," he said, sitting on the lid of a toilet seat and staring into a mirror, in the bathroom just outside the doctor's office where he was diagnosed. He folded and refolded a postcard he had gotten that morning from his father, which was inscribed with more of the quotation by Saint Cyril his father had been running past him for weeks, like a miniseries. "We go to the father of souls," it said, "but it is necessary to pass by the dragon." Eddie wrote a lyric on his father's postcard, which he softly sang to the tune of "Frère Jacques."

> Purple lesions, purple lesions
> On my foot, on my thigh,
> Slowly multiplying.
> Does this mean I'm dying?
> No, not I. No, not I.

Eddie thought of his clinician as Dr. Fillgrave. His clinic was listed in the "Where to Find It" section at the back of the *Village Voice*. Prices were on a sliding scale, and confidentiality was assured. And it was conveniently located, too, in a low brick building in the West Village not far from the piers, and the trucks, and the old Mine Shaft—an easy commute, Eddie thought. But Dr. Fillgrave had a fixed, bland expression beneath which percolated a bilious loathing, and he treated Eddie as if he were just another cadaver. "You'll last a good two weeks, don't worry, two years, maybe six years if you're lucky," he offered, helpfully, when all the blood rushed out of Eddie's face and he thought he was going to faint, "unless of course you don't have health insurance, in which case, the quicker the better, eh?" He actually said that, like a bad stand-up comic doing "the doctor from hell." But doctors, Eddie thought, if they didn't kill you with their ignorance, they would surely try to kill you with their knowledge. That he, indeed, did not have medical insurance seemed to him merely an additional argument in favor of alternative treatments, like suicide, perhaps, or—what? "Douche with Borax," the doctor suggested, flatly, when Eddie asked him what to do about sex. For his first concern was still Merrit. He didn't know if this was a way to hang on to him, or to drive him, irrevocably, away. Though it seemed he had already lost him, for Merrit hadn't called since their last weekend together.

The lesion on his foot had shown up a few days after that. At least, that was the first time he noticed it, and for two days he pretended that it wasn't there. Anyway, it could have been a long-forgotten smudge of tar from childhood, off the streets of Fleming-ton, or indelible ink—his pens leaked, everywhere. The refrigera-tor door was stained; why not his heel? But the second lesion, a reddish-purple almond-shaped blister on the vulnerable, livid flesh of his inner thigh, was harder to ignore. Could it have been a kiss? A lover who had come to him when he was sleeping, dreaming? Merrit's tooth marks? Eddie thought not. Was it really just a bruise, then? A blood clot? Well, the one on his heel itched. Poison ivy? He bathed in scalding hot water and baking powder, but it didn't go away. At the end of the week, he found Dr. Fillgrave, who did a biopsy. They sent away to Kansas, or Lincoln, Nebraska, some-where like that, for the lab results. Eddie had gotten AIDS from Nebraska, he thought, trying to laugh. But his customary defenses were failing him.

He was a man, not a boy, alone in a bathroom, which was painted aqua blue, and made of cinder blocks, and he had AIDS. Those were the facts. How did they make him feel? He had barri-caded himself in the bathroom, to try to determine how all this made him feel. He had always thought of himself as being in touch, but now he saw that he had buried all his feelings underneath a glossy sheen of easy alienation. He had taken snapshots of his life, pictures in his head of Eddie Socket posing for the magazine spread, the Oscar acceptance speech, the close-up. He was ready for his close-up, now that he had AIDS, ready with jokes and witty comebacks to his wacky pig, but he was not ready with his feelings. They were inaccessible. Oh, he was slightly dizzy, and his skin felt cool, then hot, then cool again, but that was the surface of things, and Eddie wanted to get beneath the surface. It shocked him to think that he couldn't. A man outside banged on the door impatiently. Eddie looked in the mirror.

"That's some pair of lesions you've got there," said the pig. "Kind of a nice shade, just this side of rigor mortis."

"I don't need you."

"How come you got sick?"

"Bad luck," Eddie said. "I haven't had sex in two years. And Merrit tested negative."

"Yeah, right, and the check's in the mail, and I won't come in your mouth if you don't want me to. Took those drivers up the dirt path once too often, huh?"

"Listen, I've been perfectly abstemious for two years," he said, stuffing his father's postcard into his pocket. "K. S.," he said.

"Kill Sodomites."

Eddie closed his eyes. The pig was no excuse for feeling, anymore, he thought. He wanted to be able to know how he felt without this absurd self-dramatization. But all he could think apart from the pig, were stupid things, like wishing that he had finished reading *War and Peace,* and wondering which dick it was, which dicks (there hadn't been so many), which dollop of semen, or blood. "Semen," he said, softly. "Semen. Sea men."

The first time he had had sex was in the front seat of his best friend's car in the high school parking lot at ten o'clock at night. He thought about that. It was January, and they kept their parkas on. Eddie was sixteen, and he had been in love with his friend for a couple of years, but sitting in the car he couldn't think of anything to do. Sex did not seem to be exactly what he wanted. Fusion was more like it. They kissed, and his friend went down on him, and that was nice in a way he hadn't expected. The arms of his friend's jacket went *swish, swish* as the fabric rubbed against itself, and Eddie's thighs were cold, and also warm. He came, and his friend kissed him again, on the mouth. That was the first time he had ever tasted semen. His own, still on his best friend's tongue.

"Sex is so nothing" is something Andy Warhol once said (about Truman Capote's dick, Eddie thought, another useless piece of information), and Gore Vidal said, more expansively, that sex is the perfectly existential act. It didn't reverberate at all. Indeed, for something that transformed his adolescence (as well as his adulthood, perhaps?) into alternate periods of yearning and dread, sex did seem to Eddie sometimes like a triviality. It had no meaning, no resonance. It just occurred. And it had not even occurred, not to Eddie, as often as (probably) anyone else would have thought it had (his mother, his father, Polly, Merrit Mather), considering he had gotten AIDS. If he had known he was going to get sick anyway, he would have tried to enjoy it more. For he had never had the kind of sexual experience he wanted, the fusion he had yearned for sitting in a parked car with his best friend from high school. With Merrit, he had hoped for once that sex could go beyond mechanics, beyond the sequence of motion and fact, his mouth moving here, my leg shifting there, our bodies intersecting at a certain angle. And it had. That was the surprise. For in spite of all he knew about Merrit's narcissism, and his tendency to want to come as soon as possible, still he had been a good lover. Eddie had felt, somehow, connected, in spite of himself.

"Hey, what are you doing in there, giving birth?" said the man outside the door, turning the handle aggressively. Eddie got up, and flushed the toilet, twice, to make it sound official.

He stood outside on Greenwich Avenue, shoved his hands in his pockets, and started walking. It was May. It was spring. Spring in New York lasted exactly a day, twenty-four hours of cool, refreshing breezes and the feel of robins and crocuses, between winter's nullifying gray and the wet, thick, inescapable heat of the summer. It was spring, and Eddie was dying, which sounded like the plot for a movie starring Jane Wyman and Rock Hudson. *Magnificent Obsession.* Was he dying? People lasted longer lately, but then sometimes they didn't. How long would he last? He needed time, to do a lot of things. For instance, it occurred to him suddenly that he had never crossed the Williamsburg Bridge. Why not do it now? It seemed to him as reasonable a response as anything else, when the day was nice, and he wasn't working, or sleeping, or watching a movie. He wanted to think. Maybe the Williamsburg Bridge was a good place to think.

Because his head was stuffed with advertising slogans and images, big blocks of solid colors shaped to suggest penises, Merrit's actual penis shaped to suggest Eddie's yearning, television jingles, "Lost in Space," and literary references, and Bette Davis draining a martini and saying, "Fasten your seat belts, it's going to be a bumpy night," he didn't know how to think, or feel, but only how to avoid thinking, or feeling. And though he yearned for Merrit, he couldn't describe the pleasure mixed with pain he felt just remembering his body, every part of his body, not just his dick, but his wrists, his fingers, the way he walked, his laugh, the gray in his hair.

He yearned for Merrit. Why did he yearn for Merrit? He knew better. Merrit was nothing more than the neat result of the way that light came down on the surface of things, an atmospheric trick, a mirage. Not only that, he was a fifties kind of lay, really; he liked to get it over with quickly, then a cigarette, then sleep. But Eddie had loved having sex with him. It left him wanting. For Merrit was something he suspected he could never have, and that was what Eddie thought love was about. He thought love was not quite getting what you wanted, worshiping loss. Merrit was a smooth, flat, white, glossy surface, onto which Eddie could project whatever yearning he liked. But now it seemed important to get beneath the surface of things.

Getting beneath the surface, however, made him think of shooting up, which made him think of AIDS, and so he gave up thinking altogether, and he just kept walking. He walked south through the Village, then east through Soho. He was trying hard to be an adult about this, but all he felt was "Oh, shit," as if he were nine, and had broken something irreplaceable of Doris Day's. Well, maybe he had. But getting AIDS to reach his mother wasn't a very effective strategy, and anyway, he hadn't gone out and done it on purpose. It was not even like reaching for a cookie jar he knew he might break. It was just bad luck.

So he bought some cigarettes. He stopped at a newsstand in quotes, a tin-sided shed surrounded by crew-cutted white men in oversized suits and skinny ties, who were glancing self-consciously at Caribbean magazines. Eddie bought a package of Old Golds, something his first roommate at Oberlin had smoked. His roommate was from Alexandria, Virginia, and played bluegrass on his guitar, Dan Hicks and His Hot Licks, and he was sexy and he really smoked Old Golds, and saved the coupons. Eddie wished he had the coupons now. Seven thousand saved and he could buy himself—another chance? A total blood transfusion, like Keith

Richards of the Rolling Stones? "I can't get no," Eddie softly sang, "blood transfusion." He lit a cigarette and walked farther east, pretending he was Jean-Paul Belmondo. French people didn't get AIDS, and if they did, well, they probably pronounced it beautifully.

He turned down Mott Street, where someone had spray-painted R O M A across a corrugated aluminum door. It was a lament, a yearning, Eddie thought, plaintive and sad, and he laughed, and stopped in the doorway with his cigarette. He stretched his arms out and hung his head, and said, "I thirst. Who am I quoting?" But he was disgusted with himself. It was another photograph. He was tired of posing for photographs. He tossed the cigarette into the street and shook his head, scolding himself. What was he yearning for, anyway? Joseph Stalin would love to hear about his yearning, he would call it the mind-body split, and start to philosophize. Doris Day would say, "Don't be pretentious. Just get a job." What would Doris Day say now, really? He didn't want to think about that. He started walking faster to the Williamsburg Bridge, which was his destination, after all. Doris Day was not some metaphysician, twanging in the dark. She was practical, and scorning. She would ask about his medical insurance. She would not concern herself with anybody's yearning, especially if Eddie himself didn't know what it was. Yearning? For what? Something lost, like a father? R O M A, the door said, in black fuzzy letters, ribbed and rattling like the aluminum. Was he yearning for Rome? He didn't want to be flip, he wanted to know what it was he felt he had lost, long before AIDS had come along to supply an easy metaphor for loss. Was it Empire? Homeland? Native tongue? Merrit Mather?

He was halfway to Brooklyn, suspended over the East River, when the sun dropped into New Jersey. He watched it go, and then he held to the side of the Williamsburg Bridge, to one of its rotting cables, and was thankful again that he lived on this side of the Hudson. For he had yearned, all his life, for New York. There was the nineteenth-century city, represented by the bridge, with its charming amenities, its walkway and midpoint way stations. It had been built for carriage horses, after all. And there was Robert Moses' city, rising just at the base of the bridge, a lot of blinking housing projects lined up like dominoes, face to expressionless face. That was the modernist world of New York, which aged badly, turned to slums or just industrial waste, had to be removed like the Westside Highway, or abandoned like the World's Fair out in Queens, where the Unisphere was still rusting visibly from the

Grand Central Parkway. Eddie had been to the 1964 World's Fair, with Joseph Stalin, in his yellow Mustang convertible. Doris Day rode in the front, and smoked cigarettes, and wore a scarf, and stockings. That was a whole world, his mom and dad in the car, a bright new yellow car, in the late summer heat of the city, at nightfall, ashes from her cigarettes catching in his eyelashes and nostrils, and, later, the New York State Pavilion with its nifty elevators climbing the sides of mushroom-tipped towers, from which he could look at Manhattan.

Of course, that was a five-year-old's fantasy, a tacky, showy mass of slick new interconnecting highways, and fast cars, and white people in beehives and scarves. But to think of his mother now as the sort of woman who wore stockings made him feel absurdly nostalgic, in spite of himself. Everything made him feel nostalgic, sometimes for things he had never even had—his mother, his father, Merrit, New York City, the lights of which, exciting to midwesterners and children, were, Eddie thought, always the notes of a song by Rodgers and Hart.

He fell in love with what he wanted, but he always got something else. He got what really was there, not what he projected onto things, and the discrepancy between the two was devastating. Manhattan. Merrit Mather. He was still infatuated with Merrit, and New York. He reached the middle of the bridge, and made a circle, slowly, looking at all of the city. Maybe this was being an adult—this deeper wisdom, right? This something far more deeply interfused, which was to see the nature of things beneath their beauty, and to learn how to handle disillusionment.

He realized resentfully that he had come to New York for no particular reason, except that it had never occurred to him to live anywhere else. One did not choose not to live in Rome, when one grew up a mile down the Tiber. He lived here because he had always known he would. He hadn't chosen the city, the way Polly had, cutting her ties and leaving Ohio behind. He had just ended up here. Indeed, he thought, *ended up*. He had given his life to the city, and he wondered now what he had gotten for himself, in return. A life in quotes. A weekend with Merrit, who hadn't called and didn't answer his phone (Saul did, but Eddie couldn't talk to Saul, not now). AIDS. What else did he have? A lot of snapshots, but they couldn't even be glued to a scrapbook. Doris Day had scrapbooks, and if she posed for her life, she didn't let on. But Eddie posed, and now he thought that he had learned it from New

York. All that glamour, chrome and glass, had been a pose, and it depended on people like Eddie to think it was lovely, and to sit in their rooms and dream up further poses, to wander through Soho taking pictures of themselves, to live as if in a world in which they were famous, and healthy, and rich.

Merrit and AIDS? And New York. A kind of trinity. Which was the father, which the son, which the holy ghost? Which was fact, and which was fiction? Which was the accident, which the punishment, which the stroke of luck? Could he even speak of his luck? Merrit and AIDS. Which one could be cured, he thought, his obsession with Merrit, or the thing that had moved directly into his cells? Was there a difference, love or disease? Yes, there was a difference. He had read Susan Sontag, after all, and, goddamnit, there he was quoting again. The whole fucking world was in quotes. Was death going to be in quotes, too? Something had to matter, and if death didn't matter either, why be disaffected at all? He suddenly wanted to die, to feel something that mattered. And that seemed to him the most fucked-up thing of all. It was the worst kind of cliché. But it scared him.

He stared at Manhattan, and the whole priapic length of the island glinted back at him and Eddie thought, *That's it, that's the one, the dick. That dick.* He gave head to New York, he thought, and it had given him AIDS. And if that was an irrelevant thought, well, then, the hell with it, he couldn't do any better. "New York made me," he said, "AIDS undid me. Who am I quoting?"

He turned to Queens, and watched the Domino Sugar sign. He said, "I thirst. Who am I quoting?"

He stared at the sign, which was red and white and blue and blinked an indifferent response.

The Gentleman Is a Dope

Polly and Brag sat yards across from each other, at a big wrought-iron table meant for six, in a chic patisserie halfway between the East and West Villages. Polly knew the area as a strip of lower Broadway that used to be sleazy and now had Tower Records, but Brag called it Noho. She was bothered by the feeling that she had eaten here before, though she couldn't think when, or whom she was with. Brag picked negligently at the chocolate mousse pie, as if determined that she alone should bear the burden of its calories on her hips and thighs. Dessert had been his idea, after all, and for him now to lay the responsibility of eating it solely on her seemed to Polly a sign of some inner lack of generosity. But she took this discovery about his personality—the dessert factor—as a kind of gift, a sore point to focus on, and about which to feel relieved when he told her, as (surely) he was about to any minute now, that he wasn't interested in seeing her anymore.

He was dressed a little too neatly tonight, and nibbling his fingernails. He wouldn't meet her eyes directly. He sat there with a fixed look of slightly wounded sympathy on his boy's face, and watched the dessert.

She got the breakup call last Saturday. "I'm feeling out of touch with you," Brag said. "Let's have dinner in about a week." As if that weren't portentous enough ("Why not tonight?" she had started to ask, but she knew the answer to that), he had left it up to her to choose a restaurant. Whenever a man called up and said, "I want you to decide where we should eat," it meant he wanted out. Polly had learned this from hard experience. So she had guided Brag, mischievously, to her favorite Indian restaurant, on First Avenue around the corner from Sixth Street, and intentionally ordered dishes she knew would clash. (He had already admitted that he was slightly wary of Indian food, though he had never tasted it.)

When they portioned out their servings, it had seemed to Polly a combination much like Brag and herself, radically different flavors from out of the same cuisine—two white, middle-class Americans, both midwestern, but with some essential differences between them, Polly thought, differences more subtle than just their appearance, her bushy bangs, his business suit. They were both distinctly American suburban, homogenized by television, officially liberal but secretly rather conservative, though generally uncomfortable with politics; they fluctuated wildly between strict pragmatism and rampant idealism; they liked to be reflective, but when they acted, they acted on impulse. They had never learned to clean up after themselves. But where Brag had gorged on his successes, Polly had cultivated a sense of guilt, even shame, which had nothing to do with some Jewish stereotype. She was more white American than anything—affluent white American— whether she lived up to her parents' standard of living now or not. Yet she had this feeling of guilt. Often, she was not even certain what she felt guilty about.

But Brag felt nothing but need, or maybe it was greed. He only wanted. It never crossed his mind to wonder whether or not he deserved. There he sat, Mr. Instant Gratification, trying to figure out a way in which to discard her, like a disposable razor. He had a male's sense of entitlement, and though he was cynical about money, he believed it to be his proper reward—money and possessions. Polly wanted, too, but without the slightest intimation of deserving. It was unthinkable to her to imagine that her indulgences (credit card purchases, movies and plays, books, expensive clothes) were justified, not merely in a world in which people were warring and starving and dying, but in any world at all. No one in the history of humanity had consumed in a lifetime as much as Polly had consumed the previous week, possibly even the previous day. It made her sick sometimes with satiety, as if she had eaten a bushel of overripe strawberries.

Of course the migrant workers who picked the berries, at a dollar an hour, were much worse off than she was, but that was only part of the point. She was worried about the natural order of things. She believed in a natural order, in which she figured as essential, not preeminent, and maybe that was the difference between her and Brag, who still hadn't spoken. He understood the order of things as dependent solely on him. So did Eddie. Men seemed to have this delusion of being the center, the head and the shoulders, the ordering factor. Eddie felt overwhelmed by his delusion, and he collapsed. Brag, in contrast, was motivated by it. Eddie had a great disorder whirling always around him, but Brag, who saw that the world was chaotic, had imposed on it a violent order, which was, quite simply, making money. He was good at making money. It did not require him to depend on his emotions, which he couldn't verify, or even his ideas, which he didn't entirely trust, but merely his impulse to increase the flow of cash in all directions. "It's better," he confided once, "than masturbation," which, he explained, sometimes resulted only in gism, without any feeling of pleasure. "Just glop that sticks to your hand," he said, "a mess to clean up." Polly remembered that mess. But money, Brag said, which always made a mess, never failed to give him a thrill. Money shot off all by itself, with merely a phone call, and cash was always, always hard. His sexual analogies went on and on. True love was something he said he could come to in time. He never doubted he would.

Polly doubted it, forking another stale slice of mousse pie into her mouth, and chewing resentfully. He still wasn't talking, and she wanted to leave, but something kept her there, waiting to be rejected. Was it his body? Well, his body was nice enough, perhaps even beautiful, but that was all that could be said for Brag. After their first date, she decided she would stay around only for another couple of fucks (she was stingy about fucks, saving even the undesirable ones, the way some smokers saved their butts, against that desperate night), but those fucks had passed, and so had her interest in him. Yet some perversity, a deeply rooted emotional inertia perhaps, together with her inability to be the one who did the rejecting, kept her in this mousserie, this patisserie, where she knew she had been before (when? whom with? what for?), waiting for him to find the gentlest words with which to send her away. She would not go until he had certified himself unavailable.

What was it about her, she wondered, what childhood experience, what lesson imparted by Depression-era parents or grandparents ("Waste not, want not"), what socially imposed impression of femaleness, that she was unable to walk away from a still-available man? She was never the first to leave, no matter how insensitive the man became, no matter how boorish in bed, no matter how undesirable, ultimately. With every man she could remember, it had ended this way: she lost interest, but she waited, and waited, and waited until he told her to go. At last, she had to endure the peculiar humiliation of being rejected by men she knew she no longer wanted, though she clung, nevertheless, to the fiction of loss. She always played the loser. She pouted, she sulked, she begged for one last night together, she regretted the loss officially, while privately she had wearily counted the days or weeks or even months to their parting.

Brag touched the side of the dessert plate, stroking it sentimentally. He was pretty, kind of dumb, and he would never be hers. Why did she put herself through these entanglements? The worst thing was her conviction, despite everything else she believed, that if only she had come to the relationship with a different frame of mind, she could have uncovered his hidden wonderfulness. If only they had had a moment of feeling together, even a gesture, a sigh, it could have worked out. But she was there to witness the drama of his leave-taking now, and, like a man, he was going to make her endure his pronouncement. She had wanted this to happen quickly in the open, out on the street, after curry, possibly on Second Avenue, which, for Polly, was just a short walk home. But Brag was set on dessert. He was, after all, the kind of man who went out for cappuccino. She thought he looked very young tonight, earnest and diligent and young. In his blue pin-striped suit (number six? number three?) and a new haircut that drew attention to his ears, he looked like a William, not a Brag, tonight. William Boleslawski, nice midwestern boy, caressing Polly's dessert plate, looking silent and pouty and sculpted, like Ramon Novarro, reluctant to enter the era of sound. He still said nothing.

Then she remembered, of course, who it was she had been here with before. It was another William, her first New York lover, Brag's

110

namesake. She remembered that it had been the end of a terrible evening in which they had gone to see *Persona* or *The Silence,* or maybe it was *Winter Light*—some awful Bergman thing in which the crows flew black against the ashen sky and no one talked, and the women looked like girls who hadn't bathed for days and had kept to their rooms in a snit, with red eyes and pouty expressions and long, stringy blond hair. She hoped she didn't look that way tonight, though she suspected she had eight years ago, with William the First, when she was pouty about everything, including the movie, which she hated. But he was a film student at Columbia (she remembered laughing, "Columbia? Not NYU?" and that had been her first mistake), and he found the movie's pathos or its bathos or its some-damned-os profoundly moving. Perhaps he was not unaware of staging a suitably Bergmanesque scene afterward, between the two of them, in this patisserie, with her tears, and his cold withdrawal. That made him Max von Sydow, which wasn't right—he was terribly callow and terribly clever, and anyway, she never cast people as effectively as Eddie did. She didn't have the right sensibility. Though she could see now where it would be helpful to think of her life as a Bergman film—then she could laugh at her own pretension, and walk away from the current encounter, with William the Second, comparatively unscathed.

She laughed then, but what she was feeling right now was in fact the pathos in her own life, the unhappy string of correspondences that brought her back and back and back to the same overpriced not-East not-West Village dessert bar with the same-but-not-the-same William, to experience again the rejection for which she had been setting herself up all her life. Brag was even looking sulky now, the way all men looked sulky when they were about to be patronizing, or abusive; he wanted to be simultaneously heartless and pitied.

But he still wasn't ready. While Polly was waiting (almost done with the pie), another ghost came into the restaurant. It was one of her peripheral people. She had about half a dozen peripheral people, mostly women, but a few men, too. They were all about her age, and they had come to the city around the same time she had. At least, she assumed they had. For they had all been there, during her first year in New York, looking pouty, like her, and somewhat lost, going to the gym, walking through the park, standing in line for a movie. She never spoke to them, or even acknowledged them with a nod or a glance, but they were aware of each other. She counted on seeing them, after a while, and supposed, rather sentimentally, that they counted on seeing her.

They went through their twenties together. She watched them get older, suddenly appear with lovers, then disappear, then return alone, or engaged (she saw the rings), or even pregnant; she watched their dress evolve from postcollegiate to precorporate; some remained doggedly the same, year in, year out; and some disappeared completely after a few years, and she was glad she didn't know why (she liked to think of them as having gone to Houston). They formed a comfortable background, against which she measured herself. How was she doing? Well, the woman who appeared tonight, tentatively, in the doorway (looking for a friend?) looked rather jaded. She did not look old, exactly (she couldn't have been much older than Polly), just tired, somehow, inured. Polly remembered having first seen her on the uptown Number 6, and she remembered her face distinctly. The face the woman had tonight had clearly passed through some kind of loss. She looked as if she had become an adult, in spite of herself. She looked surprised, not pleased but not pouting.

That must be my face, too, Polly thought, the face she presented to Brag.

She decided suddenly that she could not stand to wait any longer for him to reject her. But just as she was about to break her pattern, and tell him she wanted out, he spoke up, as if anticipating her.

He put down his cappuccino and said, "Polly, I don't think that this is working out."

"This what?" she said, annoyed. Now that he had said it, she was on the defensive.

"Us," Brag said, gently. He was trying to be chivalrous, which irritated Polly even more.

She said, "I think I've had this conversation. In this very room."

Brag looked rather hurt. He stared down into his cup, and then he looked at her, not speaking for a couple of minutes, until he said, rather carefully, "You are the only person I have ever met who seems to feel trapped by reality."

Polly thought of Eddie, and William the First, and Brag, William the Second, and all the Richards and Henrys and Johns in between, and she thought about every stale forkful of chocolate mousse pie she had ever eaten waiting for a man to tell her that he didn't want to fuck her anymore, and she thought about how things add up, after all. Brag had clearly been waiting for a response, but she wasn't going to help him. So he got rather quickly to the point.

"If this is going to be any work," he said, "well, then, frankly, I don't want to bother. I'm sorry if that sounds callous." He had the decency to blush, and to spill a drop of cappuccino on his tie. "Shit," he said, suddenly more concerned about the damage to the silk than any insult or injury to her. His attention to the details of his dress, Polly thought, was almost the most touching thing about him. "Can you ask that waitress for a glass of water?" he said, holding his tie up to the light.

The waitress was dispatched, the water presented, and Brag began dipping his napkin and then scrubbing his tie, his attention focused single-mindedly now (he had boyish concentration, all red-faced self-absorption and obliviousness, which was cute on a boy but rude, Polly thought, in a man, given the circumstances), when, suddenly, abruptly, he stopped, sat up very straight, held his palm flat to Polly urging her not to speak, and whispered, "Listen."

"What?" Polly said, leaning forward, whispering also, with that genius for accommodation to a male's needs that had been imparted to her by—whom? Her mother? Nancy Reagan? Donna Reed?

"The song," he said, solemnly.

"What song?"

"Shhh," Brag warned, and a glazed look came into his eyes.

Polly listened to the song that came over the cafe sound system. It was Judy Collins singing "My Father," a sad, sentimental piece about a father's broken promises, which was on the album "Who Knows Where the Time Goes?" Polly had played the album herself so many times her freshman year of college that she could not now listen to this song without anticipating the scratches and skips that had been worn into her recording. To have it played in its unadulterated version seemed a kind of betrayal. Eddie, of course, had cured her of her Judy Collins obsession ("Talk about sophomoric," he said), but now that she heard the melody again, she felt a certain nostalgia, even a welling in her throat, which she dismissed as improbable. Then she noticed that Brag was getting very slightly teary.

He was, there was no mistaking it. He was holding the tie in one hand, his wet napkin in the other, and, with his head cocked a bit to the side, he was quietly reminiscing, his face pinched and his eyes red, if not exactly wet.

He put his hand across the table then, the hand that had been holding the tie, and took her hand, and looked at her, guilelessly, almost for forgiveness. And Polly understood, for the first time, that this was a man who believed he had some kind of internal life. Maybe his pinched expression was grief for a father who neglected him, maybe something else. But there was feeling, and pain he wanted to express. And Polly, sitting across from him, her bag on the floor between her legs, and in it her diaphragm, her spermicide, her lubricant, her condoms, her dental dam, her cellophane wrap—all the articles of intimacy, for God's sake, the only kind of intimacy she ever really had with men, all at hand in case Brag decided after telling her to go away that one last fuck would be appropriate—Polly sat there with the last of Brag, the half-used box of condoms, in a bag between her legs, and realized that she had gotten more than she had bargained for. Brag was sharing his innermost life, however he could, without a word.

And she wanted to laugh, because he was almost absurd. She wanted so much, and he had so little to give. All the men she had ever known—even Eddie—were so limited; they offered a sigh when a hug was required, and acted as if they had made some kind of big contribution. She had to laugh at him.

Because now was the time, according to his scenario, for her to squeeze his hand and say, "Let's try, all right, let's try." She could have touched his gorgeous cleft chin and said, "I want to try," something dumb like that, and he would have finished with his teariness, and then they would have paid the bill and gotten into a cab, or merely walked, just walked, to her apartment, where they had never been together, and where, tonight, they would sleep, perhaps in their clothes, just clinging to each other.

She thought he was absurd. She had never taken him seriously. It made her feel guilty now, for he clearly imagined that he had feelings. Suddenly, she felt a bit callous, and she wanted to go.

But Brag wasn't finished, not yet.

He said, composing himself, "I wasn't going to tell you this, Polly, but, actually, I've met someone."

"Oh, really," Polly said, never losing a beat. This was appalling. Why did he tell her? But she said, reflexively, "Who?"

And he said, "Well, it's a man."

"A man?"

"I'm sorry."

"Oh God," she said, stricken briefly with the premonition that it was Eddie.

"I'm really sorry."

"Well, I hope you have better luck with them than I do."

Brag smiled, reassured. "I wanted to tell you because I thought you could understand. I want you to know that I like you a lot. I think you're the only woman I've met who would understand this, which is why I'm telling you. It's not that I don't want to work. I do. But I want to work, you know, I want to work at a man. I thought it was better to hurt you now, than later. We're going to Paris together. I'll be away for a while. I know this is hard for you."

It was hard, but not in the way he was thinking. She said, reaching for her bag, "I wish you'd—"

"No, but listen," he said. "I want you to have my car."

"I'm sorry?"

"While I'm gone. I don't want to lose you, Polly, and I know that if I leave my car with you, at least I'll see you when I get home. I feel a real affinity for you. I feel a connection. I might even say I love you. I think we could have a lot together. Maybe sometime we could be lovers. But for now, I need to do this."

He pulled the keys out of his pocket, and laid them on the table, with cash for the bill.

"There's a note here with all the instructions. I park it in Queens. It's cheaper out there. All right?" He kissed her cheek. "I'm meeting him later tonight," he said, checking his watch. "Wish me bon voyage." But Polly was crying, in spite of herself, and she let him go without saying good-bye.

Into the Woods

Eddie was at home with the cats, choosing a cemetery plot. He had temporarily abandoned the project of thinking about his life. He was thinking about how his mother would respond to his death. He didn't want to leave any untidiness behind. "Clean up your mess," his mother always said. Well, he would. He was making a will, having already decided that he wanted to be buried in Woodlawn Cemetery, "resting place of the famous." Merrit could pay the expense. Why not? He was rich, and besides, if he wasn't going to call, at least he could spring for a coffin. Why hadn't Merrit called? It was kind of inconceivable (or maybe the opposite, too predictable, even for Merrit). So Eddie was having his Barbara Stanwyck moment. Dying and abandoned, he retreated into toughness, pragmatism. He had a map of Woodlawn spread out on the floor, beside him, matter-of-factly. It had a key on the back that listed all the most prominent residents—Duke Ellington, George M. Cohan, Fiorello La Guardia. There were others. Why not Eddie Socket?

He decided to be buried next to Herman Melville, who understood yearning and obsession (and running away), and who had loved Nathaniel Hawthorne, a beautiful, icy man with an ivory-sculpted brow, and a big, big barn. They had lain together in that barn, idly stroking one another in the cold New England sun; they had their moment, like Eddie and Merrit. Then Nathaniel sent Herman away, and he went off, rejected, and wrote *Moby-Dick*. What would Melville's mother have thought if she learned her son had AIDS? Back then, it would have been tuberculosis, or, considering Melville traveled on ship, scurvy.

What would he say to his mother? How would she respond? She had a westerner's ability to make do with what was at hand; she knew how to handle herself in a crisis. Eddie did not. He realized for the first time in his life that he had self-confidence, because he suddenly felt himself losing it. He had had the kind of confidence, anyway, that kept him from wondering whether tomorrow would mean an attack of pneumonia, or shingles, or thrush, more lesions, meningitis, tumors, or tuberculosis, toxoplasmosis, or something as innocuous as a runny nose.

Doris Day would know what to do, and Polly would know what to buy, but when Polly came home, unexpectedly (Saturday night, she should have been out with the trader), and leaned on the tub, her face a mask against intimacy, it occurred to Eddie sadly that they were long past sharing confidences. They had fallen out of like with each other. Yet they had been together seven, eight years, longer than most marriages, he thought, and with nearly as much sex. They had arrived in New York together, driving cross-country from Ohio, when they were both twenty-one, and had just finished college. Eddie had been in the car with Polly when she saw New York for the first time. And she was the only woman with whom he had ever made love, just once, in a dreary, expensive room in the Times Square Motor Hotel their first night in the city.

That was when it was still possible, Eddie thought, to establish a lifelong friendship in the course of a ten-hour drive. In New York, it sometimes took ten years just to say hello. Polly was plump and earnest and midwestern then, and Eddie had very long hair and a long overcoat, and an ambivalent sexuality. They were awkward with each other, but not secretive, whereas now they were painfully honest, and dangerously smooth. They had both learned the New York trick of being officially open, but privately mistrusting. For Eddie sensed now, despite whatever Polly said, that he had fallen from grace, or from authority, with her. He remembered telling her, when they left Ohio, that she reminded him of Natalie Wood in *Splendor in the Grass*. "I don't know what that means," she said, "but it sounds just awful." Her credulity was flattering, and when he rewarded her by quoting, impressively he thought, from *The Great Gatsby*, on "the bored, sprawling, swollen towns beyond the Ohio," she had beaten her hands against the steering wheel enthusiastically, and said, "Yeah, really."

But she was no longer Natalie Wood, and he felt he himself had not gotten much further than Sal Mineo in *Rebel Without a Cause*. She was now wearing a beret that he had given her a long time ago. It was the color of soft green grass, a shade off the deeper tropical green of her eyes, and it reminded him of how much more he liked her than any of the men he ever pursued, including Merrit. He liked women better than men, actually, perhaps because he didn't set them up to disappoint him. Wanting friendship was not like wanting sex; it didn't involve all that yearning, or maybe he meant jealousy. But wanting Polly hadn't gotten him what he needed right now, which was to be able to tell her about his illness.

Because it was too late, he thought, to jump back into intimacy with "Guess what, I've got a terminal disease." He wanted her to know, but not when they were stationed at opposite ends of the room, Eddie on the floor, his usual inert mass, Polly perched tensely on the edge of the tub, looking like a bird about to fly off into the night. She would think he was kidding. "Polly, I think I'm dying." "Me, too," she would say. "Our whole generation is dying." They would talk in snappy public relations chatter about being members of a "blank generation": too old to revolt, too young to conform, trapped between Yippies and yuppies, children of the nonexistent seventies, their president was Gerald Ford, their music was the Bee Gees, their movie star was John Travolta, and so on. They no longer got any more intimate than this *People* magazine stuff. Yet he had been closer to this woman than to anyone else in his life, except his mother, and he was sorry that he felt unable to tell her. If he couldn't tell Polly, how would he ever tell his mother? Maybe both at once, he thought, sliding his map under the rug, and smiling tentatively.

"I was just remembering the way we spent our first two hours in the city," he said.

"Yeah, parking," Polly grunted. She had not taken off her coat. Eddie wondered if she might be going out again, whether she had come home to get her things—her diaphragm, her tax forms, whatever she did for fun with a trader—and then return, uptown, to Brag. But she didn't move. She sat on the lip of the tub, crossing her arms over her chest and breathing evenly, deliberately, as if recovering from shock.

"No," he said, "I mean, we had coffee. You had coffee, rather; I had tea. It was in a diner on the East Side somewhere, and I said the east side of Manhattan always reminded me of my mother, and you said that it kind of reminded you of New York. You hit your fist on the table—I remember people turned to look—and you said, maybe even something like 'Gee, golly,' first, or 'Holy cow,' and said—you were midwestern, really, I don't mean to torture you, Polly—and you said, 'This is exactly the way that I would picture, um, New York.' The pause was the part that made it so perfect, that 'um.' You said it with your hand to the side of your head, the way you do when you're considering, or making a joke. It was the 'um' that cracked me up, and you laughed, too, and we both laughed so hard we had to go, except we couldn't figure out how much to leave for a tip. And it turned out we only had enough to cover the tea and the coffee, anyway, so we didn't even leave a tip. It sounds like I'm making this up, doesn't it?"

"I never said 'Gee, golly' in my life," Polly said, resisting. She sat still on the tub, not moving, refusing to be drawn into the game.

"You looked like someone who would have said it."

"You told me I looked like Natalie Wood."

"You do remember. You were offended."

"I don't remember being offended. I remember being worried. I thought, 'If he thinks I'm her, what happens when he finds out that I'm really—' I don't know," she said, putting her hand to the side of her head. "Who would have seemed just plain dull to me then? Um—"

"Sandra Day O'Connor."

"I mean, I always thought Natalie Wood was sort of beautiful."

"Well, that's what I meant."

"You didn't mean that, Eddie. I know what you meant. You meant terribly earnest, and a little bit ridiculous."

"Did I mean that?"

"I gave up doubting a long time ago that you always meant the most insulting thing." She dropped her arms. "I just spent my last shred of integrity on a trader," she said. "I don't feel like being glib about it, or chatty, or analytical, or smart, so please don't ask me any questions, okay? Or torture me with reminiscences. I always have to work so hard to keep up with you. Nihilists are too demanding."

"I don't think of myself as a nihilist."

"You see, already you're quibbling."

"I was missing our friendship."

Polly pulled off her beret and looked at him mistrustfully. "Is this some kind of a game?"

"No, it's not a game. Why does everyone always think I'm playing a game? I was just thinking, we really used to be friends."

"We're still friends."

"Oh, yeah, look at us," Eddie said, "eyeing each other across the room like a couple of dogs."

"Where is this coming from?" Polly said. She went to the refrigerator, unbuttoning her coat. "I want ice cream," she said, opening the freezer.

"There's yogurt," Eddie said, sheepishly.

"You finished the ice cream," she said, throwing her coat on the stove.

"Careful, you'll burn something," Eddie said, remembering Merrit.

"Sugar," she said. "I want to burn some sugar."

"Polly," Eddie said, trying now for confidentiality, "he dumped you."

She turned slowly, and reached into her coat, pulling out a set of keys which she threw on the floor. "That's what's left of Mr. William Boleslawski. He's going away. With a man. All right? Don't ask me why he gave me the keys to his car. He's twisted and weird, and I'm a cold-hearted bitch. I don't want to talk about it."

"Polly," Eddie said, softly, "I've sort of gotten jilted, too. I mean, he was married, so what did I expect? Married to a man, I mean. But still."

"You've fallen in love?" Polly stopped with her arm halfway into the refrigerator, drawn into the conversation for the first time.

"I kind of did."

"You never fall in love."

"Yeah, I don't know what happened. He's pretty unavailable. I haven't seen him in a couple of weeks, and he doesn't answer his phone. I mean, of course, I've sort of been preoccupied the past few days," he said, half to himself, "maybe he's been trying to reach me. Maybe I've missed his signals."

"If he hasn't called, he isn't sending signals. I mean, except 'good-bye.' "

"You've gotten cynical."

"I know." She put her hand to the side of her head, and said, "I'm sick of New York."

"You think it's New York?"

"It's crossed my mind."

"Mine, too. But I mean, where do you think it's likely to go better?"

"I don't know. At this point I would say New Jersey."

"New Jersey," Eddie said. "Well, if you've got a car," he said, hopefully, "you know, we could drive there. I mean, it's just across the river. You could meet my mother."

"Your mother?"

"No kidding."

"We can take his car."

"That's what I said."

"It's a BMW—"

"No, let me guess the color: burgundy."

"You're not thinking money. Emerald green."

"I bet he never uses the ashtrays."

"For change."

"We'll spend it. We can buy ice cream cones and spill them on the interior. Stick bubble gum under the seats. Let's leave now."

"Now?" Polly said, punctuating their conversation with a definite yawn. "We'll go in the morning," she said. "Maybe this is what I need."

She went into her room and shut the door, and Eddie, satisfied that something lost had been recovered, lay back on the rug, and thought about the drive. It would be his first time in a car with her since Oberlin. In eight years, they hadn't even shared a cab. Perhaps he could coax her into a nostalgic mood, and then somewhere around Somerville he could tell her he was dying.

But the next morning he remembered with a familiar misgiving what it meant to visit Mom, and Flemington, New Jersey. He woke up early feeling sick to his stomach, slightly headachy, and dry at the back of his throat—not ill, but nervous, like a boy in grammar school on his way to a spelling bee in which he would be tested on words that had, for him, uncomfortable meanings, words like Sally, faggot, homo, queer, all the words that had been used against him in grade school and high school. When he used these words himself, now, they were in quotes. But in Flemington, New Jersey, their meanings were simple and direct: A faggot was a faggot was a faggot. It was safe to be gay in New York. At least, it

121

used to be safe. He touched his dick as if it were an endangered species, and briefly considered whether it was better to be attacked outright, with fists and knives and nasty names, or subtly undermined by the local government and medical community. No one liked faggots, he thought, that much was clear. But the only place he had ever been called a faggot (relentlessly) was New Jersey.

"Ah, New Jersey," he said, an hour later in Brag's car, as they came up from the tunnel in Weehawken, "an oozing swampland, unwittingly appended to the capital of the modern world, like snot clinging tenaciously to a great man's nose. The light at the end of the Lincoln Tunnel."

Polly drove ferociously. The suburbs hadn't numbed her completely, Eddie thought, admiring her fine, long neck and her green fingernails, which were clipped short. "You don't know how I depended on women for survival, out here, Polly," he said, remembering all his girlfriends in grammar school, "though by the time I got to high school some of the girls I used to play jump rope with were calling me a faggot, too. They had started wanting boys, I guess, like I did, and in order to get boys you had to play their nasty games. I wanted boys, too, but they tortured me. I hate what I'm attracted to," he said, blowing his bangs. "Who am I quoting? Maybe Merrit Mather."

"Who's he?"

"The boy I want. Do you hate men as much as I do?"

Polly rolled down her window and stuck her elbow out into Jersey. "That's just it," she sighed. "I'm beginning to think I do."

"So what if you do?"

" 'Would a convent take a Jewish girl?' " she sang.

Eddie laughed. Cars made him happy, and Polly did, too, and now that he felt he could probably tell her, he didn't want to at all. He didn't want to spoil their moment. Anyway, Doris Day, unlike Polly, would probably guess. Minutes after he walked in the door, she would say, "You've come to tell me that you're dying, right? and now I have to sell the house to pay for it?" She had guessed things before. She had known, before he told her, that he was gay. He'd invited her out to a fancy restaurant on the Upper West Side for lunch, but she took one look at the room and said, "So, I suppose you're going to tell me that you're homosexual?" Then she ordered a gin and tonic. He hadn't known whether to be relieved or angry. At least she hadn't cried, or raved, or turned stony and refused to speak. But his sexuality was one way in which he hoped to distinguish himself from her, and appear as an adult, and she had taken that away from him. She didn't banish him, or lecture him, she didn't disapprove; she just treated him as some-one whose actions couldn't have serious consequences for her own life. "Oh, yeah, that," she said, as if it were merely a colorful feature of his general insignificance. He had wanted to accomplish something that would make her really notice him. Well, he thought, bitterly, *here was his chance—he was dying.* Surely it was something she wouldn't wave away with a giggle. But he didn't want to risk finding out.

"I think we're in the boondocks," Polly said, brightly.

They were on Route 78. "Whoosh!" Eddie said, cheerfully (if he could not confide, he could entertain), "into New Jersey. Not just plain Jersey, but *New* Jersey, 'a keg tapped at both ends,' who am I quoting? Rural northwestern New Jersey. 'Even the weeds here have the look of being on welfare.' Who am I quoting?"

"I want to see boondocks," Polly said.

"It doesn't start officially until we get to Somerville," he said.

"I'm dying to meet your mother," she said.

"Yeah, well, anyway," Eddie said, and after that he was quiet all the way to Clinton.

But when they turned off the highway onto Route 31, Eddie started babbling. It was the Clinton Point Theater that did it.

"That was practically the only movie theater in the entire county, when I was growing up," he said. "They showed Disney and por-nography, alternating weeks of *Debbie Does Dallas* and *Chitty Chitty Bang Bang.* Then after the movies there were just two places to go, the Daz-O-Del, a sort of prehistoric McDonald's, for a dip-top cone, or an old red barn across the street, where men used to jerk each other off, I guess, after Debbie did Dallas."

"Actually I think *Chitty Chitty Bang Bang* is a much racier title."

"Well, maybe they went there after that one, too. I was never in that movie theater. My mother hates Disney. And my dirty movie days were still ahead of me."

"When were you ever in a dirty movie theater?"

"Alas, my innocence," Eddie said, evasively.

"I can't picture you in a dirty movie theater."

"Yeah, well, the pure products of America go crazy. Who am I quoting? All right, now we're passing a famous bar, the one with the antlers on top of the roof, The Hunter's Rest, where all the high school boys hung out, the ones who called me faggot, with their chicks. That's what they called them, their 'chicks.' And in my sophomore year, I think, the football team got busted there for drinking underage, and afterward, the quarterback, his name was something German Protestant, an Alpaugh or a Hockenbury, drove his father's steel-blue Dodge Dart into the side of the local police station, as revenge, while getting blown, it was said, by the prom queen. No one could prove it but she had her jaw wired shut for a year, and he, not disgraced but visibly missing at least his throwing arm, if not other limbs, moved to Hampton after graduation and started a cabbage farm."

"You're making this up."

"Not me. Not Flemington," Eddie said. "I'm not that clever. That's spelled p-h-l-e-g-m, by the way, Phlegm-ington, New Jersey. Flum-dum. It's one of the little ironies of my childhood that my mother, who grew up in Sacramento, came out here looking for California. Go figure. It was New Year's Eve, it seemed like a good idea. Who am I quoting? Actually, I'm quoting her, and it was Halloween. She was living in Tarrytown with Joseph Stalin, before the Great Schism and his escape to New York. They had a big black Pontiac convertible. She got the dogs in the back, the Yorkies, and the cat, whose name was Quagmire, and while Dad was at work, editing textbooks, I think, at the time, Mom got the real estate section of the *New York Herald Tribune*, and, looking like Kim Novak—"

"In a swimsuit?"

"Looking like Gloria Grahame in *The Bad and the Beautiful*, but in Levi's."

"This sounds rehearsed."

"I have to keep telling it to myself, in order to get it right. She turned on the radio to Perry Como singing 'Mountain Greenery,' or maybe it was Matt Dennis, and she crossed the Tappan Zee, and took the back roads—no highway then—straight to Flemington. Where she found this house. On a dirt road. In the middle of the woods. Miles from civilization, with a burned-down barn way back in the trees, from which she gathered smoke-damaged siding with which to patch the holes in the walls of this big, dilapidated farmhouse made of stone and rotting clapboard, and held together entirely by ivy, which grew up through the bathroom floor. She trained it around the shower."

"It sounds charming."

"Well, I suppose it was charming. It was just in the middle of nowhere. And I was gay. There was no Institute for the Protection of Lesbian and Gay Youth in Flemington. You know, and then there were my parents, their relationship. They kept breaking up, and getting back together, and there was always something sad, ineffably sad, about my mother, and my father is inexplicably angry. He's always been angry, and she's always been sad, and if there was ever anything between them other than her nostalgia, and his rage, I don't know. I think at first she found him scrupulously fair, and he thought she was loving."

Polly nodded. "The thing you love first about a person always turns out to be what drives you crazy later on," she said. "Finish your story."

"There isn't a lot more. The highway came through Clinton in 1965, they sold half our road to developers, and they put up rows and rows of little boxes. My father used to sing that song, just before he left, his exit music. 'Little boxes, little boxes,' how's it go?"

" 'And they're all made out of ticky-tacky, and they all look just the same.' The whole road?"

"Just from my mother's property on. There were still a couple of miles of woods leading up from the bottom of the road that couldn't be developed. So it's, like, Hansel and Gretel's forest, and then my mother's big gingerbread house, and then, pow, suburbia. And off my father drove, down the new highway, as if it had been laid especially for his escape, away from the crumbling eaves, the sad wife and homosexual son, the Yorkies, the plumbing that froze in the wintertime, the cold slate floors in the summer, the dragonflies and irises and lilac bushes and the daffodils and lily-covered pond and banks of myrtle, most of which were spoiled by erosion when the new development upset the area's ecosystem. Don't get Doris Day started on ecosystems, please. He threw on his old blue high school letter sweater and got into his yellow Mustang convertible, the top was down and the visors were up and it looked like a wing-tipped shoe. I think I made that last part up, but that's how I remember it, and I remember the Beatles singing 'Baby's in Black,' on the car radio, as he pulled out the drive. They're still married," Eddie sighed. "That's the part I wish I'd invented."

They turned off the highway onto a narrow paved road, marked

125

by a red Victorian house with peeling paint and hanging shutters. Rows of apple trees stretched back out of sight on either side of the road.

"Eddie, this is lovely," Polly said. The road, his road, had been cut out of the side of a hill, rather informally, Eddie thought, as if no one had seriously expected to use it. It was just wide enough for an old Ford pickup carrying a load of hay, and it hung off the hillside like a loose bale, balanced precariously over a brook that lay three hundred yards below. It curled back on itself several times, following the course of the brook, until the water rose slowly up to the level of the road, and crossed just beneath, under an old stone bridge.

"It's a half a mile from here to my house," he said. "I used to walk down here with my cat, Batman. He followed like a dog, and I sat in the sun, and thought about the boys who lived in the development. Some of them were very sexy, and I hated them, and wanted them, too. It felt like self-betrayal. I mean, my sexuality."

"Don't get me started on self-betrayal," Polly said.

"The trader?"

"It's just, I know exactly what you mean, Eddie, when you talk about wanting something that you don't approve of wanting."

"Well, these boys came from farming families, who had moved off their land into what looked like Day-Glo pink and orange shacks, and people like my mother moved into the roomy farmhouses they left behind. No wonder they resented me, but I didn't understand this when I was twelve. I only knew they taunted me, and threw rocks at the dogs, and I hated them. I hated farmers and gas station attendants, truck drivers and car mechanics, and I hated the woods, as if, you know, prejudice came from the woods, and homophobes were all born in New Jersey. I'm really a snob about fields and farmers. It's hard for me to admit even now that it's—I don't know, you said, lovely, I guess. I mean, not to mention Mom. You'll probably think she's lovely, too. Just to gall me."

But she was, even Eddie could tell. She came to the porch as they pulled into the drive, and she was barefoot, holding a dog in each arm, wearing a pair of faded blue jeans and a man's white shirt, her face tanned, her hands long and masculine (dirt under the nails, he knew), her hair cropped short and streaked with gray, brushed back from her face, which was soft, and delicate, and lovely. She wasn't Doris Day at all. She was Rita Hayworth glamorous, crossed with Tom Joad in *The Grapes of Wrath*, far more

126

comfortable in the country, after all, than in the city. She watched them get out of the car, clearly pleased, Eddie thought, to see him with a woman.

"Hot wheels," she said to Eddie. "Is that really your style?"

"It belongs to a trader," Eddie said, mysteriously. He was in the mood to withhold information.

"What's he trade?" his mother said. "Not Green Stamps."

"It's mine for a couple of weeks," Polly said, introducing herself. She stretched out her arm, placing her green-painted nails in Doris Day's callused palm (which she extended awkwardly, out from under wriggling Yorkie tails).

"I would have thought a Volkswagen was more you," she said, over Polly's shoulder, to Eddie. From the moment he stepped out of the car, she directed all of her chatter at him, though tacitly acknowledging Polly's presence with an occasional turn of the head. "A ratty old Bug, with a convertible top, the kind that explodes when you put it too quickly in reverse, which you would probably do."

"We came for lunch," Eddie said. They were still on the porch. No move had been made on anyone's part to enter the house.

"I'm on a diet," his mother said.

"Some lemonade, maybe?"

"I've got grapefruit, water, and some cottage cheese."

"Or we could just sit."

"Well, come on in," she said, dropping dogs, and swinging through the door, the torn screens of which had been patched with gray electrical tape.

"Welcome to Tobacco Road," Eddie whispered to Polly, just loud enough for his mother to hear.

"If you had grown up on Chagrin Boulevard," Polly said, "in Shaker Heights, you would think that this was absolutely delightful."

"Polly's from Cleveland," Eddie said.

"I've been to Cleveland," his mother said, in a way that precluded any further conversation on that topic. In any case, their chatter was overwhelmed by the appearance of a dozen yapping, panting Yorkshire terriers, inside the door. Their sharp little nails clacked over the hardwood floor, and over Polly's shins and Eddie's knees.

"That one wants to mount you, I think," Eddie said.

Doris Day went straight into the kitchen. "Don't sit on the

couch," she said. "It's glued. The dogs ripped it up, at the corner. It's still drying. I used Elmer's and some heavy-duty paper clips, Wally, what do you think? Don't touch it," she shouted, from the other room.

"Very ingenious," Eddie said, wondering, as he watched five dogs jump onto the couch and turn in circles, how it was that he was hazardous to newly glued corners, and they were not.

"Where can we sit?" Polly whispered. She was suddenly the wholly obsequious guest. It was strange to see someone else intimidated by his mother. But Polly had folded into herself, temporarily, and Eddie, looking around his mother's house, suddenly understood why. It was a place in which no concessions had been made to physical comfort—at least for people. It was entirely a dog run, in which the incidental appearance of humans could have occurred only as a kind of regrettable necessity. Someone, after all, had to feed the dogs.

The hallway opened into the living room, which was furnished with mission oak—the couch and a couple of chairs, with cracked, dark red leather upholstery—and a drafting table, against the wall. The fireplace (slate hearth) was piled high on either side with logs, and the room ended in a big stone wall that swept upward to a cathedral ceiling. The wall above the fireplace was decorated with a collection of rifles and handguns, relics from what Doris Day referred to satirically as "my unfortunate western heritage."

It was a room, Eddie thought, in which you stood nervously alone, waiting to be called upon to perform. His mother liked to be entertained, and it was work to distract anyone from the dogs, who were always doing something urgent or interesting, fighting or howling or getting sick all over Doris Day's stack of *New Yorkers* and *Opera Digests*, which lay in a pile on top of an old trunk that had traveled west with her grandmother (who climbed trees at ninety and was married seven times), and then back east with her. It was the closest thing Eddie had to an heirloom, and it was worn through at the corners with the tooth marks of a thousand dogs.

His mother came out of the kitchen with a tray of Ritz crackers, and a half-empty container of cottage cheese. "Turns out I've got some Coke," she said. "Or are you still on some weird macrobiotic thing?"

"Coke is fine," Polly said.

"Wally?"

"Coke is very exciting."

"A simple yes or no will do," his mother said, turning back to the kitchen.

Polly sat tentatively in one of the chairs. "Your mother's so—"

"Butch," he said.

"I was going to say pretty."

"She's butch."

"She's very direct."

"She hasn't looked at you once."

"She's trying to figure out our relationship."

"She knows our relationship. She doesn't like the competition. She doesn't know it, but she's secretly grateful I'm gay. She'll never have to fight with another woman for my attention."

"What is it you do like about her?" Polly whispered.

Eddie pushed three dogs off the couch, and sat down, anyway. "I like the smell of her furniture," he said. "She likes musical comedy. It never occurred to me not to tell her I was gay, even though I know it makes her unhappy. She's beautiful. She was— you ought to see the pictures—she had—oh, gosh, she was exquisite. Like Grace Kelly, if Grace Kelly had been able to say 'fuck.' She's outrageous. She can be very fun, if she's in a good mood, especially for kids. It was like having a pal, when I was twelve, who just happened to have possession of the car keys. She never baked. She never sewed costumes for the high school marching band. She's almost completely unsentimental, and I have entirely her sense of humor. Whatever makes me laugh, it's because of her. She always knows who should have been in the movie. Every book in the house, she's written down the perfect cast on the inside back flap. She had *Ship of Fools* cast years ahead of Stanley Kramer, only better. She'll walk into a room and say the three embarrassing things everyone else is thinking, and get away with it. God, she was a relief sometimes at Fourth of July picnics, I can't tell you. She never let me join the Cub Scouts. She plays 'Musetta's Waltz' badly on the piano, and 'Someone to Watch Over Me.' Sometime when I'm sixty and she's dead, I'll hear 'Musetta's Waltz' in some disgusting bar somewhere miles away, and weep. Except, oops—"

"Except what?" Polly said.

He was going to say, "Oops, except I forgot, she's the one who's going to be weeping at sixty for me," but it seemed wrong to say, even if Polly had known he was sick. It was just too sentimental.

Early death? Judith Traherne, in *Dark Victory*? *Not my scenario,* he thought, as his mother came back into the room, glaring, and handed him a glass of Coke. He got up quickly off the couch, and said, "Nothing."

"Nothing what?" his mother said.

"Nothing sentimental," he said.

Doris Day handed Polly her glass, and went to the drafting table, where she had set up an old Smith Corona, which Joseph Stalin had gotten as a high school graduation present, and which Eddie, because he was, his mother said, "mechanically inept," was not allowed to touch. He kept waiting for her to turn around and look at Polly, and say something brittle and smart, like "So, I suppose the two of you have decided to have a baby together and you want to borrow my turkey baster." But she didn't seem to care why he had come, which was both a relief and a disappointment. She pulled a sheet of paper from the typewriter, and held it out to Eddie.

"I'm writing for *The Backyard Horseman* now," she said. "You want me to read you something? It's about boggy hock."

Polly said, uncertainly, "Boggy hock?" She was struggling with one of the dogs—Eddie thought maybe it was Rudolfo—who, indeed, had attached himself amorously to her ankle. He walked to the drafting table, and eyed Joseph Stalin's typewriter. It was still missing the *Q* key, which he had broken off when he was nine.

"I hope it's not an article about quarterhorses," he said.

"Welsh cobs," his mother said.

"What's boggy hock?"

"Big swollen ankles."

Polly discreetly kicked Rudolfo, who yelped.

"Knock it off," Doris Day said. She was talking to the dog, but it was clear to Eddie, turning quickly to Polly, that she thought his mother meant her. She got up from the chair and went to the fireplace, sipping her Coke. Rudolfo pursued.

"Is it an incurable disease?" Eddie asked.

"It's incurably funny," his mother said. "I had to sit through seven hours of film about it, where the narrator sounded like he had boggy nose, and left big pauses between his words." She held her nose and demonstrated. "This," she said, grabbing Eddie by the ankle and tipping him backward. "Is. Boggy. Hock." She pinched his skin, and pushed him over the drafting table. His head hit Joseph Stalin's keyboard.

130

Suddenly Polly, who had picked up Rudolfo and held him, wriggling, in her arms, said, "Really, Eddie, I don't know why your father left, this house is charming, and the dogs are so welcoming." She laughed, to cover her embarrassment.

But Doris Day, with her son's head tipped back into her husband's typewriter, as if about to compose a veterinary tract on his temple, let go of Eddie's ankle, and rushed across the room. "You bastards behave yourselves," she said, grabbing Rudolfo away from Polly and tossing him onto the floor. "He's been like this all week long," she said, "with half of the bitches in heat. At the end of the month I'm calling the vet, he's coming over here with his syringe to give them all a mass abortion. Thank God there aren't any doggie right-to-lifers. Leonora," she shouted. "Settle down."

Eddie mimed to Polly, behind his mother's back, "You said the magic word." She shrugged, and he mouthed, "Joseph Stalin."

But then his mother turned, and held out her palms, to her son. She said, "They've scratched me all to hell."

And her hands, and the insides of her wrists, were covered with thin red scars, toenail scratches from little, odious dogs.

Eddie said, "Oh, gosh," and went to give her a hug, which she half refused, laughing. "You should have Labradors," he said. "They don't jump up." She laughed, and pushed him away. She said, "I can take care of myself."

They were like married people, Eddie thought. She let him have her feelings, and then when he expressed them, she was free to wave them away, as if they had come from him, not from her. But Eddie felt the loss; he was left with her sadness, whatever it was.

She turned to Polly and said, "My son is oversensitive." Eddie shrugged. This was his mother's official version of him. (It was also his.)

He said, "My mother can't have feelings. They're like indigestible food, she can't process them."

"Where's Woody Allen, while we're saying these pretentious things?" his mother said, laughing. "Is he this arrogant with you?" she asked Polly, who was standing by the fireplace, smiling bravely.

And it was clear, Eddie thought, in this exchange, why he wouldn't be able to tell his mother he was sick.

On the Waterfront

So he decided to do the reasonable thing, and tell Merrit. At least, in some scenario, it made sense, like a sex-education film shown to high school students, in which two young adults sanely discussed their having been infected (alas!) with a venereal disease. It was a sharing, mature thing to do. And though Merrit was neither sharing (he hadn't called now for weeks) nor, in many respects, especially mature (Eddie was beginning to feel more responsible than most of the people he loved—Merrit, his mother), still, he was the closest thing Eddie had to an intimate partner in life. They had held each other's dicks, no more than a month ago, and talked about literature, and art. That had to count for something.

"Yo, dove," Merrit said, when Eddie finally reached him on the phone (it hadn't been easy) at his office downtown. "How've you been?" His voice was neutral.

"Oh, gosh."

"Poor little dove. You live in your own world, don't you?"

"Is that a criticism?"

"I don't think so."

"It feels like criticism. Listen, Merrit, but I kind of want to talk to you."

"Right now?"

"In person. Somewhere alone. Nowhere near Saul."

"Well, that won't be easy."

"It's important."

"You're insisting?"

"Yes," Eddie sighed, "I'm insisting."

"Well," Merrit said, "I'm free for fifteen minutes at eleven-forty-five. Can you come by my office?"

"It's going to take a while. And it can't be at your office. It has to be on neutral territory."

"It does?"

"Maybe outside. In the park."

"Which park?"

"Whichever one you like."

"Can it wait?"

"It can't wait."

"You see, because I'm leaving town."

"You're what?"

"I'm going on a business trip. Of sorts. Well, anyway, I'm going overseas. A couple weeks."

"How soon?"

"This after—" Merrit cleared his throat. "Excuse me. This afternoon."

"You're leaving town this afternoon?"

"For Paris. And Florence. And Rome. On business. Look, I've got to put my car in the garage, and see to a few other things before I go. Can I call you when I'm back?"

"Yeah, right, if I'm alive."

"Eddie," Merrit said finally, "you sound upset."

"I am upset."

"Did I hurt you somehow? Are you in trouble?"

"Christ, Merrit, it's not like I'm pregnant. I need to see you. Isn't that enough? I mean, my God, I said I loved you, and I had your penis in my mouth. Isn't that worth something?"

It was worth half an hour, Merrit said. He agreed to swing by Eddie's place in his car. And this time, Eddie wasn't late, and his socks were clean. He had even combed his hair. It lay slick against his scalp, parted in the middle, and he thought he looked like Scott Fitzgerald. He was wearing Merrit's shirt, a purple polo shirt, which he had snuck into his knapsack during their weekend in the country. It smelled like Merrit, tar shampoo and plain white soap. His trousers were newly washed, and he had sponged his pink sneakers. He had decided not to rehearse a speech. He was going to get into the car, and hope that Merrit would understand immediately, without having to be told, that he wanted to be held. He would be able to cry, if Merrit held him. Then he would take him to Paris. They could go to the Pasteur Institute and the Luxembourg Gardens. Eddie could go on AZT, and at night they would eat at Aux Deux Magots, like Hemingway. Or, God, not Hemingway, like Gertrude Stein. Where did she eat? He blew at his bangs, but they were plastered to his skull. He checked his wallet. He was prepared to buy dinner, if that was what it took to hold Merrit's attention for more than thirty minutes. He had fifty dollars, plus the fifty he already owed him. *One hundred dollars an hour,* he thought, *I might as well be seeing a psychiatrist.*

Merrit was half an hour late. Eddie was sitting on the stoop, his elbows on his knees, his head in his hands, when Merrit pulled up and honked.

"I thought this was going to end like that Judy Garland movie *The Clock,*" Eddie said, getting into the car. "She goes into Pennsylvania Station, looking for Robert Walker, with whom she's had a brief and passionate affair. But he never shows up. I can't remember if he got killed in the war, or what. She doesn't sing in that movie. Hi. You look terrific."

He leaned across the seat, and kissed Merrit on the mouth, and complimented him automatically. It was what he wanted to hear about himself, that he looked fabulous. But he knew Merrit wouldn't give it to him, so he gave it to Merrit. It was a trick he had learned from dealing with his mother. But of course, Merrit did look great, that was the rub. He was a bit older than Eddie remembered, but very handsome. He was the completely attractive white man. It was almost galling.

"I got blocked in by a delivery truck," Merrit said. "I tried to call, but you were out."

"Outside, waiting for you."

"Well, I guess our timing's off. Listen, my garage is up at Sixty-seventh Street. After I leave the car, I have to run off. You understand, don't you, dove?"

"Actually, I was thinking maybe we could get some, you know, peaches or something, and go for a walk in the park," Eddie said, sounding rather plaintive, he knew. Merrit made him feel sixteen.

"Oh, Eddie," Merrit said. "I told you on the phone."

"Listen, this is urgent."

"So is my trip."

"When is your plane?"

"This afternoon."

"What time this afternoon?"

"Actually, I think they moved it up a bit."

"To when?"

"Oh," Merrit said, adjusting the rearview mirror. "Nine."

"Then there's time."

"I need to be there early, though. The flight could well be over-booked. Something like that."

"You get there at seven-thirty, that's plenty of time. Leave here at six. That's two and a half hours from now. You can spare some time for me."

"You've gotten so assertive," Merrit said, touching Eddie's cheek.

It was hardly true. He felt anything but assertive. But if Merrit thought he was, so much the better. "I know what I want."

"I guess," Merrit said, perhaps satirically.

"I owe you money," Eddie said, reaching for his wallet. He handed Merrit two crisp twenty-dollar bills and a ten, and that settled it, to his surprise. Merrit said, "Dove," delightedly, and they drove to Riverside Park.

They parked near the Soldiers and Sailors Monument, and walked to the boat basin, at Seventy-ninth Street. Merrit's hard-heeled shoes (the same black wing-tipped shoes he was wearing when they met) made a staccato sound on the marble steps as they walked down to the mall along the Hudson. Eddie liked to watch him move. In pleated linen trousers and a gray and white patterned shirt, a ventless blue cotton jacket, and cranberry socks, he was so fastidious, a little bit square. Would he still do it with a man who was HIV positive? For Merrit hadn't taken him in his arms, and wasn't even very reassuring. Suddenly Eddie wished he had prepared a speech, with which to affect Merrit deeply. The hell with spontaneity. *Merrit, there's something I think you should know.* No, too Warner Brothers, Eddie thought. Too drab. Something flashier. *Kiss me, you fucking preppie, I'm dying.* Who was he quoting? Ali MacGraw? Christ, how could he be so flip?

The mall ran out into grass, and they followed a path into the bushes, along the fence, where people sometimes jerked each other off. Eddie swung over the fence, and dropped down to where the blocks of granite formed a bank along the riverside. He sat on the stone, and dangled his feet, which hung a few yards above the water. Merrit took off his jacket and, handing it over, hiked up his trousers to straddle the fence. Eddie saw the stretch of naked skin between the tops of his socks (they were silk, with a fine cream polka-dot pattern against the cranberry, Eddie noticed) and his cuffs, two inches of skin between trousers and socks, a vulnerable span of flesh. Then the rest of Merrit landed beside him, and Eddie's tenderness vanished with the exposed skin, which disappeared as Merrit's cuffs fell back down to his shoes. He rearranged himself, quickly palming his crotch, brushing his shirt. He leaned down cautiously and swept clean the granite, then daintily sat. He reached for his jacket, which Eddie relinquished sadly.

"All right, now," Merrit said.

"Look at the river," Eddie said, beginning to wonder if this had been such a good idea, after all. Merrit was treating him like a trick; Eddie had the awful, dry-mouthed, headachy feeling of having awakened in a stranger's bedroom at dawn, and been offered coffee, rather diffidently. Merrit was ashamed of the noises they had made the night before, and now he wanted Eddie to leave, but he was too polite to say so. If this was true, Eddie thought—well, it only made him more determined to have his moment, here at the water, with Merrit, whether it was owed or not. "I wonder what it's like to live with a constant view of Jersey," he said. "It must be sort of comforting. I mean, to know that it's there, and you're over here. With all the floating Hudson garbage in between."

Merrit swept dust from his shoes.

"You know the smell the West Side has?" said Eddie, breathing in audibly. "That coffee smell? I used to think it was something to do with the stone they mined to make those prewar buildings up and down West End Avenue. That dark, dark stone. I thought, the wind against that stone, the salty river wind, corroding—you know, something like a chemical reaction, stone and salty wind, and then you get that smell. I didn't know that it was coffee grinds from Jersey, their scent, wafting across the Hudson. Coffee stench, aroma, from the Maxwell House plant. 'Chemical air sweeps in from New Jersey, and smells of coffee.' Who am I quoting? I'll give you a hint. He was a poet who died of homosexual panic. In a cab. He tortured his wife."

"You read a lot of poetry?"

"I used to."

"You don't let on."

"It doesn't matter. Poetry doesn't matter."

"What matters?"

"You matter."

"Listen, now, Eddie," Merrit said, dropping his voice an octave, assuming authority. Clearly, he had come with a prepared speech. This was it. "Listen, dove," he said, pressing for intimacy and sanity, simultaneously, "I think you know what I'm about to say. No, let me finish. I can understand that you're infatuated, and it's sweet. I've been infatuated, too. I think I have—I hardly remember. I thought a lot about us, after our time together. I talked to Saul. Well, yes, I tell Saul everything. He wasn't very helpful, really, as you can imagine, but he did remind me that I have a way of developing scenes in my head that don't play out. I have a reality problem. I can't exactly mediate between my fantasies and how things are. I choose the wrong people, the wrong set of circumstances, get my hopes too high, and then I'm disappointed. This has been very hard for me, I hope you understand. I get so disappointed. It's because I'm as-iffy. That's what my therapist says. She says I have an as-iffy personality. I'm as-iffy, Eddie, I can't help it. I think because of my parents. They were socialites, always performing. So am I. You see? I picture the kinds of feelings I should be having, then I act as if I were having them. But I'm not having them, really, at all."

Eddie wanted to say *Just hold me.* He thought of his mother and wanted to say *Where's Woody Allen?* He said, "You didn't like being with me?"

"I like you a lot."

"But if you're as-iffy . . ."

"Well, it's a clinical term. Sure, though, I can tell that I like you a lot."

"We had a good time?"

"I think you're very sweet. I care about you."

"And I'm handsome?"

"Yes, you're handsome," Merrit said, touching the back of his head.

"We had good sex." Was that what mattered to Merrit? Was sex supposed to be good?

"It could have been better, actually," Merrit said, as if reading Eddie's thoughts, withdrawing his hand, and pulling a piece of lint from his trousers.

"You didn't like it?" Eddie said. He was really sounding eleven.

But he wanted this to matter, he wanted to make some connection to Merrit. Whenever he was completely in earnest, he was a boy. He didn't know how to have authority; he was either comically jaded, or completely naive. All that Merrit saw, clearly, was that he was a boy. But for once he wanted to seem like a man, to Merrit if not to himself.

But Merrit said, "I think you're too young. It isn't your fault."

"But you're not having sex with Saul. He's not young."

"Saul understands me."

"Saul hates you."

"Eddie, don't be ridiculous."

"It shows in his voice, when he's talking to you."

"When have you heard him talking to me?"

"That night at the movies. The night that we met. March fifteenth—"

"Eddie, you don't understand. A lot of our friends are sick. We've been pretty tense."

What do you know from tense, Eddie wanted to say. It sounded like Saul, who had lots of authority. But he was unhappy with Merrit, too. Maybe the guy was just impossible to reach. But this was Eddie's moment, now, to make a connection. Here was a chance to recover something lost, to take himself seriously, to force Merrit to do so as well. "You can't lose something without finding out first what to replace it with," someone said to him, once. He seemed suddenly in a position to lose a lot—Merrit's attention, for instance, not to mention his own life. But his life was too much to consider losing. Merrit was easier to concentrate on. What could he replace Merrit with? Self-respect?

He said, "Well, what about me?"

"What about you?"

"What if I were sick?"

Merrit laughed, patronizingly. "You are a melodramatic dove."

"Well, what if I were?" Eddie said.

"Oh, Eddie, don't be outrageous. It's manipulative of you even to suggest it. I've lost seven, eight, nine friends since this time last year. I won't sit here and listen to your belittling that, or using it in any way."

"I wasn't using it," Eddie said. "Maybe it's true."

"Don't be such a child. All right? We understand each other, now let's leave it at that." He got to his feet.

Eddie grabbed at his cuff. "Don't leave," he said.

Merrit looked down at Eddie as if discovering he had slept with the Bad Seed. "Jesus, this whole exchange just confirms what my therapist suggested," he said, brutally. "Saul suggested it, too. I didn't hear it then, but now I'm clear. I'm clear it was a mistake, to be with you."

"It wasn't a mistake."

"I'm clear about that, Eddie. It was a mistake. It wasn't even much good, really." He checked his watch, and put on his jacket. Then he hoisted himself onto the balustrade. "Not even the sex was very good. Maybe it was good for you, but not for me." Now he was standing on the other side of the fence, looking down at Eddie. "I've got to go. Are you coming?"

"I'm not coming."

"Suit yourself."

He started to go. It was awful, how he could call Eddie's bluff, like a taunting older brother. But Eddie followed. They walked together silently all the way back to the car. Eddie couldn't believe he was going to let Merrit go without telling him he was sick. They stopped at the car, where Merrit mopped the windshield with an old, ratty glove.

"Merrit," Eddie said, watching him work, "listen, I wanted to say something."

"Keep your voice down," Merrit said, mopping.

"I want you to stop a minute," Eddie said, taking his arm. "I wasn't kidding," he said. "I've got AIDS. Merrit, it's true, I have, I got the diagnosis just a couple weeks ago. I've got K.S. I'm going to die."

"You're sick," Merrit said, more quietly than anything Eddie had ever heard, more penetrating. "You're sick."

"I am."

"No, I mean you're sick," Merrit said. "In the head. I didn't see it, but I do now. Do you know what's wrong with you, Eddie? You're irresponsible. You don't want to take responsibility for anything you do in life. You criticize the world, you criticize the way I live, by implication, yet you're happy enough to take advantage of the things I have, when they come your way. You think you're in love with me? Well, I didn't get to be the way I am without assuming some responsibility, and working in the world, and making a life for myself. You haven't got a life of your own. You're so wrapped up in self-pity that you're paralyzed. All you do is go to movies, and obsess. Lie around the house, that awful empty white apartment, how can you live in a place like that? Don't you care about your life at all? Your life is empty, Eddie. Movies, and your masturbatory fantasies. You're so full of perceptions, you're so full of opinions, well, it's just bullshit. The whole of it is bullshit. I hate your bullshit. I hate your fat stomach. I hate your irresponsibility. What do you have an education for? So you can sit around idly and say things like 'poetry doesn't matter'? So you can make jokes about something like AIDS? What kind of decadence is that? I never should have gone away with you. I'm clear on that. It certainly won't happen again."

He got in the car.

"You don't believe me," Eddie said.

"I've got to go," he said.

"When are you coming back?"

Merrit said nothing.

"You're going alone?"

He put the key in the ignition.

"There's someone, isn't there?"

"Yes, there's someone," Merrit said. Eddie grabbed his glove, which he had left on the hood.

"Who?" Eddie said, offering the glove.

Merrit ignored it. He said, "For Chrissakes, what do you care?"

"I want to know who."

"He's in finance," Merrit said, starting the engine. "I met him at the Health and Racquet Club."

"What is this, cliché of the month? Health and Racquet Club? What is he, straight or something?"

"As a matter of fact, I think he's bisexual."

"You don't have permission to go with him. You don't have permission to go."

"You lower your voice. Shut up."

"I don't give you permission."

"Shut up," Merrit said, slamming his door.

"Yeah, that's right," Eddie said, stroking Merrit's glove, "why don't you run away?"

"I'll see you," Merrit said, rolling down the window.

"Yeah, okay," Eddie said. "You run away. You run away because you think it matters. You think life matters. But it doesn't matter, Merrit, not to me."

"What matters to you?"

"Nothing matters."

"That's bullshit."

"You matter."

"Eddie, what we had was a weekend, that's all, and we both enjoyed it. So let it go. All right?"

"I've got your glove."

"Just let it go."

"You're going to leave without your glove."

"It doesn't matter."

"You see? You agree with me. Come on, what possible difference could it make to anyone that I devote myself to anything? The world goes on, you know, and people live and die, and nothing matters. 'I have found the answer, and it's nothing.' I'll tell you who I'm quoting, that's Joan Didion."

"I have to go," Merrit said. "Good-bye."

"Yeah, good-bye," Eddie said.

"All right?"

"No, it's not all right, Merrit, because you think it matters, but it doesn't. You know, it's just a discrete, individual experience, added to a lifetime of experiences, each with equal weight or lack of weight. It doesn't add up to anything. You have to carry out these scenes with real-life conviction, you have to find a way to feel something about it afterward, bad, angry. Or to fail to feel bad, and then feel bad about that. But I don't feel bad. I don't feel anything. So drive off, Merrit, I don't fucking care."

But that was just defensive psychobabble, and not a word of it was true. Eddie had been posing a long time. It mattered to him more than anything now that he had chosen people who couldn't be trusted with his feelings. Because he was in love with Merrit— kind of. He felt completely abandoned, watching Merrit drive away, yet, perversely, he had never wanted him more.

Dreams About Clothes

All right, now you know, the schmuck ran away with a banker, a trader, a financier, bisexual, too, deposits anywhere, and likes it rough—he's into stocks and bonds. Let me tell you, now you have to understand, I heard his message on the phone machine, his voice, even when he's giving basic information, meet me here, lunch with me there, he sounds like a member of the National Conservative Political Action Committee recommending the removal of a liberal from elective office. It's just what I've always feared: what Merrit wants in his heart of hearts is a European trip for two, a foreign affair, with a hot young straitlaced laconic massively ordinary financier with a big, big bank account and all the major credit cards at hand. Not that Merrit ever wanted money. But, I guess you go with what's familiar.

So how do I avenge myself? I play with sweaters. Merrit's sweaters. That'll show him, right? I pile them on the bed for a little appraisal, you know, style, and period, and approximate worth, and sentimental value, of course. I mean, do you get it? He's on the Grand Tour with a cross between Lance Loud and David Rockefeller, and I'm cataloging his sweaters. There's a powder-blue lamb's wool crewneck, Constantine and Knight (repairs to the shoulder), great sentimental worth. It was the first thing I gave him, and the first casualty of one of our earliest fights. I sewed it up where Merrit ripped it in the fracas, but it's never been worn since. That's just one. There are thousands, like he's Imelda Marcos, only not with shoes but sweaters.

Some of them stop me completely. There's the sweater from L. L. Bean, which he bought with me in Maine, to give to a friend who later died of AIDS. The friend never got the sweater, because Merrit decided it looked better on him. Well, it did look better on him. There's the one he wore the weekend after we met, our first whole weekend together. We went to the beach, the end of October, to roll and play in the sand, with the dog. Everybody has these moments, right? and later it's a sentimental journey. Merrit wore a cable-knit white wool sweater woven in Ireland, with a rollover V-neck collar, and he sat way back on the beach and watched me play with the dog. He was under a blanket. He was feeling old that day, and later we got home and he ran me a bath. This was in his apartment on Eleventh Street. I slipped into the bath—it had authentic brass Victorian era claw-and-ball feet—and he went into the other room and played Chopin waltzes on his piano. Ah, well. I thought that this relationship was going to be my work of art. I thought the two of us were going to learn to be him, magnificently, beautifully. Who knew he would turn out to be this road company Morris in *Washington Square?*

Ah, but I too can be cruel, for I have been taught by a master. This is what I'm thinking later when I go to Uncle Charlie's, which of course is across the street from where we met. "A cigarette that bears a lipstick's traces." Tonight I'm ready to settle for an imitation, something in the school of Merrit Mather, or after the style, or in the manner of. And I'm in luck, a man walks up to me, he's wearing a navy-blue blazer with a seal over the breast pocket, and he has a pair of white duck trousers and a pink silk shirt, and a cobalt-blue bow tie with a cream polka-dotted pattern, and newly chalked white bucks, and whiskey on his breath, and a boy's unlined complexion slowly sliding off his dissipated skull. He's a 1940s college weekend movie musical alumnus, the sort of man whose white shoes disappear into the closet after Labor Day, a nifty Mather clone.

We sit together on a carpeted bench against the wall, staring absently at videos of long-haired men in high-drag makeup swinging pipes and chains and clanging on guitars. They're squeezed into stone-washed preshrunk jeans from the Paramus mall in Jersey, I believe, and moaning low like troglodytes. My buddy—I'll call him Bobby Van—turns to offer me a drink, a bottle of beer. It pops out of his inside breast pocket like he's offering a wad of bills in order to induce me to perform specific, unforgettable acts with him in his Pierce Arrow, in the light of the moon, the silvery moon, to Lena Horne singing "Prisoner of Love." " 'Alone from night to night you'll find me,' " Lena sings, while Saul bends over the running board, " 'too weak to break the chains that bind me.' "

"Gee, no thanks," I say, my hand out flat. But this is difficult. Obviously, the guy's drunk, but I have a hard time turning him away. You know why? Because I'm susceptible to clothes. I mean, my big secret is that I got involved with Merrit because he wore saddle shoes and argyle socks. After all, I'm trained to respond to something quite specific, which is Gregory Peck, *The Man in the Gray Flannel Suit.*

So I'm not out prowling for sex. I'm prowling for trousers. Reluctantly, I send away Mr. Bobby Van, and look around the bar for something similar that doesn't drool. So I appraise the remaining merchandise. There's a pair of nice suspenders by the door, and an old, old high school letter sweater, the kind with leather elbow patches, in the corner. Discouragingly, the suspenders leave with a studded leather jacket. No accounting for taste. Then the letter sweater comes my way, I start to hope. Except it's hanging from the back of an Adonis, and he doesn't notice me. Clothes, I can negotiate. But when it comes to bodies, beautiful bodies, I'm out of luck.

You know why? Because, physically, I'm a B person in a world full of A's. A's are the ones in all the magazines, they lean against the walls, they have their legs cocked so, their hair so neatly clipped, a basketball between their thighs, a pair of swollen lips, their hands continually busy with their bangs. B people, on the other hand, don't have perfect teeth, they can't stand totally immobile more than twenty-seven seconds, they get nervous when they know they're being watched, they go to bed with strangers dreaming sadly of love, faithfully imagining it's more gratifying than masturbation. A people don't go home with B people. Merrit is an A person who made the mistake one night of going home with me, a B, and he's been punishing me ever since.

I don't go home with A's anymore, you know why? Because the only thing they want, they want a flat, flat stomach. They tell you that they love your mind, they love your creativity, they love the way you think, the way you dress, the way you comb your hair;

they love your talking intelligently about art, for Chrissakes, they love the way you whistle when you come. Or whatever it is. They say these things. They take you in their arms, they take you by the ears and hold your head to their chests as if you had just come in from the cold, they reach down with their palms to touch your stomach, and, brother, if it isn't flat, start counting. And all your chatter, whether you can comment thoughtfully on Eisenstein, or Caravaggio, enjoy Madonna, sing the score from *March of the Falsettos*, quote Cavafy, quote James Merrill, argue the difference between the use of the word *homosexual* as an adjective or as a noun, the various possible sexual preferences of tennis stars and classical musicians, cook Indian, cook French, psychoanalyze as if you had a Ph.D., I swear to God, it couldn't matter less within eleven seconds of removing your shirt, because if what you've got below your breasts is flabby, then forget it. Gay men want the world. They want the fucking world. I swear, I sometimes wish I were straight.

So I don't go home with Bobby Van, or anyone. I leave the bar, and go to a movie, a midnight showing of *Rebel Without a Cause*, which is a movie I never really got, not then, not now. I mean, James Dean, so what? It's not just that he's not my style—obviously I go for the more repressive types, I like my men angry but submerged—but that all that grunting and scratching never spoke to my soul. Give me Gary Cooper any day, circa 1930, around *Morocco*.

But tonight, I'm connecting with the film, because of Dean's jacket. It's red, but they dipped it in a can of black paint to mute it, I read that somewhere—it glittered, and the film's in color and they couldn't have it casting a reflection. Well, they failed, because I can't take my eyes off this absolutely luminous jacket. It reminds me of the ones my butchest high school classmates wore in the sixties. They were the boys with rolled-up jeans and T-shirts, cigarette packets folded into their sleeves, wearing wonderful jackets, palming their crotches, smelling and walking like a parody of masculinity, perhaps, but sexy. Even I, who was secretly waiting for someone refined, Ramon Novarro, could tell they were hot.

Anyway, it's hot to me now, because the jacket is making me hard. It gets passed around. Dean wears it, poor Natalie Wood in a devastating bra wears it, Sal Mineo also wears it. Jimmy Dean is promiscuous with his jacket. It's the mantle of his budding masculinity, which everybody wants. They don't want him so much as his jacket, and I want it, too. That's what's so moving. I yearn for this jacket, like I yearn for Merrit's sweaters—different versions of who I have wanted to be. It ends up finally on Mineo, who, after he declares his love for Jimmy Dean (not in so many words, of course), pathetically dies. In fact, he's assassinated, but he's got the jacket, which Dean, having had *his* rite of passage (he gets to knock nipples with Natalie, whose breasts look surgically pointed), has cast aside. Sal gets the coat, and dies, and Jimmy gets the girl, and they procreate. The jacket has become a shroud, it clothes the dead, Sal Mineo, the homosexual.

So Jimmy Dean becomes a man, at Mineo's expense. Why couldn't he have made it up with Sal, adopted him or something, saved him, rescued him, made love to him, moved in with him and Natalie? I wanted that, I wanted Sal to live. But then there was this sacrifice, it shocked me. Why couldn't Natalie have died? Or Dad? Or Mom, who is, predictably, the real villain of the film? Or the chief of police, for God's sake? No, the faggot had to die, he died with Jimmy's coat, and Dean reached down to him, the corpse, and put his shoe in place, his penny loafer. And he turned, and there was Natalie, and two years later he was working in a corporation, probably, and she was vacuuming.

Well, all right, I'm walking home, I'm thinking of the movie, and my adolescence, and the clothes that I've become attracted to, and the clothes I used to want, and being homosexual, and yearning for Merrit, and being a man, and you know what happens to me? I have sex in the park. I'm thinking, Sal Mineo and Jimmy Dean, I'm thinking, Eddie Socket, who wears jackets like the one in the movie. I'm thinking, *East of Eden,* Merrit's favorite film—anything with deathbed reconciliation scenes between a father and son, mother and daughter. I mean, all right, I've told you once, I'll say it again, he's forty-five years old, his parents still don't know he's gay. They think he's Jimmy Dean. They think he only hasn't given up the coat, he hasn't put his childhood aside. His homosexuality. They don't know that it's possible to be a man and not deny your homosexuality.

But me, I'm doing it with strangers in the park. And why? Because this is Merrit's territory, that's why. "It makes me feel like an adult," he says, casual sex. Isn't that a contradiction in terms? "Casual sex"? Not for Merrit. He's in the park with strangers and his pants around his knees because he doesn't have a Natalie to put his arm around and say to Dad, "I want you to meet my girl." I mean, I'm the girl. And I won't do. And I think, I would also like to be an adult. Now, all this happens very quickly: I walk toward the entrance to the Ramble and just pick out the first guy who looks reasonably sane. It happens that quickly. I decide not to think at all about his clothes, or anything, I just want a face among the shadows, and I find one.

In the light spilling over from the streetlamp I can sort of make him out. He's wearing running gear—blue shorts, and a tank-top T-shirt, running shoes, athletic socks. No clothes to criticize. At last. He's just a man, generic homosexual, he could be anyone at all. He could even be straight to the world, and only a fag in the park.

But he knows what I want. There isn't any need for conversation, second thoughts, debate. "Down here?" he says, gesturing with his head down a slope, where a dirt path winds into the underbrush.

"Is it safe?" I ask, slightly breaking the rules. To ask is to remember that you live in the real world of cause and effect. But this is surreal.

He says, "It's safe." He asks, "Are you okay?"

I say that I'm okay.

We walk down the hill. He takes me in his arms. We're standing on a slope. He's shorter, and I move so that he's standing uphill from me. Leaves are in my face and brush against my arms. There's moonlight, and a trickle of water somewhere down below. He tries to kiss me, but I pull away.

He says, "Okay. Are you okay?"

He has a little bit of a beard. I wonder maybe if he also has a knife. But no, he's rather gentle, actually, and he wants to hug. He puts his arms around me, and we hug. He unbuttons my shirt. I touch his back, his ass. He pulls my shirt away, and licks my nipples. I don't like it very much; I mean, I'm just not sure. I don't know what to say. I'm really only good with words. But he wants to hold me tighter, and he puts his tongue inside my ear. He carefully undoes my trousers, pulls them down around my knees, and tugs my underwear, until I'm naked from my shoulders to my knees. He wants to suck me off.

I say, "No, that's not a good idea," and he says, "Are you okay?" and I say, "Yes," and he says, "I'm okay," and then I know that we're discussing AIDS, and I say, "Oh, not that, you never know," and he says, "Okay, is there somewhere we can go?" It's the middle of the night. He has an innocent, pleading quality, a boyishness, which is rather sweet. He wants to please me, I suspect, he touches me as if he likes my skin. He strokes my back, my shoulders, and it feels weird, and I don't like it very much, except I also do, it's nice to know he thinks that I'm attractive. I don't want to marry him, but I don't want him to leave me, either.

So when I tell him I would rather finish up right here, and he says, could I please lie down, he wants to come on me, I think, okay, I'm okay, I lie down in the dirt, on my shirt, and he squats over me. There's moonlight on his face. He looks at me, he's squatting over me, he smiles and he says, "You must know that you're beautiful." He touches my dick and says, "I'd love to take you in my mouth." He says, "You have a wonderful ass." He says, "You're very beautiful." I say, "Well, thanks," and then he comes, it splatters on my chest, as if my beauty is enough to bring him off. He says, "Are you okay?" I nod, and then he jerks me off. I hardly notice coming, but it isn't really what I wanted, anyway. I got what I wanted.

So when I get home—I'm thick with semen, in my trousers, on my chest, I'm cloying, sticky, wet—when I get back to the apartment, there are all of Merrit's lovely sweaters on the bed, like something too symbolic in a neorealistic incest tragedy by Tennessee Williams. Saul, I think, is this the kind of homosexual you're going to be, after all? Maggie the fucking Cat at home, Blanche DuBois in the park? Trapped between an ambivalent dick and the kindness of strangers?

Because sex is really nothing. That's true. It isn't Merrit's cock I want to suck, though I wouldn't mind, as long as he reciprocated. It's this: I fell in love with a sweater. As far as Merrit goes, I think I made him up. I don't believe in Merrit Mather anymore, but I'll tell you this: the Merrit I don't believe isn't punishing, insensitive, aloof. He's warm, and loving, and honest, and kind. That's my particular neurosis. I'm nostalgic for a past I never had.

Good-bye to All That

With his failure to confess to anyone he truly cared about, Eddie gave up all hope of telling, and shifted into the mode in which his life was pure performance. He had, he thought, three choices: he could sleep away the rest of his life, he could find a miracle cure, or he could leave. And his runaway kid encouraged him to go. Eddie's runaway kid had been around since he was nine years old, when Eddie lost his mother's C.P.O. shirt in the spring, and suffered through the summer terrified of the first cool autumn day when she would ask what he had done with it. He never told her he lost it; his runaway kid got in the way, and kept him from admitting his guilt. "Don't tell," said the runaway kid. "And when she asks where it is, play dumb." Of course, she never asked until about five years later, and then it was too late to care. But Eddie's sense of guilt had lasted all that time, to the point where, though he had forgotten specifically why, he knew that he deserved to be punished. He had been waiting now for years to receive his punishment, he realized. Was that why he had gotten sick? Because he lost his mother's C.P.O. shirt? It was too outrageous an idea, even for the son of a Catholic.

But when the runaway kid said, "Flee, all is discovered," Eddie, from old inclination, got out his father's army duffel bag (a worn green sack, with the name WALDO JEFFERS U.S. and the numbers 3151226 stenciled in black against the fabric), and started to pack. It was the beginning of June. He was going to find northern California, as his mother had hoped to find it in New Jersey. He was going to take her journey, but he was going to get it right.

He blew at his bangs, and packed what he wanted to die with. He packed his beat-up copy of *The Complete Poems* of William Butler Yeats, which he had had since college. He had broken the binding late one night in his senior year when he threw the book down his dormitory stairs, in frustration over an unavailable boy. "There is some historical precedent," he said. He took his toothbrush. He took a copy of *Playgirl* magazine, the issue with the model Kelly Coffee posing naked in a doorway. Kelly looked like Merrit—they had the same dick. He packed *Play It as It Lays*. He got together six cartons of strawberry yogurt, a plastic spoon, three small metal traveling containers of Anacin, and a map of the western United States, which he had gotten free at the Exxon Building. He packed the biography of Montgomery Clift he had gotten from his mother. He took his father's postcards, and he packed Merrit's glove, which he first held to his cheek.

When he was done, he showered and shaved, flossed and brushed his teeth (after unpacking the toothbrush), put on Polly's underarm deodorant, clipped his fingernails, cleaned his ears, stepped into a clean pair of peach-colored Jockey shorts (they had belonged to some boyfriend of Polly's), and dressed as neatly as possible. He wanted anyone discovering him dead on the highway to know that he had been a nice boy from New Jersey. He laced his pink sneakers tight.

He kissed the cats before he left, calling their names and groping blindly, Bette Davis again in *Dark Victory*. Yes, he would be sentimental, after all. "Darth, *2b*," he said, and held them up to his nose, each in turn. Then he poured out water for them, shouldered his big green sack, and walked all the way to midtown, to say good-bye to New York.

It was just getting dark when he reached the booth for T-K-T-S, and stood below the big red billboard advertising *42nd Street*. He faced uptown. Tourists behind him were buying tickets to see *Les Misérables*. To the east he could see the three identical towers on Sixth Avenue, the Exxon, Celanese, and McGraw-Hill buildings, and, turning west, the sky over Jersey, which was orange and yellow and blue and darkening fast. There were big new holes on Broadway that used to be sleazy arcades, and porno movie theaters. New red girders poked out of the holes, which were sealed behind blue plywood walls, covered with posters, and graffiti. Rush hour was over, but curtain time was still an hour away, and the dealers, and cabbies, and whores, and three-card-monte dealers, and the tourists, and Hare Krishnas, and hustlers, and the men in business suits headed off to a guilty hand-job, and the street musicians, and pretty boys in tank tops, and women in open-toed, spike-heeled pumps, and visitors from Germany and Japan, were quiet, and mellow, and things were moving rather slowly, Eddie thought, as the sun took the heat into Jersey, but not the humidity, which clung to his skin like an extra piece of clothing, and brushed his face in the wind coming east from the river, and up from the trains underground.

He had wanted the city to know him, had wanted to be known to all of New York, and he had failed. He had also wanted to be known to Merrit. He had been known, but not loved. That was his great disappointment—the city he yearned for, and the man he loved, had not been impressed by his yearning, and loving, nor finally had they been what he wanted. He walked to the Port Authority and got a ticket on a Greyhound bus, hating the sense of leaving without being prevented, just for a moment, from going, by an ardent lover, or friend. Merrit had rejected him, and Polly didn't follow in his footsteps anymore. His father was out of the question. And Saul must have thought of him as the other woman. So he called his mother.

"This is your good-bye call," he said, calling her collect from a pay phone just outside the loading ramp in the basement of the Port Authority. His bus was warming up, and he could smell the exhaust fumes. "I'm standing in the Port Authority with Joseph Stalin's bag, his army bag. I'm going on a trip."

"What kind of trip?"

"A trip to California."

"California's a big place. You don't just take a trip to 'California.' Where, exactly?"

"San Francisco. I want to see where you lived."

"Where I lived."

"Yeah, what was your address?"

His mother paused. "Wally, this is idiotic. You don't just pick up suddenly and drive across the country to see a building."

"I think my bus is leaving," Eddie said. "I'm holding the phone out. Can you hear the motor? That's my bus. It's honking. What was your address?"

"Wally, where are you really?"

"I told you. In the Port Authority."

"You're on drugs somewhere in Brooklyn."

"If you want to know the truth, I'm sort of running away from a man."

His mother was quiet again.

Then she said, "Maybe you think that no one else has ever been infatuated, Wally. I ran away, too. Careful, or you'll end up in New Jersey." She sighed. "Eight-six-eight Ortega," she said. "Off Twenty-third."

"Mom," Eddie said, "there was something I sort of wanted to tell you. I wanted to say it the other day, when I was there with Polly."

"What?"

"Oh, I just wanted to say," Eddie said, stalling. "Well, *que será, será*," he said, finally. "Just *que será, será*."

Then he hung up the phone.

He arrived in Chicago the following day, with an itinerant drag queen from Staten Island named Eulene. They met on the bus outside Erie. She performed at bars across the country, moving by bus from city to city like a migratory bird. She was in civilian drag when they met ("my civvies," she called them, cut-off jeans and a sweatshirt); she had been sitting way in the back of the bus, trying to get Eddie to jerk off with her. ("It breaks up a long ride," she said.) But she ended up modeling some of her wigs, one of which came together in a bun at the nape of her neck, and made her look, from the eyebrows back, Eddie thought, like Olivia de Havilland in *The Heiress,* while from the neck down she was James Earl Jones, resonatingly large. Her voice went from deep to shrill, depending on the conversation, sometimes coming across sardonically with a raspy New York quickness, sometimes slowing to a stagey Tennessee Williams drawl. She could be Blanche DuBois, or one of the Dead End Kids, though her middle range, Eddie noticed—Eulene in repose—moved and sounded like a coupon-clipping mom from Todt Hill, slightly fussy, chatty but preoccupied, and, despite the occasional queeny grandeur (or, perhaps, because of it), deeply conventional.

She touched him a lot, stroked his wrist and pushed his bangs back out of his face, perhaps flirtatiously, which Eddie sort of liked. If she had Merrit's dick and Saul's bow tie, he thought, he would ask her to marry him. But they were just girls together. That was how it felt. They sat together and giggled, told little jokes and shared confidences, and eyed all the boys in the back. It was hard for Eulene to be discreet, particularly modeling wigs. She snored noisily when she napped, and when she talked, her laughter was loud and continuous.

She was merely a piece of his luck, Eddie thought, a part of the excitement between leaving and arriving, which was just the trip itself, the going. As long as he was going, going, going, through Erie, Pennsylvania, and the towns of Ohio, the state with the prettiest names, Ashtabula, Sandusky, Toledo, and Indiana's gastrointestinal diseases, South Bend, Mishawaka, and the first names, Hobart, Porter, Gary, leading on to Chicago, at last—as long as the green signs of the freeway flickered by, luminescent in the dark, and Eulene slept beside him, snoring loudly, Eddie felt safe, and warm, and he didn't have to think about his sickness, and he didn't have to remember his parting words to Merrit, and Merrit's to him.

Merrit was Captain Bringdown, that was clear. Eddie alternately wanted to punish him and to prostrate himself before him, neither one a reasonable option. But he couldn't find the middle ground.

He reached into his sack for a pen and paper, and, careful not to wake Eulene, who was still napping, he tried drafting a letter:

Artists do not need criticism they need praise is something Gertrude Stein said once. I am an artist, Merrit, and you are a philistine, and if I die needy and impoverished it doesn't fucking matter. You are leaving things behind, things. I am leaving behind my soul.

He folded the letter in half, and wrote another:

Dear Merrit,

I've been thinking you are probably right about my irresponsibility and now I feel rather chastened, and guilty. I have a habit of remaining vague about my own reality; I never act; I never decide. There are reasons not to decide,

153

and maybe that's what you don't understand. But anyway. Thank you and I love you very much.

Always,
Your dove,

Eddie

"What are you writing?" said Eulene, sleepily.
"It's a boy I sort of like," he said, slightly embarrassed.
"Oh, a boy."
"Yeah, he kind of jilted me."
"So you're telling him off?"
"Yeah, that, too. And sort of apologizing."
"I used to write a lot of letters to men, but honey, once, when I was forty, I sat down and read them all. I mean, I had copies, I'm an organized person, maybe you noticed. I read every single one. And you know what? They were all the same. Twenty years' worth of the same goddamned letter."
"Maybe you wanted to keep writing it until you got it right."
"Oh, well, that's a thought." Eulene laughed. "But in that case, I failed." She pushed his bangs out of his eyes. "I grew up on the Kill Van Kull, in Staten Island," she said, "under the Bayonne Bridge, and when I started doing drag routines, I used that name, I called myself Miss Kill Van Kull. And one night after a performance at The Grapevine, Forty-seventh Street—that was probably before your time, a drag bar, Lauren Bacall had her own drag show then just across the street, *Woman of the Year,* she's a man, I'm not kidding—one night after my number, a gorgeous man with aluminum teeth came up to me and introduced himself as Arthur Kill, and we were lovers after that for nearly a year. I used to introduce him just before my routine, which was an interpretive dance, with feathers, to Dinah Washington singing 'What a Difference a Day Makes.' I'd say, 'That's my man, girls, keep your fingers to yourself,' and he would smile and his mouth just glittered. Oh, honey, he was hot. When he was gone, I cried for a couple of months, but I hardly remember him now. Sometimes I lie awake in bed at night and list them all, all the men, and try to remember —what was it? What the hell did he do? And I can never remember. All I know for certain is, at the time I thought he was hot, or at the time I thought he was not so hot. But sex? Who remembers? It's a good thing, too, because if anybody really did remember,

from one time to the next, what it was like with a man, well, who would want to do it again? So all I'm telling you is, if he was good, you've already got your reward, and if he wasn't, why get him back?"

Then she went back to sleep, and Eddie left his letters crumpled on the floor. It didn't matter. There were others in his knapsack.

But Chicago, Eulene said, was a city for switching, and, indeed, she took him to a drag bar somewhere on the South Side, where she performed. She disappeared right away to get into her costume, and left Eddie sitting alone at a table with three of her friends. Their names were Hank and Dawn and Louise. Dawn and Louise were in miniskirts, and Hank was in a pair of sharkskin trousers and a tank-top T-shirt, which richly displayed his fabulous pecs. Eddie kept reminding himself that, as far as he knew, they all had dicks.

When Eulene came out to perform, Eddie had to stand up in his chair to see. Dawn got up on Louise's shoulders, which were very broad, and Hank stroked her thigh. She slapped his hand away. Then he turned to Eddie and patted his ass, which was sort of disconcerting, but Eddie smiled, wanting to be friendly. Hank offered cigarettes all around, and Eddie smoked, and they watched Eulene dance in a red flapper dress and cranberry pumps to Elvis Costello singing "(The Angels Wanna Wear My) Red Shoes."

Then she kicked off her shoes, and danced to "Boys," by the Beatles, but Eddie missed the performance, because of an enormous white man in blue nylon shorts and a baseball cap, leaning against the wall. His ass was as neat and small as a button, and his legs were unconscionably long, and a woman standing next to him reached up inside his shorts, and pulled on his dick. She was wearing hot pants, and she had extremely toned and muscular calves and upper arms. She had the most beautiful arms Eddie had ever seen, sinewy and obscenely defined shiny black arms. She pulled on the white guy's dick and he smiled, slyly, privately. Where had Eddie read that men who smiled privately in public were premature ejaculators? He watched until the man's dick slipped into view, out from under his shorts, and then he blushed hotly, and got down off his chair. Dawn elbowed him and giggled. She said, "I tried him, once. I gave it a pull and made him an offer. But he's pre-op. You wouldn't know to look at him, but he is. He said, 'Baby, the thing you want is what I'm trying to get rid of.' I said, 'So leave it with me.' Anyway, I see he still has it." She laughed. "Maybe you could coax it out of him."

"I think not," Eddie said, laughing a little too loudly. He had never been very comfortable in bars where sex was out in the open. He liked dark places, movie theaters, where he couldn't quite be seen, or recognize himself. When he went out prowling for sex, it was like going into a different room in his head, where the doors were sealed securely against his better judgment. He had sex in that room exclusively, where he was allowed to do whatever he liked, to be with men he wouldn't ever speak to normally, to ask for things which might embarrass him to repeat in the actual world. Sex with Merrit was the first time in years in which he saw himself doing it, as Eddie, out in the open; he could have had his mother watching, she would only have said it was what anyone else would have done. Indeed, Merrit was the kind of man you took home to meet your parents; even Joseph Stalin would have approved. That was the big disappointment with Merrit —that he could bring sex with him out of that room, and into the rest of the house, and still feel disconnected, finally, and lost. Because sex for him had never been what he was promised, a greater intimacy. It was either a performance or a disappointment. What he really wanted was just to be held.

"Will you hold me?" he said to Eulene, when she came down off the stage.

"Not until we've bumped pussies," she said, taking his hand. "Let's go out on the roof." She led him through the barroom, to a door in the back, where they climbed six flights of stairs and then a narrow rung ladder.

She stood on the roof in her bright red flapper dress and cranberry pumps, and in her yellow Marilyn Monroe wig she looked like a tasty wad of cotton candy on a big red stick. The night was clear, and they could see a part of the moon, and it was steamy, and hot. All around were the flat tops of tenements, and the sounds of radios in the street.

"Come away with me," Eulene said, spinning around. "After I finish this gig."

"I'm going to San Francisco," Eddie said.

"Perfect," she nodded.

"I've never been there," he said, "and I thought I would go now. Now that . . ."

"Now that what?"

156

"Now that I'm going," Eddie finished.

"Well, that's wonderful, that's fine."

She moved to Eddie, and put her arms around his shoulders.

"I've got people in St. Louis," she said. "Do you want to stop with me in St. Louis, first?"

"I don't know," Eddie said, pulling away. He liked her, but he didn't want to be flirtatious. After all, he had AIDS. He didn't want her to know, but he was still more afraid of rejecting than being rejected. "Maybe."

"Well," she said. "Well, you haven't told me how I look in red."

"I love your wig."

"You do?"

"It accentuates your brow."

"Well, now, there's an idea."

"No, I mean, you have a wonderful brow. A Coriolanian brow. Who am I quoting?"

"I don't care who you're quoting. What the hell does it mean?"

"It means very high."

"Oh, like way too big."

"It means distinguished."

"Gargantuan. Right?"

"It means elegant, and noble."

"Oh, yeah. Like I'm just this enormous drag queen. Right? That's what it means. I'm a big black drag queen, honey, and you're a sculpted little white boy, and you probably don't even shit."

"I'm not a white boy."

"What do you call it, then?"

"What do you mean, what do I call it?"

"I mean the color of your skin. Faded Nancy Reagan red? Plantation peach?"

"I don't think of myself as white."

"Think harder."

"Oh, well, anyway," Eddie said, turning away, as if to look at the moon. He hated confrontations. But Eulene still pursued.

"What the hell are you doing out on the road, anyway?" she said. "Don't you have any folks, somewhere out in Fairfield, Connecticut, who worry about you?"

"My parents don't worry about me."

"Sure, you've got a mansion back there somewhere, you don't have to worry about nothing. They let you out on the road without your chauffeur?"

"Just because I'm white," Eddie said, "doesn't mean I'm rich."

That broke the tension; she laughed.

"Honey, I like you," she said. "Tell me again what you think of my dress."

"I won't fall in love with you."

"Is that supposed to be news?"

"I can't have sex."

"Did I mention sex?"

"I can't, because, you know, I mean I could if you wrapped me in plastic. I mean sex is scary, right? I could be sick, for all you know. For all I know. And I don't want to give you anything. We can't even kiss."

"Who the hell mentioned kissing? I mentioned my dress."

"It's great."

"Don't be so expansive. It's gorgeous. It's good for my breasts. Couldn't you hug me in this, take me drinking, dancing?"

"Not if you want to ingest my bodily fluids."

"Don't flatter yourself. I know all you white boys, you'll be coming Perrier. I've got no taste for your gism."

"What's the most humiliating thing that ever happened to you?" Eddie said.

"The most humiliating thing? This is a little humiliating."

"Eulene, that dress is absolutely you."

"Liar. I wish I had more of an ass."

"You know what's the most humiliating thing that ever happened to me? He told me I was fat, and he pushed me away."

"Honey, if you're fat, we're all in trouble."

"I think it was because he wanted to help. I think it was love. Anyway, he's beautiful. He looks like Franchot Tone."

"Franchot Tone never once told Joan Crawford she was fat. And if he did, I guarantee you, sweetheart, he would have been out on his ass."

"But what if he was right? About me?"

"He could only have been right about you if he mentioned your extraordinary beauty."

"You're sweet."

"I'm stating facts."

"You're flirting."

"Why shouldn't I flirt? Because I'm wearing a dress?"

"Because you're sort of a man."

"You don't flirt with men?"

"Not if they like me."

"Honey, you've got to learn not to beg where you won't get a bone." She turned around. "Unzip me."

"You do it," Eddie said, shyly.

"Don't think I won't." She drew the zipper down to her ass, exposing her back, and the tops of her rounded buttocks.

"Eulene," Eddie said, "can I ask you a personal question?"

"I wish you would."

"Why are you wearing a dress?"

"Because," she said, turning around, throwing out her arms, and tipping her head to the sky, "because I look goddamn good in chiffon."

Sanctuary

Eddie went to church, in Chicago and St. Louis, with Eulene. He went reluctantly at the beginning, then later, almost contentedly, he went alone. But the first time, he sat with Eulene in a big Catholic church, resenting his father. Eulene was remarkably pious, and Eddie thought she never more resembled a proper middle-class woman than when, plainly dressed as a man, she crossed herself humbly, and knelt down for prayer. She shifted her great body forward as if she were balancing a spectacularly decorated hat, encrusted with feathers and grapes and perched on her head as a sign and test of her strength. Afterward she sat back slowly in the pew, with a judging, self-satisfied glance at the room, folding her arms on her bosom.

He felt weightless beside her. He needed an object of worship or faith all his own, to balance her intense involvement with something outside herself. For she thoroughly lost herself in the ceremony, but she got back delight. Maybe she was truly committed to God, Eddie thought, as corny as that sounded. He might have been willing, even now, to make that leap of faith. But he was bored with the mass, which held no resonance for him. He had never been to church, despite his father—*to* spite him, perhaps, for his mother had never allowed him to go. She had fixed forever in his mind a prickling atheism, not based on principle or science, but posed in scathing opposition to organized religion, and bishops and popes. "Pope Pius the Twelfth was a fascist," she wrote to her Catholic husband, in the only piece of correspondence Eddie knew of that had passed between them. He had picked it out of the mail, when he was twelve, and steamed it open, to see what his mother sounded like when she thought that only Joseph Stalin was listening. But it was full of codified loathing, which he couldn't decipher.

She would have been appalled to see him in a church, a Catholic church. That was a naughty, niggling pleasure for Eddie, like drinking illegally when he was still an adolescent. But his father would have been thrilled, and Eddie took some private delight in realizing that his father, who often said that all he wanted for his only son was that he become "some kind of religious," would never learn what godly or ungodly acts he committed out in the fields of the republic. Eddie might genuflect, he might confess, he might be transubstantiated for all that Joseph Stalin would ever know.

He tried to convey the logic of this to his mother, on the phone from East St. Louis, where he was on his way, alone, to Sunday morning service. Eulene was still asleep, and maybe his mother would be, too, he thought, slightly wanting to annoy her with this news of his going to church. But he knew that she was in allegiance with him against Joseph Stalin, and he thought she would feel, with him, his pleasure in thwarting his father. But his mother's only concern, when she got on the phone (having been awake, she said smugly, for hours), was that Eddie not be converted to anything. As usual, where Joseph Stalin was concerned, she missed the point, and her customary sense of humor failed her.

"You don't take Communion, do you?" she said.

Eddie stood at a pay phone a block from the church, not far from the Mississippi River, which he couldn't see. But he could smell it. It gave off an offensive stench, nothing like the Hudson smell of coffee beans. For the first time on his trip he was conscious of being lonely for New York.

"Why would I take Communion?" he said.

"Just please don't" is all she said.

"It's a sacrilege or something?"

"Oh, I don't care about that. Sacrilege? What do I care about that?"

"So what's the problem?"

"Especially not in a Catholic church."

"I'm just on my way into a Catholic church. That's the point. The point is for Joseph Stalin not to know that I'm attending Catholic service. What would he care if he didn't know I was attending a Methodist service?"

"Jesus, Wally, don't you have any sense?"

"Of course I have sense."

"Don't you know about Catholics?"

"What's wrong with Catholics?"

"Oh, I don't know," she said. Eddie could hear the dogs yapping in the background, ten of which were bitches named after tragic sopranos, Tosca, Mimi, Violetta. It was a house full almost exclusively of women, with which he was self-consciously male enough to sometimes feel excluded, though he disdained this response. "Girls," his mother shouted. "Girls. Be quiet." Then she said, "What are you calling first thing in the morning for, anyway, to say you're going to church? Do you think I care?"

"You seem to care."

"Look, Wally, Catholics. They're weird, they're like—listen, anybody with the letters r-e-v in front of his name, I don't care if he's black, white, young, old, liberal, conservative, anybody who believes in God—"

"Catholics don't call themselves reverends."

"—is fanatical. All religious fanatics, all of them. I don't care if it's Robert Redford, all right? People who believe in God are either fanatic, or lying. Shit," she said, and Eddie heard her dropping the phone. "Mimi, Norma," she said. "You bastards. Get the hell off the couch."

She was hostile, and profane, Eddie thought, two characteristics he had always sort of admired. She hated anything dogmatic and male. She didn't hate men, but she hated male authority, and Eddie hated it, too. When men were allowed to be in charge, they ruled arbitrarily. That was why she hated the pope, and that was why she swore like a trailer, which was a combination, he decided, of a trucker and a sailor. He realized for the first time that he had never heard his father swear; he never said anything saltier than "nuts." No wonder his mother found him intolerable, a man who never said "fuck," not even for the hell of it. She called him "a pillar of goodness." "You and your goddamned moral rectitude," she said. Eddie had grown up in a house where people expressed dissatisfaction with each other by saying things like "You and your goddamned moral rectitude."

162

But Joseph Stalin must have had something for her, though Eddie never knew what, unless it was just the rhythm of partings and reconciliations she enjoyed. They had ended and renewed their marriage so many times that Eddie could no longer tell the difference between separation and reconciliation. Their marriage was not having a marriage. When they were together, he could feel only the inevitability of their coming apart, and when they were apart, it was just a prelude to their getting back together. Each phase was its opposite, until their relationship just canceled itself out, completely. In all, there were moments, sometimes lasting no longer than a conversation, sometimes going on for several days, or even weeks, in which they seemed to be conventionally involved. And though Eddie didn't mind the stigma of their not being married, or divorced, in any ordinary way (indeed, he almost enjoyed the notoriety), he got tired of the wonder, the conviction, with which both his parents expressed, at each successive turning, their faith that the marriage was finally over, or destined, at last, to work out.

They couldn't get along, that was all. Eddie was used to it now. But when his father withdrew from his mother, he withdrew from Eddie, too, and his absence enraged them both. Eddie suspected that he and his mother were both focused self-defeatingly on spiting and resenting a man who possibly no longer knew, or even cared, how they conducted their lives.

Joseph Stalin, after all, passionate postcards notwithstanding, was perhaps the most aloof, emotionally scrupulous man Eddie knew. He had never seen his father cry, or laugh, or raise his voice, except in prayer. He was Irish Catholic from deepest Queens, without any colorful New York idiosyncrasies, neither Tammany Hall aggressive nor West Side Y harmless and quaint, but sort of Don Knotts crossed with Walter Pidgeon, erect and slightly foolish, stern but rather absurd. Of course, he was attractive enough; he looked like Dick Haymes singing "The More I See You." His boyish good looks concealed a steely resistance to feeling, yet Eddie and his mother continued to believe in him, or else to need not to believe in him. For faith needs an object, after all, Eddie thought; they were attached to his absence from their lives. They were emotionally dependent on him as they never would have been if he had always been around.

"I can't keep spending money on your phone calls," his mother said, back on the phone. "They started showing up on the bill, and this is costing me an arm and a leg. In fact, it's costing me three full articles in *Yorkie Tales,* if you want to work that out mathematically. I get paid by the line. We've just talked about twenty-five lines. I'll give you ten more, then I'm hanging up."

"I just wondered what your big objection was to my attending church."

"Go on, attend," she said. "Go dance around a maypole if you like, burn incense, wear a hair shirt. Just don't call me collect to tell me about it."

"I'm calling all the way from St. Louis, Missouri, the gateway to the West, the city in which *The Glass Menagerie* is set, for God's sake, Mom, to share something of my life with you, and now you don't have time for me?"

"I don't know what you want from me," she said, sounding resigned.

"I want to tell you about church," he said, plainly. He knew she could deal with facts.

"All right," she said. "You win. Tell me about church."

"Well," Eddie said, pleased to have won this little battle, "it's sort of fun to watch. I never pray, or sing, or anything. I mean, when everybody stands, I stand, that only seems polite."

"To strangers in a church, he's polite. However, to his mother—"

"Okay, I'll hurry. What I like, I like collection. That's when they get out all of these baskets, and they have eight men in blue passing them. Anyway, they did in Chicago. The men went down the aisle, almost as if they were fishing, casting their baskets into the pews, and reeling in big bundles of money."

"Wally," his mother said, abruptly, as if finally he had said something that truly captured her attention, "you don't give them money, do you?"

"What?"

"I said, just don't give them any money."

"You missed the point," Eddie said. "I was sharing with you, and you missed the point."

"And don't take Communion."

"I told you, all I do is watch."

"Don't give them money, and don't take Communion, all right? That's how they get you, with Communion. Promise me."

"You're too absurd."

"Don't call again unless you promise me."

"All right. I promise."

164

But he lied to her. He hung up the phone, and went to church, where he took Communion. He wanted to know what it would be like, a strange man putting something on his tongue. He had seen Eulene do it several times, but she wouldn't discuss it with him. "Something has to be sacred," she said, adjusting her wig. The church was nearly full. The women were wearing hats and flapping paper fans, and the men, in suits, were sweating. The mass had already begun when he arrived, but he liked walking into a church late and alone, like a prodigal son, cavalierly showing up in the middle of a family reunion. They would know that he was Eddie Socket, who had strayed from them, perhaps, for a time, to make his own arrangement with God, and who now came and went as he pleased, pious only after his own satisfaction. It gave him a sense of control, imagining all this, as he moved to a pew.

He sat in the back beside a man in a white shirt and tie whose neck bulged uncomfortably from his collar and dripped bright droplets of sweat onto his shoulders. The man had laid his suit jacket carefully down beside him on the pew, but even taking this precaution against the heat, he was sweating right through the back of his shirt, and wetly clasping his thick hands together on the back of the pew in front of him. He was big like Eddie's father, with a similarly bulbous nose, and he kept his clear eyes open all the time, even when he dropped his head in prayer. They were bright, watery eyes that stood out luminously against his rather haggard face, and as his forehead dripped sweat down his cheeks, it looked to Eddie almost as if the man was crying.

When it was time to stand, the man rose slowly and sang unabashedly, though his voice was not especially strong. Eddie stood, too, politely, though he didn't sing. He liked for the man beside him to decide perhaps that here was someone who was free to pick and choose among the aspects of a pious life. Certainly his father would have had him singing the hymns, Eddie thought, and his mother would have had him picketing out in front, or merely thumbing his nose.

If he felt like an adult, standing, not singing, in church, was that because adulthood was merely the freedom not to do what would have been required of him when he was a dependent boy? But he had not done many things, the past eight years, had not paid his bills for months, had not done his laundry, logistical things but also personal, spiritual things, had not thought at all of his life as something to lose, the way he lost track of time, or his keys, or the cats. He had mistaken the freedom not to act for being an adult, he thought. Some things, of course, were not to be done, like voting Republican or drinking Coors, but he saw now, alas, that he might have made some decisions peculiarly his own, even decisions based on his anger with his parents.

For his parents were incapable of joy. His father had no sense of pleasure in life; his mother was self-indulgent and then self-denying, and between them, Eddie thought, he had learned to alternate between periods of incredible indulgence followed by months of punishing abstinence and withdrawal. He binged emotionally. He binged sexually, too. It was not exactly irresponsibility. It was a failure to imagine a world in which there were any options other than the ones his parents presented; it was having learned not moderation but guilt, fear rather than joy.

But now in a Catholic church in East St. Louis, with his parents far away, he thought he would make a genuine decision, based on his own desires, and so he took Communion. The church was so large they couldn't have everyone up to the front; a man in a robe walked halfway down the aisle, and served the back of the room. There was no kneeling involved; there wasn't even wine, which disappointed him. He would have liked to drink wine in a church, when he never drank it anywhere else. But there was a line forming now. The worshipers collected single file in front of the priest, taking bits of bread mechanically, as if absolution, too, had been modernized by the principle of assembly line production.

He hesitated before joining the line. He wanted to see how people took the wafer. Did they hold out their tongues, or take it in their fingers first? There were many variations, for all of which the priest seemed prepared. Eddie got up and shuffled slowly forward. He decided to open his mouth and stick his tongue out flat. The priest was deft; he put the wafer on his tongue without touching his fingers to any part of Eddie's mouth. The wafer was thin, and dry. He held it in his mouth strangely. He didn't know now whether to suck, then chew, or chew and then suck, so he held it on his tongue, his lips closed gingerly, and carried it back to his seat, where he watched the others, again, to see what they did.

Everyone, returning from the priest, held their hands clasped closely to their chests. But some looked straight ahead, and some turned their heads from side to side, and some held their mouths absolutely still, as Eddie had, around their pieces of actual flesh —for it was not a metaphor, right? It was actually supposed to be

166

someone's body—and some chewed daintily, and some looked terribly satisfied, and some looked humble, and the choir members, who were last, were giggling furtively, holding their hands to their mouths so as not to spit out the Host. When everyone was done, Eddie simply swallowed the wafer; that was easiest.

Because, he thought, there was nothing to define himself against, no lover, no family really, no community, only New York, and his homosexuality, and he had not emerged in one, and he had not taken pleasure in the other. And though God was nowhere in his life, not even in his father's scrawled epigraphs; though God did not seem to be present (could not, he thought, really have been present) in his having gotten sick; though he did not believe in a benevolent omniscience, or even a malevolent omniscience, or an omniscience of any sort—the world seemed too fractured for that, and who could possibly know, and see, it all, and if someone could, why had he not been warned to take that dick, whichever dick it was, out of his mouth right now, before he caught something he couldn't get rid of?—though he didn't think that God existed, still, it was nice just to sit somewhere with people who believed that he did. He had been promised a whole world and had found himself living in a shattered one, and maybe being an adult was just learning to pick up the pieces that seemed to apply, and go with little bits, and don't disdain wholeness when it offers itself, even if it comes in the guise of a church. It was a moment of patience, at last, a moment of sanctuary, inside their world but not on their terms, just for himself.

The Eqoist

Florence was tiny and crowded and hot, and it reminded Merrit uncomfortably of Boston, its many, many banks and shops and cemeteries all bound to the centuries with a leaden, immovable weight. The sidewalks were narrow, and it was difficult to see the Duomo from a reasonable perspective without stepping into the street and risking being run down by cars and motor scooters. The city compared unfavorably to everywhere else he had been in Europe. The Florentines were not as chic as the Parisians, or as friendly as the Romans. They refused to give directions, and they loathed tourists, even circumspect American tourists with money to spend on generous tips, if they were so moved. No one moved Merrit. He felt disliked. The men refused to flirt, the women hurried past with babies, or bundles, or baskets. And the peasants were merely contemptuous; for them, he didn't exist. Nothing was as picturesque as he expected, the green hills in the background, the replication of the David all over town, the art-worshiping travelers who camped out at the Accademia, sharing Renaissance secrets. Somehow, they kept to themselves, and the city remained a locked heart. Moreover, the Duomo was cracked and needed repair. The papers were full of the debate, how best to preserve the landmark. Merrit found it depressing. Everywhere he went in the world, the known community was deteriorating, buildings and people and paintings. In Rome the Sistine Chapel, under restoration, looked like a naked baby's bottom, between changes of diaper. It even smelled ammoniac, like urine.

He was in Florence with an earnest younger man named William Boleslawski (he was twenty something) with a textbook physique and an immense penis. It was nice to be wanted by a perfect specimen, the man every self-respecting gay man wanted (flat stomach, nice suits, good job), but it wasn't enough. His interest in William had diminished almost as soon as they were truly alone together, in a hotel room in Paris, which indicated to Merrit—well, something. The best part of his trip, so far, had been the flight from JFK, alone (he and William took separate flights), when he was able to look out the airplane window, down at the city, and see it falling away, Saul and Eddie and his dog, and his apartment, and AIDS falling slowly away. Then he closed his eyes and slept to Paris, meeting William at the airport. Their first night together was good, the sex was good, but William liked to be watched. Although gentle, he wasn't very giving. Merrit liked a lot of attention in bed, as long as it wasn't clinging and needy, like Saul's. If Saul had William's body, Merrit wondered, would they still be lovers? But Saul was too angry for sex, and it wasn't very sexy to be constantly, constantly blamed.

Yet when Merrit closed his eyes and thought of William, with his big dick, squatting eagerly over Merrit, he wanted to run. That was too much. After Paris he asked for separate beds, and he spent a lot of time alone, writing letters with the pen William had bought for him at Tiffany's before their trip. It was slender and smooth, and gun-metal blue in the light. He wrote to Saul, he wrote to Eddie. He wrote every day, on whatever scraps of paper were available when he was overcome with the urge to communicate, for he was being romantic in Europe, and he liked to write.

To Eddie, he sent a couple of postcards. They were short, and he wanted them to be funny. They meant "Please, get over it," or "Don't blame me." "Dear Eddie," he wrote, his handwriting slanting up from left to right (he was left-handed, and postcards were hard), his big, looping letters anxiously scraping each other, "Even if I were twenty-four, and you were rich and lived in Paris, it still wouldn't work." Actually, he didn't really care whether or not it could work. That wasn't the issue. But he wanted to throw Eddie a fish, at least—he had come down pretty hard on him in New York.

He wrote voluminous letters to Saul, line after tightly scrawling line on sheets of tissue-paper blue from the Hotel Meurice in Paris, small square note-sized pages from the Hotel Columbus, in Rome. And the odd, sentimental scrap:

> Dear Saul, you might think this is a romantic gesture, writing to you on the back of a poster I tore off a wall, but the problem is I have not been able to find a blank piece of paper in my satchel. I found a postcard for Eddie (do you mind my mentioning Eddie?) with a picture of Gertrude Stein and Alice B. Toklas on the front. Eddie needs to be in therapy. William works a lot. Our trip has not been successful, and I wish that you were here. You'd know how to talk about the art, the sculpture, the outfits worn by the Italians! Perhaps we can reconcile still. You know I need my flirtations, so forgive me William and this silliness. The pen is soaking through the paper now (as you can see), and I will sign off lovingly here.

But in Florence he was dogged throughout the city by the presence of ghosts. His ghosts, not Italian ghosts. They were American ghosts, from New York City, and from Massachusetts. He would be sitting in front of a church, perhaps the Santa Croce, writing a letter to Saul, and there would be someone he knew, from the past, sometimes a death from AIDS, sometimes an old high school crush. They all looked wounded, and vengeful, and pathetic. They weren't necessarily dead, but they were people he hadn't seen, or thought about, for years. They turned up, glaring, everywhere, and nearly spoiled his trip. He was followed around by accusing memories. He didn't know what they wanted.
Saul would have known.

> Dear Saul, I think I must be getting old. I'm sitting at the Santa Croce, right out front, and I think I can see the girl I took to the senior prom, wrapped around the statue of Dante. I remember her name, Hilary Slunk. Remember, you laughed at her name, a long time ago when you liked me, and we laughed together a lot. I wonder why Hilary Slunk is clinging to Dante. I wish you were here, because you would laugh, and make an explanation. William doesn't laugh very much. He dresses very well. He bought me shoes. They're ordinary, banker shoes, you wouldn't like them very much.

What does Hilary want? The year I took her to the prom, my brother took his wife (when she wasn't his wife, they were just going steady), and she was prom queen, too. They were queen and lady-in-waiting, or queen and queen mother, or something. The newspaper printed a column, and the heading was this: "Mather Brothers Go for Queens." That was long before I met you. I'd like to write to that newspaper now! What would they say if they knew? I'm married to you. I miss you, dove, I miss the way we were those first few weeks years ago, when you couldn't think of anything bad to say about me. I miss your telling me what Hilary wants. You would probably say something like "She wants your balls. She wants revenge." But I don't hurt everyone. Only when they want to be hurt. I wish you didn't want so much to be hurt. William wants us to go to Venice, but I'm thinking of leaving here alone, and traveling by myself, a little while. Too bad we can't get along! You're my dove. Love.

When he wasn't writing to Saul, he was staring blankly at William, and trying to connect. There was nothing wrong with him, he was genial, and fairly intelligent, and relatively kind. But Merrit pulled further and further away. They stayed at the Hotel Excelsior, along the Arno, in their separate beds, but in the morning, just before the heat, when it was barely light, William crawled onto Merrit and took his pleasure. He liked to come on his chest, and his face twisted shut and he shouted, and shook out his big dick like a dog shaking water from its back. He wanted Merrit to suck him, but Merrit was scared about AIDS, and he wouldn't even let William take him in his mouth (ruefully remembering Eddie), though it would have been nice. After William came, he squatted over Merrit and watched him jerk off, and then Merrit waited with their semen on his stomach while William went for a towel, and wiped him dry. Then Merrit rolled over and slept. In the afternoon he wandered the city alone, followed everywhere by jilted lovers. There was a line that connected them, from William (for he was already discarded) back to Eddie, ending at Saul, and maybe from Saul back to—someone. His father, his mother, someone. His therapist would know, but she was also on vacation (Lisbon, Barcelona, and Madrid). Saul would know, too.

"Yo, dove," he said, calling Saul long-distance, from the concierge's desk, at three in the morning, U.S. time.

171

"Don't get patronymical with me," Saul said.

"Patro what?"

"Nicknamey."

"I miss you, dove," Merrit said, thumbing through the guest register.

"Yeah, when you're thousands of miles away. Why are you calling?"

"Saul," Merrit sighed, "I'm having a terrible time."

"Which you wanted to share with me. That's very considerate, Merrit."

"I haven't been happy."

"So the trader isn't holding your interest?"

"Don't make jokes. I think I'm too old for this. He wants to go dancing at night, you know, and I like to sleep."

"Play with the teens, dance to Madonna. Those are the rules, sweetheart."

"Don't be mean," Merrit said. There were three people staying at the Excelsior, he noticed, named Kurtz.

"Who's being mean?"

"He's really rather mature."

"Can we have an age here? Can you estimate? Which side of nineteen? The legal side?"

"He's perfectly adult."

"Unlike you. Merrit, why did you call? Is Goldfinger paying for this, your little financier? Or maybe I shouldn't say 'little.' "

"We're not spending too much time together."

"He's not beautiful? He's not warm? You don't like to sleep with him, either?"

"I always liked sleeping with you."

"As long as we didn't touch."

"Well, anyway," Merrit said. He closed the guest register, and scratched his thigh. He was wearing William's Dartmouth boxer shorts, and a V-neck T-shirt.

"Merrit, I want to ask you a question. This boy?"

"Don't, Saul."

"No, really. This boy, this trader, this young man, is he very attractive?"

"Well, yes, I'd say that he is. Objectively, I mean. His body, his face. His lips are kind of thin—"

"I never trusted a man who didn't have lips. Don't tell me, now, he hasn't got a penis, either, right?"

172

"No, he has a penis."

"So what's it like?"

"Saul, I didn't call to talk about this."

"You woke me up, asshole. You woke me up to talk from fucking overseas about your little fling, this Richie Rich, this financier, so now you have to answer my question. That's the rule. It's in all the handbooks, believe me."

"What was the question?"

"Well, what's it like? You know, 'it,' the light fantastic, pillow talk. Is he hot, or is he not?"

Merrit adjusted his shorts. "He's very exciting, I guess."

"You bastard."

"Saul, you asked."

"Yeah, well, you could have lied."

"He's very exciting, but . . . "

"But what?"

". . . it isn't enough. He isn't very giving, that's the thing. He's doting, but he isn't giving. You're very giving, Saul, when you're not angry. It's something I like about you."

"Yeah, well, I'm giving, and where are you? Here by my side?"

"Well, it's different with him, Saul. You know? Maybe you were a little too giving. He's kind of cool. He likes to be admired."

"So I should have made you admire me, is that it? I shouldn't have given, I should have made you admire?"

"He's nothing like you."

"That's comforting."

"Saul, it's not about you."

"So call someone else at three in the morning, after you've flown far away," Saul said, and hung up.

Saul was too angry to be helpful, and Merrit continued to be trailed by his ghosts. "I didn't come all the way to Florence to peel you off the statuary," he told one of them, who had been hanging off the David. It was something Saul would have said. Saul made connections with people, he knew how to talk, and analyze dreams, and make explanations of things. Merrit walked along the Arno, lining up his ghosts along the water, hoping to find the point at which a theme emerged, as if from out of the river. He expected the theme of his life to surface out of the water, and take him on its back, and pull him in a straight line out to sea, and back to New York. But nothing emerged, no connection was made, as long as he walked, as deeply as he considered.

He wondered what Saul would have said, if Saul weren't so angry. He was sure it would have made sense. He was sure that Saul could have explained the connection between William, and AIDS, and Hilary Slunk, and Eddie Socket, and all the deaths in the past few years, and his unhappiness. But it wouldn't have helped, because Saul would say the connection was this, that Merrit was never going to die. He was going to live forever, he was never going to die. And everyone he knew, whether from AIDS, or heart disease, or cancer or sadness or boredom, gunshot, napalm, radiation poisoning, sniper fire, political assassination, rape, evisceration, childbirth, hard-heartedness, bad luck, good luck, poverty, insanity, or rage, everyone he knew would die, and he would not. For Merrit did not believe in mercy. He did not even particulary believe in justice. What he believed was that under the surface of any gesture, loving or angry or sad, was a fist clenched in willful defiance. That was the shape in the river he waited for, a clenched fist. That's what Saul would have said. It lay at the bottom of all, the base of his life, holding his soul in its grip, a tightly clenched, indomitable fist.

Greetings from San Francisco

My son called, from San Francisco, collect. He said, "I'm standing on the corner of Ortega and Something. Which house was yours?" I said, "Are you going to call me collect each time you have to cross the street, from now until the day you die?" My son is twenty-eight years old, and I have failed him. He cannot find his way out of a paper bag. He said, "I might." I said, "You're standing where?" He said, "I'm standing on Ortega now, and Polk is running—north and south? Or something, up and down. Which was your house?" And I said, "Twenty-third. Ortega and Twenty-third." He said, "It's lovely here. I've been walking all over town." "I know it's lovely there," I told him. "I always said that it was lovely there. Didn't you believe me?" "I'm trying to figure out how come you left. I mean, this guy you followed to New York, he must have been hot." My son is impertinent. I raised him to be polite, but he grew up impertinent. I don't know how this happened. I said, "That's none of your goddamned business." He said, "We crossed the mountains, getting here." "Of course you did. We who?" "Eulene and me. The mountains were wonderful. We crossed them in Colorado, and then later there were more." "Who's this Eulene?" I said. "I called to say it's lovely here," he said, "and sad. A lot of single men on Market Street in antique cars. I have to think their lovers died. It feels like during a war.

175

War widows. You know, that movie, *Since You Went Away,* with Claudette Colbert, Jennifer Jones, Shirley Temple in her first adult pair of pumps, all waiting for their men to come home. It feels that way here." I didn't respond to that. I have never liked this touch-me feel-me, which my son is suddenly so intent upon. "Eight-six-eight Ortega," I said. "I just wanted to say, greetings from San Francisco," he said. "I wanted you to know that I'm here." Then he hung up.

I went outside, and sat down on the porch, and stared at the road. I'm fifty-seven years old. I have lived over half my life in New Jersey. I left Sacramento in the early fifties, and I stayed in San Francisco two years exactly, of which I remember mostly the nights. I remember Puccini, Irish coffee at the Buena Vista Cafe, and Don Lorenzo. He was an opera singer, a bass. Later on he sang *Don Carlo* at the Met, but in San Francisco he was Colline, the philosopher, in *La Bohème.* How many times did I hear that passage where he talks about his coat? He held it open and sang to the lining, praising his coat, which of course he was going to have to sell for nothing, sell for no reason, I mean, because the medicine he buys for the price of the coat is not going to bring the soprano back to life. After all, it was opera, and she had a terminal disease. But Don Lorenzo sang to his lining night after night. I never told him that he shouldn't have sung to the lining. He tucked his nose into the crook of his arm, and it looked like he was sniffing his armpits. I should have told him that.

He had terrific legs, and he wanted me to give birth, with him, to the perfect American child. He was Italian. He said that I could go to Italy, and have the child, and leave it with his mother, who would raise it as her own. I said, "How old is your mother?" She had to have been sixty, at least—he was thirty-seven. I was twenty-three. "The neighbors would know it wasn't hers." Not that I care about neighbors. He said, "But you must agree. She will be a lovely child." He was sure it would be a girl. "She will have your looks and my talent." "That would be nice," I nodded. "Unless she has *your* looks and *my* talent. There's no guarantee." Of course, he never mentioned marriage. But looking back at it now, I might have accepted. Because I went to New York, and I did get married, and I did have a child, with my looks and his talent, but the child isn't happy, and the husband didn't stay, and they both might just as well be far away in Italy, for all the joy I feel. Joy is something I have never understood. I thought it was just my generation, but I have raised a joyless son.

"It's so sad here," he said, the next time he called. "So full of distance, and loss."

"Don't try to be lyrical, not with me," I said.

"The houses are wonderful colors. Eulene likes to sleep in the late afternoon, so I walk around the city, starting at five until the sun goes down."

"Do I get to know about Eulene?"

"Do you want to?"

"Eulene is a woman?"

"I'm not sure I believe in those categories anymore," he said.

Only a boy without a job could afford to be so goddamned cavalier, so flip.

I said, "When I was twenty-eight, I had a baby and a house in the woods, and pipes to unfreeze in the winter, and a husband to feed."

"Eulene is a man," he said, "but we're not doing the wild thing. We're sleeping together. We're sharing a bed in a room in a tiny hotel. It's cheaper that way. But we're not going into the wilderness together. She's a drag performer and I like her very much. But, Mom, I only called to tell you about the colors, and the light. I walk around until the sun is gone, and watch the light fall onto the buildings, shadows and light."

"I know about the light," I said.

"Pacific light."

I said, "I remember about the light." I wanted him to know that. I wanted him to know that I'm not so easily shocked, that he can call me up collect, call his mother collect and talk about things like drag performers and "the wild thing," and still not scare me away. I don't care what he does. I don't think he believes me, but I really don't care what he does. I just don't want him to end up—what? Dependent on me. His father was dependent on me. He still is. Wally doesn't know this, but his father calls me once a week. Sometimes I pick up the phone, and sometimes I don't. I don't like to be clung to. But now my son is calling, too. At least his father doesn't call collect.

"The shadows are wonderful, too," he said.

Well, I remember. There's a lot to remember that I wouldn't want to discuss. I remember Sacramento, but I never went back. I had a

177

boyfriend there who was out of this world. His father was Swedish and looked like Laurence Olivier in *Hamlet*. His mother was Italian, and she looked like Sophia Loren. So you can picture a cross between that. I was forbidden to see him, but I saw him anyway. I crept out of the house, and we went driving together in an old Pontiac. Old now. New then. We were engaged to be married, but none of our parents allowed it. We drove into the mountains. I got sent away to Santa Barbara that summer, and when I got back, his parents had moved.

My son would treat this now like some kind of joke. He'd say, "That's so William Inge." My son is so goddamned clever. But I can assure you, it mattered quite a bit at the time. It doesn't matter now, but at the time it did. He followed me around with a shotgun once, for a week, when I tried to break up with him. He wrote obscenities all over my high school yearbook, which I couldn't show my parents, of course, because at that point we weren't supposed to be seeing each other. Thank God we didn't get married. The last I heard, he owned a golf course somewhere east of Denver, and was terribly rich. Or maybe it was fat.

I don't have any kind of philosophy of life, but if I did, if I had a philosophy and liked to talk about these things, the way my son likes to talk all the time about his principles, or lack of principles, his nihilism, which as far as I'm concerned is just an excuse not to work—if I had a rule to live by that I wanted to share, I'd say it was this: I cut my losses. That is the easiest way, in the long run, though it takes some discipline. This is something men never learn, how to let go. Don Lorenzo pleaded for months. He wanted a child. Others chased me with guns. Wally's father calls me once a week. They don't know how to let go.

Wally would say that I don't let go, either. He'd say I'm still married to a man I didn't love. But I would point out to him that his father's Catholic, and he simply wouldn't divorce me. Wally would say, "So you divorce him." But Wally is a boy, he doesn't understand about the slow accumulation of debris, how things gather dust, and magazines get piled in the corner, and marriages go on and on when there's no particular reason to end them, even when you're no longer married in any way that makes legal, or personal, sense. He would say I have led a limited life. All right, I made some mistakes. But I have kept my feelings close to myself, and I pay my own way, and the road, from my porch, is idyllic, and if I turn my back on the pink and orange Day-Glo houses up the

178

road, I can look out on the myrtle on the banks along the drive, and please myself.

"But Mom," Wally said, "how could you have traded this for New Jersey?"

So I sat up late downstairs last night, and I thought, all right, I'll try to remember. Just in case he calls again. I got out all my old scrapbooks, and I played some old records, Jo Stafford, Frank Sinatra, Keely Smith. I drank a couple of glasses of wine. I looked at the pictures. There I was with Debbie and Lynn, my roommates, all of us looking like Maggie McNamara in *Three Coins in the Fountain*. Well, actually, just Lynn. Debbie looked like June Allyson, and probably still does. I looked like Kim Novak. I'm not boasting—I don't like Kim Novak. The pictures are in black and white, but I distinctly remember that Debbie wore pink. I hated pink. I had dyed my hair that year, to be a brunette, but the dye faded strangely, and my hair turned bright orange.

None of this is in the picture. What is in the picture is three awkward girls dressed up for a night with the boys and probably some clarinets, because San Francisco was a good place for jazz, at the time. I remember now that Debbie was a Mormon, and she married once and then converted to Presbyterianism and married again, and now she has another husband somewhere in prison (last I heard), and a business of her own, cosmetics, I think. Lynn still writes to me. She says her children are yuppies. "Somehow this is the last thing I would have expected," she says. I haven't told her yet my son is homosexual.

The pictures have captions, which are written in chalk in what must be my handwriting. The one of the three of us says, "How To Marry a Millionaire." There's another picture with everyone nearly asleep at two in the morning, Lynn with Howie, whom she married, Debbie with Lark (she is the sort of woman who would marry a man named Lark), and me with Steve Grant, another singer, a tenor. He was thirty-five and divorced, and I was in love with him. I thought. I followed him to New York. That was as far as we got. Our shoulders are bare in this picture (my shoulders, anyway—he is wearing a shirt and a tie), and people are smoking. People don't smoke anymore, which is something I miss, as long as I'm listing regrets. The caption here is embarrassing. It says, "Too Bad About Dien Bien Phu." You see, I understand Eddie. I was nihilistic once, too.

But you grow out of that, and anyway, we laughed a lot. My son doesn't laugh. Who did we laugh at? Mort Sahl, Don Sherwood, Jack La Lanne. That's right, Jack La Lanne. I worked for him for a while, in a television studio, KGO. We were all at a party once, and he was wearing tights and talking about "abstemiousness"—a little ahead of his time there, a prophet in something, after all. You couldn't take him seriously. He was a funny man in tights who talked about not fucking, and he said he didn't drink, either. But he spoke to my breasts all night, and offered me a sip of his drink, which was straight gin.

Who would have thought, with all the talent in the city, who would have suspected: Jack La Lanne? That's the way it goes. For instance, on a larger scale: Arthur Godfrey, John Wayne, Eisenhower, and Nat King Cole. They all got sick at once, and which one died? I know it's terrible to say, but the nerds prevail. Don't get me started on the Kennedys. "I'd rather mow lawns in Golden Gate Park" was what Don Sherwood said when the network tried to move his show to Chicago. He didn't leave and he never regretted it, as far as I know. Don Sherwood was David Letterman years ahead of his time, and he would have been a sensation. He stayed where he was, and now who remembers him? That's in the past. And if he had gone, what then? But maybe this is the point, don't look back. Or, never leave home. Or, never go east.

"Guess where I am?" Wally said, much too late for him to be calling. He sounded out of breath. I was on my third glass of wine.

"I don't know, where?"

"I'm standing across from the Buena Vista Cafe. It's filled with yuppies. You have to tell me, now, were you a yuppie? Prototypically speaking."

I told him the truth. I said, "I was a chick, on the lam."

"From what?"

"How do I know from what?"

"Steve Grant?"

All right, so he knows the button to push.

"He dumped you in the Oyster Bar," he said. "So what?"

"So I married your father."

"There must have been other options."

I said, "I don't like it when people call me at three in the morning from the Buena Vista Cafe."

Steve Grant. The last time Wally was home, he came with his friend, a girl with bright green fingernails, driving a bright green car. They looked at scrapbooks, and he talked to her about my life as if it wasn't mine, but his. Steve Grant. "This one was her boyfriend in Sacramento," he said. "This was the guy who wanted to father her child." All right, I've shared some facts with him, over time. But he sat on the couch with the dogs and this girl, and talked about my life as if it now belonged to him. I was in the kitchen when I heard her ask this: "She's still in love with him?" It was as if he felt my life was his, to share however he liked, with whomever he wanted, and I will not, goddamnit, sit here now and think about Steve Grant. My son wants me to talk about these things, Steve Grant, his father, New Jersey. What about my feelings? he wants to know. What about them? I don't remember. Did the pioneers have feelings? Did they stop every two hundred yards and think how they felt about what they were doing? No. They just got into their wagon trains, and went. Lewis never said to Clark, "How do you feel about going hungry today?" you know, or, "How do you feel about walking fifty miles with your heels bleeding?" or, "Sacagawea? Aren't there any other options?" What is so important about feelings?

I married his father for a very particular reason. I married him in order to raise a child. I mean that perfectly sincerely. I wanted to teach my way of looking at things to a child. I thought that I could set another person going in the world, a person with some common sense, a man who wasn't a fool, an idiot, abusive or abandoning, or just plain silly. But I have failed. My son has been calling for weeks. I don't know what he's doing all the way across the country. I don't know why he's sleeping with a transvestite. I don't know where he gets his ideas. I don't know anything about him.

I said, "Wally, listen to me. Here's what you do. All right? Listen to me. You take the cable car up Powell, to California Street. You do it late at night, because that's when you see all the lights. Take a sweater if you can, because sometimes it's cold at night, even in June or July. Ride all the way to California, which is where you get off, and then you go to the Fairmont Hotel. Look in the lobby. It's nice. Have a drink. Have a whiskey sour. It's a terrible drink, but that's what you have at the Fairmont Hotel. Then go to the Top of the Mark. That's in the Mark Hopkins Hotel. It's close to the Fairmont. I don't remember how close exactly, but close. Go to the top, on the elevator. Take someone with you. Take Eulene. When you get to the top, don't have a drink. Look at the view. Look at the city from the Top of the Mark. Wally? All right? Steal me an ashtray."

Then I hung up.

Since You Went Away

Eulene got a regular gig at a club in the Tenderloin, doing a drag medley from *Carousel,* which Eddie watched from the back of the crowded, smoky room. He was a band wife. He sat through all her shows, and waited for her afterward, sometimes until two or three in the morning, when he would take her out to a bar somewhere with some of her friends, and let her unwind. They would usually end up at breakfast at a McDonald's on Market Street, before going home to bed, just after sunrise. Eulene slept, but Eddie, who was suddenly insomniac, lay awake a few hours, and then went out walking. He was starting to get sick, though he hadn't quite acknowledged it. He was dizzy, and frequently cold. He had gotten the sweats, a couple of times, in the middle of Eulene's performance, and had to sit them out on the john. It occurred to him at breakfast one morning, after three weeks in San Francisco, that the time had probably come to tell someone that he had AIDS.

He was chewing on a Golden Arches swizzle stick, and staring into his tea, which was acid green. The only people who knew that he was sick were Dr. Fillgrave and a couple of lab technicians in Nebraska. He knew Eulene would be sympathetic. He watched her aggressively peppering her Egg McMuffin, and wondered why he didn't want her to know. She was a big, incisive woman, after all, with a wonderful set of shoulders and a functioning penis, who was nice to sleep with (when he slept)—he curled up to her stomach with her arms wrapped around him, and snored, she said, like a dog.

She would probably take care of him, if that was what he wanted. But he wasn't sure it was. No one had ever done that for him. He had been lectured, and scolded, and pampered, and indulged, treated like an irresponsible boy, accused of dependency by people who often themselves seemed more insecure than he was. His mother, for instance, could only take care of herself, and Merrit was proving to be the same. His father, too. They all had this idea that if Eddie was allowed, he would become monstrously needy, and burdensome. But in fact he had gotten from point A to point B, or failed to, entirely on his own. Perhaps he had made a mess of things, but he did it without anybody's help. If Eulene wanted to mother him now, he wasn't sure he could stand it.

"Where have you been lately, guy?" she asked, between bites of her Egg McMuffin. She licked her fingers thoughtfully. She was the sort of person who always cleaned her plate. "I've been waking up alone."

"I like it when you call me guy," Eddie said.

"Three nights running, I've been up at sundown, all alone. Where were you?"

"I think it would be great if my name actually were Guy. It would be like never being alone. I could go into a delicatessen anywhere in the country, and the man behind the counter would say, 'What'll you have, guy?' And I would wonder how I had made all these friends, without having to be a movie star, or something."

"Maybe you fucked them all somewhere before," Eulene said, a little nastily.

"If that were true," Eddie said, with forced bravado, "they wouldn't know my name."

But Eulene wasn't merely playing catty repartee. She was testing strategies. When there was something she wanted to know, she would try every tactic she could think of, until Eddie gave in.

"What gets you up in the middle of the day, when you should be sleeping with me?" she said, directly.

"Oh, you know, I've been walking around."

"Walking around doing what?"

"Thinking. Calling my mother, just to torture her. Stuff like that. Actually I was sort of wondering about Los Angeles. I mean, as long as I'm here, in California, maybe I should make all the stops. What's Los Angeles like?"

"Queens," said Eulene, wiping her mouth, and watching Eddie intently. "With mountains. You look pale."

"It's the lighting in here. 'A person is entitled to the lighting he needs.' Who am I quoting? No, I'll tell you. Andy Warhol." He took a sip of tea, so as not to have to respond to whatever Eulene was planning to say. But she was momentarily quiet, as if reconnoitering. Did she know that he was sick? He was hardly ready to admit it to himself. If she asked him, would he say yes? "When were you ever in Los Angeles?" he said, to keep the conversation off himself.

"I wasn't."

"Then how would you know what it's like?"

"It's knowledge we're born with," she said. "Like everybody knows they have to sleep, at the end of the day. When are you sleeping?"

"I'm just not very tired," Eddie said.

"You look tired."

"Thanks." He broke his swizzle stick in half. "Actually, I was wondering if Los Angeles was a little more real than this, you know, than San Francisco. I can hardly look at the place without my mother's version getting in the way. She's very romantic. All my life I've had the expectation of romance, but the actuality of—I don't know, just this," he said, spreading his arms to the room. "Just a McDonald's. Maybe it's AIDS," he said, matter-of-factly, as if the word held no particular resonance for him. "I thought that San Francisco would be completely different from New York, but it feels pretty similar, a place full of gaps like missing teeth, where people used to be. AIDS has made these two cities the same."

"And Los Angeles is what, hermetically sealed from loss, and disease?"

"I just thought it might be a little more real than this. At least, I wouldn't have my mother tracking me down all over the city, in a pair of stockings and stiletto heels, looking like Dorothy Malone in *Written on the Wind.*"

"California's all the same," Eulene said. "Just one long New Jersey." She folded her Styrofoam carton, slipping its flaps carefully into their slots. She was meticulous. She said, "Let's go home, and sleep."

"I can't sleep."

"I'm running you ragged, the way I live."

"I like the way you live."

"You're holding out on me, Blanche."

"I'm not holding out."

"I know where you were last night, during my number."

"I was out front. You sang 'Soliloquy.' I'll tell you my favorite part. 'My boy Bill, I will see that he's named after me.' No, that's not it. It's when you stop, and suddenly say, 'Wait a minute, what if he is—a girl?' I love that."

"You were in the john, I know."

"How do you know?"

"You don't go into a drag bar looking nineteen and delicious and not have your every movement registered by seven devouring queens, five of whom report back to me. You were in there a long time."

"I was lost in thought."

"Yeah, what about?"

"I don't know. Los Angeles. My mother," he said, hoping to distract her with a story. "She's just like this 1940s movie, you know, *Since You Went Away*. She came from Sacramento. She had boyfriends, and they drove along the river roads, the Sacramento River, the American, listening to Harry James, and Helen Forrest singing 'Skylark,' which you should put into your act, Eulene. It's got a squeaky part, before she starts to sing—he plays the trumpet and he makes the note go up." He raised his hand and pointed with his finger. "The note goes really high, and then she sings. That's what my mother was listening to, along the river, in a Buick, making out with a boy, smoking Chesterfields and drinking, I don't know, Pabst or something, Schlitz?"

"Do you look like her?" Eulene said, apparently diverted.

"Do I? I don't know. We have the same nose. The same—"

"Looking at you, I could imagine she was sort of Ann Revere."

"Looking at me?" Eddie said, incredulously. He was laughing.

"Well, your eyebrows."

"They're my father's," Eddie said, pleased to have found a topic that transferred control to him.

"Your coloring, then."

"That's his, too."

"The shape of your face."

"Ann Revere?" Eddie said, holding on to the moment as long as possible. "My God, you might as well have said Maria Ouspenskaya."

"Oh, I don't know, you all look the same to me, anyway," Eulene said, chagrined.

"You'd know the difference between my mother and Ann Revere, I can assure you," Eddie said. He quickly reached for his tea, but the cup was empty. He tore nervously at its rim, shredding it, and looked around the room. He had to remind himself where he was —in San Francisco, farther west than he had ever been, alone, except for Eulene. He was suddenly scared. It was way past sunrise now, and the three people with whom they normally shared the McDonald's at breakfast—the babbler, the scratcher, and the washer (who dipped all her food in a glass of water and dried it thoroughly before she put it in her mouth)—had left, replaced by people on their way to real jobs, to whom Eddie and Eulene, a pale, scruffy kid and a big flamboyant man (still wearing eye shadow, from her performance), were the freaks. To watch people in business suits carrying newspapers back to their tables or just rushing out with coffee in Styrofoam cups made Eddie feel lonely.

"You're the only person in the world right now who knows exactly where I am," he told Eulene. "The only one who knows specifically, anyway. My mother knows in general." He tore his Styrofoam cup methodically to bits, as if he were spirally peeling an orange. He said, "I thought if I could get far enough away from anyone who knew anything about me, to a place where I didn't recognize myself at all, where I hadn't spent every Sunday of my life since I was three, like in New York—I thought I would be someone else."

"Who?"

Someone who didn't have AIDS, he was going to say, but he didn't. He still wasn't sure how it would feel to share that information. At first he had wanted someone to know—Polly, Merrit, his mother—but since he had been on the road, he had forgotten about it. Sort of. Maybe he had just chickened out. *If I lay a trap for myself, right now,* he thought, *and make it impossible not to tell her, or make it so clear she has to figure it out*—but still, he hesitated. He pulled the bottom off his cup, and wrapped it around his thumb. "I don't know, maybe in Los Angeles . . . "

"Maybe in Los Angeles, what, babe?"

"It's just it's nowhere I have ever been, or anyone I know has been, and I was thinking . . . "

"You were thinking what?" Eulene said, annoyed. "That you would find it, whatever you think 'it' is, on Sunset Boulevard? You want to keep running for that unavailable dick, is that it, babe? That something unattainable and perfect? You think you'll catch it floating in the bottom of the bowl, Los Angeles, down there at the bottom of the world, drag queen dregs on Hollywood Boulevard, you're looking for the word, the word is 'yes.' Yes, I'll have you back. Yes, I'll suck your dick. Yes, babe, I was just abusing you, but now I'm ready to be everything you ever wanted, Tyrone Power, Gary Cooper, I'm your hero, baby. Yes, it all makes sense. Yes, you are a work of art, capable of love, lifted to the truth, stretched right out to beauty. Is that what you were thinking, maybe? Or was it something more immediate, something more expedient, some other reason you're wanting to leave me now, for Los Angeles?"

"I want to be somewhere that things I expect are somehow correspondent to the things I really get. I just don't want to hope anymore for something I'm not going to get. I don't want magic anymore. I want the truth."

"Well, my God, there have to be feathers," said Eulene, playing the wise man. "What am I without the feathers? A fat black drag queen."

"You're not," Eddie said. "You're a beautiful black man. Don't ever call yourself fat. I think you're beautiful."

"Oh," Eulene said, looking, for a second, like a very shy small boy. But she recovered herself. "Now listen, guy, I want to know what it is. Just—something, just tell me something. What it is you want from me. You want a mother, a father, a lover, a friend? I don't mind sleeping with you, darling, without having sex, but I do not like not sleeping with you and not having sex and not knowing what it is. Because I'm too old now to be following boys, just adolescent boys."

"I'm twenty-eight."

"Going on—" She shifted in her seat, agitated. "You are just completely . . . " she said. "You let everybody . . . is it a kind of a game? Don't play with me."

"I can take care of myself."

"Of course you can. Everybody can."

"I don't want anyone to take care of me."

"That's not what I meant."

"I'm very strong."

"The kind of strong that you get other people to do for you. That's a kind of taking care of yourself."

"No one ever does for me."

"But people want to, darling," Eulene said, reaching across the table for his hands, which were sweaty and cold. "I want to." She stroked his palms. "You're wet."

Eddie closed his eyes. What he had wanted, for as long as he could remember, was to be held, not taken care of, but held. But he didn't pick demonstrative people to love, or pursue. Obviously, he didn't have a choice about his mother. But he stayed away from men he knew who could give him what he thought he wanted, which was to have his palms stroked, and his forehead checked for fever, as Eulene was doing now.

"Why don't you tell me what's been going on," she said, dropping all poses.

Eddie kept his eyes closed. He was going to tell her, but obliquely. He didn't know how to say it directly, which was really his problem. He had gone through life not knowing how to say important things, or ask for what he wanted, directly. But he trusted Eulene to figure it out.

He said, "My life has been this, like, totally projected thing, this fantasy experience, which takes place either in the past, which is my mother's, or the future, which was supposed to have been mine. And they're both completely romantic, only mine is worse because it's so naive. My mother's the war teen, World War Two, watching melancholy movies in the forties, *Since You Went Away,* where Robert Walker dies, he doesn't come home from the war, to be with Jennifer Jones. Shirley Temple gets to wear her first pair of grown-up shoes in that movie, but it doesn't matter because of all these pretty boys, Guy Madison, Robert Walker, who die. I'm a war teen, too, except I never really knew that people died. My mother knew. Her father died in the war. Well, I never remotely knew anyone, except for David Alpaugh's second cousin Earl, who came back and told us how his having been a wrestler in high school helped him in a Viet Cong detention camp. It wasn't a real thing that was happening, to be sentimental about or even patriotic, it was a big surreal thing, to be angry and idealistic about, even optimistic, because you could tell it wouldn't happen again, that was its point, that this was the last time. So I'm this completely optimistic person, this white deluded person. I never really knew anyone died. And for all the pictures I saw in *Life* magazine, and on the television, it was unbelievable. My mother, she had *Since You Went Away,* and I had this funny optimism, or idealism, that the world, in spite of this horror, was a perfectable place, where

189

people didn't die. And so you see, I'm the optimist, and she's the cynic, that's the final twist. In real life my mother knows that people die, and I do not."

"Babe," said Eulene, getting it. She moved around the table, and stood next to him, holding his hand.

"The reason I haven't been sleeping is because I've been dying, instead." He had shredded his cup, now, irredeemably. "Is that too melodramatic?"

"You be quiet now, finally," she said.

"You figured this out, right? I've known for a while. I was diagnosed in, I don't know, April or May or June . . . "

Eulene pulled him to his feet. She said, "Come on now."

"Where are we going?"

"You need to lie in a bath."

"I want to take care of myself."

"Shut up and give me your arm. I'm going to give you a bath."

"I don't want you to do this for me. I want to do this myself. I want to take care of myself."

"Then what the fuck are you doing out on the highway traveling to California in the middle of the night with nothing but a big green bag of junk to hold against whatever comes up? Who do you think you are? Some kind of indomitable something? You just opted out of any claim to being a sane and reasonable being, and I don't care how white you are, baby, it doesn't make you immune."

"I guess I figured that out."

"I guess you haven't."

"I want to go home."

"We'll get you home."

"I want to go back to New York."

"We'll get you back."

"I miss New York," he said, leaving with Eulene, as their table was taken up by three earnest white lawyers who looked like they worked for Bank of America.

*   *   *

Eddie called his mother one last time, from San Francisco International Airport.

"Mom," he said, calling from a pay phone near the booth for Hertz, which had a big, yellow luminescent sign. "Mom, I have something to tell you. . . . Don't hang up, please. I'm still in Cali-

190

fornia, which is like New Jersey except the ocean's on the wrong side. That's a joke. . . . Mom, don't hang up now, don't leave me. I was thinking that you came from here, from northern California, and I'm from New Jersey, and there are thousands of miles between us. It's no wonder we can't communicate. Because . . . no, listen, I'm not being critical, sorry, I didn't mean that—because we can't even talk until the two ends of the continent get pushed together, you out here and me back there. Except this time, and I'm getting to the point, Mom, here's the point, this time I'm out here, and you're back East, and now that I'm the westerner and you're the easterner, and our roles are reversed, just briefly, well, I think that I can talk to you. . . . "

He said, "You know that movie, *Since You Went Away*? . . . No, please, just wait, it isn't trivial, the thing I have to tell you, Mom, it isn't trivial at all, it's just I have to tell it this way. Look, it's as if I were Montgomery Clift, all right? and calling on the phone, I've got Clark Gable and Marilyn Monroe waiting for me in the car while we have this final conversation. Not that it's final," he said, swallowing, "you know, because I'm coming home. But some things are easier on the phone.

"Listen, now, that movie, *Since You Went Away*, we watched it once together. There's that famous segment. Jennifer Jones and Robert Walker, they're saying good-bye. He's been home on leave, and they have fallen in love, it's World War Two. Now he has to go back overseas. . . . Well, all right, you've seen it, but I have to tell it, now. I have to get it right. I want to get this one thing right. Okay? They're both, like, nineteen years old. They go to Grand Central Station, I think, and he gets on the train, and hangs his body out the window, and they wave good-bye to one another. She runs down the platform, following the train as far as she can, before it disappears out of sight, taking him with it. And he says, 'Good-bye.' And she runs down the platform, crying, and she yells, 'Good-bye.' He says, 'Good-bye, good-bye.' And she just says, 'Good-bye.'

"Mom, you asked me once what made me nihilistic, but the thing is that I'm really not. Because I figured out, in California, that I'm really just this, I don't know, quote, disappointed romantic. . . . Okay, that sounds pretentious, why do you think I put it in quotes? Why do you think I put anything in quotes? The difference between you and me is that you don't mind it that your feelings are clichés.

"My feelings are clichés and that bugs me, so I try to hide it with

191

other, slicker clichés, and with everything in quotes, at least I can remind myself that I know better than my feelings, which are really the drippiest, most sentimental, self-pitying things. You're tougher than that. So listen, now, and here's the point, I'm on the train, I'm riding down the platform, and I'm waving and waving good-bye. I want this moment to be sentimental. This is my David O. Selznick moment, Mom, because I have a terminal disease. . . .

"No, no, Mom, listen. Look, I've got the ticket and I'm coming home, I'm nearly on the plane, Eulene is funding me, don't worry, you can torture me when I get back, right now I want to have my sentimental moment. I'm on the train, it's riding down the tracks, I'm waving and waving. And this is what I'm thinking. They don't tell you in the movie what Robert Walker is thinking, because it's film, and it's Hollywood, and it's not like that. But lucky you, you're talking to your son, and this is his internal monologue. I've been saving it for you. I'm on the train, I'm thinking this. I'm thinking that I want my life. I have to be corny now, I have to say I really want my life. I want it whole, and I want it complete, I want its texture and its spirit, I want its internal rhythms and its external shape, I want it all at once and forever, and I want it now. I want it now that it's going, Mom, and that's the final reversal. 'The tables have turned with a vengeance.' That's Tennessee Williams," he said. "Good-bye."

Then he hung up.

PART 3

Indeed

The Return of the Native

You lean," he says to me. All right? "You lean." Shocked the hell out of the doorman, let me tell you. "I had stepped outside," the doorman says, his eyebrows radically arched, discreetly signaling distress, "to hail a cab for a lady. The young man was waiting here when I returned, asking for you." And I mean, let me tell you now, you have to understand, this description of Eddie as a "young man waiting," well, it's rather a circumspect depiction. If I didn't know my doorman better, I would suspect him of irony. Because we're talking scrambled eggs here on the floor of the Prasada, scrambled Eddie, who looks like nothing so much this morning as the prone, lamenting personification of AIDS. I mean, of course it's AIDS, what else could it be, I ought to know by now the look of someone dying from AIDS—for he's come to my lobby to die. This is my call, my wake-up call for Eddie. And I have to give him credit, it's a very dramatic variation on a tiresome theme, Eddie collapsed on the white marble floor, at eight o'clock in the morning, asking for me, no kidding, not Merrit, but me. All right, my luck, I'm not the one you come to for sex, I'm the one you come to for solace, with your go-right-away personality. And I can already tell that Eddie is going to go right away. Some people hold on for months, some for years, some even forget that they're sick, then, bang, one morning they're gone.

But some fall apart in a week. Eddie's one of those. I can tell. I'm writing his eulogy now in my head.

"All right, butch," I say, helping him onto his feet, "how long has it been? How long have you been wandering around in this condition?"

He says, "You lean."

"No," I say, draping his arm over my shoulder, "*you* lean."

"I should have stayed with her."

"Stayed with who?"

"I should have stayed with Eulene."

All right, so this is a name.

I say, "Who's Eulene?" We sit on a padded *faux* mahogany bench in a corner of the lobby. I want to tuck in his shirt, which is hanging out in the back. That's his style, I remember, early disheveled. God, he's dying, I'm contemplating his fashion aesthetic. But I'm remembering now that I like him. When Merrit took him up, I put him away, forgot who he was. But sitting in the lobby now with me, he's Eddie again, the kid who never showed up on time to do my work, the boy in pink high-topped sneakers, which he's still wearing. I remember liking his audacity, and suspecting that it masked his vulnerability. Now his vulnerability is masking everything else.

"Who's Eulene?" I ask him again, straightening his collar and brushing off his sleeves. He's a mess. He smiles and closes his eyes, and slowly, almost incomprehensibly, I get the story, the diagnosis from a doctor he calls Fillgrave, and Eulene, and San Francisco, and phone calls in the hills to Doris Day. Then the plane ride home. He's making this up?

"I really didn't get sick until the plane," he says.

"That must have been lovely for the airline."

"I want Polly Plugg," he says.

All right, I'm thinking, Dr. Fillgrave, Doris Day, Eulene, and Polly Plugg, he's living in an Archie comic strip. To hell with what he wants, I get him into a cab. We're going to Lenox Hill Hospital. He says he doesn't believe in hospitals. I say, butch, it really doesn't matter what you believe in right this moment, if you don't get about a hundred quarts of blood inside of you, you won't see noon. He says, all right, then can we stop for Polly Plugg. I realize this is an actual person, so we detour all the way down to East Eleventh Street, and this rather plain-looking woman who bears an odd resemblance to Patty Duke, circa 1965, gets in the cab, and they have this touching reunion while we make the schlep back up to Lenox Hill, during the course of which it turns out that he doesn't have any medical insurance.

I say, "Eddie, goddamnit, you're staggeringly predictable, do you know that?"

"Please," he says, "I've already had this conversation with Merrit."

I'll bet he has, I'm thinking, vaguely gratified, in spite of myself, at the image of Merrit dealing with Eddie's logic. But getting Eddie a hospital bed is like a Nichols and May routine that takes place in Bedlam. And Polly and Eddie supply a perfectly absurd commentary in their conversation, which they pursue all the way up in the cab, and into the hospital lobby. They discuss Michael Jackson's latest surgery. "What about his nose," Eddie says, "you think it's Diana Ross?" "Actually," Polly says, "I think he passed right through Diana Ross, and now he's on to Eartha Kitt." "I think his nose is Candice Bergen," Eddie says. "What about his helper cells?" I want to scream. "What about his spleen? Who do you think his spleen is? Perry Ellis?" But I keep my mouth shut, quietly guiding these two emissaries from the blank generation to a couple of molded plastic chairs in the emergency waiting room. They make me feel very old, and responsible, the only adult in the room.

"Who might be the party to whom you are referring," says the emergency room receptionist, slowly, tonelessly into her hand, which she holds to her mouth as if hiding a zit along her lower lip. She sits behind a plain gray metal desk and directs all her questions to a point in space just over my left shoulder.

"My friend's name is Eddie Socket," I say, already defeated, I know. But the woman doesn't register any surprise.

"Could you spell that please," she says, giving each word equal emphasis. She's working religiously on a piece of chewing gum, which I would seriously like to extract from her mouth and paste to the sole of her shoe, sticking her there in place behind that dreary steel desk for all eternity.

"It's 'Eddie,' " I say. "Then after that, it's 'Socket.' "

The woman raises her left hand.

"Just a minute, please," she says, holding her palm flat, the pencil tucked under her thumb. "Just repeat that slowly. Eddie."

"E. Double d."

"E," says the receptionist. She notes that. I turn around. All the way across the room, Eddie is sliding out of his seat, as if his ass were greased. Polly keeps pulling him up.

"D," says the receptionist. She has six-inch fingernails, painted blood red, with small black paste-on spots. Her fingers are lady-bugs. She waits.

"D-i-e," I say.

"D . . . i . . . e," says Ladybug, cracking her gum. I look over my shoulder again, at Eddie and Polly. Why am I suddenly reminded of *Lassie Come Home*? Then the android behind the desk speaks again, and I feel more desperate than ever.

"Last name?" she says.

"Why don't you just give me that sheet?" I say. "I'll write it down."

"I'm sorry, sir," she says, "but we have our regulations."

"Look," I say, "I need to get my friend a bed. That's all I want. He's terminally ill. Do you want me to spell that for you? Terminal, as in train station, as in last stop. Ill, a three-letter word. Bed, another one. B-e-d. You probably have one at home. Am I right? You do sleep, don't you? Or are you wired to your desk lamp?"

"Perhaps you'd like to speak with my supervisor," says the receptionist.

"Please. Please. Just anyone."

I wave to Polly, and shrug. She has her arms around Eddie, who looks as if the last eleven of his red blood cells are about to be devoured, tasty morsels, by the killer virus.

"Just one moment, please," says the receptionist, which has to me the sound of famous last words.

Twelve hours later—we could have sat through a performance of the *Ring* cycle, for God's sake—Eddie has a doctor and a bed. He says, "It's falling in a dream," as we tuck him neatly into his rollaway bed like an oversized shoe tree, he's there to keep the shape and stiffness of his sheets, though considering how thin he's gotten in the past few weeks—the past few hours, for all I know—he's not going to keep much of anybody's shape for long. We get him plugged into an IV and a TV, and I scream for blood (literally), and we sit with him through the transfusions, which lethally indifferent nurses administer. Then I scream some more and get sedatives, which another nurse injects into one of Eddie's pale, almost fleshless buttocks, while a doctor stands by, ineffec-tually. When he's finally asleep, we tiptoe to the elevator, not wanting to attract the attention of any more sick people, not to-night.

So we're standing in the hallway, waiting for the elevator, and I'm rubbing my temples, my head is splitting, I'm sensitive to fluorescent lighting and neutral colors, and what am I thinking? I'm trying to remember the clinical definition of tragedy. I think if I can find the right combination of words to describe Eddie's situation, everybody's situation, that would help, you know, a timely utterance to give my thoughts relief. So, what I'm thinking is hubris, pity, and catharsis, and the oldest who have borne the most, such that we who are young shall never see so much, nor live so long. I mean, I had my Shakespeare in the Bronx, except that Shakespeare got it wrong. Because we who are young have seen an awful lot the past few years, and if we live so long, we'll just see more. If Shakespeare's tragedy is limited to kings and aging men and tortured princes, well, that leaves the queens out altogether. What do you call a roomful of dying queens?

Because it's not convincing, not dramatically, it doesn't play for all these twenty-eight-year-olds to die. They have to learn about their lives, they have to have catharsis, something has to come from their despair, some kind of knowledge, maybe wisdom. Let me tell you, I think that Eddie is a charming kind of waif, illogical perhaps, but cute. But wise is not a word that I would use to describe him. How can he be wise at twenty-eight? So if you're learning wisdom from a tragedy, what happens when you suffer terminal disease and death, and all you learn is that you're falling in a dream?

So I guess that makes this comedy. Or maybe a tragedy reframed? A crisis at the center of an unflappable world, a hot subject in a cold frame? Or the other way around, a cold subject in a hot frame. It's a disproportionate response to ordinary circumstances, or an inappropriate response, you know, to tragedy, because the woman at the counter asked, she said to me, "Have you ever had the chicken pox?" My friend is dropping platelets the way some people drop names, she's asking me about chicken pox, and I wonder, if this is a comedy, why do I have this acid in my stomach? And I reach into my pocket, and pull out a packet of Tums, still waiting for the elevator, and I offer one to Polly, and she looks at me, and says, "Tums?" and the two of us start laughing, and we can't stop. We don't even speak, we just laugh, we hardly know each other and it's kind of intimate. When the elevator finally arrives, the two of us are holding each other, laughing so hard we can't even stand up. We laugh onto the elevator, which is full of glaring orderlies, and sad-looking women in overtailored suits, and we laugh all the way down to the lobby.

But when we're in the lobby, Polly says, "Oh, shit."

"Oh, shit, what?"

"I think I'm going to cry. I'm sorry, laughing always makes me cry." She sniffles. "He just looked so pathetic," she says, searching in her shoulder bag. I offer her a Kleenex, which she takes gratefully. "Fallout shelter is my middle name," I say. "I was always the class monitor in air raid drills."

"We had air raid drills in kindergarten." Polly blows her nose. "Then they sort of ended."

"Yeah, they stopped worrying that blowing up the world was a tragedy. I want a drink."

"I was thinking the same thing," she says.

"Come on, Oscar," I say. "Let's you and me go get drunk."

Which we very rapidly proceed to do, at my apartment. I'm on the floor, Polly is on the couch in the living room, talking about Eddie. "What I really like about him," she says, after her third gin and tonic, "is his belly." She is stretched across Merrit's green Edwardian couch. She is the only person I have ever seen who looks at ease in the awful thing, with its arched serpentine backrest above outscrolling arms, on reeded, tapering legs. The way she sprawls, it seems like a beanbag chair. I like her for that. "His belly," she repeats, "is, or rather, was, slightly distended, outwardly sloping, curving roundly over his cock, which is inset deeply, almost feminine the way he carries it, his hips highly arched, his pubic hair growing thickly, and his penis held within, protected."

"Oh, dear," I say, a bit drunkenly perhaps. She does wonderful things in the air with her hands when she talks.

Merrit's clocks chime the hour, twelve gongs from five different clocks. Polly keeps on talking. She is sweet, and sorry, and terribly out of place, like a gray wool skirt in an underwear drawer. Her vowels are wide open like the plains, and she seems guileless. What is she doing in New York? I want to put her back on the train to central Ohio. Women are legible, written out like missives in distinctive script, clear when clarity helps, mysterious when you yearn for an enigma. They are beautifully ordered, subject to misinterpretation certainly, but wholly there on the page.

"Men," I say, "for Chrissakes, Merrit. Scrawly, cramped mosquito-writing Merrit. Letter after long prevaricating letter he sent me from Europe, making pledges, swearing his allegiance. God, his thoughts aren't even there between the lines, they're underneath the lines, his real wants, demands. He has to be translated out of his own recondite language into something like human symbol and meaning. And then he's free to deny every word as something you invented and put in his mouth."

"He left you?"

"He ran away to Europe with a financier."

"A banker?"

"A trader, I think."

"Where is he now?"

"Drowning in the Arno, I hope. He fled to Florence and Paris and Rome. He called me from Florence. Reversed the charges. New Englanders are like that, darling, stingy."

"That's funny," she says, "because I had a trader, I dated a trader, and he ran off to Europe. His name was Brag."

"Funny name."

"Yeah, well, not his real name. He ran away to Florence and Paris and Rome. With a man. His real name was—"

"Mine, too. Merrit. Ran away. With a man. To Florence and Paris and Rome. His name was—"

"William Boleslawski."

Which makes me nearly slice my tongue in half. "Wait, stop. How did you know?"

"How did I know what?"

"How did you know that Merrit Mather ran away with William Boleslawski?"

"He did?"

"Darling, can we stop here and now and just take inventory?" She nods. "All right. If your boyfriend is Brag, who ran away with a man—"

"To Florence, and—"

"Yes, the place has been established, please. And if my boyfriend is a man who ran away with a trader named William Boleslawski—"

"Oh, I'm getting this."

"—and if Brag and William Boleslawski are the same person—"

"I think I'm really getting this. I'm not liking it, but I'm getting it."

"It's a tautology, see? If A went with B, and C went with D, where

A and D are actually Brag and B and C are Merrit Rowlandson
Mather—"

"Merrit Mather?"

"Then, honey, you and I are very nearly related."

"*The* Merrit Mather?"

She sits up, with this absolutely terrifying expression spread
across her face.

"Wait," I say, holding up my hand. "Honey, I don't want to know
he's diversifying. He fucked you, too?"

"Merrit Mather with wonderful gray temples and an unforgettable
dick?"

"Oh God. Is everyone in my life going to have fucked Merrit,
from now until the day I die? His dick is going to pursue me to the
grave."

"I'm only quoting."

"Quoting whom?"

"I'm only quoting Eddie." She touches me now, compassion-
ately, as if this piece of information will be somehow more than I
can stand. "They were lovers," she says, very softly. She holds my
arm a long time. I don't want to spoil her moment.

Then I say, gently, "No kidding."

She looks at me intently. "You knew?" She is barely audible.

"Of course I knew."

"You knew and yet still you did all that today? For Eddie?"

"I did it all for myself. I don't like messes. Even other people's
messes."

"No, wait, stop," she says. "That bastard!"

"Which one?"

"Well, both of them. If I may."

"All three of them, perhaps."

"My boyfriend jilted me for—"

"My boyfriend. Polly, I feel we've been in therapy together, or
something."

"Oh my God, I could just SCREAM."

"Well, you know, New York. Only so many nice white men to go
around."

"Oh, men," she screams.

"Oh, please," I say, "don't get me started on men. I hate men.
You want to hear a secret? I think the reason I'm gay is because of
how much I hate men. I know, we're supposed to hate women,
but who I really hate is men. What does that make me, a gay man

who hates men? Does that make me a woman? Merrit is a straight man trapped in a gay man's body."

"Brag is a Ken doll."

"I used to play with Ken dolls. Barbie dolls, too. My cousin had a set with the change of clothes. We visited her, and she went out and played in the street with the boys. I stayed up in her room and dressed up the dolls."

"I used to mutilate mine," Polly says. "Good-looking men are the worst." She's needling me. I swill down the last of my drink and say, what the hell, like Tallulah, "Men over forty are worthless."

"Any man from thirty-five to almost fifty," Polly says, "unless he doesn't have a sense of entitlement. Middle-aged, middle-class men have such a terrible sense of entitlement. And then it's your fault they don't have everything they want, or think they deserve."

"So then they start depriving you." I laugh. "With ten-year sexless breakdowns."

"Sex is the first thing to go. I don't believe that men like sex at all. I think they're making it up, every word, their sexual pleasure. I've never been with a man who didn't fake his pleasure, and then hate me for not faking mine. Who but a man could make up the image of the vulnerable, weak, simpering woman who doesn't like sex if it's dirty, or fun? The perfect fifties woman is a total projection of male sentimentality. Even the whores they adore are visions of themselves. Marilyn Monroe weeping is actually the perfect image of the soul of an aggressively masculine man—sad and dependent and sorry, and helpless and scared."

"Men who have never gotten fucked are not to be trusted," I say, emphatically. It sounds like a non sequitur, like everything else at the moment, now that we're drinking and Eddie is dying and Merrit is gone, and Polly fucked with William Boleslawski, who fucked with Merrit, who fucked Eddie, who lives with Polly, who is now in my house, and I begin to feel as if I'm living in a tiny world of two hundred white people aged twenty-five to forty-five, all of whom have either shared a bed or shared a therapist within the last ten years.

I say, "We *are* related."

But she's still hating men.

"Men who went to Dartmouth," she says.

"Merrit went to Dartmouth."

"So did Eddie." She pauses. "So did Brag."

203

"Eddie went to Dartmouth?"

"He transferred out after a semester."

"Oh," I say. I lie down on the rug, finally tired.

"Men with nice dicks," Polly says, joining me on the floor, putting her head next to mine.

I say, "Men with nice sweaters. All gay men."

"All straight men," she says.

"What's the difference," I say, "when they're all jerks?"

I close my eyes. "The schmuck ran away with a trader. Maybe I should leave him."

"Oh, Saul," says Polly quietly. "I think that's best." She hugs my head to her chest. "You've got beautiful skin, you know," she says, stroking my neck. I bury my cheek in her breast. I can hear her heartbeat. She is suddenly warmer, and closer, and more reassuring than all the men I have pursued in order to work out my anger with Merrit. I fall asleep in her arms, wondering, if I'm not a straight man, and I'm not a gay man, what does that make me? Maybe, I think, nearly asleep, my face to her chest, maybe I'm really a lesbian.

Animal Maqnetism

Everyone but Merrit (not including Joseph Stalin) came to
Eddie's bedside. Saul, especially, was there, his personal
savior at last. After weeks of "truly, truly Kafkaesque absurd-
ity and circularity with the world of health insurance, forms inside
of forms inside of forms, like a Chinese box," Saul had said, "and
I'm not quoting Woody Allen, I mean Kafka-fucking-esque, except
American, *The Trial* crossed with *Double Indemnity,* performed by
Imogene Coca on 'Your Show of Shows,'" he had gotten him
Medicaid coverage, and insurance benefits, and a larger room,
which Eddie shared with a man named Fong, who didn't know any
English. The nurses condescended to him, speaking MGM-version
Chinese. "How you today?" they shouted. "Would you rike a ritter
dlink?" Eddie, deeply offended, apologized to Fong, when they
were alone. "It's just American hegemony expressing its imperi-
alistic self," he patiently explained. "It's not about you, Fong. Don't
feel hurt."

Eddie himself felt like Rudolph Valentino in a casket, surrounded by aggrieved, adoring fans. He was missing only the mysterious veiled woman, though Saul volunteered to dress all in
black, and kneel in pumps and a veil to mourn. "Pinstripes and
loafers would be more to the point," Eddie said, and they both
knew he meant Merrit. They were uncomfortable discussing him.

Eddie asked careful questions, which Saul as carefully answered. Eddie was sorry Merrit didn't come, but Saul was almost preferable. Polly smuggled in his cats for a visit, and his mother came. His fifth-grade English teacher somehow found him out. Lots of people brought flowers—gladiola, lilacs and forget-me-nots, green-stemmed amaryllis with bright orange blooms the texture of crepe paper hearts.

He was surprised by a visit from some fellow word processors, a scornful, caring woman who reminded him of Eulene, and a cuddly, effusive straight man who had tried once for a month to interest him in becoming a communist. They brought fruit and copies of *Workers World*. His very first high school crush called every morning for a week before he would finally say who he was, and then he cried for fifteen minutes on the phone, while Eddie reassured him. "It couldn't happen to you," Eddie said. "I know it couldn't," said Eddie's first love. "I'm married and I live in Pequannock." Even the president of the Oberlin alumni association, New York chapter, paid a courtesy call. Eddie was the first member of his graduating class to be stricken with a terminal disease, the woman explained. They were writing it up in the alumni bulletin. He posed for pictures that afternoon with Polly and Saul, a flower tucked behind his ear.

Indeed, his life passed in and out of his room, ominously, portentously, a daily procession of luminaries emerging from out of his past, bearing gifts, like the Magi. With Darth and 2b sometimes there, it was a bit of a manger. And Polly was Mary and Saul was Joseph, and AIDS was the Immaculate Conception. "Because I never got this disease," Eddie shouted at his pig, late at night, when all his visitors had left and Fong was shitting quietly in his sleep and the nurses didn't answer his calls and the television didn't even work. "I never did anything to get this disease. A dove brought it." "A dove who likes analingus," said the pig. "A dove with a nasty infection."

"I have been asleep a long, long time," Eddie said to his mother, one day, after he had been in bed a few weeks. He would, he realized, be living in the hospital from now on.

"Well, it's not very cheerful here," said his mother, tensely. She was dressed for Indian summer; she wore white leather sandals and a cool blue dress, and carried a kid leather purse, which snapped open and shut with a click that satisfied Eddie. He asked her for gum in order to hear the snap of her white leather purse.

"I've never admitted this to anyone," he said, taking the gum, but not unwrapping it, "but when I was five and you were out of the house, I liked to put on your shoes, and scuttle across the floor." He turned red. "You had a particular pair. They were gold, with very pointed toes and slender heels. Their arches were terribly high. They must have been hell for you to wear."

"Your father had a thing about shoes," his mother said, smiling, and waving her hand in the air as if to dispel an unpleasant odor. "I used to call it a fetish."

"I liked your handbags, too," said Eddie. "All the big square blue ones that hung on your arm, the kind that Jackie Kennedy carried around. They were like boxes for holding equipment, and the fasteners were silver, or brass. The insides were lined with fabric, and when you opened them up, and rattled inside for a change purse or a lipstick, there was a dull rumble."

His mother crossed her knees and sat on a chair beside the bed. She smiled nervously, perhaps on the verge of tears, or fighting a cough, or a sneeze coming on. Her dress ended just at her knees, and it was tight at the waist and sleeveless, with a scooped neck. Her arms and a circle of chest shone bare and brown, her collarbones chiseled and fluted under her skin, like the delicate bones in the outstretched wings of a bird. Her mouth was set against the encounter with her son, but her face was gentle and soft. She looked defensive and bewildered.

"Funny things to tell your mother," she said.

"I wonder what wouldn't be," he said, lifting his arms from the bed and making a circle, his fingertips touching, "under the circumstances."

She looked at her feet.

He had never discussed his phone calls with his mother, and he spoke with her awkwardly now, almost embarrassed at having been so intimate with her, long-distance from California. But she never referred to the calls, either, not even to complain about the phone bill. They were careful not to talk about what had been said, or felt, almost like lovers, Eddie thought, the morning after a one-night stand, who were a little ashamed of what transpired in the dark, when they couldn't see each other.

"I like what you're wearing," he said.

She stroked the inside of her elbow. "I'm meeting a client for lunch," she said.

"You're taking a meeting?"

"The *Maltese Times* is thinking of starting a regular column. Maltese as in dogs, not as in Malta."

Eddie laughed. "A columnist for the *Times*. My mother the columnist."

She tucked her chin, defensively. "It isn't poetry," she said.

"I didn't say it was."

"I'm not an intellectual, like you or your father."

"If I were so fucking smart," Eddie said, "I'd think my way out of this."

She brushed her hair from her face, and pulled at her dress.

"What do you do all day long," she said, "to keep from getting bored?"

"I talk to Fong," Eddie said, pointing over her shoulder. "I swear at the television set. I talk on the phone. I get a lot of phone calls. I count things: all the books I've ever read, the number of women who have gotten two Academy Awards for Best Actress. The number of classes I cut in college. The number I actually attended. The amount of times I've gotten anywhere when I said I would. The animals we had."

"The animals," she said.

"I counted twenty-seven."

"All at once?"

"From as far back as I could remember."

"We'll count from when you were born."

"Were there any before?"

"Of course there were, the puppies," said his mother. "There were seven, and we gave away five."

"You and—"

"Me and your father, yes. There was the cat."

"That's one."

"Quagmire. And the puppies were named for saints. There was Agnes, and Francis—oh, and Gary Cooper."

"Gary Cooper?"

"It was a joke at your father's expense. Actually, though, he looked like Gary Cooper, long and thin and kind of lumbering, and he had very big ears, and short brown hair, and he barked in yups and nopes. 'Yup, yup,' he barked. 'Nope, nope.' "

"Well, anyway, I don't think they count. The only ones who count are the ones that you kept."

"There were only two. Aggie and Frannie. Their mother died. That's three."

208

"And the strays."

"You're counting the strays?"

"I'm counting the chipmunks and birds," he said, "the rabbits."

"Well, there was Mackie."

"Jesus," Eddie giggled. "Four. Immaculata. That awful big black-haired mutt, with beagle brows and a Labrador lope."

"His tongue," his mother said, shivering.

"His hard-on."

"He tried to mount the Yorkies," his mother admitted.

"And the guests. Whenever there were guests."

"No one was sad when he died."

"So Mackie is four," said Eddie.

"Yes, and Quagmire died."

"He wandered into the woods?"

"He didn't come back."

"He must have got hit by a car."

"No, he was old, he might have gone, the way that Eskimos put their old people out to die."

"That's what I want, when I'm ready to go."

"Oh," she said, catching her breath. She rubbed a finger over her lips. "Then your father," she said, quietly, "left and there was Misfit, and the cats."

"But Misfit didn't stay, so she doesn't count."

"Strays don't count?"

"Not if they don't stay. Misfit doesn't count, and there were eleven cats, including the three who died in the hall. The ones we found in the pond, their heads stuck in cranberry cans. You laid them out on the floor heater in the hall," said Eddie, "on a blanket, drying them out. I remember watching them, and not quite understanding they would die."

"I've got thirty-two," his mother said.

"Anyway," said Eddie, "most of them are dead now. When I saw you last, out there, I didn't recognize a soul." He smoothed his sheets. "When Joseph Stalin left," he said, "I had that chipmunk, you remember? Yeep? He made that noise. Yeep, yeep. He was so sick, but he would have lived, except that I forgot to give him water. We drove to the city one afternoon, and I had forgotten to water him. That's why he died."

"So you blame your father and me," said his mother. "That's why you're sick."

"I didn't say that."

"Your father went away, and I didn't suckle you long enough, and that's why you're sick."

"I never even said that I was sick."

His mother got up from the chair. She walked to the window, and adjusted the blinds. "I don't think your air conditioner is working," she said. She looked at her watch.

Eddie said, "My life revolves around the smallest moments. You ask what I've been thinking, how I keep from getting bored. I've been thinking how my life revolves around the smallest, smallest moments. I don't have to think about colonialism, and I don't have to think about hunger, and I don't have to think about poverty and war. I'm not a victim of racist attacks. I live in a white cocoon. My skin is white and my friends are white and my world is whiter-than-white. I'm an ad for a laundry detergent."

"Expand your world," his mother said, turning around. The sun coming through the blinds cast her shadow across the brown linoleum floor.

"I moved through my life so easily up until now. Too easily, I think. I've been complacent. The hardest decisions I've ever had to make were whether to sleep an extra hour, whether to masturbate or not."

"You're trying to shock me."

"I don't have enough information about the world."

"Then read the *New York Times.*"

"All I have is my dick, and my mouth. A hole, and a plug. If I could stretch far enough, I'd have a solution."

"Now you *are* trying to shock me."

"I'm not."

"You are, but I'm not that easily shocked. You want to even the score with me, I can tell. That isn't shocking, it's wearying. I don't know what, or whom, you begrudge. You haven't had such a miserable life. Oh, I remember now, when you're twenty, even thirty, you can still afford to be hurt. But somewhere along the line you grow up, and wounds start to heal whether you want them to or not. That's the big revelation about becoming an adult, the things that used to hurt don't bother you anymore, and all of your anger and blaming is pointless and vague."

"Why don't you divorce him?" Eddie said, abruptly.

"Wally, let's not have this fight."

"Eddie."

"Wally." She looked at her hands. "I could never get his approval," she said, not looking at Eddie. "He was too good for me. Or thought he was. Or *I* thought he was. I had him back and back and back in order finally to win his approval. I'm not used to losing. I don't mind losing *things,* but I don't like to lose. I kept hoping his scorn would go away, but it didn't. Oh, but what the hell. That's over now. You'll see what happens, when you start to get old, past forty-five, your parents are dying, and your kids are fucking up, and generally speaking you're done with the great themes of your life, you've gotten over the pain. And then you can't afford to fight anymore, or be uncommitted, or whine, or complain. Because the real things have started to happen."

"I think this is real," Eddie said, quietly.

"I only raised you in the world," said Eddie's mother. "I'm not responsible for your sadness. I'm not interested in your happiness, either. Don't you understand? Just because I made a choice to have you doesn't mean I care how your life goes."

"But you do care."

"Of course I care. Why did I come today? You don't think I care?"

"I do think you care," he said.

"You truly don't think I care?"

"I know that you care."

"Well, all right, then."

She sat down, on the side of his bed, drained of conversation. Her weight made a small indentation in the mattress.

"Are you going to die without admitting—"

Eddie said, "Shh."

She put her palm to her brow. "I'm sorry you're sick," she said.

And Eddie said, "Shh." He gathered his bed sheet in his fingers, and, folding the material back, rearranged his legs. It was a momentary gesture, but he was naked long enough for them to see, concretely, what had happened to him. His legs were pale and bluish in spots, and covered with lesions that multiplied daily. His feet were scaly and dry. His hips were stretched with skin that sagged and bunched almost like the hospital shift. His penis hung sadly, grotesquely flaccid, and brown. His ribs were like the cartoon carcass of a fish, licked clean of flesh. He rearranged his legs, and stretched the shift until it covered his genitals. But quickly, before he covered himself, he looked in his mother's eyes. He knew that she saw. For in the instant he was naked, he could see her recoiling as if she had been shot. He felt her intake of breath, saw the childish look of disbelief that flickered across her face.

211

She held her arms to her sides and straightened her back. He had caught her sharp look of pain and incredulity. And in that brief exchange, lasting no more than an instant—the sizzling tip of a match, just extinguished, against her wrist, or fingertip—she said, so delicately that both of them were uncertain afterward whether it had been an echo in their own heads, or something projected into the silence between them, briefly, "I love you."

He pulled the sheet to his neck. She got to her feet, and leaned to his brow, kissing his forehead. She left the room without a word.

Sometime in New York City

He who is not busy being born is busy dying" is a queer line from an old Bob Dylan song that Polly had, nonetheless, repeating in her head, all the while she was thinking, *Maybe so, but no one is busy dying quite as rapidly, as unexpectedly, as my friend Eddie Socket.* She went to see him twice a week at the hospital (after a month he was still too sick to leave), and twice a week she walked home slowly, stopping here and there to buy a candy bar. She had become the kind of woman who wandered the streets alone throughout the late afternoons, arguing with Bob Dylan songs and eating a Snickers. The walk reminded her of her first job in New York, temping as a filing clerk in the personnel department at (coincidentally) Lenox Hill Hospital. She worked in a brownstone with six white women who commuted home to husbands and pools in Bergen County. But she herself was so poor (putting up a month's rent, a month's security, and a broker's fee for their apartment had left both Eddie and Polly almost destitute for months) that she walked to work and then home again along Park Avenue. On Fridays she left the hospital early to pick up her check at the temp agency, then rushed to a check-cashing office, a storefront room with dingy tiles behind Grand Central. Standing in line on the sidewalk with a hundred anxious-looking others, tensely clutching her meager paycheck and beating her hands in the cold, she felt vaguely criminal, or at least desperate, a "yellow-ticket girl" from out of *Crime and Punishment*, walking the streets to feed an alcoholic father, a consumptive mother.

That was February, and she wrecked her shoes in the snow which Eddie had assured her never fell in New York City, not for more than fifteen minutes. Because of him, she left her boots in Ohio. It occurred to her now, walking home from the hospital, that Eddie had gotten everything wrong, the boots, the snow, their ineluctable rise to fabulous easternhood, her inevitable Manhattanization. Granted, she had boots now, for walking in the snow, and she had constant free-lance work, which paid enough to keep her out of check-cashing agencies and desperate, moneyless moods. She had New York in September, the smell of the Hudson River even reaching the East Side in the breeze, the shorter days, the twinkling lights up and down Park Avenue. But Eddie was looking more and more like a figure in a newsreel of the Holocaust. He was going to die, and she would once again be Polly-from-Parma, no longer Holly Golightly, as Eddie sometimes fantasized. For it was his version of their lives that she believed in. Now that he was dying, she began to see the facts of her existence in New York.

If she was going to lose him, she thought, she wanted him to go in a way she could control, a move to Dallas, or to Rye, New York, where she could call him, or neglect calling him, depending on how they had parted. But to lose him completely, permanently was cruelly not what she expected. Suddenly she wanted a refund on all the time they had spent together. She wanted their moments returned. She wanted Eddie carefully extricated from her life, her entire life, air-brushed out like a Soviet diplomat excised from history. She didn't want to remember his presence, so she wouldn't feel his absence. But he kept reminding her.

"Do you remember," he asked, one afternoon, before she walked all the way home, "do you remember your triple 'I Love New York' day?" He was in white in his bed, on top of the sheets, and his legs were skinny and dry. She lotioned his feet. He had been moved recently into a private room, and Polly at last felt as if their conversations weren't being monitored from the other side of a drawn curtain. Though the privacy was sometimes oppressive. His beard was starting to grow (he had shingles, which made it hurt to raise his arms to shave), and he looked scruffy, and lanky, and small. "We were sitting out on the roof, with friends from Oberlin, do you remember this? We'd been in New York about nine months, I met you at a party on the Upper West Side, above the museum, Central Park West and—"

"The Alden," Polly said. "We sat on the roof of the Alden."

"Christ, what a terrible party," Eddie said, turning his feet so Polly could reach the insides of his ankles. "Six other people I don't remember liking."

"It was dull."

"It was deadly," he said. "I could have thrown myself from the roof, for boredom, only you arrived, at last, and you had had your triple 'I Love New York' day. Do you remember?"

"Why were we out on the roof?"

"It was dark up there, and no one had to stare at anybody's bland expressions of boredom and loathing. We didn't have any real friends in the city, not yet, just people from college we didn't want to see. But they were better than nothing. And you sat down in a chair, one leg tucked under you, the other crossed over it, sort of like—"

"You don't have to show me, I know."

"Sort of like . . . " he said, trying to shift in bed.

"I haven't finished with the lotion," Polly said. "Don't move."

"It fucking hurts to move."

"I know. Don't move."

"Oh, well, anyway, you know how I mean, one leg tucked under, one crossed over, and your hands went up in the air, one hand to the side of your head, and you just talked and talked, because that morning you had seen—"

"Caroline Kennedy, right."

"No kidding, in a coffee shop. When she was fat."

"Be nice."

"And after that you saw her mother."

"Jackie Oh."

"Wearing her glasses, and a scarf. And then after that . . . "

Polly was giggling now. "Miss Diana Ross," she said.

"Your triple 'I Love New York' day. But that didn't matter, Polly, that wasn't really the thrill, it was the way you told it, you were absolutely charming. The way you moved your hands, and stuck your tongue inside your cheek, you knew exactly how little it mattered who you saw in the street, but it didn't depress you to tell it.

215

You were ecstatic, because you love the ridiculous. It doesn't entrap you, like it does me. You know where to put Jackie Oh in the world, to keep her securely in place."

"You're making a philosophy out of chatter."

"I never know what to do with Miss Diana Ross," Eddie said. "The whole concept is just overwhelming. I put her in quotes, I end up in quotes myself. I take her out of quotes, I have to cope with her absurdity. Why should I have to spend half my life liberating myself from Diana Ross?"

"You're not making sense."

"I'm sorry," Eddie said. "I'm sorry. I don't know, they give me Percodan, I go to sleep at night, I dream about Diana Ross, and wake up gasping for breath."

He was gasping now. He grabbed a clear plastic mask, which fit over his nose and mouth like a dentist's mask for local anesthetic, and he sucked in, not gas, but oxygen. Polly watched, not knowing whether to pretend she wasn't concerned, or to ring for the nurse. But he dropped the mask, and frowned.

"You know what I've been doing here," he said, "to pass the time? Singing Rodgers and Hart, of course, in my head, you know, 'all alone, all at sea, why does nobody care for me?' because I've been so lonely. I'm not afraid to admit it now, you know. I just picked people who could not respond to me, like Merrit, and I'm wanting to be this torch singer, just to get over the pain. I'm Barbara Cook. I'm pretending Merrit loved me, and I'm singing this. I'm singing. 'I didn't know what time it was, then I met you. Oh, what a lovely . . .' " His voice trailed off.

"Polly?" he said, putting down the mask, "can I make a confession? You won't think it's weird, or perverted? I mean, maybe you will. But I was thinking, lying here, 'Two loves have I,' I'm Josephine Baker, I've had two real loves in my life. Only two. This is going to sound pathetic now. But I don't mean lovers. I would say 'relationships,' but Merrit hardly counts as that. Two loves, let's say, and one is my mother, and the other one is Merrit Mather."

Polly started to respond, but Eddie closed his eyes and said, "That's enough now. That's enough. You can put the lotion away." His transitions were abrupt, almost hurtful. But he waited until she was ready to go, as if he had been watching her gather her things, before he said, "And you, too, Polly. I think you're the most charming person in the world."

So she walked home, and stretched out on the floor of Eddie's

216

room, and listened to his old Rodgers and Hart recordings. He had
a stack of old, scratchy records, thick black discs with the names
worn away from the labels. Each one featured a different thin-
voiced singer, sometimes offering incongruously lighthearted in-
terpretations of what were essentially songs of remorse and sadly
unrequited love, with titles like "Glad to Be Unhappy," and "It
Never Entered My Mind," and "He Was Too Good to Me," which
had the unintentionally funny lyric, "I was a queen to him, who's
going to make me gay now?" She nibbled chocolate bars (she had
brought home a stash of Milky Ways) and lay on the floor, thinking
that she had missed the point about Eddie, all along.

For a man who could sing as much of "I Didn't Know What Time
It Was" as he could manage between gulps of oxygen—well, there
was no getting around his sentimentality. Eddie Socket was a sen-
timentalist. He was not "in quotes," as he claimed, not at all. He
had merely been embarrassed by his own romanticism.

If anything about Eddie was in quotes, she thought, listening to
his records, it was his nihilism, which was merely his defense
against his need to be wanted, and loved. But she herself had
believed, all this time, and rather simplemindedly, in his existen-
tialist pose; she had even organized her life around the statements
he made about purpose, and meaning, and hope. He wanted to
live without hope, he said, because hope disappointed, but he sat
in his hospital bed and romanticized his mother, idolized Merrit,
turned Polly into the world's most charming woman. She was essentially the pragmatist, while he was the romantic, after all. She
had tried to live according to his perceptions—his surface-not-
substance, his sequence of motion and fact, his lack of faith in
action, any kind of action, as effective, or even possible. "Actions
don't reverberate, they only are," he had told her. "They're isolated,
and inherently without value." He sounded like a psycho killer,
lacking conscience, living outside of himself. But though she had
struggled against his influence, she partly believed him: he could
make ennui seem attractive, and chic, and it helped to think of all
her bad relationships with men as isolated episodes, unconnected
to something consistent, or continuous, within her life. Yet here
he was singing "I Didn't Know What Time It Was," yearningly, out
loud.

She slept on the floor that night, and the following morning she
called in sick to her job, and took his bicycle out for a ride. It was
propped against the wall, a big yellow bike with an iron lock slung

over the seat, and a bright red horn which made a terrible noise and frightened the cats. She carried it down to the street, and started out for Queens.

They used to go there a lot, when they first moved to New York. Eddie had a big map of midtown Manhattan from 1963, with neat renderings of all the buildings, including Penn Station and the old Metropolitan Opera House. On the back were maps of all the other boroughs, which, she remembered, he wanted to fill in. He wanted to ride his bicycle across every single street in all of New York City. He took her on a lot of trips to faraway places, bundled up in coats and scarves and gloves for cold March excursions to Breezy Point and City Island, Orchard Beach, and La Tourette Park, on Staten Island. Polly had an old blue beat-up boy's bike, which she later abandoned—they chained it to a lamppost one afternoon, and left it out to die. But for about a year she pedaled it after Eddie into every crease and wrinkle of the city. After their trips they went home to his map, where he colored in their route in felt-tip pen. He had an elaborate system of color coding, green for what they covered on their bikes, red for where they went on foot, and so on. He never got the map completely filled. Polly stopped going with him, and he seemed to lose volition. He rolled up the map—it was big enough to hang on the wall over the tub—and shoved it into his closet. Polly no longer went to places like the peeling remnants of the 1964 World's Fair, in Flushing Meadows Park, where you can find the largest map in the world of the state of New York, laid out at the bottom of the New York State Pavilion, across the dewy flats of Queens, in red and white and blue ceramic tiles.

He especially loved industrial waste, and he taught her to appreciate it, too. The first summer they were in New York they read a long biography of Robert Moses, so that they could go out together on educated Robert Moses field trips, to admire dying roads and bridges. There was something, Eddie said, enormously touching about the Henry Hudson Parkway, pinched off at Fifty-seventh Street and peeled from the earth in segments down to the Battery, like some kind of shellfish brutally eviscerated, its red remains of shell washed up onto the waterfront. They bicycled to the Bronx, to Crotona Park, and stared down into the Cross Bronx Expressway, to admire its thick concrete walls, oiled with exhaust. Polly tried to moralize about the effect of cars and highways on people and whole communities, but Eddie called her provincial, and bland, and said, "It has an ontological significance all its own."

218

He took her to the Penn yards, at Seventy-second Street along the Hudson, where they wandered through acres of abandoned railroad siding, and switching tracks, and turntables; they went out to the piers, and took pictures of Eddie standing like Christ, his arms straight out to his sides, among the rusting girders. He said he loved the failure, the audacious disaster, of industrial New York —the city, not as it was in its greatness, but just after, a remnant. He said he loved it because it was falling apart, magnificently.

She believed him then, but now she wasn't sure. She rode his bike to Fifty-seventh Street, and wondered whether he had been in earnest. What an irony if he had only been posing, she thought, because she had taken his word as fact, and now she saw that it was probably fiction, the fiction he told himself about his life. For she had fallen in love with a city in ruins, and learned to respect its decay. But Eddie was falling apart magnificently, too, and she could not imagine that even he would say that his decline was somehow more exciting, more resonant, than any other period in his life.

Polly rode out to Queens on the Queensboro Bridge, where she shared the bicycle lane with outgoing traffic, because the car lane was closed for repairs. It, too, was rotting, crumbling. But "the city seen from the Queensboro Bridge is always the city seen for the first time, in its first wild promise of all the mystery and the beauty in the world." That was from *Gatsby,* which Eddie had quoted all the way east from Ohio, eight years ago. She was headed out of the mirage now, into the gray, ashy wasteland, wanting to find industrial waste, wanting to love the city again with renewed feeling, bicycling to Queens the way old married couples return years later to their honeymoon suites, to recapture their passion, and love.

But she got lost. She couldn't find her way, without Eddie. She gave up rather quickly, and pedaled close to the waterfront, along a line of old factories that blocked her view of Manhattan. A gap opened up when she was halfway to the Williamsburg Bridge, and the city appeared suddenly over her shoulder, beyond a big empty lot, across the river. "There it is," she said, stopping abruptly. She got off her bike and walked slowly to the edge of the river, to look.

It still had the power to move her, that skyline. She felt a familiar pang in her stomach, not entirely pleasurable, like meeting an old lover in the street and realizing that, in spite of everything, you still think he's beautiful. She remembered scenes with Eddie, sitting

219

with him at dusk out on the roof of a building on Third Avenue, drinking beer, and wondering how they were going to begin their lives, against the certainty that Ronald Reagan would initiate a nuclear war. They watched the sky get dark, the big, pink neon New York City sky that never shows a natural color, not even at night, not even in the rain.

But she hated it now. She thought she had always hated it. Perhaps she had, perhaps she had only loved it for Eddie. She hated it passionately, the way a nineteenth-century maiden hated her vile seducer, who offered sweets and affection, but wanted nothing more than her defilement. She hated Eddie's sentimentality, his real love for the city, and she hated his hiding his feelings behind decadence, his love of ruin and decay.

"You're having your Joan Didion moment," Eddie would have said. She knew his preoccupations too well. "It's when you turn twenty-eight, and you put on dark sunglasses and an old string bikini, and discover that the past is irrevocable."

She had just turned twenty-nine, and didn't have sunglasses or a bikini, but she knew what he would have meant. For she had Eddie Socket in her life, irrevocably, and as much as she wanted to unweave her past, to have them unraveled from each other, still, there was no way she could lose him. He was going to die, but he wouldn't be lost, and she wanted to lose him now, very badly. She didn't want to stare at the rusted remains of his life, their lives together, anymore; she didn't want to feel the waste. She had loved him for all the wrong reasons, had missed the things about him that mattered the most. And now he was going to be a big, aching wound in her past, a choice she made without thinking, a person she loved for what he had not been able to do. He was romantic, he was sentimental, he was Rodgers and Hart; she was left with industrial waste. That seemed to her a particularly ironic reversal. She turned away from the city, and started for the Williamsburg Bridge.

Sorry-Grateful

Merrit is back from Europe at last, sans financier, and he's returned with this resolve, which is, incredibly, that we can work it out. We're in a cab downtown, headed for another memorial service at St. Francis Xavier's, on Sixteenth Street, where they book AIDS services the way the Ramada Inn out in Parsippany does wedding parties. Merrit is looking very black and white in a nice new suit, very RKO, and I'm more MGM, I hope, in something linen and cool, something in which I might be asked to dance with Peter Lawford.

Merrit says, "I'm getting way too old, I want to start again with you. We'll sell the apartment, leave New York, go anywhere you want. Tell me what you want. I'll do anything you ask."

And he believes that he means this sincerely. It's his self-deluding pattern. He goes off with someone else, as if the solution to his unhappiness were a more accommodating version of me. Then he comes home, dejected, determined to "try it again" with faithful Saul. There's always a day in which he swears he loves me more than anyone he's known in his entire life, though it would be difficult to see, from his behavior, how this is possible. I personally don't think he has the first idea how to love a soul, including himself, but I don't tell him this. I just keep my mouth shut. Because there's always a voice in the back of my head saying, "Maybe

221

this time he means it, maybe he'll make love to you at last." I never want to turn him away when he's finally pursuing me, even if I know perfectly well that I would rather stick my head in a Waring electric blender than start again with him. I haven't had the courage yet to leave, but it's gaining on me.

"Who is this funeral for, again?" he says, when we get out of the cab in front of the church, and start up the steps.

"You remember," I say. "Donald's lover."

"Donald who? I know a lot of Donalds."

"This is the Donald with the dead lover."

"I know a lot of Donalds with dead lovers."

"Like who?"

"Oh," he says, "I don't know. Wasn't last week—"

"That was Arnold. He was Daniel's lover."

"Daniel?"

"You remember Daniel," I say. "Bernard's ex-lover. We saw him at the service for Herman."

"I thought he was dead."

"Herman? He is."

"No, David."

"He's dead, too."

"What was he doing at the service for Herman?"

"He died the following week."

"Oh."

We're approaching the door to the church.

"So who was Donald?" Merrit whispers.

"Not Donald," I say, "his lover. Raphael."

"Oh, that Donald. I thought he was sick."

"He is sick."

"Not dead?"

"Not yet," I say, and we enter the church. And I recognize at once, the way the boys are sitting all in front in lovely sweaters, and the family is off to the side, and the priest is young and blond and hip, that this is going to be a casual service, what I call the Reform.

The thing about funerals, AIDS funerals, is you get three types. There's what I call the Orthodox, that's strictly for the family. They fly them in from Manly, Iowa, and usually they're Catholic, or Baptist, looking very pious and disturbed, and clearly the father or the mother or the youngest brother who is currently enrolled in seven different clubs for young Republicans has not been told, and is being protected from, the cause of death. Consequently, the friends of the deceased are seated according to their unobtrusiveness, the business colleagues just behind the family, followed by the straight roommates from boarding school and college (they always dig them up, don't ask me how), then all the single women, separated into poised and butch, and finally the lovers, former lovers, friends and fuck buddies, in the back, from which, if they're at all discreet, they disappear before the service ends. And you'd be surprised how many self-respecting New York homosexuals are willing to collude in this charade, to slip in late in suits and ties and walk out early, as if someone never had a life except the one his mom remembers back in Iowa.

Then there's what I call the Conservative service, where the homosexuals are allowed to sit among the family, and even weep, but not to speak, or ask to be remembered in the priest's remarks, or the rabbi's. Afterward everybody stands in line for cupcakes at the reception, and you always know the fags because their socks are coordinated with their shirts.

The third kind of service, today's service, which I call the Reform, is strictly friends and lovers, with a pinch of family. It's basically an opportunity for brunch buddies to get up one at a time and talk a little bit about their lost whomever, you know, he was funny, he was charming, he told party jokes, we went to the movies in the afternoons, he really loved his life, he was the bravest man, plugged into tubes and boxes in the hospital room he was determined not to die, he wanted to live, it all begins to sound like an advertisement for a film with Susan Hayward, and then afterward an aging boy soprano stands up on the balcony and sings "He Was Too Good to Me," a cappella, always Rodgers and Hart, these queens, or Jerry Herman, "Time Heals Everything."

The thing about Reform services is that after about half a dozen deaths everyone begins to sound uncomfortably alike. I mean, it turns out everyone has had the same life, exactly, in New York: they brunched, they went to movies, they were always on the phone. That describes me. Maybe this happens to straight people, too. Maybe if they died they'd find out they're all the same, and they would go to one another's services and say the same nine things about one another, over and over.

So we sit through the memorial for Donald's lover, Raphael, and Merrit is crying. It's very discouraging to be involved with someone who is open with his feelings only when there's a roomful of people to be impressed. It's a version of being politically correct, his tears, an emotional correctness. He's been in therapy since 1917, I guess he's earned this little display, to be publicly in touch with his feelings. Of course, it's tastefully done. He isn't marring his makeup or anything, very Meryl Streep, a single crystalline stream from each gray-green eye. And he is so intent on his technical mastery of tears that he doesn't notice when a new group starts coming into the church, way in the back, by the doors, clearly not part of our service. They're waiting for us to finish, about two dozen people, formally dressed and looking impatient.

"I think we're holding up a wedding," I whisper to Merrit, "and won't they be surprised to find a bunch of weeping faggots in their church."

"Maybe they're waiting for mass."

"I don't think so," I say, "because I think I know these people. Merrit, look. Isn't that Randy?"

"Randy who?"

"You know, his lover's Gene."

"I thought Gene was sick."

"He was. I saw him on the street about a month ago, and he looked awful. I didn't think he'd last another six months."

And Merrit says, "I don't think he did."

And guess what, he's right. Raphael's lover, Donald, gets up and announces that we have to "terminate the service," because we've run overtime, and there's another AIDS service just coming in, for Randy's lover, Gene. He says come downstairs for the reception, we can finish the last of the service over cookies and tea, but Merrit and I just sit there.

I mean, all right, everyone is dying, but I have to ask you, back to back? But Merrit says, "We better go downstairs and finish Raphael's."

"Yeah," I say, "but let's be quick, so that we're back in time to catch the last of Gene's."

And that is what we do. We service-hop, the way we used to jump from party to party at New Year's Eve.

But then, as we're leaving, what should happen but that Merrit reaches out for me. He takes my hand. We're out on the street in front of the church, he's weeping still, he puts his arms around me, finally, and he really starts to cry. And that is when I realize that I want to leave.

He says, "We're so fucked up," and, yes, we are, because I can't tell the difference anymore between Merrit and loss. For the past three years we have played out our relationship against this background of mourning and loss. We don't break patterns anymore except at funerals. And at last, it's not enough.

So what do I do, I leave him, I go to a movie. I say, "Merrit," and he pulls away, we walk in opposite directions, like it's been decided that it's time for us to quit. What can we be holding on for? So that he'll come to my memorial, and sit in front, impeccably dressed, and talk about how we always held hands at funerals? No, I leave him, now he walks away, I turn and wave, he waves at me, I go to a movie. I'm downtown anyway, I walk to the Village, I go into the first available lobby. It's the Cinema Village, a revival house, and lucky me, the film today is *Panic in the Streets.*

This is not your standard fifties melodrama. It's got thugs and the FBI, of course, except it's set against a background of epidemic loss. A plague. It's even got a name, it's called "pneumonic plague," a weirdly lethal pneumonia, not to be confused with PCP, Pneumocystis. The good guy, Richard Widmark, is a doctor in the navy, and the bad guys are described as "probably Armenians or Czechs, mixed-blooded immigrants," and they're the ones infected with pneumonic plague. The head bad guy, who's sick but doesn't know it, is Jack Palance, and you know he's evil because he happens to be the only person in the film who looks good in a suit. I mean, I'm not inventing this, I come from back-to-back memorial services, I leave my lover in the street, I walk into a film about an epidemic disease spread by attractive men in well-tailored suits and dark-skinned immigrants from distant lands. Haitians and gays, right? And it's got a subplot in which Richard Widmark, our hero, never wants to touch his wife because he's afraid he's been exposed to the disease. And I'm thinking, I've already had this relationship. Right?

So what I do is leave the theater, it's the middle of the afternoon. I think, I want to look at death, I'll visit Eddie. I take a cab to Lenox Hill, the one place I'm assured of not encountering Merrit. Except that maybe I was wrong, because what Eddie wants to know from me, what he's wanted to know every day of these past weeks, although he doesn't say so directly, is when is Merrit coming.

I say, "Eddie, you know, wishes may bring problems such that you regret them."

He says, "Then he isn't coming."

And the two of us, we've been avoiding this discussion now for weeks. He's sitting up in bed, he's feeling mobile today, he wants a roll around the floor in his wheelchair, so I roll him. We sit in the visitors' lobby. I put my hand on his back, I can feel his spine. I want my cells to drain from my palm to his marrow. I say, "No, I guess he isn't coming."

He says, "Saul, I wonder why you're here."

"It isn't obvious?"

"I was the other woman, after all," he says, after an interim of throat clearing.

"Oh, well, there were lots of those. If I avoided every one of Merrit's tricks, you know, I wouldn't have a lot of friends."

"That's what I was, wasn't I? A trick."

"Did I say that?"

"You called them tricks."

"I didn't mean—"

"It's okay," Eddie says. "It's just I sometimes think, you know, you come here almost every day, and I was wondering, is this revenge? Some kind of sick revenge? Maybe I'm every one of Merrit's tricks you've ever wanted to—I mean, you wouldn't want to see them die, presumably—but, Saul, if that's the reason why you're coming, well, I can die as easily alone as I can die beneath your gloating. If this is your idea of revenge, then don't take it out on me. All right? Just don't take it out on me. Your altruistic frowns, they don't convince me. Your pretending to be caring. Don't care for me. All right? Just don't pretend. It doesn't help, it doesn't work, it doesn't make me any better. If you're so determined to be helpful, maybe you can put in for something easier, something you'd be better at, like dusting."

And mind you, all this time I've got my hand against his back.

We sit there quietly. And now what happens is, I guess, I start to cry. I'm thinking, fuck it, I can't comfort Merrit, I can't comfort Eddie, I can't comfort myself, I can't comfort anybody. Because Eddie is what I've given myself, instead of Merrit. That's what I'm doing here, replacing Merrit, finding someone else to love. So what, he's dying? So what, I'm going to lose him, too? At least he'll be gone. Merrit is never gone. We can't let go. We have to turn, and linger, we have to hold on to each other. It happens every time we say good-bye, leaving the church this afternoon, we turn, to wave. He walks a little farther down the street, he turns to me, I turn, we wave. It's very queer. We keep on walking, then again I turn, he turns, we wave. It goes on just like this, until we're out of sight of each other finally, even after the worst fights. It's our version of never going to bed angry, I guess. Of never letting go. I turn, and Merrit turns. We wave and wave.

Scenes of Clerical Life

Eddie dreamed he went on David Letterman. It was a camp nightmare, sort of a musical comedy cross between Dostoyevsky and *Grand Hotel*, with an all-star cast (Jane Fonda, Jodie Foster, Bette Davis, and Vanessa Redgrave, his favorite women, for the dramatic interludes) and a crucifixion scene with taps and feathers. It took place in the ice-skating rink at Rockefeller Center, where David Letterman told AIDS jokes. He turned to one of his guests, Ed Koch, and said, "Hey, Ed, do you have AIDS?" and Ed said, "Well, uh, no, uh, David, no, I certainly, um, do not," and David Letterman said, delightedly, cuing the band, "Then you're the asshole I've been looking for," and Bette Midler, strapping on a dildo like something out of *Lysistrata,* came out singing with a hundred dancing boys dressed up like tubes of K-Y jelly. Eddie entered afterward with his pig, for the Stupid Pet Tricks segment. He and the pig had a long conversation about Catholicism, which culminated in Eddie's being nailed to the hood of a 1965 Ford Mustang convertible, and taunted by the members of the Century Club, the centurions, consisting of the Reagans, the O'Connors (John Cardinal and Sandra Day), the Decter-Pods (Midge and Norm), John Simon, William Buckley, Hilton Kramer, and Christopher Lehmann-Haupt, all in togas. At the same time, he was vociferously defended by his mother, Polly, and Eulene.

Dressed in a lavender gown, and drinking New Coke from a straw, he wore a cap that said "I.H.S." (which stood, he knew, for "I Hate Sodomites") and he said, "I thirst," and "I have such yearning." Doris Day came on at the end and sang "Dream a Little Dream of Me," while Eddie asked a series of irrelevant questions, the last of which was "Father, why have you . . . "

"Why have I what?" said Joseph Stalin.

"Why have you . . . " Eddie repeated, but he didn't remember what he was going to ask, because he was awake, suddenly, in his hospital room, which always surprised him. He never quite expected to be returned to his hospital room. During the past few weeks he had had visitors, real and imaginary, from the whole of his life, from grammar school to East Village, with some *Life* magazine photo personalities thrown in. He felt as if he were living simultaneously in a dozen different time zones, like a character in the Kurt Vonnegut books he devoured in high school. To find that a bad-smelling room in a hospital ward constituted his only physically verifiable reality—well, he never quite believed it. He didn't mind dying as much as living in a hospital room. It was like having a great religious conversion in a McDonald's.

But he had a palpable visitor now. For Joseph Stalin had come into the room while Eddie was sleeping. He was sitting on a chair beside the bed, wearing a mask and a pair of rubber gloves, and a white apron tied in the back.

"Why have I what?" his father repeated through the mask, which muffled his words. "Why have I what?"

Eddie blinked. "Why have you what?"

"You said, 'Father.' You called my name, and then you asked me—"

"Why have you come?" Eddie said finally, recalling the dream all at once, and then forgetting it forever.

"Can I take this off?" his father said, indicating his mask. "I feel rather foolish."

"You can take it off."

"The gloves, too?"

"You can take off the gloves," Eddie said. "Even the smock."

"I trusted your nurses. They told me I had to wear these things, or else I couldn't come in. You must forgive me."

"My nurses lie," Eddie said. "You should have been warned."

"You must forgive them, too," said Joseph Stalin, pulling off the mask, the frock, and the gloves, and folding them neatly into a pile on the desk beside the bed. "Some of them seem very young. They hardly know better. I fear it makes them rather callous. For pain must enter into its glorified life of memory, before it can turn into compassion. You don't look especially well."

Eddie said, "Who are you quoting?"

"I beg your pardon?"

"Never mind."

His father was a large, plain man, peering over a pair of thick, square glasses which rested officiously on a generous nose. He was very proper in his speaking, but sloppy in his dress, pedantic and disheveled, like Edward Everett Horton crossed with Peter Falk. He was wearing a cardigan sweater, frayed at the collar and cuffs, and his hair, which had turned completely white, flopped down in his face boyishly in bangs. He brushed it back continually with a slow, unconscious movement of his palm, patting it into place as he talked. His voice, which was almost exactly Lionel Barrymore's voice in *Grand Hotel,* was the self-dissatisfied sound of a man with too much energy and daring, trapped in a life that offered him few challenges. For Eddie had always assumed his father had made the easiest choice, to offer himself to God. He was not aware his father had struggled, or doubted. He knew only that he was sanctimonious, and rather too eager to offer advice, in the form of aphorisms, of which he was insufferably (if discreetly) proud. This pride, Eddie thought, was his only detectable sin.

Eddie said, "They want to take away my spleen."

"Why is that?" his father asked.

"I don't know. I think my surgeon's Adolf Eichmann."

His father didn't laugh. Irony to him was like indigestible food —he couldn't process it. He had this enormous cellular blandness. Eddie had a spleen that was growing like the Blob, subsuming unsuspecting red cells into its spongy, vascular walls. He felt like a freak with his father, now more than ever, though he looked as if he might be kind, which struck Eddie suddenly as rather galling. For he knew nothing at all about straight men. He had grown up terrified of straight men, loathing and envying them, because they had the fists, and the bats they could swing at balls and butts. They were openly powerful, while all of Eddie's power was contained in subterfuge. He had no idea what it was like to have the kind of power straight men seemed to have; what did they want, how did they think, what were they like in the sack? He could not even imagine them eating—they seemed to him like creatures from the planet Louise. They were not just the opposite sex, they were a separate race.

He had modeled himself after women, because the feelings he had, as far as he could tell, matched up most closely with his mother's. He felt things, and responded, like a woman. He felt himself, by implication, to be not as good as a man, although he was a man, and so he felt better than women and worse than men, and that made him—what? Kind of confused.

But who was this man by the side of his bed? Eddie somehow couldn't recall ever having had a father, and Joseph Stalin's belated appearance suddenly struck him almost as a kind of Dickensian twist. Was he the benefactor, about to reveal to Eddie the secret of his paternity? Or—the Hollywood version—had he come to stage a reconciliation, like in *East of Eden* or *Terms of Endearment?* Eddie said, "You're Shirley MacLaine." His father said nothing. Eddie said, "Quick, go out in the hall, circle the desk, bang your fists for medication."

Joseph Stalin grinned sheepishly, in a bewildered way that made Eddie want to take care of him.

"I'm sorry," Eddie said. "I'm being flip."

"I suppose a sense of humor is important," Joseph Stalin said. He pressed his palms together as if he were praying, and looked at his shoes.

"I don't want to give them my spleen," Eddie said. It seemed like a non sequitur, but he couldn't think of anything else to talk about.

"You're on medication?" his father asked.

"Oh, yeah, a lot of stuff."

"What stuff?"

"I don't know. Percodan mostly, as far as I know, and mists and sprays, and hourly injections, and little red pills, and big blue pills. I've got a chart in the drawer, I have to mark down what I take, when I take it. That's all. I don't have to say how I like it, or why it's good for me. It's pretty easy to be dying, I guess, you lie here and no one ever asks you to explain yourself, they just say 'Roll up your sleeve.' Or 'Stick out your tongue.' Or 'Don't bleed on me.' "

"I gather you've adopted rather a passive attitude," his father said, and it was as if, Eddie thought, the single word "passive" was meant to convey a great many things. It was a question; Joseph Stalin wanted reassurance. Was that what he wanted? Or else it was an accusation, and he wanted to be vindicated. Was he scolding, inquiring? Or maybe he just didn't know what to say, either.

His sweater was the kind that can't be gotten anymore except from the closets of high school graduates, class of 1944. It had leather elbow patches and deep side pockets, and it buttoned down the front. He had buttoned it over his belly, which, Eddie thought, was a fashion mistake.

"They've been feeding me drugs that make me not want to ask about the drugs they've been feeding me. I hate hospitals."

"I never liked them, either."

He folded his arms. He had thick wrists, and the backs of his palms were newly spotted with brown.

Eddie held out his right arm. "Compare," he said.

His father looked puzzled.

"Hold out your arm," Eddie said. "Roll back your sleeve." He touched his father's sweater.

Joseph Stalin put his right arm in the air, and Eddie placed his arm alongside it. He said, "You've got bigger bones than I have," and his father's face turned red. They stared at their arms. "Roll up your sleeve," Eddie said, and his father pushed his sweater up to his elbow and rolled back his sleeve. Eddie put his hand around his father's wrist. His thumb and forefinger didn't touch. Then he put his hand around his own. "Of course, it used to be thicker," he said. "Go on. Measure."

His father very gingerly put his hand around Eddie's wrist. His hands were broad, thick, and fleshy, with short, square fingers and double-jointed thumbs. One of his pinkies bent crookedly to the right, from when he had chased after Eddie's runaway stroller, when Eddie was nine months old. His father had tripped and fallen rescuing Eddie.

"We're nothing alike," Eddie said.

Joseph Stalin held his wrist. Eddie remembered when he was about eleven or twelve and just discovering his body, his father and mother had reconciled for about a month. Every day his father came home after dark, and went upstairs to his bedroom, and changed into jeans and a ratty old sweatshirt. Doris Day was out with the dogs, and Eddie had about seven minutes to sit with his father, while he undressed. He sat on the edge of the bed, and when his father was naked (he even pulled off his clean city underwear in order to step into ratty old Jockeys, torn in the back), Eddie sat up on his knees, on the bed, and reached out for a hug, which his father supplied. Then he lay back and watched his father's penis disappear into his shorts. He was fascinated with his

232

father's body, the hair on his chest, the line of his spine down the length of his back, his thick white calves, which were hairless in back as if they had been rubbed, his penis, which wasn't circumcised, like Eddie's. He could roll it out longer when he peed, then tuck it away. Eddie discovered masturbation trying to get his penis to roll like his father's. He thought it was something he would grow into; as he got older, he would get the extra skin his father had. But the skin never came, and after a month his father stopped coming home, and the next time Eddie reached for a hug from a man, it wasn't just as a boy reaching out to his father.

Joseph Stalin let go of his wrist.

Eddie said, "I went to church out there."

"You went to—?"

"Out in Missouri. I went to church. I've never been to church before. I wasn't going to tell you."

"When were you in Missouri?"

"I went to church just after I got the diagnosis," he said. "Catholic church."

"When did you go to church?"

"I went quite a few times," Eddie said. "I went at first with a friend, and then I went by myself. I thought about you. I guess I sort of went because of you. I was angry with you. I thought that if I never told you, well, that somehow you'd be hurt by not finding out."

"How would I know?"

"That's the point. I mean, that's the catch. I went to church, and I liked it, sort of, but I didn't feel saved."

"Well, it doesn't come as easily as that."

"I wanted it to make me feel saved."

"I know you did. It just doesn't come that easy."

"I took Communion. Don't tell Mom."

His father touched Eddie's cheek.

"I didn't feel very much about it one way or the other."

"I'm sorry."

"I haven't felt much about anything, you know, for a long time. Not until this. I mean, you left, and there was Mom, and then there was Merrit—I guess you don't know about Merrit, he was this man, I sort of liked him—and then there was this. I sort of wonder where I was in all of that, it all just sort of happened, and I thought, all right, try this, try that, I tried a lot of things, but none of them—oh, fuck it, I don't know."

"I'm sorry," Joseph Stalin said.

And Eddie said, "They hated me." He said it very clearly. He said, "They hated me. I never did a thing to them. They hated me. You left me, and they hated me. They called me names. I was just myself, and that was all it took. And I will not have anything to do with their baseball-playing, straight, self-satisfying, macho, Ronald Reaganizing, churchgoing, family-sanctifying, bill-paying world. I just won't. I just won't have anything to do with them. I thwarted my entire life because they hated me. And where were you?" Eddie said. "Where the hell were you?"

He blew at his bangs. Eddie's father pushed his own hair out of his face. He sat there until Eddie fell asleep.

Bette Davis Eyes

Today is the day that they are taking Eddie's spleen away. Good title for a song, you think? I go downtown, to Fourteenth Street, and try to find him something to replace it with. You can't let something go without replacing it with something else. I know that on account of how long I lived with Merrit Mather, which I don't, anymore, I'm living by myself now in a sublet way the hell up near Columbia. It's lonely. But I'm living, and for Eddie, there should be a substitute. Not Merrit, he's a fish, and Eddie's a slug, pale and white with disease, except that recently he's got this bloated spleen. A spleen, I don't even know what it does. It's quite Elizabethan, really, isn't it? "Milady doth today prefer her spleen." Which is, like, high drag for "My pumps are killing me, can we go home?" Except with Eddie what it does is quite specific, it eats up his white blood cells at a phenomenal rate. White cells, maybe red cells. From the look of Eddie, that's some hungry little spleen.

So what would Eddie have if he were told to trade his spleen for something? Baseball cards? Decoder rings? I'm walking in and out of stores wondering, since Eddie's taste, it's not what I would call sophisticated. He thinks it is, but listen, he's wrong. When he appears in Dragnet glasses and high-topped junior Keds, it isn't irony, he really wants to be a fifties kid. Ah, but Eddie isn't Ricky

Nelson. What he is, he's a sour-smelling, emaciated, pigeon-breasted, dying little boy, with too much to think about and not a lot to do, and a scruffy growth of beard now, since the hospital, and big blue eyes, and long, skinny legs, and bedsores, and a hopeless expression, a collapsed expression, a decided, given-up expression, and a mask these days he uses off and on for oxygen, and long, long beautiful eyelashes, and thrush. Just some foam around the edges of his mouth, like a sink regurgitating.

What Eddie really loves is advertising, plastic things, suburbia. Where I come from you call it chintz. Or camp. To Eddie, it's art. All right, so I schlep from one establishment to the next, these tacky little stores on Fourteenth Street, and I find a lot of "art." I find a plastic see-through paperweight containing tiny figurines of Ron and Nancy arm in arm before the fireworks in New York harbor. They're immersed in water and their eyes roll when you shake the paperweight. It's like drowning them. It's wonderful. And I find a close-and-play model phonograph, like one I had in 1962. And something good to listen to: a recording of Mario Andretti singing "What Does He Want of Me" from *Man of La Mancha,* only with the lyric changed to "What Do *I* Want of Me." You've got to hear that to believe it, stick-shift fingers, and a pedal foot, on the down-beat. "Why do I do the things I do? Why do I do these things?" Varoom.

But I don't buy any of those trinkets. What I find for Eddie finally is plastic, and it goes around your head. It has a pair of twirly-twirlies up on top of it, and a mouthpiece where you blow and then the twirlies fill with air and make this *phoom! phoom!* noise, and stand up straight like horns. I walk away with this and then I call him from a phone booth on the corner of Eighth Avenue and Fourteenth Street.

I say, "I'm on my way." And I say it gingerly, you know, because, well, lately, he's been biting. Last few days, he's showing me his fangs. But today, he sounds a bit resigned, if dictatorial.

He says, "I want some brown rice pudding."

"Brown rice pudding? Eddie, you're supposed to be in surgery. You can't eat yet."

"For later."

"Later you'll be sleeping off the anesthesia. And anyway. Brown rice? It's not enough to want to be Troy Donahue, you've got to be the maharajah, too? Fasting, eating beans and rice?"

"You want me to put some white rice in my system?" he says. "It'll poison me."

"Sugar is sugar, brown or white. Who are you suddenly, Miss Jane Brody?"

"Just a minute," Eddie says. He's got the mask now, gulping oxygen, I hear the wheezing sound. Then a truck rattles by and I lose him. The operator cuts in, and I haven't got another quarter.

"Okay, already," I shout, over the truck, over the operator, just before she cuts me off. "So I'll get the brown rice pudding."

Well, and good luck finding it. Except I do. I find a health food store on East Eleventh Street, where outside on a chalkboard is a blurb for brown rice pudding. Inside, at the counter next to me— I'm waiting for the pudding—is a woman in a shapeless dress, the kind my mother used to wear. It's sleeveless, and it hangs to her calves. She's fifty, probably, and not exactly dirty—more like it's become a part of her pigment. The dirt is what her skin looks like. She doesn't smell or anything, but her fingernails are chipped and crusted and her face is grubby. She turns to me in all sobriety and says, "I am acquainted with well-known people in show business, and it hasn't helped me."

She gets a glass of carrot juice, and then continues.

"I know Tiny Tim," she says. "I know Jerry Stiller. I know Darryl Fucking Strawberry."

She isn't quite addressing me, exactly, but she isn't not addressing me exactly, either. Still, I'm the only person in the store who looks at her. I want to memorize her outfit, and remember what she says, to share with Eddie. Eddie loves this kind of thing, and I'm remembering for him.

"I know Ed Koch," she says. "He's in show business, too, you know."

She starts to sing "I'm Getting Married in the Morning," and she pays her check, and winks at me, and leaves.

I'm standing there waiting for this New Age tapioca, it's brown and slimy, and the man behind the counter slops it into a cup (recycled paper?), and I rush outside and hop in a cab for Lenox Hill, taking inventory. What I have for him. I have this anecdote about the woman in the shapeless dress, I have the brown rice pudding, and I have the *phoom-phoom*. A thing to hear, a thing to eat, a thing to wear. Except I just now realize that the *phoom-phoom* is a bad idea for a guy who's barely over PCP, pneumonia.

Getting him a thing to blow in. It's like buying an amputee a terrific pair of sling-heel open-toe pumps. So the pudding only, and the anecdote, and I know it's not enough. Because Eddie, Eddie is what you'd call a scrapper, a term reserved for underdog political candidates and losing pitchers. They're going to take out all his organs one by one until there's nothing left. Suddenly I wish that I knew well-known people, too. I wish I had Elizabeth Taylor breasts with which to suckle him, Rita Hayworth hair for him to twirl in his fingers, and Bette Davis eyes.

But I don't. I have my offerings. At the hospital I walk into his room without knocking and start to tell him, cheerfully, about the woman, and he stares at me and says, "I'm coughing blood." Looking up at me, he says, "Today, I'm coughing blood."

He's sitting up in bed and holding his oxygen mask, and the thrush is just a dried line of white, like sea salt, on his lower lip. His beard is even longer now than yesterday, and scruffier. His cheeks are sunken. He was always pale, but his color is definitely missing something. Or maybe it's the smell. I don't know if it's death smell or hospital smell or unwashed Eddie smell, but it's sweet and it's ammoniac, vaguely urinous but also the smell of overripe fruit, and faintly the smell of old, dried shit.

"Does anybody know?"

"Only you, and please don't tell."

"What about the surgery?"

"They canceled it."

"They canceled it?"

"That's what I said."

"Just now? I only spoke to you half an hour ago."

"Just now."

"Oh. Well. Does anybody know about the blood?"

"I said they don't. I don't want them to."

"Why not?"

"If the doctors know, I'll have to stay."

"But, Eddie, you already have to stay. There's nowhere you can go. And anyway, the surgery."

"What about the surgery?"

"Your spleen."

"Saul, I never knew I had a spleen until a week ago."

"But I mean, you have to stay a while, anyway, for surgery."

"That's right, and they can serve me more dead animals and waxed green beans in liquid shit, and poke me with needles fifteen times a day, assuming that they'll even come in here except with masks and gloves and aprons like I was, you know, the fucking It from Outer Space, and, shit, even the orderlies who mop the floors are terrified of catching what I've got, like all I have to do is quote a line from *Sunset Boulevard* and they're infected, while the doctors contemplate which of my organs are dispensable, and remove them. They want to open up my scrotum, take away my balls, and stuff white bits of Styrofoam in there to soak up the blood. What blood? I ask. The blood from the incision in your scrotum. Now is this Catch-Twenty-two or is this Nazi doctor school or what? Because, if they consider me an organ bank, they ought to know that I don't have so many organs I can spare."

He starts to cry. I am sitting by the bed still in my coat and scarf and gloves, trying to think what to say. Eddie reaches for my hand, grips my wrist, and pulls me toward the bed.

"Can I hold you just a little? Saul? I can feel my spleen just growing. I just need to have some pressure on the pain."

"You're holding on," I say.

"I want you here," he says. "In bed. You can leave your coat on, if you want to."

Well. I drape my coat across the chair, and climb into Eddie's bed. The door is open, and the nurses pass back and forth, glancing in.

"Shall I shut the door?"

"Just let me hold you," Eddie says.

It isn't very easy with the tubes, the IV, but I find a spot. I lie down with my back to Eddie, watching out the door. He folds his arm around my chest, adjusting all the tubes. He finds my hand and grabs it. Then he buries his head in my shoulder blades and cries, and slowly falls asleep.

*   *   *

So they don't take Eddie's spleen away today. I go off to work and home to sleep, but in the morning, seven-thirty, Eddie calls me on the phone and says, "Today, it's happening. Can you come over?" This time I go empty-handed. When I get there, having called in sick to work, I find him watching television calmly.

"They changed their minds. Again. They changed their minds."

"My God."

"No kidding."

He's watching "The Newlywed Game." The emcee is asking the contestants, "Husbands, if your wives hung their bras instead of stockings on the mantel Christmas Eve, what kind of fruit would Santa put in each cup?"

"Well, Eddie," I say, "it could be worse. You could be dying and straight."

"That's not a joke," he says.

I say, "I'm sorry," but he doesn't seem concerned. He says, "Who's the main character in my life?"

"What?"

"Who is starring in my life? It can't be me."

"Of course it is."

"No, I've thought about it, and it isn't. I'm just a walk-on, Saul. Not even a supporting player. Not even a cameo appearance by a long-forgotten star. I'm just an extra. No one else is starring in my life. That's why they're halting the production. It's a bad investment for the studio."

"Eddie, I think I get the point."

"I wanted to be Barbra Streisand."

"Now you've lost me."

"I wanted to make such big gestures. All my life, I grew up male, white, American. I believed that I could make such big, romantic gestures. But Saul? Americans have totally lost the talent to affect reality at all, except destructively. I won't be American like that. I won't be Waldo Jeffers, he's a Jersey boy. My name is Montgomery Clift. My name is Lorenz Hart. My name is Michelangelo Buonarroti. I'm Italian, I'm in love with Pope Julius the Second, I am working on a tomb for him. When I receive the papal semen, it is bloody, very bitter, and he utters phrases affectionately in Latin. 'Agnus Dei.' "

"Eddie."

"My name is Raskolnikov. I don't believe in justice, I believe in mercy. 'To live and to live and to live and to live! No matter how you live, if only to live!' Who am I quoting? Excuse me. I have to go to the bathroom."

He is wearing a hospital-issue shift, attached around his neck and open down the back. When he gets out of bed, with difficulty, I stare at his back, where the ribs show through. I offer to help him. He brushes me off. He makes it to the bathroom, and returns.

"Please just put that blue pad in the middle of the bed," he says when he returns. "Otherwise I'll stain the sheet."

I pick up a piece of blue material, thin and absorbent, off the top of some linen piled on a chair beside the bed. He takes it from me, placing it across the middle of the sheet. Then he turns around and backs up to the side of the bed. He puts his hands down on the edge of the mattress and tries to lift himself up onto it.

"I'll help you."

"Please stand back."

I can see the balls in the joints of his elbows, all this skin collapsed around them. He groans a little as he tries to lift himself. His ass is missing. He doesn't have buttocks anymore, just skin there, hanging on his bones like a bad fit. His anus hangs out naked down below, like a monkey's. I want him to have some kind of dignity. He has enormous dignity, but not the kind that I have, or the kind that you have, or could have. He has the dignity of falling apart spectacularly, in a way I wouldn't have thought possible. And I think, if there is integrity in what cannot be helped, this is the bravest man alive.

He raises himself up over the blue pad, with some effort. A droplet of red blood drops from his anus to the middle of the pad. It seeps into the pad, making a wider and wider circle, the way ink seeps into paper toweling. I catch my breath: one droplet of blood at the center of the pad. Then Eddie lands on the pad, too. He grunts. His arms collapse. He lies back very slowly. I look up at his face, the red stain of blood still burning my retinas like the flashbulb from a camera.

*   *   *

On the way home on the crosstown bus at nighttime I pick an empty row of seats, and who should sit down next to me but Elizabeth Taylor. I swear it is. I lean over boldly and I say, "Elizabeth? Hello."

"Hi there, Saul," she says.

I giggle, and look around the bus to see if anybody notices that Elizabeth Taylor is sitting next to me. No one does. This makes no sense to me, and she's wearing something on her finger, too, a rock, not big, but not that small. Ah, but who's to figure? I smile and I say, "Gee, you're beautiful."

"Knock it off," she says.

"Your eyes, they're really blue."

Because of course they are, they're every bit as blue, as violet, as you would think, and she is just as beautiful as I expected. Even more. She's sitting perfectly straight like an absolutely old-time lady with her knees together and her hands folded in her lap, and she isn't coarse, and she isn't loud, and she isn't fat, and I say, "Liz, you're looking fabulous, you've taken off some weight."

"Thank you, dear," she says.

"What's it like," I say, "to be perhaps the most beautiful, the most famous woman in the world?"

She lowers her voice and leans close to me, and she smells terrific, and she isn't wearing any makeup and her skin is smooth and clear, and her breasts are warm against my arm, and she says, "It's wonderful, Saul. It's every bit as wonderful as you would think. Oscars. Limousines. All the caviar you can eat. Young heirs making passes. Gambling at Monaco. It's heaven."

Then she starts to laugh. She tips her head back and laughs, and I am thinking, well, here is a woman, after all, who has had intimate knowledge of portions of Eddie Fisher's anatomy, and doesn't she look great. Which makes me think of Eddie, my Eddie, and his anatomy.

"I'm sorry about your friend," she says, reading my thoughts, taking my hand.

I start to cry. I cry and cry and cry. Elizabeth Taylor takes my head into her arms and presses it to her bosom. I'm vaguely aware that I'm getting snot all over her Technicolor breasts, but it doesn't matter, not to her, she's real. She holds me, and rocks me.

"Saul," she says. "Oh, Saul. Oh, dear Saul."

She holds me for a long time, I rest my head on her breasts and cry a long, long time. She strokes my hair. I look up into her beautiful eyes, and I say, "I want to be the color of your eyes." She giggles lightly and says, "It's contact lenses."

"I don't believe you," I say.

"No, it is," she says, still gently, "Look."

Well, I look, but I don't see, and then she—laughing, she pokes her fingers in her face and pulls her lenses out. I sit up then, and look again. And she's right—really, she has the plainest steel-gray, boring eyes you ever saw. Tired, hopeless eyes, like Eddie's.

She says, "You think the rest is real?" and she slowly starts to pull herself apart. Her chin, her cheeks, her breasts. Her breasts, where I have only just now lain. Her left buttock, her right kneecap. Piece by piece she pulls herself apart. She's a walking prosthesis, everything is rubber and it comes off in her hands. I look around again to see if anyone is watching. No one is. Just me and Liz. Finally she is sitting in the seat beside me with a pile of rubber parts on the floor between us, and I recognize her, all diminished now, as the woman in the health food store, the one who knows important people. That's who she is, the lady with the dirty fingernails. She starts to sing again, "So Many Men, So Little Time," and singing this, she gathers up her limbs and parts and stuffs them into a shopping bag and hobbles off the bus.

And now I have to ask you. If nostalgia is a longing for the past that never was, what is it when you miss the future that will never be? I miss my life ahead of time. You see, because of all these deaths in New York City. And because of Elizabeth Taylor, and the woman with important friends, and the "Newlywed" contestants with their fruit and bras, and Ed Koch, and Doris Day, and Darryl Fucking Strawberry, Monty Clift and Barbra Streisand, Ron and Nancy Reagan, Mario Andretti, and Kip Noll, starring in a fuck film at The Works, a gay bar on Columbus Avenue and Eighty-first Street, where I stop and watch the video—Kip Noll slowly beating off, it's taking him a long, long time, he doesn't look like he's enjoying it or anything, just pulling, pulling, pulling with Buddhist concentration, and he must be sore, I'm thinking, and I wonder, who is getting out of this? is anybody getting out of this? the widening red circle, everywhere I looked in that hospital room I saw it, that deepening, widening red circle. I still see it.

He Wishes for
the Cloths of Heaven

Polly found Eddie on the floor of his hospital room, splayed and still, as if dropped there. She didn't recognize him right away. He was no longer close to resembling the boy she had known since college, once slept with, always loved. His body had assumed a shape that represented something else, she couldn't say what. But she felt she didn't know him anymore, and realized, in the moment before she moved to help him to his feet, how much she had depended on his always occupying a consistent and particular space, actual physical space, in her life. He lay splattered on the floor now, like a bird thrown up against the windshield of a car, not reduced to his essential humanity, but transformed to something messy, and pathetic. She could hardly think that this was what she had in common with everyone, the way the body falls apart with sickness and disease. It would never happen to her.

"Please don't help me," Eddie said, when she bent to him. His voice had changed, too, aged, perhaps mellowed. The whine was gone. He sounded almost wise, almost forgiving, if not self-forgiving. "I sort of like it here, the floor. It's cool, and I've been so hot."

"Come on, they pay nurses to take care of you." Polly headed

244

back out the door. "What the hell are you in a hospital for, anyway? You can fall down at home."

"Don't call anyone. Please. I think at last I've found a spot where I'm comfortable. In bed I turn, right side, left side, everything hurts. My spleen. It's gotten so big it sort of hangs off the edge of my skin, like a giant, misplaced breast."

"How long have you been lying there?"

"I don't know. Hours, maybe days."

"Well, what were you doing, for God's sake?"

"This is upsetting you."

"I mean, you could have broken—"

"Do you think that matters now?"

"People are not supposed to get worse in hospitals. They're supposed to get better."

"I guess it hasn't worked for me."

"Eddie, you can't lie on the floor."

"I said I like it here."

"I'm calling the nurse."

He lifted his chin. "Please don't. I'd rather lie here. Polly, please don't leave. It's so good to see you. The only thing I was missing was company. I don't mind the floor. I got up to go to the john, it sort of leapt at me, you know, the tiles sort of hugged me, pulled me down, and it's cool down here, and anyway I've never liked chairs, or beds, or—"

"And what about the john?"

"I got there anyway," he said, sourly. Then Polly noticed a circle on the floor, somewhat brighter in the light than the surrounding tiles, and the twisted dampness of Eddie's hospital shift, tangled around his waist.

"Oh my God."

Eddie laughed. " 'For God's sake, let us sit upon the floor, and tell sad stories of the death of kings,' " he said, quietly. "Or maybe I mean queens. Who am I quoting?"

"Please don't be literary now, all right?" She put down her knapsack, and draped her coat on the back of a chair by the bed. "You can't lie there in your own—"

"Don't call a nurse."

"Well, someone has to—"

"Can't you take a hint? They hate me, all right? My urine? I mean, listen, they don't even like to take away my tray when I've finished

245

eating, do you think they want to come in here and—" He stopped. He dropped his head back to the floor.

"Oh, Eddie, I'm sorry," Polly said. She put her hand to the side of her head.

"I haven't even had a bath," he said, closing his eyes.

"Oh, I'm sorry," Polly said.

"You're sorry," Eddie said. "I'm wet. And where I'm not wet, I'm sore. And where I'm not sore, I'm numb. And where I'm not numb —which is a lot more of me than if I had my way—I itch. And where I don't itch—"

"I'll give you a bath," Polly said. Then she relaxed. At first, she had wanted to run, then to take him in her arms, then to break a flowerpot over his head, and bring it all to an end. She had wanted all these things in quick succession. She had wanted to escape the smell of his room, of plastic fitted sheets and shit, and HandiWipes. But her need to go made her guiltily loving. Then she was angry, then sad. But when she stopped responding, and decided just to clean him up off the floor, she felt relieved, and knew she could stay.

"You'll get infected," Eddie said.

"Don't be stupid," Polly said, pushing the sleeves of her shirt over her elbows. She picked a towel off a stack on a chair by the side of the bed, and dropped it onto the floor, to soak up the urine. Then she undid Eddie's shift at the back of his neck, and pulled it gently away.

"Careful where you touch that thing," he said.

"I know what I'm doing," she said.

"Ms. Pioneer," Eddie said. He was naked now, but Polly didn't like to think of what she saw as Eddie's body. She gave it other properties, in her imagination, endowed it with a particular volume and weight, as if it were something familiar to her, if not exactly human. The voice coming out was Eddie's, but that was coincidental. The body was like something she had known about, but never discussed.

"Be quiet," she said.

"You're like my mother," Eddie said. "Draw all the wagon trains together in a circle. Western toughness in a crisis."

"I have to pick you up," Polly said. "Do you think you can stand?"

"Shouldn't you be wearing gloves or something?"

But she had made up her mind not to be squeamish at all. She wanted him to see she wasn't afraid of him, even if she was. "Please let me do this, Eddie. If I lift you from behind, my arms under your armpits, and support you, can you stand?"

"I can try."

Polly crouched down, then straightened her legs and pulled him up from the floor, stretching him out full-length like an unfolded crepe paper Halloween skeleton. In places, his skin had turned almost orange. "Into the bathroom," she said.

He sat on the john precariously, while she filled the tub. Then she helped him over the side, into the water.

"People always want to wash me," he said, smiling shyly. She had seen him naked thousands of times, had touched his penis erotically once, long ago, massaged his shoulders, pressed her cheek to his back falling asleep. But she had never felt, not with him or anyone, the terrible hush and hotness of intimacy that she now felt, looking at his ruined body. He blushed and pressed his knees together.

Neither one of them spoke as she washed his hair. The shower-head had a long attachment, the tip of which she held close to his head, and wet and lathered and rinsed and lathered and rinsed Eddie's hair, which had turned thin and soft with his sickness, almost textureless. She soaped his arms and chest, and legs, and his back, very gently, and she drained the tub and rinsed him everywhere, between his toes, his pubic hair, the backs of his legs. He watched her hands when he could, and grunted softly. Then when they were done, she helped him again to his feet, and wrapped him in a towel, and he sat on the john while she went back into his room and finished cleaning the floor. She changed his linen, dropping the sheets and soiled towels in the corner, with his soiled shift. She helped him walk out of the john, but he had to be lifted into his bed, where he pulled the fresh white sheet across his legs, and held Polly's hand. She sat beside him on the bed; he didn't want to let her go.

"How do I look?" he said.

"How do you look?"

"There's a mirror in the bathroom, but I always look away. Usually I can see it in your eyes. I haven't looked in an actual mirror more than once all this time."

"Maybe that's the right idea," she said, gently.

"Well, I've never had the right idea about anything," he said. "Why start now? Do you have a pocket mirror? Something?"

She dropped his hand, and went to her pack. She had a compact shoved inside the zipper pocket, way down at the bottom. "Here," she said, returning, and she watched him open it clumsily and hold it to his face. He held it at arm's length at first, then closer, looking at his face in bits and pieces: his teeth, then his chin, then his nose, his forehead, finally his eyes.

"No pig," he said, softly.

"I'm sorry?"

"I'm not. I said I think my pig is dead."

"I can't tell when you're talking nonsense," Polly said.

"African swine flu virus, maybe," Eddie muttered.

"You have beautiful eyes," Polly said.

"My nose is still enormous."

"I've always wanted your eyes."

"I'll leave them to you," he said. "Shit." The compact fell out of his hand; the mirror shattered on the floor. "Shit," he said. "It's all right," Polly said. "Don't clean it up," he said. "Shit." He took her hand again and squeezed, and Polly wanted something—wanted to embrace him, hold him, stand him up, dismiss him, tie him down and shoot him full of drugs to make him better, or to make him go away. She didn't want to touch him. She didn't want to need him, or to have to wonder how it would feel when at last she lost him. She wanted to scream. She wanted to know how this was going to feel twenty years from now, or twenty minutes. He lifted his legs across her knees slowly, and she put her hand around his ankle. That was all that she could think to do. Most of him was spread across her lap—there wasn't much of him. She stroked his ankle, and he talked softly.

"I was never really very good at it, you know," he said.

"Never good at what?" she said.

"You know, it. You know, the wild thing, oh ha ha ha. You spell that with an *e*, I ever tell you that? For gays, I mean, the Wilde Thing. As in Oscar—"

"I get it."

"—Oscar Wilde. That's the joke. I never even liked it very much. Should I be laughing now?"

"Don't laugh," she said.

"I mean, I did it often enough. Not like it was the only thing in my life, though sometimes it was. Sometimes it was just the mild thing. But sometimes I got close to thinking, yes, this really is a pleasure, isn't it, the freedom to demand exactly what you want, to be the center of attention, to address a guy directly and forget his personality and say, 'I like this.' "

"You're making me uncomfortable."

"My legs?"

"Not your legs."

"I want to tell this."

"I'm scared."

"Your hands are cool. I want to tell this." He shifted his weight. "Still uncomfortable?"

She nodded. "Yes." Then she said, "All right."

"That's what I was thinking on the floor," he said. "I was remembering. How almost nice it sometimes was to be a body wanting only pleasure, and to have it gratified. For a time I used to do it just with dudes. Jersey dudes. I think I got the closest then. I felt that I belonged. You know, I mean that they were bros, like from the locker room, they said 'Yo, buddy,' you know, and they asked me stuff, like what did I do, I said I was a poet, what the hell, and they believed me, in a barroom in the back somewhere, or on the piers, or in the park, they were entirely from Jersey. Not the way that I'm from Jersey, as if I were some kind of artist, but, you know, seriously Jersey, Irish Jersey City and Bayonne Italian, Cuban Union City, black working class, and I'm this white, white boy, they're baseball-playing guys, the kind I've always hated, but they liked me, they respected me, and they touched me, and they put their dicks inside of me, and it was wonderful. It was like a baseball game. I mean they coaxed and coached, you know, like all the playground boys who used to try to teach me how to swing when I came up to bat. These gorgeous, butch Jersey voices, only they were not abusing me, not 'Easy out,' but giving pleasure. 'Great butt,' they said, and 'beautiful skin.' I felt like one of the guys. For an hour of my life, one night a week, for months, I was like one of the guys, a straight guy playing baseball really well, and pleasing everyone. I had to have sex with twenty guys to feel like a straight man, finally. What kind of irony is that?"

Polly stroked his shin. The skin was dry. "Except," she said.

"Except?"

"Except you never really . . ."

"Never really," Eddie said, relaxing more and more of his weight onto her lap, into her arms. "Never really even did it very much. Like once a month. Or every other month. Then not at all the last two years—"

"But enough."

"Oh, well, what's enough? I got sick, I got unlucky, that's all."

Polly nodded. "But I didn't know," she said.

"I wasn't sharing. Not exactly."

"Oh, well, yeah, I guess."

" 'How was your day, honey?' 'Oh, fine, I just jacked off in Central Park with someone I don't know.' Right?"

"Men are lucky. Gay men. If they want it, they can go and get it easily enough."

"Straight men would do the same, if they could. Do you ever want to?"

"Sometimes."

"Yeah, well, don't bother. Because, you know what I discovered? That it's just another thing that doesn't matter. All those dicks."

"Oh, please."

"I mean, it's nothing to do with their personalities. Not at all. What they're like in sex is not at all to do with their personalities. Like, that really surprised me. Because I didn't want their personalities, not right away, but anyway I just assumed that they would be the same as when—"

"Well, that much I know. They're not the same."

"They're never the same."

"Sometimes they're not."

"Personality and sex are two completely different things," Eddie said. "I learned that from Merrit. Because it seemed to matter to him, but I guess it really didn't. The only problem was, it mattered to me. I think that was the only time it ever mattered to me, was with Merrit. I'm full of ironies."

"I don't know," Polly said, thinking how, finally, their roles had truly been reversed. For Eddie's ramblings, even his presence in the room, his weight in her arms, felt real to her, perhaps too real, and she didn't want to feel what was happening to her. She didn't want to understand the connection between them. She felt herself watching. She felt herself suddenly watching. As Eddie reached to her, as she hugged him to her chest and tangled in his bedclothes, inextricably, as at last she felt the kind of connection she had wanted with a man, with someone, it frightened her, and she withdrew. She looked only at the appearance of things, Eddie's "exact sequence of motion and fact," a quote from someone, though now she would never know whom. That was their lives, she thought:

their feelings left out of the frame, they were just an arrangement of figures and facts, posed as if in pity, but only "as if."

But Eddie kept talking. He said, "Do you remember Patrick Dean?"

"Patrick Dean?"

"At college. You remember?"

Polly nodded, but she was hardly listening.

"Patrick was beautiful, and he believed in God. Do you remember? He was beautiful, and he believed in God, and he was gay, I know that because I slept with him that night before we left Oberlin. I never told you, Polly. Do you know why I slept with him? Because very late one night, in his room, he quoted poetry to me. Is that too queer? It was something from Yeats, I didn't recognize it then, he didn't know the title. He lay on his bed and said he wanted me to be his lover, but that God would not approve or something, and he said, I swear, he lay down on his bed, his room had sayings from the Gospels written on construction paper circling the walls, he took my hand and said, 'Tread softly because you tread on my dreams.' Which meant, 'I'd sleep with you if I were not so scared, and don't be angry.' I found the poem the next day, wrote it down, and left it under his door, and we didn't speak the rest of the year. Until the night before I left. And then I went to his room. He insisted I stay in his bed while he slept on the floor. We held hands across the space between us. Then he asked for a back rub. A back rub! Then he said I gave a lousy back rub, and he got into bed with me and showed me how. Then we lay together, Polly, then he took me in his arms. Then I tried to kiss him, and he wouldn't be kissed. Then we jerked each other off. He got back into his sleeping bag after that. Our semen dried against my stomach. I think he went to Haiti after graduation. I hugged him once the next day. I wonder where I'd be right now if Patrick Dean and I had not been so afraid. Would it have made any difference? Polly? Do you think? The poem went like this: 'Had I the heavens' embroidered cloths, enwrought with gold and silver light, something something half-light, I would spread them under your feet.' " He closed his eyes. " 'But being poor I have only my dreams; I have spread my dreams under your feet,' " he said, but that was as far as he got.

He lay on Polly's lap and turned his head away from her and draped his legs and dropped his arm, and he died. She held him, and she had the appearance of things. And the appearance was this: she sat very still, supporting him. She was tangled in his bedclothes. She tipped her face to his and watched him. He was very thin, and with his dying breath his soft white body and the muscles of his stomach and his chest, pigeon-breasted with his reddish nipples, and his naked arms, quite long, and thin, his boy's knees and his slender calves, and feet, second toes longer than the first, and narrow shoulders, ample hips, and vulnerable belly crumpled, bent in the middle, and his fingers clutched the bed sheets at her knees. She watched him, held him, tenderly. His last hot breath condensed like steam upon her cheek.

Ballad of a Thin Man

errit was on the uptown Number 1, from his office down near Battery Park. He was on his way to visit Eddie, finally, in the hospital, when he stopped to make a panic call to Saul from the Forty-second Street station, before he changed trains.

He said, "How do you survive all this?"

And Saul said, "I have my gay moment."

The uptown express came into the station, and another uptown local arrived, discharging its mouthful of greasy passengers. Merrit was edgy, and nervous. "Speak louder," he said. "What if I buy him some shoes?"

Saul laughed.

"I mean, I don't want to arrive there empty-handed," Merrit said.

"Oh, I know, the need for a prop," Saul said, conciliating. "They don't always help. Just have your gay moment."

"Jesus, Saul," Merrit said. "I'm not being flip."

"And neither am I. You know what a gay moment is? Merrit, relax. It isn't so hard. I keep on visiting Eddie, week after week he gets thinner, and sadder, and harder and harder to see. I just remember that movie, Judy Garland in *I Could Go On Singing.*"

"Oh, please," Merrit said.

"All right, I'm a queer."

"Maybe I should call him up and ask him whether I can bring him anything."

"It's not a dinner party. Listen, Merrit, this will help you. Judy Garland plays a concert performer, oh coincidence, and she wants to adopt the son she had ages ago out of wedlock with Dirk Bogarde. And I mean, if you can imagine Dirk and Judy doing the wild thing, as Eddie would say."

"I never got his slang."

"Close your eyes and relax. He wants to see you."

"I'm worried more about me."

"It's like finally paying a bill, to be crass. You'll be glad."

"The last time I saw him we fought. He tried to tell me he was sick. I didn't believe him."

"Why don't you forgive yourself? You had a fling, it didn't work out, and then he got sick. It isn't your fault. You want to hear about this movie, or not?"

"Okay," Merrit said. "But talk loud. The trains keep rattling in."

"All right, so one afternoon, the day of her final performance in London, she realizes that she can't have the kid. It wouldn't be fair. He's happy with Dad. She gets out of bed, and shouts to her dresser, Aline MacMahon, 'Get me my black dress, I'm going out!' "

"Dove," said Merrit, "can you hurry? My quarter's running out."

"Don't you have more change?"

"I do. Just hurry."

"Oh God, it's my favorite movie, too," Saul said. "So Judy goes out and gets drunk, and winds up in an emergency room, hours later. Not AIDS, just her ankle, it's bandaged, and she has a sadly self-indulgent, drunken, belligerent stammer. Eddie has thrush, by the way."

"I don't need the vivid parallels, please."

"Sorry. It's just that you should know that he has thrush. Around his lips. Just look at him, Merrit, that's the mistake everyone makes, they act like nothing is wrong. Look at him squarely, and flinch if you want, and let him know that you see. Don't pretend he's not there."

"We just had one short weekend," Merrit said. "I don't understand why I matter so much."

"Because you're beautiful," Saul said, impatiently. "Don't you know that? God, and he's never been in love. Don't you know that you're beautiful?"

The phone clicked intrusively.

"They're going to cut me off soon."

"Give me your number," Saul said. "I'll call you back."

"Just finish the movie."

"All right. Dirk—a doctor, of course—shows up at the hospital and says, 'You've got to go out and perform. You're already late.' And she says, 'Oh, the hell with the audience. I don't sing for them, I sing for myself.' He says, 'Then don't sing for them. Sing for you.' 'I don't want to sing for anybody,' she says, alcoholically. He says, 'Sing for me, or just sing.' Which is what she does. He takes her to Albert Hall, she walks to the wings, and just before she struts onto the stage, she stops and looks at the lights, and tips her head way back. The audience is pounding and shouting, they're angry, she's terribly late. She tosses her head, briefly and defiantly, just for herself, right before she goes on. She does it for herself. That's her gay moment."

Then the mechanical operator cut in, asking for more money.

Merrit shouted over the voice. He said, "I need you, dove."

Saul said, "Have your gay moment, Merrit. That's what gets me through. Remember that you're a queer. It's helpful in life. Stop outside of his room, think of how he will look, of how much of him will be gone, and whether he'll be breathing alone, or plugged into boxes and tubes. Affirm yourself, and go on. You're beautiful, Merrit, remember."

Then Merrit lost the connection.

But he didn't transfer to the crosstown train; he couldn't go on. He thought about buying some shoes. Would Eddie like shoes? Maybe calling ahead would be better, but then, he didn't want to interrupt if Eddie was resting, or busy with somebody else. He found another quarter in his pocket, and dialed the hospital number. A woman picked up the phone. He asked for Eddie's extension. She said, blandly, "Are you family?" He said he was, which was true, in a way. Then she disappeared for quite a while, and more trains came into the station. Merrit watched another uptown local arrive. Then, against the rattle of the train departing, she came back on the line.

He thought he heard her say "expired," and asked, "What?" He held his hand to his ear and furrowed his brow and tipped his weight to the girder supporting the pay phone, as if leaning would help him to hear what she said. But when she spoke again, over the noise, he heard her distinctly enough. She said, "The patient has expired." It was that simple. He stood in the station with the

255

phone to his head, a leather satchel clutched between his knees, his London Fog raincoat open down the front, his suit with razor-sharp creases in the trousers, even his boxer shorts, he thought, green-and-black–striped and immaculately pressed, and he understood, with angry resignation, that the order of his life was not a guarantee against this kind of moment. Something, at last, had escaped him. He held the phone receiver until the woman on the line said, "Sir?" and a man beside him, dressed as he was, glanced impatiently from the pay phone to the subway tracks and back again, reminding him of what was expected of him now.

He broke the connection with his thumb, hearing the soft crackle of disconnected lines before he placed the phone receiver back in its cradle. He lifted his satchel from between his knees. In one smooth movement, he checked the change slot, smiled vacantly at the man he had kept waiting, and headed for the steps that led to the exit. There was no point getting on the other train, now.

Merrit was "that unbroken series of successful gestures upon which beauty depends," Saul had said, teasingly, once. Now, suddenly, he had nothing to do, except think. She hadn't told him how it happened—had he died in his sleep, was there blood, was there pain? He stopped at the newspaper stand at the head of the stairs, and read the tabloid headlines: PROSTITUTE BITES FATHER OF FOUR, HELD IN AIDS MURDER RAP. In the middle of the concourse, a bright-haired boy Eddie's age with a midwestern twang and a yellow cardboard display preached Dianetics from a fold-out metal table-top. "Merchants of Chaos," he shouted at Merrit. "Learn to resist the Merchants of Chaos." He held out a book in his hand. "Follow the word," he said, "herein. You can learn to be Clear."

Merrit shook his head perfunctorily.

It would be nice to be clear, he thought, pushing through the turnstile and heading up to the street, emerging into the above-ground Times Square traffic. It would be nice to have a word.

For there wasn't a word for fourteen, sixteen, thirty people dead or dying, each of whom knew fourteen, sixteen, thirty people—oh, and so on. There wasn't a word that said, "I just got off the phone with the ghost of one more twenty-five-year-old who should have passed out of my life in a normal, healthy way."

Times Square was full of gaps where, once, familiar billboards hid buildings that had recently been leveled, revealing big new chunks of sky and empty space. Maybe the Iroquois saw the city

256

like this, the sky visible from everywhere, Merrit thought, stopping at another pay phone on the crowded southwest corner of Forty-second Street. Maybe they would have had a word. Maybe Saul would have one, too. He dialed Saul's number, hoping he was still home.

"You know, you've been the one great love of half a dozen different lives," Saul had said, the last time they talked about Eddie. Merrit didn't understand why it was so important for Eddie to see him. "You attract the sort of person," Saul went on, "who falls head over heels in love. Look at your picture gallery, Merrit, hanging there in the hallway. Your photos of lovers, and boy-friends, and girlfriends, your dog, your car, and your wife. I saw you put me up there next to your old car, the one you had in 1962. Don't you see what you do? You make people give up their lives, but then you only want them for trophies, to hang on the wall. You don't want the person at all."

Saul knew the histories of all of Merrit's former lovers, but the truth was, Merrit didn't quite remember anymore. Saul was the one who kept track. Oh, Merrit remembered not getting along with his wife. He remembered the first man with whom he had ever had sex. It was in Washington when Merrit was thirty, and he had walked one night into a bar he had somehow always known about. When he ended up in a strange apartment, with a man who taught the second grade and lifted weights (he had barbells under his bed), Merrit came before he was even touched. He recalled one scene from his high school romance—pulling up his underwear and running across the hall to hide from his girlfriend's mother.

He told these things to Saul, who hoarded them, almost per-versely. He was flattered by Saul's attention, but it offended him, too. He liked to be watched, not recorded. For it wasn't just the dirty parts, like sections copied out of novels by adolescents, that fascinated Saul: he wanted the progression from one departure to the next, how all the lovers had gone, or how he had sent them away. "What was it like with a woman?" Saul wanted to know. "When you started with men, was it like love starting over, a sec-ond chance to begin? Was it the beginning of love, or just a play with a new set of props to manipulate?"

Saul asked too many questions. Sex was always the same, and men were like women because they all left him, and he was alone. He treated them badly, he withdrew, and then when he believed that he could never convince them to go, they finally left. Afterward

257

he tried to keep in touch. He had them all to his parties at Christmas, and they stood together, all his former lovers, and drank and eyed his current flame, and made uncomfortable jokes. Saul was right, he fell for people who couldn't let go. His high school crush held on for years; his wife still sent anniversary cards; a woman in Vermont who had a son his age and had joined the Peace Corps sent long, apologetic letters blaming herself and remembering his penis; his first male lover and the woman Merrit was seeing at the same time had moved in together. One after the other he had stopped wanting them, too soon, and without explanation.

Well, he loved Saul the most, he thought, standing in Times Square, waiting for him to answer the phone. It wasn't the sex, he thought. That hardly mattered. Saul was boyish in bed, his flesh was too pink, he wanted too badly to please. It made Merrit uncomfortable, and he responded to Saul as if he were in a therapy session, with periods of resistance followed by yielding, resistance, and yielding, until they were awkwardly through. Merrit liked his lovers to be selfish like him, and quiet, and proud of themselves. But Saul never loved for himself. He kept on talking, and asking, and trying to please. Early on, when they first met, he had talked about God, and that was alarming, and sweet. Later he wanted a grade. "How was that, was it good, is it better with me than with Bob, or Wendy, or Sue, or Brian or Tony or Steve?" Those were questions that didn't have answers. Didn't he know that? He must have known that.

But Merrit loved him the most, because he never went away. Only now he was gone, and Merrit couldn't quite believe it. He stared at the awful marquee of the Marriott Hotel, and waited for Saul to answer his phone, but he didn't. Had he gone out already? Heard about Eddie? It wasn't like Saul to insist on a life of his own. Merrit wasn't used to that at all. "Shit," he said, hanging up. He hurried east, along Forty-second Street.

He had to have something to do. He could stand to be alone, as long as he had something to do. He decided he would still buy Eddie some shoes. He knew a clothing store across from the library, upstairs in an old Fifth Avenue building. It was a slightly nineteenth-century place, with personalized service, and oak-and-glass display cases with rows of oxford cloth shirts and silken bow ties, and suspenders. They had studs for tuxedo shirts, and straight pins with colored enameled heads, for the asking. All the old gentlemen who worked there were gay, in the old-fashioned way, that is, secretly, tastefully homosexual, though not above flirting. When Merrit was fitted there once for a suit, the fitter dipped down to his knees, touched Merrit's penis unabashedly through the new material, and said, with aching propriety, "What side, sir, do you dress on?" Merrit smiled now, remembering.

He crossed Sixth Avenue, and found the entrance to the store. He climbed three flights of narrow, rubber-matted stairs. No one could have found this place without knowing exactly where it was. He liked that. He liked places no one knew about, undiscovered beaches, plays that three people saw, empty restaurants the first two weeks they were open for business. But when he got to the top of the stairs, and walked down the hall to the entrance to Best Clothing, he was shocked to find the store in a state of disarray.

They were going out of business, that was apparent. Cases were empty, and the floor was piled with boxes. Shirts were strewn over counters, sweaters on shelves were coming unfolded. Tissue paper had been scattered as if by a litter of rambunctious kittens. The floor was covered with sawdust. Shoe boxes seemed to have exploded, in a pile in the corner. No one but Merrit was around. The room was too brightly lit, the salesmen were gone, the windows overlooking the street were covered with cardboard curling in the corners.

Merrit walked slowly through the debris. He looked at some ties that hung from a lamp, and waited for someone to come and ask him if he needed help. Finally a figure emerged from the back, a dignified man in trousers and a vest, his shirtsleeves rolled over his elbows, a watch fob strung across his corpulent belly, his thinning hair combed straight back from his brow.

"We're closing," he said, jovially.

"For the day?"

"We're closing it out," he said, gesturing for Merrit to stay and browse if he liked. "We're closing the old dame out," he repeated, pushing a toothpick contemplatively between two lower teeth, and rubbing his free hand liberally under his nose, which was bulbous and red. "You can't keep up with Alexander's," he bellowed, and laughed too heartily. Merrit smiled uncomfortably.

Then a small, spare, gray-haired man with round, wire-rimmed glasses and an aggressive slouch shuffled into the room, and called out, "Ezra!" He was also in a vest and shirtsleeves, but his gaze was fixed on the floor, and his tone was pathetic and mad. "Ezra," he shouted again, and Merrit thought he had walked onto

259

the set of *Death of a Salesman,* as the round, upright man turned away from him to talk to the crouched, unhappy one.

They stood in the corner, and chatted under their breath. Merrit glanced quickly around the room, and saw a pair of saddle shoes by the window. They were lying loose on top of the pile of boxes and shoes. They were black and white, and he smiled when he thought of how they would have looked on Eddie's feet. Eddie would have said, "Those shoes are absurd," and laughed out loud. When he laughed he threw his arms up in the air, and leaned way back until Merrit thought he would break. Then he crumpled over forward, clapping his hands. He moved like a puppet, all the way back and then over forward again, as if he had no bones, only loosely wired joints.

Merrit looked in the corner and saw that the men were still talking, arguing softly. He walked over to the pile of shoes, tucking his satchel under his arm. Then he reached out quickly to the saddle shoes and slipped them under his coat. He hardly breathed. His face was hot and he felt very young, and excited. He pulled his coat closed, his satchel clamped to his side on top of the shoes, and walked to the door.

"Well," he said, too casually, to the men in the corner, "good luck to you."

Hardly noticing, the men waved him away. He went through the door, and made himself walk nonchalantly down the stairs to the street.

It was October, nearly Halloween, and the sky grew dark so quickly now. When Merrit came out on the street, flushed and exhilarated, the shoes still clutched to his side, he walked briskly through the too-early dusk, threading through shoppers and commuters, and a boy on a skateboard in ratty old jeans and a T-shirt, who didn't look cold. Merrit wasn't cold, either. He liked the change in the weather, and the shoes burned a hole in his heart, keeping him warm from his neck to the top of his head, and down to his groin.

He hurried up past Saks and Rockefeller Center, smelling the coffee smell from New Jersey that blew across town on the breeze from the Hudson. Eddie had described that smell, the day he tried to tell Merrit he had AIDS. Merrit hadn't believed him then, and he never went to see him after he knew it was true, but that was all right. Saul needed things to be seen, to be told. He thought that Merrit had a secret. He always wanted to know what it was—had

260

he slept with his mother, murdered his father, what could it be that kept him so quiet, so cool and withheld all his life? He could never tell Saul that his secrets were easy, and small. He read books not for plot or character, but page number—he liked to count the pages more than he liked reading them. When he sometimes ran in the park, he told himself that he had a fence attached to his spine, with which he marked off lands as his own, with each successive stride. His grandfather used to operate a junk shop in his dining room, collecting damaged goods in fire sales and evictions, and Merrit thought as a child that he had been gotten in a similar way. When his parents first started out, they ran a motel, which was where he grew up. Now they operated a chain that stretched from Massachusetts to California; Merrit got his money from the kinds of places seventeen-year-olds went to lose their virginity. He didn't like sex very much. Those were his secrets, which wouldn't have satisfied Saul.

Saul thought the world revolved around a moment of irretrievable loss, in which he wrapped his soul, as if loss could encompass, and hold. He had been holding himself inside that moment for years. But Eddie was dead, and Merrit was relieved. He never went to visit him, but he didn't have to. He knew all the time that he was dying.

For I know what death feels like, he thought, the coffee smell in his nose, the saddle shoes under his coat. Death is relentless, and dull. You wait for people to die. You wait and wait, and sometimes they get better, for years, and sometimes they go very quickly, and you're almost surprised. But the whole time, you rehearse. A little bit at a time, you go through the feelings of loss. And then when they finally go, you've already lost them in stages, and there isn't any grief to be aware of. How do you let go of a person, Merrit wondered, a relationship? You just rehearse the losing carefully, until it doesn't matter anymore.

Frequent Flyer

All right, dear," the teacher said. "When you're ready."

It was a combination lost object–preoccupation–fourth wall–phone call exercise. She had to walk into a familiar setting, with a specific objective in mind but focusing on something else, establish a sense of privacy (that was what the imaginary fourth wall was for), conduct two separate phone calls (one outgoing, one incoming) with people with whom she had completely different relationships (and with an objective in mind for each call, as well as an exact awareness of the contents of each conversation), then discover she was missing, and subsequently search for, something so important to her life that to go on without it would be to induce paralysis, insanity, or death.

"Five seconds," Polly said, checking the set one last time before she went out into the hall for her entrance. She had set up just a bench and a phone on the floor, for this was Eddie's room, and props were unnecessary. The bench was doubling as a trolley, and she endowed it with flatness, and whiteness. It already rolled. Underneath she had placed her lost object, Eddie's ashes. They were in a plain white canister. Her objective was to get the ashes and leave, for she was on the way to Eddie's funeral. The phone calls were to be from Eddie (one last lament from the beyond) and Brag, whom she hadn't seen since she returned the keys to his car, months ago. Her preoccupation was the possibility of seeing Merrit at the funeral. He was the man, after all, to whom she had lost two sort-of lovers—Eddie, the lover who wouldn't have sex, and Brag, the lover with whom she couldn't be friends (and who wasn't so good with sex, either, for that matter).

"Will you ever be ready?" said the teacher.

"One more second," Polly said. She stared at the back of the classroom, and established the fourth wall of her make-believe room, imaginatively hanging Eddie's pink shoes on the red exit sign above the windows. Actually she still had Eddie's shoes in her knapsack. They were hers, he said, to give to Merrit, and his father; he had also given her his old volume of Yeats. She held the knapsack now, and smoothed her dress, an elegant, black tea-length frock with a sweetheart collar and a drop waist, which she wore over chalky gray stockings. She was wearing black shoes, and elbow-length black gloves with bone ivory buttons. Her hair was twisted neatly in a knot in back. She had a black wool coat with an imitation sable collar. She actually was on her way to Eddie's funeral—as soon as she finished the class.

"All right," she said, confidently.

The teacher nodded, perched over his pad punctiliously, playing with his pen. The other students yawned, and shifted in their seats. Polly turned coolly and went out into the hall. She closed the door, shut her eyes, and started wondering what Merrit would actually look like. As soon as she felt a tense wad of anxiety in the pit of her stomach, she opened the door and walked onto the set.

"Make it real," the teacher breathed, once, lightly, as she came through the door. She held the knapsack and her keys. She knew where she had been, and where she was going. She set down the knapsack on the trolley, with her keys. She threw off her coat, and searched in her pocket for her cigarettes—brand-new habit. All her life she had wanted to smoke. She felt that Eddie's death was an excuse, and fuck the irony. She lit a cigarette, fumbling with the matches ("Always have an obstacle," the teacher counseled, "keep your obstacles convincing, and surmountable"), took a deep drag, and exhaled.

She dropped ashes on her skirt. Panicky, surprised, she brushed her thigh quickly, then checked the fabric for holes or burn marks. She didn't want to appear in front of Merrit—or Eddie's mother, for that matter, or Saul, or even Eddie's father—looking as if she'd been up all night long injecting heroin.

"Injecting!" she said, wondering where that thought came from. (It was also a talking-to-yourself exercise.) She took a last, deep drag on her cigarette, then dropped the butt to the floor. She was still self-conscious about smoking. She tried to look like Bette Davis, but she knew she didn't do it right, she didn't hold it properly. Crushing the butt beneath the sole of her shoe, she dialed Brag's number. She had rehearsed this; she knew what would happen. But now she had to forget. She had to hear Brag's voice in her head, and feel surprised. But his answering machine picked up.

"Oh, shit," she said.

"This is 555-7250," Brag said. (She had never actually heard his machine, but she could imagine that his message was factual, and short.)

"All right," she said, after the beep, "I'll talk to your machine."

She looked at Eddie's shoes, hanging on the fourth wall. Eddie had never met Brag, which was just as well.

Quickly, she said, "Don't stay here." She put her hand to the side of her head. "That's all I wanted to say. Don't let it stick to you, don't stay here. Take it from me, I know." Then she rattled off a quote from *Gatsby,* about how unprepared midwesterners were for the life they found in New York. She said, "I do feel trapped by my reality, and you will, one day, too." Then she hung up.

"Oh, yak yak yak," she said.

Then the phone rang again. She had rehearsed this one, too.

"Hi, Polly," Eddie said.

"Oh," she said. "What a surprise." (She wasn't to give away who it was on the phone. That was one of the rules. "Don't say his name, just have the call," the teacher had said. "We don't need to know who, or what it's about.")

"Yeah," he said, "we get to make just one long-distance call."

"I've got your things," she said. "We're, you know, taking care of it this afternoon. Your mother, me, your father even, Saul—"

"And Merrit?"

"Him, too."

"Well, good."

"I miss you."

"Yeah, I miss me, too."

"You know what I've been doing? I've been lying on the floor of your room, and I've been making phone calls."

"That's unusual?"

"It's the kind of phone calls I've been making."

"Dialing for Dollars?"

"1-900-555-HUNK."

"What does that mean?"

"Dirty phone calls."

"Oh, Polly."

"Dirty homosexual phone calls."

"With women?"

"No, not with women. With men."

"Don't you have enough trouble with men?"

"Straight men. These men were gay. They said."

"Oh," Eddie said.

"Well, goddamnit, I got lonely, and you—well, I guess I don't have to remind you what happened with you. So I called this service. Just to talk. It was either that or Dial-a-Confession. Sometimes I scare them away. Once I gave my number to a guy, he called me up and tried to get sexy."

"I'll deck him."

"Don't bother. Anyway. A lot of guys were sympathetic. You know, they'd lost roommates, too. And I learned a few things."

"Like what?"

"Like I learned that if you ask a man, any man, about the size of his dick, he'll tell you it's eight inches long. I mean, unless it's possible that every gay man in the New York City area is equally hung."

"Polly, what did you want?"

"Well, I've figured out what I'm going to do. I'm going to leave. I'm going to go to California."

"You're taking the cats?"

"I'm saying good-bye to you now, because I'm leaving. I've got this frequent flyer ticket somewhere, from my father, months ago he mailed it. It's under all my stuff, lost in a corner of the room. It was meant as an inducement to go home to Cleveland for the weekend. But I was thinking maybe San Diego. Because, you know, I found out something I had not anticipated. Getting and wanting are really the same in the end. I saw what happened to you."

"You won't avoid it out in California. People die, wherever."

"Yeah, well, not like you. And anyway, I'm scaling back my expectations. But listen, I wanted to ask you. I mean, listen, I had nothing to do with what happened."

"What happened?"

"What happened to you."

"You mean I got AIDS."

"Nothing to do with me, really. Not that it matters. But it really did have nothing—"

"Nothing at all."

"I couldn't have—"

"Done anything at all. Except what you did. You were there."

"Yeah, I know. I know I was there."

"And that was enough."

"It was?"

"Sure it was."

"Because I've had this feeling. You know, that—"

"Hey babe. Relax."

"You think?"

"I think. Listen, they're signaling me, you see, it's a pay phone and there's a line. All right? Good-bye."

Polly said, "Good-bye," and hung up the phone. Then she picked up her keys from the trolley and the knapsack, but before she left, she stopped at the door. What was she forgetting? She looked out at the audience. She had the shoes, she had her keys, she had her cigarettes. She had a subway token, in the pocket of her coat. What else did she need? She was going to Eddie's service, she needed—

"Oh God, Polly."

She put down the knapsack, opened it up, looked inside. She walked from one side of the room to the other. She went to the door, looked out into the hall. She ran back to the center of the room, and stopped.

She said, "My name is Polly Plugg. This is the life I am having. This is my life," she said, going to the windows, checking the ledges. She moved very slowly around the room, then more quickly, then slowly again. "I am feeling this way now because of how my parents raised me, in a certain place and time, in this century, America. I have these feelings. It's heredity, and it's environment, and I believe I have free will within certain limitations. I am free to act within those parameters."

She got down on her hands and knees.

"I have political beliefs," she said out loud. Searching on the floor, she carried on the rest of her monologue silently, in her head. "I grew up with a certain understanding of myself as female, and American. I have this peculiar relationship to my genitals, and my body grew a certain way, and I have become attracted to a various array of people, based on how I was afforded love when I was growing up."

She said "growing up" out loud. She crawled toward the trolley, carefully holding up her skirt and moving on her kneecaps so as not to get too dirty.

"And if my friend has died," she thought, "if Eddie died and I have this response, I have a certain kind of physical response, emotional response, and it's because of how we interacted according to the lives we led and who we were in the world."

She saw the canister under the trolley, and shouted.

"Who we were in the world," she said, out loud. She got to her feet, set the container on top of the trolley, brushed her knees, straightened her dress. "I'm beautiful, and sensual, and intelligent, and I know who I am in the world."

Her knees took a lot of rubbing. She had caught the hem of her dress on a nail and pulled a thread.

"He was Eddie Socket," she said silently, standing in the center of the room. It was her moment. She had earned it. Now she stood very still, and had her moment. She thought, *My name is Polly Plugg.* She looked at the audience. *I'm beautiful. And if I have a certain chemical and emotional response to Eddie's death, then it's because of all these things. And when he died my cells were readjusted, rearranged, and all the cells in all the world were rearranged, and now the energy that he released has been reapportioned, like an excess of profit redistributed among the needy. Eddie's energy. My cells. His cells.*

She took up the knapsack, the canister, and left the room. She reached the hall, she heard the teacher speak. He said, "I have no criticism."

The Art of Losing

I didn't have to end that relationship, because everybody died. Oh, Merrit didn't die, and I didn't die. But everybody else. We were just the last two remaining pieces of the puzzle. We fit together, but it didn't matter anymore; we had no context, no landscape, no frame. I try to explain this to Merrit. We're having lunch. Today is the day we're burying Eddie, so to speak. We're spreading his ashes later; now we're sitting at the table in the kitchen that used to be mine, eating hummus. I got it from a Middle Eastern restaurant, somewhere nearby. We're eating it out of a tin. I'm talking, and Merrit is nodding, quietly grunting, tearing pita bread into flat beige strips, which he dips in the hummus. He flicks green flecks of food from his fingers nervously, and eats. He says he still loves me, "in spite of it all," but that's not very reassuring. Then he breaks his tooth, while I'm lamenting the loss of the kitchen, my favorite room in the house, which Merrit is having remodeled. He wants to buy new appliances, throw out Rose, the old white enameled stove, take down the big wooden cabinets, put in Formica and fiberglass.

"I love this room," I say, "it gets the light, and the floor creaks underneath your feet, and it's spare, and masculine. Like you, I guess. Is that too absurd? The room reminds me of you."

Then Merrit's mouth goes crunch. He holds his jaw still, and puts his hand to his chin. He's gotten a haircut today, for the service, and he's wearing a sweater I don't recognize. It has blue and green stripes, against black, and it buttons up the front. The buttons are shiny, and brass. It isn't his style at all.

"That's it," he says.

"That's what?"

"Christ, I'm getting old."

"What happened?"

He moves his jaw slowly, in circles, and, putting two careful fingers in his mouth, pulls out a gray-white, smooth porcelain chip, with a raw, jagged edge.

I say, "That's kind of intimate."

"It's just a tooth," he says. "I just had it filled."

I take the small piece of bone.

"It's sort of like holding—" I say. "I don't know." I put it back on the table. "I don't like it."

Merrit scoops it into his palm, along with the pit of an olive. "I broke it on that," he says, dropping the tooth, the olive pit, the rest of the bread into the tin, which he folds in half and tosses in the garbage. "Do I need a tie for Eddie?" he asks, leaving the room.

"Doesn't it hurt?"

"It's mostly filling already. Now I'll have to get it capped."

"Leave it to me to offer you food riddled with dangerous alien objects. An olive pit. I ought to get my money back. Hell, I ought to sue."

"I never met his family," he says, shouting across the hall. "Will they require a tie?"

"His mother is kind of butch," I say. "His father is hollow, and scared. I hardly know them at all. His roommate's kind of sweet, and maybe a little flamboyant. The countercultural thing. She's trying too hard. Green fingernails, kind of like Sally Bowles. Her name is Polly Plugg. All right? She's just a kid, a nice girl from Ohio. No, you don't need a tie. For Eddie? He could hardly ever tuck in his shirt. It's not exactly formal."

"I don't understand how suddenly his family emerges, out of nowhere."

"They've been around," I say, wiping the kitchen table, from habit, the once and future wife. "You're the one who hasn't been around."

"He was your friend, mostly," Merrit says, coming back into the kitchen. I'm rinsing the sponge in the sink.

"Right, and you only slept with him.'"

"How is this tie?" he asks me, trying to change the subject. I turn around, my back to the sink, and pointedly say, "The sweater is nice." I mean, it came from a boy, some boy, all right? I know what Merrit buys for himself.

But he's still being coy. "What about the tie?" he says.

"I hate the tie," I say. Then I remember his mouth. "Aren't you hurting at all?"

"I can feel the hole with my tongue," he says, undoing his tie. It's draped around his neck. "Why don't you pick one for me?" he says.

But I want to play doctor, or nurse. I say, "Open your mouth, I want to look."

I put my hands on his beautiful cheeks, and tip his head way back. He drops his jaw, and points with his tongue. I remember his tongue.

"I don't see anything."

"I told you, there's nothing to see."

"Where'd the sweater come from?"

"Is that what this is about?"

I've got his head in my hands, I could be vicious now. But I let him go. "Oh God," I say, "I miss this."

"Miss what?"

"You know, having a person around to whom to open your mouth and say, 'Look up inside, and tell me what you see.' Being that person. It isn't the sex that I miss, or anything else. There wasn't any sex. It's this, just staring into your mouth. You know what I mean?"

"You left."

"That's not the point."

"I think it is."

"Well, there we are. We couldn't agree."

"What about the tie?"

"All your ties are terrible."

"Are we going to have to talk to his parents or anything?" Merrit says, leaving the kitchen again. "Eddie and I were not exactly very close, after all. You were the Florence Nightingale."

"Tending to my lover's mistakes."

"We're not getting into that."

"Really, I wonder why I ever got involved. He was your trick,

270

right? He shows up on the doorstep, you were away, and suddenly I've got this maternal impulse?"

"Well, you knew him first." He's back in the room. "How's this?"

"God, he was only a boy."

"That boy was twenty-five," he says.

"Twenty-eight."

"And it's not like I defiled him or anything. We just had a couple of nights. I thought the reason you left was so we wouldn't fight anymore. Why are we fighting?"

"We're not fighting. You're feeling guilty."

"I wasn't under any obligation to visit."

"Just because he was dying."

"So was everyone else."

"You didn't have sex with everyone else."

"If I had to go to the hospital room of every man I've slept with in the past ten years . . ."

"Yeah, well, maybe you should have thought of that ten years ago."

"Are we getting political now? Just because you were a virgin until the age of thirty-seven."

"Excuse me, twenty-nine. As opposed to the whore of Babylon at twelve."

"Which isn't the truth about me. But anyway, I'm not sick."

"And neither am I."

"So, there you are. So don't play 'You Were Trashier' with me, Saul Isenberg. For that matter, Eddie hardly did anything at all, with anyone. And now look at him. So what about the tie? Come on, we'll be late."

All right, so I step away, he stands in the light. His haircut emphasizes the gray in his hair. He's newly shaven, and immaculate, in pleated wool trousers, a button-down shirt, silk socks, and penny loafers, and a delicate old flat-faced watch with a brown leather wristband, classic Merrit, but older. For the first time since I've known him, I think, he looks his age.

I tell him the tie's okay. I mean, I have to let go. He wants to leave the house in a sweater like that, it isn't for me to deride or censure his looks. I say, "The tie is wonderful," he smiles. He's easily pleased. At least, in some respects. He says, "I'm ready." He wants to know where we're going. The whole thing has been my suggestion, after all. But he does seem to want to go.

I get my coat, I look around the kitchen. I'm watching the old wooden clock that ticks on the windowsill, wondering where it will end up after the renovation. I say, "His father's a priest, a bishop, or something. Right? His mother's agnostic, she says. His roommate's Jewish. Everyone had a suggestion to make, including Eddie, who wanted to be buried in Woodlawn, no kidding, he actually left those instructions. As if there were room there for him. But Polly's suggestion was almost as good—she wanted his ashes to be spread at the New York Pavilion of the 1964 World's Fair."

"In Queens?"

"That's what she said. Then she suggested that we drop him into the Hudson, just below Riverside Park, where Donald Trump now wants to build his building so tall it takes you twenty minutes just to reach the lobby from your panoramic view of Jersey. So we settled on that. At least it isn't Queens."

"You're making this up."

"Which part of it sounds invented?'"

Merrit has his keys, he's wearing his blue cashmere coat with the Joan Crawford shoulders. I mean, it's November, just the first, and finally cold.

"Ready, dove?" he says.

"Don't change this room too much," I say.

"We're going to be late."

"Don't put in carpeting, please, or something like that. You have to promise. Merrit?"

"I promise," Merrit says, taking my arm.

We've been to a lot of funerals in the past few years, Merrit and me, but neither one of us knows quite what to make of Eddie's. It's held on the site of the old Penn Central Railroad yards, which have, until recently, been a monument to industrial waste. Old trains and rusting roundhouses, and turntables set in the ground, and railroad cars have lain abandoned for years. But now they've already started to strip away the debris, in order to construct their postindustrial worlds. It's just a lengthy strip of valuable real estate, waiting to be exploited.

The family and friends are standing in front of a chain link fence, below the West Side Highway, right on the river. Eddie's mother is there, and his father, whom I haven't met. They stand on either side of Polly, who smiles at me, but not at Merrit. No one makes introductions. Merrit clears his throat; we stand awkwardly, long

272

enough for me to decide that Eddie looks like his father, after all, sort of Mr. Peepers crossed with Montgomery Clift. Of course, his mother is beautiful, which is not a surprise. Eddie was right about that.

Polly speaks first. "I've got him," she says, shouldering her knapsack. She points to a hole in the fence. "We have to climb through there."

His mother, wearing black slacks, and chewing on her nails, goes first. She seems distracted, and a little bit nervous. Eddie said that people made her uncomfortable. He said she was Mary Tyler Moore, in *Ordinary People*, icy, and dissatisfied. But that could describe any one of us this afternoon, and Mary Tyler Moore would never say "shit," as Eddie's mother does, when she catches her sleeve on the fence. I decide that I like her. "He's laughing at us," she says. "He knew about the goddamned fence."

Polly shrugs, and follows. Then me and Merrit. Then Eddie's father behind. He's wearing too many layers of clothing, as if prepared for a storm, and staring at his feet. The ground is still soft, and the dirt, which is black, clings to everyone's shoes.

Merrit says to me softly, "He looks just like his mother."

"Not at the moment, he doesn't."

"You know what I mean."

"I think he looks more like his father. All but the nose."

"They don't look married."

"They're not. I mean, they are, but they're not."

"Sort of like us."

"Oh God, I hope not. They've been married thirty years. Eddie said they can't give it up."

"I told you, just like us," Merrit says, holding my arm.

Then Polly gets to the water. Eddie's mother stands beside her, and his father stands next to Merrit, who doesn't let go of my arm. I think, again, he holds me here, when people have died, but it's sweet, I like it today. Polly turns to Eddie's mother, who shrugs, and says, "Who's first?"

"Hold this," Polly says, passing Eddie's remains to his mother. Then she opens her knapsack and pulls out Eddie's sneakers. No kidding, his pink high-topped sneakers.

Merrit says, "Jesus."

His mother says, "This is a joke."

His father doesn't say a word.

"He asked if we could dump these in the river," Polly says. She gives the shoes to Merrit. "He would have wanted you . . . " she says, and doesn't finish.

And I mean, you have to understand, the look on Merrit's face. He takes the shoes, I think that it's a good thing that he never visited Eddie. He holds them like—well, if there were some way to modify "gingerly" almost to the point of losing it. I think, he'll pass them on to me, and then we'll have this game of hot potatoes. But he turns to Eddie's father, and gives one of them to him. They both hold on to their shoe, looking equally nervous, and young. Eddie's father looks particularly touching. He's the sort of man who probably played stickball in the streets of Astoria once in high-topped sneakers. Though certainly not pink ones.

Then Eddie's mother opens the canister holding her son's remains. "Do we all put a hand in this, or what?"

"I think not," Polly says, simply.

"Let's get this over with," his mother says.

Without looking at her husband, or Merrit, or me, she puts her hand inside the white container and undoes the tie on the plastic lining. Her fingers are long and masculine, and her knuckles are bruised. When she comes out with a handful of Eddie, and sprinkles him into the Hudson, to float downstream to the bay with all the turds from Yonkers and the old Chevrolet submerged in the water just below the bank and the tugboats and the catfish and the bass, some of the ash gets under her nails, where it will linger for days. She doesn't waste any time. She dips her hand again and again into the bone chips and ash, and pulls Eddie out in white fistfuls. Some of him blows in the breeze against Polly's dress. Some dapples his mother's slacks.

Merrit unloads his shoe. It falls in the water with a plop. The other shoe follows, from nowhere, it seems, for Eddie's father has hardly moved. When the canister is empty, we stare at each other, embarrassed. It is the worst kind of loss. We stand around Eddie's mother, unable to move, each of us hating the moment, staring at the empty canister.

"Somebody must have a poem or something," I say.

Merrit lets go of my arm. Eddie's mother stares dumbly at the white container in her arms, which she cradles very gently. Polly sweeps her hair out of her eyes. Merrit turns away, and walks slowly east. Eddie's father clears his throat as if to speak, but he doesn't. I feel so empty, so fucking bereft. For this is absurd, an absolute loss, but not in a way that would have made Eddie respond, or giggle, or gloat. He would have felt the hollow I feel now in the back of my head, the aching up-all-night cavernous feeling of emptiness. Not even pain.

*   *   *

Back at Merrit's apartment, Merrit heats milk on the stove. "Good old Rose," I say, watching Merrit lift the pan and pour it off into a chipped mug. "So throwaway chic," I say, wanting to comment on something. We sit at the table, and pass the mug back and forth, taking tiny sips. I hear Merrit's lips and tongue make a delicate sound against the side of the mug. Then I remember something.

"Merrit," I say, "what's today?"

"November the first."

"It is. Of course it is."

"Of course it is what?"

"Mather, it's our anniversary."

Merrit takes another sip of milk. He looks at his hands. I say, "What the hell," and kiss him on the cheek, which is cold.

"Four years?" he says.

"Six."

"Six years. I don't remember anything."

"You're getting old."

"Don't remind me." He hands me the cup. "Well, then," he says. "How shall we celebrate?"

"We could have sex, and both of us could like it."

"You don't give up."

"I guess this is it, then," I say, getting up from the table. I lay my hand on the back of Merrit's neck, and smooth a tuft of hair where, night after night, I had once laid my cheek. I look around the kitchen, which is too familiar, mine but no longer mine. So many things are lost, I think. Door keys are lost, and wallets are lost, and houses and cities are lost. Friends are lost, too, eleven in the past nine months, and lovers are lost. Even grief is lost, finally, and then you mourn the loss of that. I pull my hand away from Merrit's neck, and walk around the room, touching everything. The clocks, the pinewood cabinets. The old white china, and the pantry door. The floor creaks comfortably under my feet. I move around and around the room, as if to memorize the final setting, the placement of objects, Merrit's arrangement of all the things of his life. Even losing Merrit, I think, is easy enough, if only I put him in his place in the room, among the fixtures of a life that I no longer lead, there at the table, preserved, wearing a sweater that doesn't belong, nursing a tooth, and drinking heated milk.

New York City
1985–1988

John Weir grew up outside of Califon, New Jersey, with horses and dogs, and a couple of cats. He has lived in New York City for ten years. This is his first novel. His writing has appeared in *7 Days* and *Harper's* magazine.

JOHN C. MAXWELL

LEADER SHIFT

WORKBOOK

MAKING THE ESSENTIAL CHANGES
EVERY LEADER MUST EMBRACE

TWELVE LESSONS

HarperCollins
LEADERSHIP

LEADERSHIFT WORKBOOK
© 2019 by John C. Maxwell

Published by HarperCollins Leadership, an imprint of HarperCollins.

Published in association with Yates & Yates, www.yates2.com.

Scripture quotations are from *The Message*. Copyright © by Eugene H. Peterson 1993, 1994, 1995, 1996, 2000, 2001, 2002. Used by permission of NavPress. All rights reserved. Represented by Tyndale House Publishers, Inc.

ISBN 978-0-310-10988-4 (softcover)
ISBN 978-0-310-10989-1 (ebook)

First Printing September 2019 / Printed in the United States of America

CONTENTS

Acknowledgments 5

LESSON 1: Why Every Leader Needs to Leadershift 7

LESSON 2: Soloist to Conductor 23

LESSON 3: Goals to Growth 39

LESSON 4: Perks to Price 57

LESSON 5: Pleasing People to Challenging People 71

LESSON 6: Maintaining to Creating 89

LESSON 7: Ladder Climbing to Ladder Building 107

LESSON 8: Directing to Connecting 125

LESSON 9: Team Uniformity to Team Diversity 143

LESSON 10: Positional Authority to Moral Authority 159

LESSON 11: Trained Leaders to Transformational Leaders 175

LESSON 12: Career to Calling 193

About the Author 211

Endnotes 213

ACKNOWLEDGMENTS

I want to say thank you to Charlie Wetzel and the rest of the team who assisted me with the formation and publication of this book. And to the people in my organizations who support it. You all add incredible value to me, which allows me to add value to others. Together, we're making a difference!

WHY EVERY LEADER NEEDS TO
LEADERSHIFT

Change or die.

I've been wanting to write a book on the idea of *leadershifts* for a long time because a lot has changed in the decades I've been studying and practicing leadership. In the 1970s when I was new to my career, I could find very few books on leadership. Back then, *management* ruled the business world and Peter Drucker was the king. That started to change toward the end of the 1980s, as a few authors were starting to write leadership books. People eagerly bought and read them. Why? Because they could feel that life was moving faster, change was becoming normal, and they needed a way to navigate the world's complexities, which were becoming more challenging.

People need to learn leadership to be successful. The principles of management, which had been taught for years, depended on stability and known factors. As expressed by Eric J. McNulty, director of research at the National Preparedness Leadership Initiative:

> Management systems and processes tend to be linear. They assume that similar inputs will result in similar outputs. In many situations, this

holds true. Leadership, however, requires a more nuanced view of the world because it involves people: what motivates them, what their interests are, and how engaged they become. Mechanical systems may be linear but as soon as the human element becomes involved the system becomes both complex and adaptive.[1]

Where management took stability for granted, leadership provides principles that work in the face of the unknown. Back in the eighties, people were looking for leaders to guide them, and people running organizations recognized the need to become leaders themselves. As they began to apply leadership principles to their world, they thrived. That's why for the last thirty years, leadership has ruled the business world.

FAST IS FASTER—FORWARD IS SHORTER

As fast as the pace was in the 1980s, when I look back it seems slow by today's standards. Life moves *much* faster now. The rate at which we must deal with change and uncertainty can seem insane.

For several years one of my organizations, the John Maxwell Team, has asked me to do short videos they post daily called Minute with Maxwell. My team will set me up in front of a camera and then give me a word or phrase, asking me to react to it or teach on it for a minute or so. It's fun and the video gets posted online as a kind of mentoring moment. Recently, for one of these sessions, the phrase they gave me was *fast forward*. What immediately came to my mind were the words *faster* and *shorter*. Here's what I mean.

The future seems to be coming at us faster than ever. It is not going to slow down. Would anybody seriously consider the idea that tomorrow will be at a slower pace than today? Technology, social media, and the rate of change will never allow that to happen. To go forward, we need to move faster. And as leaders, we need to stay ahead, we need to see more than others, and we need to see before others.

Traditionally, in athletic races, the first three finishers are recognized, and all three receive prizes. Today, outside of sports, it seems as though only winners get recognized and rewarded. As the saying goes, coming in second means you're the first loser. That's why speed and agility are so important.

Forward is also shorter. As a young leader, I was taught that to be effective in leading my organization, I should create a long-range plan of ten years, a medium-range plan of five years, and a short-range plan of two years. That seems absurd now. Today a long-range plan may be two years. Technology and innovation move so quickly that everything is going forward in a shorter time frame. As leaders, we can't drag our feet or take too long making assessments. We have to change, reread our situation, and change again. And *continue* changing.

CONSIDER

In what ways do you feel the speed of life? How does it challenge you or negatively impact you?

_____

_____

_____

_____

How does a leader do more than just hang on and survive in such an environment? The key is to learn how to continually make *leadershifts*. What is a leadershift? It is an ability and willingness to make a leadership change that will positively enhance organizational and personal growth.

Educator and author Bruna Martinuzzi cited a study conducted by an organization called the Economist Intelligence Unit. It identified the top three leadership qualities that will be important in the years ahead: "the ability to motivate staff (35 percent); the ability to work well across cultures (34 percent); and the ability to facilitate change (32 percent)." All three of these qualities require adaptability. Martinuzzi likened this to the Chinese proverb that says that the wise adapt themselves to circumstances, as water molds itself to the pitcher. Perhaps at no other time in recent history has adaptability been more important than it is now. "*Adaptability*—the ability to change (or to be changed) to fit new circumstances—is a crucial skill for leaders."[2]

A more recent study conducted by Right Management and published in *The Flux Report* made it clear that the need for adaptability is only increasing. They asserted that 91 percent of future recruiting in the workplace will be based on people's ability to deal with change and uncertainty.[3]

LEADERSHIFTING IS THE ABILITY AND WILLINGNESS TO MAKE A LEADERSHIP CHANGE THAT WILL POSITIVELY ENHANCE ORGANIZATIONAL AND PERSONAL GROWTH.

Good leaders adapt. They shift. They don't remain static because they know the world around them does not remain static. This has always been true, but it's never been more obvious than today, nor has the ability to change quickly been more important. Adaptable leaders who make leadershifts lean into uncertainty and deal with it head on. I like what Paul Karofsky, executive director emeritus of Northeastern University's Center for Family Business, said about this, though he used the word *ambiguity* instead of *uncertainty*:

> Ambiguity may keep people up nights, but anyone seeking exquisite simplicity in his or her career ought to look for a non-leadership position.
>
> Leaders, by definition, have followers. Followers need direction. Direction requires decision-making. Decision-making requires consideration of options. And consideration of options involves dealing with uncertainty.[4]

If you want to be successful as a leader, you need to learn to become comfortable with uncertainty and make shifts continually. You need to be flexible and deal with uncertainty without losing focus. Leaders who leadershift must be like water. They have to be fluid. Water finds a way, then makes a way. First it changes with its circumstances. The environment dictates the change. But moving water is also forceful. It first moves around an object, but at the same time it begins moving the object. It can wear down solid rock over time. A seemingly small shift can make a big difference. Simple and obvious it may be. Trivial it is not.

ASSESS

On a scale of one (poor) to ten (fantastic), how comfortable are you with uncertainty normally?

1   2   3   4   5   6   7   8   9   10

On a scale of one (poor) to ten (fantastic), how flexible are you naturally?

1   2   3   4   5   6   7   8   9   10

On a scale of one (poor) to ten (fantastic), how well are you able to remain focused when facing uncertainty?

1   2   3   4   5   6   7   8   9   10

On a scale of one (poor) to ten (fantastic), how confident are you while changing and dealing with uncertainty?

1   2   3   4   5   6   7   8   9   10

CONSIDER

How do you think these characteristics will impact your ability to leadershift?

_____

_____

_____

_____

_____

_____

_____

_____

The truth is this: *every advance you make as a leader will require a leadershift that changes the way you think, act, and lead.* If you want to be an effective leader, you must leadershift. You cannot be the same, think the same, and act the same if you hope to be successful in a world that does not remain the same.

As Malcolm Gladwell said, "That's your responsibility as a person, as a human being—to constantly be updating your positions on as many things as possible. And if you don't contradict yourself on a regular basis, then you're not *thinking*."[5]

YOU CANNOT BE THE SAME, THINK THE SAME, AND ACT THE SAME IF YOU HOPE TO BE SUCCESSFUL IN A WORLD THAT DOES NOT REMAIN THE SAME.

Leadershifting moves us forward in the face of the natural temptation to be mentally rigid. It prompts us to become more innovative and get out of our comfort zones, question conventional wisdom, and welcome change. Every leadershift you make has the potential to make you a better leader.

ARE YOU READY TO SHIFT AS A LEADER?

Before I talk about the practices involved in leadershifting, I want to lay the groundwork by describing the mind-set needed to leadershift.

ASSESS

YES	NO	
☐	☐	Are you ready to change?
☐	☐	Are you willing to start asking more questions instead of giving more answers?

❑ ❑ Are you willing to become a better listener?

❑ ❑ Are you willing to become a better observer?

❑ ❑ Are you willing to rely more on your intuition and your creativity?

If you answered no to any of these questions, you are resisting change and will need to adopt a new mindset in order to leadershift.

Leadershifting will require you to rely on values, principles, and strategy, but it will also push you to rely on innovation, to seek out options, to harness creativity. You'll also need to let go of some things and be dedicated to getting better.

Leadershifting is not easy, especially when you first start doing it. Often you leave behind something that has worked to pursue something untested. You'll have to deal with the tension between the stability that gives security and the adaptability that opens up opportunity. That will empower you to get better, to become someone new before you can grow into something new. The desire to improve will drive you to keep learning. But here's the good news: learning to leadershift will make you a better leader!

YOU'LL HAVE TO DEAL WITH THE TENSION BETWEEN THE STABILITY THAT GIVES SECURITY AND THE ADAPTABILITY THAT OPENS UP OPPORTUNITY.

HOW TO LEADERSHIFT

As we move forward in this book, I'll take you through eleven major leadershifts I've made in my leadership journey. But before we do that, I want to teach you seven things you must do to leadershift successfully. Embrace these practices daily, and you will be ready to face every leadershift situation with flexibility and confidence.

1. CONTINUALLY LEARN, UNLEARN, AND RELEARN

I've already discussed the pace at which our world is changing. I recently read an article published by the World Economic Forum that brought light to this.

> To quote Harvard Business Review's "Mind the (Skills) Gap": "The lessons learned in school can become outdated before student loans are paid off." As it points out, the skills college graduates acquire during a bachelor's degree that used to provide enough basic training to last a career, today have an expected shelf life of only five years. . . . Or, as lynda.com author Mark Niemann-Ross states bluntly: "In four years, you'll have to relearn 30% of your job."[6]

How are leaders to thrive in this environment? We must learn, unlearn, and relearn. This process is essential for leadershifting. We have to embrace change every day. We must be willing to let go of what worked yesterday and learn new ways of seeing, doing, and leading. We cannot afford to be in love with any one technology or methodology. We keep learning and changing, or our leadership dies.

2. VALUE YESTERDAY BUT LIVE IN TODAY

Baseball great Babe Ruth is rumored to have said, "Yesterday's homerun doesn't win today's game." Isn't that fantastic? It's a good reminder for us to focus on today. What we did in the past may look good on a resume, but it won't help us win today.

For years I had a sign in my office that said, "Yesterday Ended Last Night." I put it there to remind me that all the good I did yesterday won't guarantee a good day for me today, nor will all the bad that happened yesterday mean that today has to be bad. Today stands on its own. If I want a great today, I need to do what's necessary now. I can and should be grateful for yesterday, but I have to focus on today.

3. RELY ON SPEED, BUT THRIVE ON TIMING

Having to move quickly in today's climate isn't really a choice if you want to succeed. However, timing is. As a leader who leadershifts, you need to understand the context of your environment. What is happening around you determines whether you hold fast or move forward. Leading is like knowing when to eat a pear. It's said that there is only one day in the life of a pear when it is perfect to eat. As a leader you must be able to recognize the right timing of leadershift moments. When does a team member need an encouraging pep talk and when do they need to be challenged to step up? When is the right time to add a new product or to retire an existing one that has already seen its best days? When should your organization use some of its cash to seize an opportunity, and when is that a bad idea? For leaders, timing is critical.

4. SEE THE BIG PICTURE AS THE PICTURE KEEPS GETTING BIGGER

My journey leading people really began when I first understood that everything rises and falls on leadership. This truth became the foundation upon which I built my life. It continues to be the catalyst for my personal development and my training of others.

When people started asking me to speak on leadership, I didn't have much to teach. Later when I decided to write a book on the subject, I thought it would be my only one. Now I've been leading people and training leaders for more than forty-five years, and my perspective has been enlarged tremendously. The more I learn about the subject, the more I recognize I don't know enough about it. The more leadership experiences I gain, the more I realize I would benefit from more experience. There is no finish line when it comes to improving, and there is no complete picture of leadership that can be mastered. As long as I'm growing, my leadership picture will continue to enlarge. If you keep growing, yours will too.

I like to think of this process as layered learning. Each time we learn a new lesson and connect it with the many things we've already learned on the same subject, we gain depth and we see more of the big picture. This process requires time; no one can learn all the lessons at once. Putting together lessons requires intentionality, but when you do, you expand your knowledge.

5. LIVE IN TODAY BUT THINK ABOUT TOMORROW

Leaders have a natural bias toward action. They have to be proactive today for the sake of tomorrow. However, the longevity of their leadership is determined by how they think and see the future. Staying ahead of the team comes from thinking ahead of the team. If you think ahead, you can stay ahead. As political columnist George Will said, "The future has a way of arriving unannounced." We cannot recover yesterday, but tomorrow is ours to win or lose.

How can we do that as leaders? What can we do today to ensure we have what we need to lead tomorrow? We have to practice what I call advance attraction, which I discovered in the 1980s. I concluded that I could experience a positive future only if I had a good dream and a good team. At that time, my dream excited me, but my team did not. How was I going to attract the team I needed to fulfill my dream?

The first step toward getting a better team for the future was to know what I wanted and needed. I started by writing down the qualities of the team I wanted to have. This developed an increased awareness in me that promoted advance attraction. Here's how this works.

> When you know who you are and you know what you want, you then know the kind of people you will attract, and the things you will discover.
> Your mind will think things that will help you get what you want.
> Your eyes will see things that will help you get what you want.
> Your heart will feel things that will help you get what you want.
> Your attitude will believe things that will help you get what you want.
> Your mouth will say things that will help you get what you want.
> Your actions will attract things that will help you get what you want.

As I attracted and discovered the kinds of team members I needed to realize my dream, I began to experience positive results. Today I'm abundantly reaping the benefits of this leadershift.

6. Move Forward Courageously in the Midst of Uncertainty

Life expands or shrinks in proportion to our courage. When leaders fail to make a necessary leadershift because of fear or uncertainty, it only increases their fear, which results in frustration. The greater the inaction of the leaders, the more opportunities they lose because opportunities are always surrounded by uncertainty. All good things include uncertainty, and overcoming uncertainty requires courage.

I like what Brad Lomenick said about courage in his book *The Catalyst Leader*. He quoted my friend Andy Stanley, a wonderful leader who founded North Point Church. Andy was speaking to Catalyst leaders, but his words also described leaders who leadershift:

Many, many great things have begun with a single act of courage, through-out history and today. A person steps out and makes one courageous de-cision and that one domino starts many other dominoes falling. We have to step out and take that first step, and we may never know the ripple effect of that one courageous decision. Catalyst leaders—your decision to do something courageous may result in something greater than you ever imagined. Step out. . . .

Fear in leadership usually is connected to the uncertainty about the future. But uncertainty about the future is never going to go away. I tell leaders all the time—uncertainty is why there are leaders. Uncertainty gives you job security. Wherever there is uncertainty, there will always be a need for leaders, which means always stepping out into the unknown, always requiring courage.[7]

Betty Bender, former president of the Library Administration and Management Association, said, "Anything I've ever done that ultimately was worthwhile initial-ly scared me to death." When faced with uncertainty, as leaders we need to move forward courageously.

7. Realize Today's Best Will Not Meet Tomorrow's Challenges

If you want to become good at leadershifting, you need to keep getting better, because tomorrow's challenges will not be won with today's abilities. Here's my strategy for getting better. My goal at the end of each day is to feel satisfied be-cause I gave my very best, but my goal at the beginning of each day is to be dissat-isfied enough to try to improve on yesterday. This interplay of dissatisfaction and satisfaction creates a tension that makes me want to improve.

As I approach a new day, I try to be my best. That will make tomorrow bet-ter. The best way to have good choices tomorrow is to make the right choices to-day. The best way to realize the changes we want tomorrow is to make the needed changes today. The best way to meet the challenges of tomorrow is to do our best in the challenges of today. I can't skip today and hope tomorrow is better. So every day I ask myself, "Is this the best I can do today?" In this way, I'm following the advice of my hero and mentor John Wooden, who said to make today your masterpiece.

At the same time, I don't rest on my best. You've heard that good is the ene-my of great, but best is the enemy of better. I have to cultivate the dissatisfaction required to get better. I purposely create that tension every day. The question, "Is this the best I can do today?" helps me to make the most of today. The question, "Am I getting better?" spurs me on to change. I want to grow into tomorrow's challenges, not just go into them. If I keep getting better, I can leadershift better tomorrow. Yesterday's best is the foundation for tomorrow's improvement.

ASSESS

If you want to keep getting better so that you can become a better leadershifter, then

- *Learn something new:* Ask yourself, "When's the last time I learned something for the first time?"

  Your answer: _____

- *Try something different:* Ask yourself, "When's the last time I did something for the first time?"

  Your answer: _____

- *Find something better:* Ask yourself, "When's the last time I found something better for the first time?"

  Your answer: _____

- *See something bigger:* Ask yourself, "When's the last time I saw something bigger for the first time?"

  Your answer: _____

Keep in mind: everyone can improve, and everything can be improved. Every day has improvement possibilities. Now you understand the framework for leadershifting:

- Continually Learn, Unlearn, and Relearn
- Value Yesterday but Live in Today
- Rely on Speed but Thrive on Timing
- See the Big Picture as the Picture Keeps Getting Bigger
- Live in Today but Think About Tomorrow
- Move Forward Courageously in the Midst of Uncertainty
- Realize Today's Best Will Not Meet Tomorrow's Challenges

COMMIT

Are you willing to commit yourself to becoming someone who leadershifts? If so, sign your name to this commitment statement:

I commit myself to this process. The first leadershift I will make is in the way that I think about leadership. I will continually learn, unlearn, and relearn. I will value yesterday but live in today. I will rely on speed but thrive on timing. I will strive to see the big picture even as the picture keeps changing and getting bigger. I will live in today but think about tomorrow. And I will move forward courageously in the midst of uncertainty. I will continually make leadership changes that will positively enhance both organizational and personal growth.

_____   _____

Signature   Date

The rest of this book focuses on the most important leadershifts I have made over the years. Without a doubt, these shifts have strengthened and sustained my leadership. Each has changed my course, setting me in a new and better direction. Each has allowed me to gain new leadership territory and grow inwardly. Each has shed light on my leadership journey, and I believe they will help yours. Even a small shift can make a big difference.

However, these are *examples* of leadershifting, not a blueprint. The leadershifts you need to make will be unique to your journey. While it's true that some of yours may be similar to mine, many will not be. But don't forget: *every advance you make as a leader will require a leadershift that changes the way you think, act, and lead.* When you make a leadershift, it will make you a better leader.

As you go through this workbook, you will need to continually shift from action to reflection. I will ask questions and present challenges so that your best leader can emerge. The leadershifts in this workbook will not take you from bad to good. They will take you from good to better. If you try to make some small shift in that direction every day, you can and will reach your leadership potential.

WHY EVERY LEADER NEEDS TO
LEADERSHIFT

DISCUSSION QUESTIONS

1. What causes you the greatest frustration when it comes to the need for speed and innovation in the workplace? Why?

2. Do you tend to be a proactive catalyst for change or a reactive adapter to change? How does this impact your leadership?

3. Which of the seven daily practices listed below do you think will be easiest for you to adopt? How will it help you?

   - Continually Learn, Unlearn, and Relearn
   - Value Yesterday but Live in Today
   - Rely on Speed but Thrive on Timing
   - See the Big Picture as the Picture Keeps Getting Bigger
   - Live in Today but Think About Tomorrow
   - Move Forward Courageously in the Midst of Uncertainty
   - Realize Today's Best Will Not Meet Tomorrow's Challenges

4. Which of the seven will be the most difficult to adopt? Why?

5. In what area of your current leadership are you sensing a need to make a leadershift? Why do you believe you need to make a change? How are you hoping change will help you?

NOTES

SOLOIST TO
CONDUCTOR

THE FOCUS SHIFT

One is too small a number to achieve greatness.

THE LAW OF SIGNIFICANCE

One of the first and most important shifts anyone must make to become a leader is from soloist to conductor. You can be a successful person on your own, but not a successful leader. I began to learn this lesson and make this shift in 1974 when I heard Zig Ziglar for the first time. Zig, who later became a good friend, made a positive impact on millions of lives, and mine was one of them.

That first time I went to see him speak, I was mesmerized. He was so dynamic. I had been trained to speak and had been speaking for about five years, but Zig was different. He moved back and forth on the stage. His delivery was distinctive with his Southern drawl. He paced his words for impact. He had charm. At one point, he even knelt to make a point and connect with us.

I loved everything about what he did that day, but what made the greatest impression on me was a statement he made. It became the catalyst for taking my leadership mind-set from soloist to conductor. Zig said, "You can get everything in life you want if you will just help enough other people get what they want."

Those words struck me like a bolt of lightning. Immediately I realized that my leadership focus was wrong. I was like a soloist who wanted the entire orchestra to serve me and my agenda. Instead, I needed to act like a conductor who worked to bring out the best in everyone around me. My agenda needed to change to how I could help others, not just myself.

Over the next couple of years, my focus shifted from me to we and I made a discovery. My increased effort to first focus on others and add value to them increased the energy of those I led—and it increased my energy while I was leading them. That's when I discovered that it's wonderful when the people help their leader, but it's even more wonderful when the leader helps the people.

> **MY INCREASED EFFORT TO FIRST FOCUS ON OTHERS
> AND ADD VALUE TO THEM INCREASED THE ENERGY OF THOSE I LED—
> AND IT INCREASED MY ENERGY WHILE I WAS LEADING THEM.**

Recently I read an article about four musical soloists who have transitioned to become conductors. South Korean Han-Na Chang, who has enjoyed a successful international career as a cellist, recently became a full-time conductor. When asked why she began conducting, she replied:

> I am drawn to the great symphonic and operatic literature, and also by the music-making and collaboration that exists between the conductor and the orchestra. . . . Collaborating with the orchestra is tremendously rewarding: Every orchestra is different, so the conductor is always trying to find the most effective way of conducting that particular orchestra, in order to unite the group behind a common vision and interpretation.[1]

Chang pointed out that conducting is completely different from being a soloist. "When I play my instrument," she said, "what I think quite naturally and instantaneously translates into sound; when conducting, I'm making sound with a group of individuals. The possibilities and the potential of the sound of an orchestra are virtually limitless, and this is truly fascinating to me."

Challenges Leadershifting from Soloist to Conductor

The potential of a group is always greater than that of an individual. People working together possess limitless possibilities. They can work together to do something greater than themselves. And when they bond, they enjoy the journey of working even more. However, that doesn't mean that working together doesn't have its own challenges. When you transition from soloist to conductor, there are some realities you have to face:

1. Going Slower So You Can Go Farther

You've probably heard the old expression "it's lonely at the top" applied to leadership. But think about that statement. If you're at the top all alone, where are the people you're supposed to be leading? Shouldn't they be at the top with you? If you're at the top alone, it means you took off ahead of your people and left them behind. If you climb the peaks of success alone, you're not a leader. You're a hiker. You're a leader only if you have your people with you. Your pace will be slower, but you will journey together.

Good leaders don't go to the top alone and then yell down, "Hey, people, come on up—if you can figure out how to make the climb." They make a conscious decision to slow down. They carefully choose their steps so that they can help others make the climb with them.

Think about how this must have been for cellist Han-Na Chang when she shifted from soloist to conductor. As a musician she could pick up her instrument anytime she wanted, play any music she wanted, and do so however long she wanted. She could focus on any part of the music desired or on any aspect of her technique, with no regard for others. Now, as a conductor, she can't do that. She has to make arrangements. She has to be on other people's schedules. She has to take into consideration the abilities and personalities of a large group of people. She has to communicate her vision. And in the end, she bears responsibility for their success or failure.

As I've already mentioned, leaders have a natural bias for action. Good leaders see more than others do, and they see before others do. It's in their DNA to move quickly and decisively. So their natural inclination is often to run fast on their own, to climb as high as they can. But to lead others successfully, leaders need to travel with their people, not run or climb ahead of them.

2. RECOGNIZING THAT YOU NEED OTHERS

Another reality you must recognize when transitioning from soloist to conductor is your need for other people. You can't produce the music of an orchestra when you're trying to be a one-man (or one-woman) band. Before I heard Zig Ziglar speak and realized I needed to make a leadershift, I only thought of how people needed me. I believed I was the key to their success. But after I started focusing on helping others, I began to understand how much I needed them. Only by working together and helping one another would we be able to become successful.

Once I made that discovery, I began creating an environment where people worked together to add to one another's strengths and offset one another's weaknesses. I asked others to come alongside me and make up for my leadership deficits. I, in turn, worked to apply my strengths to their weaker areas. I made it my goal to cultivate an environment where we put completing one another ahead of competing with one another.

CONSIDER

Look at the difference between the two attitudes and mark the one on each line that most often describes you:

COMPETING
- ☐ Has a Scarcity Mind-set
- ☐ Thinks Win-Lose
- ☐ Practices Single Thinking
- ☐ Excludes Others

COMPLETING
- ☐ Has an Abundance Mind-set
- ☐ Thinks Win-Win
- ☐ Practices Shared Thinking
- ☐ Includes Others

A completing culture creates wins for everyone. It lifts morale. It encourages team members to make one another better. People enjoy working in such an environment.

As I worked to create a culture and environment where completing was valued, I better understood how I needed others. I also began enjoying what we were doing together.

3. Making the Effort to Understand Others

Many entrepreneurs and high achievers are able to work alone. Like good soloist musicians who choose to play in the subway, they can create music without the assistance of any other musicians. It's also true that some soloists are so talented that others are willing to work with them, even if the soloist is egotistical and inconsiderate. But no one can become a good conductor without making the effort to understand other people.

I have to confess, in my early years of leadership, I didn't give enough attention to the people I was leading. As a soloist leader, I thought the symphony was there simply to accompany me. I only wanted people to understand and embrace my vision, my agenda, my journey, my talents, my heart. To make the leadershift from soloist to conductor, I had to consider everyone else. I needed to understand and embrace their thoughts, desires, talents, contribution, and journey.

Several years ago I was speaking in Buenos Aires, Argentina. One evening my host took me to a large ballroom where we watched a huge exhibition of people dancing the tango. There must have been two hundred people out on the floor in beautiful costumes. They were fantastic. Their sense of movement and rhythm was wonderful. I greatly enjoyed watching them.

Years before, my wife, Margaret, and I had taken ballroom dance lessons, so I had a little bit of appreciation for how difficult dancing is. The tango looked very complicated and difficult to execute with precision. I knew that my host was an excellent dancer, so I asked him, "What enables them to dance so flawlessly and effortlessly?"

He said that the key was understanding your partner's point of view. "To be able to lead properly," he said, "you want to understand how it feels to be led. In the tango, you cannot lead without having the sense of the follower." That made sense to me. The follower has to be able to trust the leader, and she must be able to move with him in time with the music. Only together can they accomplish the dance. That cooperation and understanding also applies equally to good leadership.

4. Wanting Others to Shine More Than You Do

My host in Argentina also shared another insight about the tango that applies to leaders who shift from soloist to conductor. He explained that the dancer who leads sets up the dancer who follows for success. The leader provides the foundation and makes it possible for both of them to successfully execute the intricate serpentine steps and kicks. As a result, the follower gives the tango its full expression. The more secure and solid the leader is, the more the follower is able to shine.

Good leaders who conduct rather than go solo want the people who work with them to shine. Every day I look for opportunities to lift up people. To do it, I follow a simple formula:

- see the possibilities in all people,
- honor them in front of others,
- invite them to help achieve the vision,
- notice what they do well and compliment them, and
- thank them to make sure they know they're valued.

None of these actions takes brilliance or a high degree of skill. But they do all require intentionality. If you want to become a good conductor, give them a try. Help others to shine.

5. Helping Others to Become Better Every Day

To become a successful leadership conductor, you must go slower so you can go further, recognize that you need others, make the effort to understand others, and want others to shine more than you do. But you will also need to learn how to do things every day that help the people you lead to improve. This requires taking the focus off yourself and looking for ways you can help others reach their potential. Sometimes that can be a challenge.

A few years ago, I was getting ready to speak to a large group in Kiev, Ukraine, and my interpreter and I were in the green room getting acquainted. We had never worked together, but as we chatted, it became clear that he was familiar with me because he had read a lot of my books.

About ten minutes before I was scheduled to go out onstage, I could tell he was wanting to communicate something important to me. He said, "I know you teach a lot about leaders adding value to others, but you need to know that message will not work here. For three generations, people here have been under leadership that has taken value from them, not added value to them."

As he left to prepare for our time onstage, I sat in my chair and realized that I had a big challenge ahead of me. How could I expect the people to help others when the only model of leadership they'd ever seen had leaders who took from them and added value only to themselves? How could I connect with them?

That night I walked out onstage and asked, "How many of you are suspicious of leaders?" It looked like every hand was raised.

"How many of you have been hurt by leaders?" Once again, hands were raised everywhere. Then I said to the audience, "Everything rises and falls on leadership. For three generations, you have experienced leadership that makes everything fall. Tonight I'm going to help you learn how to help people, add value to them, and help them rise under your leadership."

I went on to give them the three questions followers ask of their leaders:

1. Do you care for me?
2. Can I trust you?
3. Can you help me?

As I said each question, I asked if it resonated with them, and each time they affirmed that it did. Making the shift so that you're doing something every day to add value to others makes good leadership possible.

REFLECT

How would the people you lead respond to these three questions? Would they say they *know* you care for them? Would they say they *know* they can trust you?

(continued)

Would they say they *know* you can help them and want to? What evidence do you have that they believe you are entirely trustworthy as a leader?

_____

_____

_____

_____

CHANGE YOUR FOCUS FROM RECEIVING TO GIVING

As I've already mentioned, as a young leader I was focused on how people could help me, not on how I could help them and add value to them. My thinking was selfish. It was also shortsighted. Having lived in a farming community early in my career, I should have known better. I should have thought about the sowing and reaping principle: sowing always precedes reaping.

As leaders, our question each day should not be, "Will I reap a harvest?" Instead, it should be, "Have I sowed seeds today?" I know—I'm changing my metaphor from music to farming, but stay with me. Said another way, am I trying to add value or take value? Am I focused on receiving or giving? As a soloist, it's very easy to make everything about myself: How am I performing? Is the orchestra making me sound good? Is my technique as good as I want it to be? Is my audience appreciating me and my performance? Is this moment helping my career?

Good leaders shift from being self-focused to others-focused. They give more than they take. They focus on sowing not reaping. As leaders, we need to maintain a seed-sowing mind-set. What does that mean? It means we should . . .

- Focus on adding value daily.
- Add as much value as possible as often as possible.
- Never wait to add value.
- Give without keeping score so motives stay pure.
- Welcome any return as an unexpected blessing.

I want to spend the remainder of this Lesson on the idea of adding value to those we "conduct." I want to drill down on each aspect of this mind-set so that you can embrace and practice it as a leader. So let's tackle each one in turn:

1. Focus on Adding Value Daily

Every day I look at my calendar and ask myself, *Where can I add value today?* This question prepares me mentally to be ready to add value to others within the framework of my day. I review the scheduled meetings and activities to discover where I can be intentional about helping people.

I also ask myself, *What additional opportunities to help others will be given to me today?* When I ask myself this question in the morning, I usually don't know what the answer will be. But by asking it, I create positive anticipation, which prepares me mentally and emotionally to seek out and identify moments when I will be able to sow positive seeds in the lives of others.

My experience over the years has convinced me that we receive what we believe, and that applies to opportunities to add value to others. Because I expect to have many opportunities, I'm able to act on them.

CONSIDER

What are you normally focused on as you begin your day? Is it on adding value and sowing seeds? Or is it on receiving value and reaping a harvest? How does this impact the opportunities you receive?

_____

_____

_____

_____

_____

_____

2. Add As Much Value As Possible As Often As Possible

It's clear that there is a direct relationship between the seeds we sow and the harvest we reap. The amount of value we add to others determines the possible return. The fewer the seeds, the smaller the harvest. The more the seeds, the greater the harvest. This seems obvious. So, I have a question for you. Why do so many people sow so few seeds? Why do people not give more generously to others? Why do people not help others more? Everyone would like to reap a great harvest. I would, wouldn't you? How can you hope to have a big return with a small investment? The foundation and core of every realized dream come from sowing positive seeds. As leaders, we must stop wishing and start working. Instead of looking for the "secret sauce" of success, we must start sowing seeds of success.

> **AS LEADERS, WE MUST STOP WISHING AND START WORKING.**
> **INSTEAD OF LOOKING FOR THE "SECRET SAUCE" OF SUCCESS,**
> **WE MUST START SOWING SEEDS OF SUCCESS.**

CONSIDER

What is preventing you from being more generous with your time and resources? What can you do immediately to change that?

_____

_____

_____

_____

_____

_____

3. NEVER WAIT TO ADD VALUE

Too many people wait to do good. It's as though they're waiting for permission. Or inspiration. But we should never delay sowing seeds that benefit others. Instead, we should follow the motto: be the first to give or add value to another person when you can.

When you add value to others—especially when you do it early and unprompted—you inspire others with your example. I know I've been inspired by the positive actions of others. For example, when my mentor Les Parrott shared with me that the reason he wrote books was to add value to people, I was inspired to start doing the same. Going back to my childhood, when I watched my father walk slowly through the crowd to touch the lives of others, I could see how people positively responded to him, and I wanted to do the same. These examples inspired me to be more giving, to sow seeds into the lives of others.

Don't hesitate to help another person by sowing a positive seed in his or her life. Add value as early and often as you can. Help others to "play music better." You just might become the leader someone remembers for encouraging them to greatness.

CONSIDER

What most often keeps you adding value to others? What small change can you make to speed up your giving?

_____

_____

_____

_____

_____

4. Give Without Keeping Score so Motives Stay Pure

I know that I've already explained how we can't reap a harvest if we don't sow seeds, and we can't get a return without first giving. But receiving should not be our motive for giving. We live in a tit-for-tat culture. People are willing to scratch our backs if we're willing to scratch their backs. As leaders who add value to others, we should never keep score. We should sow seeds because it's the right thing to do. That's the only way to be sure our motives remain pure.

My thinking has changed over the years in this area. In the beginning, I was motivated by the return I would receive. I was focused on the harvest. I already shared how Zig Ziglar's quote about helping others changed my focus. But over time, I realized that placing emphasis on the return was diminishing the joy of helping others. I was thinking about how much and how long I had to give, not on how I was helping. Besides, when you add value to others, there isn't a guaranteed return.

My attitude began shifting when I remembered the words of Jesus, who said: "Whenever you did one of these things to someone overlooked or ignored, that was me—you did it to me."[2] Because I'm a person of faith, those words convicted me. But they also assured me. God sees the value we add to others, and it's like we did it for him. That finally brought me to the correct belief about helping others—that it is the right thing to do. It's always the right thing to do—anytime, anyplace, anyone. And the right way to do it is any way you can. Any day we are giving is a good day—and we should never keep score.

5. WELCOME ANY RETURN AS AN UNEXPECTED BLESSING

When my leadership mind-set began focusing on adding value by sowing positive seeds in the lives of others, I became more creative about how I could do that. I started my career by speaking once a week to my tiny congregation. Soon I started creating resources and sharing them. In time, I added writing. I started teaching at conferences, and later I started hosting my own events. I trained leaders so that they could train the people who followed them. Beginning in 2009, I expanded to include social media. I started companies that develop leaders in businesses and corporations. And I started training coaches.

All that time, my focus was on adding value. My goal was only to sow seeds, but I have to say, the return has been incredible. The influence I have been given and the value I've added is far greater than I ever imagined it could be. And it feels as though the harvest has multiplied way beyond the seeds I've sown. That has been a great blessing. If you keep sowing seeds and you do it while focused on the giving rather than the receiving, I believe you, too, will receive a harvest of unexpected blessings.

* * *

These are my thoughts on adding value. And that's what leaders do who shift from soloist to conductor. They focus on helping others to be their best. In the end, can you be a successful person as a soloist? The answer is undoubtedly yes. Can you be a successful leader? I would say maybe, but only in a very limited way. To reach your leadership potential—and more importantly, to help others reach their individual and team potential—you need to make the shift from soloist to conductor. If you are willing to make that shift and do the work of leading others well, then you might have the opportunity to live a life like the one described by author Matthew Kelly, who wrote:

> In a land where there are no musicians;
>> In a land where there are no storytellers, teachers, and poets;
>> In a land where there are no men and women of vision and leadership;
>> In a land where there are no legends, saints, and champions;
>> In a land where there are no dreamers,
>> The people will most certainly perish.
>> But you and I, we are the music makers;
>> We are the storytellers, teachers, and poets;
>> We are the men and women of vision and leadership;
>> We are the legends, the saints, and the champions;
>> And we are the dreamers of the dreams.[3]

I would add that we are the conductors, who help others make beautiful music together.

TAKE ACTION

Become a positive conductor in the lives of others. Every day this week, focus on giving rather than receiving from others. Do that by creating a plan to add value:

- *Focus on Adding Value Daily*—What do you have that you can offer to others?

_____

_____

_____

_____

- *Add as Much Value as Possible as Often as Possible*—How will you use it to add value?

  _____

  _____

  _____

  _____

- *Never Wait to Add Value*—When will you use it?

  _____

  _____

  _____

  _____

- *Give Without Keeping Score*—How can you give generously with no thought of return?

  _____

  _____

  _____

  _____

SOLOIST TO
CONDUCTOR

THE FOCUS SHIFT

DISCUSSION QUESTIONS

1. Do you naturally think like a soloist or a conductor? What examples can you give to illustrate?

2. What do you find most rewarding about working alone? What do you find the most challenging? Why?

3. What do you find the most rewarding about working with others? What do you find the most challenging? Why?

4. In addition to adding value to others, what other actions and attitudes actively promote cooperation and collaboration among people working together?

5. What is the single greatest change you need to make in order to make the leadershift to conductor? What will you do immediately to facilitate it?

NOTES

LESSON THREE

GOALS TO
GROWTH

THE PERSONAL DEVELOPMENT SHIFT

Improving yourself is the first step in improving everything else.

UNKNOWN

When I started my leadership career, I had two goals. I wanted to help the people in my congregation, and I hoped to someday—by the end of my career—grow a church to an attendance of five hundred people. I had a pretty good sense of how to accomplish the first task. I had watched my father help people every day of my life, plus I had natural people skills. But I had no idea how to go about accomplishing the second task other than to work hard.

In *The 15 Invaluable Laws of Growth*, I wrote about a meeting I had in 1972 with Curt Kampmeier, a salesman from Success Motivation. Curt introduced me to a personal growth kit that cost a whopping $799. It took Margaret and me six months to scrape together the money, and I bought the kit.

I look back now at what that kit taught, and it was really simple: the basics of goal-setting and follow-through. But it was significant to me because it helped me to create a track to run on for identifying goals, breaking them down into manageable steps, and following through with the disciplines to get them done. I spent three years working from that growth kit, and hitting goals became a consistent part of my professional life.

During that period, I read an article about the fastest-growing churches in the country, and I got excited. *What if we could make our church one of them? What if we could become the fastest-growing church in the state of Ohio*, I thought. That became my goal. It was a big goal, a huge goal for me. The church was already close to my lifetime goal of five hundred people, and I was only in my twenties. But I was willing to strive for it. I won't bore you with all the details, but we succeeded in doubling the size of the congregation in one year, and in 1975 we were recognized as the fastest-growing church in Ohio. And we all celebrated.

When you hit a goal like that, once the celebration is done, you start asking yourself the question, *What's next?* And that's what I started to do. I wondered what I should try to do next. Did I want to attempt the same thing next year? Was there a different goal I should be going after?

As I reflected and explored ideas, I came to a realization. The lessons I'd learned while working to grow the church were actually more important—and more valuable to me—than hitting any numbers or achieving the goal. In that moment, I made a shift: the personal development shift from goals to growth. The goals I set and achieved were nice, but they weren't as significant as the growth I experienced. Goals helped me to *do* better. But growth helped me to *become* better. The growth experience was giving me greater satisfaction than reaching individual goals.

CONSIDER

Up to now, where have you focused your time and attention—and where have you received your satisfaction—as you've pursued success? In the achievement of your goals or on what you've learned along the way? How do you think your attitude has impacted your life?

_____

_____

_____

_____

GOALS HELPED ME TO *DO* BETTER. BUT GROWTH HELPED ME TO *BECOME* BETTER.

There was also another great benefit. Soon other leaders began asking me how I had accomplished the growth of the church, and I started teaching what I had learned. That was the start of my career as a leadership trainer and speaker. Achieving a goal had opened the door to the opportunity, but my ongoing ability to train others and develop my career as a trainer and speaker came as the fruit of my personal growth. And I've been able to continue speaking because personal development became my focus.

GROWTH CHANGES

As I look back at the time I was making this personal development leadershift from goals to growth, I can see that I made three significant shifts in the way I approached becoming a better leader:

1. GROWTH OUTWARD TO GROWTH INWARD

When I started my career, I was motivated by my desire to meet numerical goals, and every year I set those kinds of goals for myself. I'd look at every area of my career, break each large goal down into smaller, achievable goals, and attack them. I believed that hitting numbers would automatically make me better. And I hoped that external production would increase my internal motivation. But I discovered that it didn't. Instead, the focus on hitting numbers started to wear me down. That prompted me to realize that growth on the inside fuels growth on the outside, not the other way around. I recognized I needed to make a leadershift.

2. GROWTH IN EVERYTHING TO GROWTH IN A FEW VITAL THINGS

When I understood that my focus needed to be internal rather than external, I began thinking about where and how I wanted to grow. That made me realize how unfocused I was. At age twenty-six, my hunger to grow was greater than my willingness to get specific in my areas of growth. If you'd asked me where I wanted to improve, I'd have said, "Everywhere." But it's impossible to grow everywhere all at once. So how would I proceed?

I decided to study success. My desire was to spend a year examining what made people successful and try to discover what all of them had in common. Even as I started this process, I knew what the first quality was: attitude. My father had taught me that. Not a naturally optimistic person, Dad had studied successful people as a youth and found that a positive attitude was something they all had in common. Dad had made it a regular practice to read books that promoted a positive attitude, such as the works of Norman Vincent Peale, and had paid me to read those same books as I was growing up. I would become intentional about continuing to improve in this area.

GROWTH ON THE INSIDE FUELS GROWTH ON THE OUTSIDE.

The second characteristic I quickly attributed to successful people was the ability to develop strong relationships. This was a natural strength of mine. As a teenager I had observed that people go along with people when they get along with them. I liked people and found that they usually responded well to me. So I determined to leverage this natural strength and keep building upon it.

I discovered the third area where I wanted to improve when I read the book *Spiritual Leadership* by J. Oswald Sanders. It helped me understand the impact of good leadership. It was then that I recognized that everything rises and falls on leadership.

The last piece of the success puzzle to fall into place came when I discovered the importance of equipping. In my first leadership position, I had helped my organization to grow, but within six months of my departure, the organization had regressed. I had not equipped a single person to carry on without me.

Since then I've focused my growth on these four key areas, which I later turned into the acronym R-E-A-L so that I could teach it to others: Relationships, Equipping, Attitude, and Leadership. Those are my focus when I read books and articles, listen to podcasts, and attend conferences. Those areas have also become the focus of my teaching and my writing.

CONSIDER

Where do you believe you need to focus your growth? Write at least one but no more than five growth targets for your life.

1. _____
   _____

2. _____
   _____

3. _____
   _____

4. _____
   _____

5. _____
   _____

3. Growth with a Timeline Versus Growth Without a Finish Line

As a young leader, I was focused on achieving goals. One of the questions I continually asked myself as I set a goal was, *How long will this take?* I'm naturally impatient and I was often preoccupied by how long any given task would take. But as I shifted from goals to growth, my mind-set changed. My thinking shifted onto the bigger picture, and I became less impatient. (I won't say I became *patient* because everyone I know would call me on it!)

As I made this shift, instead of worrying about how long something might take, I started asking, *How far can I go?* Instead of thinking about what I was getting and how much I had to pay to get it, I started to think about who I was becoming and the impact I could make because of it. I recognized I was on a growth journey. And I started to fall in love with personal development. What's more, at age seventy-one, I'm still in love with it.

In my organizations, I try to cultivate that same love. I do that by promoting a culture focused on growth, not goals.

CONSIDER

Take a look at the difference between the two columns below and note which of the two phrases on each line best describes your current focus.

GOAL-ORIENTED CULTURE
- ❑ Values Achievement
- ❑ Focuses on Status
- ❑ Honors Privilege
- ❑ Emphasizes the Teacher
- ❑ Target Is Arrival

GROWTH-ORIENTED CULTURE
- ❑ Values Development
- ❑ Focuses on Stretching
- ❑ Honors Serving
- ❑ Emphasizes the Student
- ❑ Target Is Growth

The more you can shift your focus from goals to growth, the greater you can increase your potential. Growth is sustaining. Growth is the only guarantee that tomorrow will be better than today.

HOW TO BECOME A GROWTH-ORIENTED PERSON

Making the leadershift from goal-oriented to growth-oriented isn't complicated, but it isn't easy either. It requires a shift in mind-set. It takes time, but it's well worth it. If you shoot for goals, you'll achieve your goals but you may not grow. If you shoot for growth, you'll grow *and* you'll achieve goals. To start making that shift, do these seven things:

1. EMBRACE CHANGE

In 1974 I heard Olan Hendrix, currently the CEO of the Leadership Resource Group, say, "Growth means change." That has always stuck with me, because I think it's human nature to desire improvement and resist change at the same time. And that's impossible.

If you want to become a better leader, a better employee, a better person, you must shift from a fixed mind-set to a growth mind-set. Why?

A Fixed Mind-set	A Growth Mind-set
Believes Intelligence Is Static	Believes Intelligence Can Be Developed
Avoids Challenges	Embraces Challenges
Gives Up Too Easily	Persists When Faced with Setbacks
Sees Effort as Fruitless	Sees Effort as a Path to Mastery
Ignores Constructive Criticism	Learns from Constructive Criticism
Feels Threatened by the Success of Others	Finds Lessons and Inspiration in the Success of Others
Plateaus Early and Achieves Less Than Full Potential	Reaches Higher Levels of Achievement

A fixed mind-set results in an early plateau, achieves less, and hinders people from reaching their full potential, whereas a growth mind-set fuels people to a higher level of achievement. Beverly Sills said, "There are no shortcuts to any place worth going." That's certainly true when it comes to growth. It's a long, slow road, but it's a highly rewarding one. And it requires us to stretch.

CONSIDER

Look at the list describing a growth mindset. Which of the seven actions do you already do well? Why? Which is the most challenging? Why? What can you do to improve in this area?

_____

_____

_____

_____

_____

_____

2. ADOPT A TEACHABLE SPIRIT

Growth begins with having a teachable spirit. What does that entail? It means having a passion to learn, possessing the intention to learn every day, and reflecting on what you learn so that you know how to apply it. It's a bit like gardening. A garden doesn't spring to life on its own. It requires planning, hard work, and the right environment. A gardener must do the work: prepare the soil, plant the seeds, water the plants, then feed, mulch, and weed. It's an intentional process, and it must occur every day.

I try to cultivate a growth environment and maintain a teachable spirit. How do I do that?

- *I Make Growth My Number-One Priority.* I am conscious of my need to learn 24/7 because a day without growth is not a good day for me.

- *I Look for Growth Possibilities in Every Situation.* No matter what I'm doing, whether succeeding or failing, opportunities to grow are there. The question is, do I see it and take advantage of it?

- *I Ask Questions That Will Help Me Grow.* Growth doesn't find me. I must find it. The fastest way to find out what I don't know is to ask questions. The best way to dig deeper and learn more is to ask questions. Are you getting the picture?

- *I File What I Have Learned.* People forget a lot of what they learn. If they want to recall it, they can't. Or they can't find it. When I find articles of value, I clip them and put them in folders by subject. When I find quotes I like, I add them to index cards filed by topic. I file what I learn so that I can always regain access to it quickly.

- *I Pass What I Learn on to Others.* Sharing something that I learn reinforces growth and prompts me to make it my own. It also allows me to help others.

I encourage you to find your own ways to remain teachable and facilitate learning. It will open you up to amazing new possibilities.

CONSIDER

What one habit can you begin practicing today—and every day hereafter—to help you adopt a more teachable spirit?

_____

_____

_____

_____

_____

3. MAKE YOUR LOVE FOR LEARNING GREATER THAN YOUR FEAR OF FAILURE

Over the years, I have experienced the fruits of failure. I don't count my losses; I count the lessons I've learned from them. I wrote _Sometimes You Win, Sometimes You Learn_ to help people to learn from their losses. Even failure isn't failure if you learn something from it. That's how you can make failure your friend.

I can remember the day that fear of failure became my friend. It occurred in Los Angeles when I was asked to speak at a conference. Every speaker on the program was more successful, experienced, mature, and recognized than I was. I was less in every way, and I was feeling it. Finally, in the green room, I confided with one of the best speakers.

"I don't feel qualified to be speaking here," I told him. I think I was hoping for reassurance. Instead, his reply startled me.

"You're not," he said. "Speak afraid. Be willing to do it afraid, and eventually you will become qualified."

That was a revelation, and it created a leadershift in me. I spoke afraid, did my best, and here is what I discovered: action reduces fear and increases courage. That realization was a major step toward increasing my love for learning and decreasing my fear of failure.

ACTION REDUCES FEAR AND INCREASES COURAGE.

Don't allow failure to be a bully in your life. It will, if you let it. Many people get intimidated by failure every day. Instead, you need to make failure your friend. How? Fail early, fail often, and fail forward.

TAKE ACTION

What significant task have you been afraid to do that you should work toward starting? What specific action can you take that's the equivalent of "speaking afraid"? When will you take it?

Specific Action: _____

_____

Date: _____

4. DEVELOP RELATIONSHIPS WITH OTHER GROWING PEOPLE

It's much easier to become a growing person if you're in a positive growth environment. I realized this when I was in my twenties, and it inspired me to write out a description of a growth environment. I observed that such environments have ten characteristics. Recently I was looking at this list and I realized that five of the ten involve other people. (I italicized them for emphasis.)

1. *Others are ahead of me.*
2. I am continually challenged.
3. My focus is forward.
4. *The atmosphere is affirming.*
5. I am often out of my comfort zone.
6. I wake up excited.
7. Failure is not my enemy.
8. *Others are growing.*
9. *People desire change.*
10. *Growth is modeled and expected.*

Much of my personal growth has come as a direct result of having the opportunity to spend time with growing people. Elmer Towns, one of the growing people who was a mentor in the formative years of my life, taught me what he called the hot poker principle. He used to say that if you keep the poker near the fire it remains hot. Remove it and over time it becomes cold. He likened growing people to fire and would often remind me, "John, stay close to the fire." That is exactly what I have tried to do.

CONSIDER

Evaluate your environment based on the criteria listed above. Mark your answer beside each statement.

YES   NO

YES	NO	
☐	☐	Others are ahead of me.
☐	☐	I am continually challenged.
☐	☐	My focus is forward.
☐	☐	The atmosphere is affirming.
☐	☐	I am often out of my comfort zone.
☐	☐	I wake up excited.
☐	☐	Failure is not my enemy.
☐	☐	Others are growing.
☐	☐	People desire change.
☐	☐	Growth is modeled and expected.

If you don't have a bunch of yeses lined up, your environment is working against you. What could you do to change or improve this?

_____

_____

_____

_____

_____

5. DEVELOP GREATER HUMILITY

"Humility is not denying your strengths," said pastor and author Rick Warren. "Humility is being honest about your weaknesses." The essence of humility is being unafraid to admit when we're wrong. It's like saying we want to be wiser tomorrow than we are today. And the more we learn and grow, the more we recognize what we don't know.

Leaders who possess humility are confident yet feel no need to draw attention to themselves. They are comfortable with themselves yet acknowledge that they need to improve. They have self-awareness. They gratefully receive criticism. And they are not threatened when others shine. They are happy for them.

Are you willing to be criticized for the sake of improvement? Are you willing to admit you're wrong in deference to your desire to change and grow? Are you willing to drop bad habits, change wrong priorities, and embrace new ways of thinking? That's what it will take to make the leadershift to growth. You must be willing to admit where you're wrong so that you can discover what is right. Anyone can make that choice, but it requires humility.

6. BELIEVE IN YOURSELF

The Law of the Mirror in my book *The 15 Invaluable Laws of Growth* states: "You must see value in yourself to add value to yourself." What you think about yourself determines the investment you will make in yourself. If your self-worth is low, then your investment in yourself will be low. If you see yourself as a two (out of ten), then you'll make a two-level investment. If you see yourself as an eight, you'll make an eight-level investment. That matters because your growth return will not exceed your growth investment.

WHAT YOU THINK ABOUT YOURSELF DETERMINES THE INVESTMENT YOU WILL MAKE IN YOURSELF.

Benjamin Franklin said, "Empty the coins of your purse into your mind and your mind will fill your purse with coins." What a great way to think about it. Be willing to invest in yourself.

7. Embrace Layered Learning

In 1954, politician Adlai Stevenson addressed the senior class at Princeton University. Here, in part, is what he said:

> What a man knows at fifty that he did not know at twenty is, for the most part, incommunicable. The laws, the aphorisms, the generalizations, the universal truths, the parables and the old saws—all the observations about life which can be communicated handily in ready, verbal packages—are as well known to a man at twenty who has been attentive as to a man at fifty. He has been told them all, he has read them all, and he has probably repeated them all before he graduates from college; but he has not lived them all.
>
> What he knows at fifty that he did not know at twenty boils down to something like this: The knowledge he has acquired with age is not the knowledge of formulas, or forms of words, but of people, places, actions—a knowledge not gained by words but by touch, sight, sound, victories, failures, sleeplessness, devotion, love—the human experiences and emotions of this earth and of oneself and other men; and perhaps, too, a little faith, and a little reverence for things you cannot see.[1]

At the time Stevenson made these statements, he was in his mid-fifties, and what he describes is what I would call layered learning—one life lesson applied upon another and another, each gaining greater insight, depth, and weight. It is wisdom acquired and applied over time, and I believe it is the best kind of learning.

If you desire to grow to your maximum potential as a person and a leader, embrace layered learning. As you do, know these things about it:

Layered Learning Requires Time and Intentionality

Any gardener knows you can't force a seed to grow faster than nature intended it to. You can't make trees bear good fruit before they're mature. You can't rush the season. Plants need to grow, and though they may grow every day, it will not show every day. It takes a lot of growing to do a little showing.

That doesn't mean we shouldn't cultivate growth every day. Small improvements over time make a big difference. Knowledge gives us a layer of learning, increasing with each added layer until it turns into wisdom. It takes years, decades, sometimes a lifetime for a person to become an overnight success.

LAYERED LEARNING GIVES YOU A BIGGER PICTURE

Layered learning is like building a picture one piece at a time. It's like receiving additional pieces of the jigsaw puzzle of leadership and putting them in place so that the picture enlarges. What you see becomes more relevant. It also enlarges you as a leader because the more pieces you receive, the better your perspective and the greater your understanding of the principles involved in leadership.

- Layered learning determines the depth of a principle.
- Layered learning determines the length of a principle.
- Layered learning determines the consistency of a principle.
- Layered learning determines the compounding impact of a principle.

You are capable of adding layers and acquiring more of the big picture than you possess today.

LAYERED LEARNING GIVES YOU A BETTER PICTURE

Recently I received the opportunity to revise my book *Developing the Leader Within You* on the occasion of its twenty-fifth anniversary. My publisher requested that I revise at least 15 percent of it so that they could call it a new edition. I relished the thought of updating the book and dove in. By the time I was done, I hadn't rewritten 15 percent; I'd rewritten 85 percent! It changed so much, my publisher decided to call it *Developing the Leader Within You 2.0*.

How was I able to make so many changes to a book that was already highly successful? Layered learning. In the twenty-five years since I had written the original version, I had continued to grow in leadership.

When you make the personal development shift from goals to growth and embrace the process of layered learning, you will never stop getting better. And your level of success can keep expanding.

* * *

I like to think of layered learning the way C. S. Lewis talked about learning. He said that learning isn't so much like a train going from one station to the next, so that we leave one place and move on to somewhere else. Instead, our growth is similar to that of a tree. As we learn and grow, we add new rings of understanding without giving up the older ones. We build, using the past to strengthen us. And create something new.[2]

GROWTH PERSPECTIVE

Few things have a greater positive impact than shifting from goals to growth. Why do I say that? Because the benefits are so numerous. Make growth your priority and . . .

- You will unlock and achieve your potential.
- You will feel good about yourself.
- You will strengthen your values and abilities.
- You will grow in humility and self-awareness.
- You will *become* more so you can *do* more.
- You will be an example for others to follow.

I want to say one more thing about shifting from goals to growth before we move on to the next leadershift. Being a goal-oriented person means having more of a short-term mind-set. We often reach for goals because we want the positive feelings that come from quick achievements. But when we make the shift to focusing on growth, it means we've begun to adopt a long-term mind-set. By focusing on growth, we go from improving in spurts to improving day after day to reach our potential. That consistency compounds. And that's important because your level of success will never exceed your level of personal development.

TAKE ACTION

Go back and look at the growth target or targets you wrote earlier in this lesson. Write those targets below along with a plan of specific actions you can take to improve in that area, how you will gauge the evidence of your growth, and the date you desire to accomplish it.

Target 1: _____

Plan: _____

_____

_____

Evidence of Growth: _____

Date: _____

Target 2: _____

Plan: _____

_____

_____

Evidence of Growth: _____

Date: _____

Target 3: _____

Plan: _____

_____

_____

Evidence of Growth: _____

Date: _____

Target 4: _____

Plan: _____
_____
_____

Evidence of Growth: _____

Date: _____

Target 5: _____

Plan: _____
_____
_____

Evidence of Growth: _____

Date: _____

GOALS TO
GROWTH

THE PERSONAL DEVELOPMENT SHIFT

DISCUSSION QUESTIONS

1. What challenges or difficulties do you anticipate facing by changing your focus from external goals to internal growth? What can you do to overcome them?

2. How do you respond intellectually and emotionally to the challenge to grow without a timeline or finish line? Does that excite you or discourage you? Why?

3. What can you do to help yourself love learning more than fear failure? How does belief in yourself come into play?

4. Do you have an example of layered learning you can share from your own life? If so, how did it occur, how did you benefit, and what did you learn that you can apply to future growth?

PERKS TO
PRICE

THE COST SHIFT

Strength and growth come through continuous effort and struggle.

NAPOLEON HILL

I've met a lot of people who desire to become leaders. That's only natural since I do so much teaching and writing on the subject. When I get the chance to interact with people one-on-one, I often ask them why they want to be leaders. Sometimes their answers reveal that their motivation is really about the perks of leading. They want to be in control. They want others to do what they say. They want a nicer office. They want a higher income. They want a better parking place.

When I started out as a young leader, my thoughts were similar. I was en-amored with my title of pastor. It conveyed to me that I was the shepherd of the flock, and I thought people would automatically follow me because they needed me. They would rely on me for direction and be grateful for everything I did for them. It seemed simple.

Then reality hit. The people of the church were kind to me, but they didn't automatically follow me. That's when I learned what I later called the Law of E. F. Hutton: when the real leader speaks, people listen. The title that I expected to be so important didn't come with any of the perks I anticipated. I learned that I would have to earn influence myself along the way.

Fifty years later, I can say that in my career as a leader, I've received just about every kind of perk imaginable. I've received titles, recognition, honorary degrees, authority, nice offices, good parking places, money, preferential treatment—you name it, I've had it! However, none of these things motivates me as a leader. I lead because of what I can do for other people. That's the best motivation to lead others. It took time to get there, but I made the shift from being focused on what I can receive as a leader (the perks) to what I can give as a leader (the price).

CONSIDER

Take a look at the kinds of questions leaders ask themselves based on where they focus their attention. Mark the question on each line that most often represents how you think. After you mark them, think about what your answers say about your leadership attitude.

LEADERS WHO FOCUS ON PERKS
- ❑ What will I receive?
- ❑ How will this decision affect me?
- ❑ How long will this take me?
- ❑ What will you give me to stay in the game?

LEADERS WHO FOCUS ON PRICE
- ❑ What can I give?
- ❑ How will this decision affect others?
- ❑ How far can we go?
- ❑ What must I give to stay in the game?

The choice to lead because of benefits, benefits no one, not even the leader. Focusing on perks won't take you anywhere worthwhile because deep inner fulfillment never comes from perks. What they offer is ultimately hollow. And they have never helped a leader to reach his or her potential. Leaders who focus on perks end up misusing their leadership, and because they love perks more than people, they are continually tempted to misuse people to receive, maintain, or improve their perks.

If you want to reach your potential, become the best leader you can be, and make the greatest impact, then you must shift from perks to price in your leadership. A price is what stands between you and your potential. If you want to be a better leader, you need to pay for it.

YOUR PRICE POINTS

While many of the specifics of the price will be unique to each individual leader, there are some common costs that every leader needs to take into account. I want to discuss three that should be part of every leader's shift from perks to price:

1. REALITY—LEADERS RECOGNIZE THAT EVERYTHING WORTHWHILE IS UPHILL

Max De Pree, CEO of the furniture giant Herman Miller, said, "The first responsibility of a leader is to define reality." Let me define the reality of your leadership potential: it's uphill all the way. No one ever coasted to success. No successful person has ever experienced accidental achievements. Nothing of genuine value is easy, quick, and downhill. All the precious things in life require that we pay a price. Contrary to the line in the old song, the best things in life are not free. Or as someone told me once during a break in one of my speeches, "If it doesn't suck, it's not worth doing."

There's a lot of difference between what we can't do and what we won't do. What we *won't* do will keep us from being successful a lot more than what we *can't* do. Poor choices, not lack of talent and ability, are the greatest hindrances to most people's success. If we want to succeed in leadership, we must do what we don't want to do, so we can do what we need to do. We must be willing to pay the price. Early American missionary Adoniram Judson is rumored to have said, "There is no success without sacrifice. If you succeed without sacrifice it is because someone has suffered before you. If you sacrifice without success it is because someone will succeed after."

As a leader, how can you prepare yourself to pay the price required to reach your potential? How do you get ready for the long uphill journey? I think you can learn a lesson from Navy Vice Admiral James Stockdale. In his book *Good to Great*, Jim Collins writes about Stockdale and what Collins calls the Stockdale Paradox.

Stockdale was a pilot who spent eight years imprisoned in North Vietnam's notorious Hanoi Hilton after he was shot down during the Vietnam War. He was frequently tortured and abused. When Collins interviewed Stockdale, the former admiral said his imprisonment was "the defining event of my life," explaining, "I never lost faith in the end of the story. . . . I never doubted not only that I would get out, but also that I would prevail."

Collins was intrigued by this man whose body, decades later, still showed signs of being broken but whose spirit was as indomitable as ever.

"Who didn't make it out?" Collins asked a little hesitantly.

"Oh, that's easy," he said. "The optimists." When a confused Collins asked him to explain, Stockdale said, "Oh, they were the ones who said, 'We're going to be out by Christmas.' And Christmas would come, and Christmas would go. Then they'd say, 'We're going to be out by Easter.' And Easter would come, and Easter would go. And then Thanksgiving, and then it would be Christmas again. And they died of a broken heart."

What Stockdale said next gave Collins the idea for the Stockdale Paradox: "This is a very important lesson. You must never confuse faith that you will prevail in the end—which you can never afford to lose—with the discipline to confront the most brutal facts of your current reality, whatever they might be."[1] Here's how Collins states the Stockdale Paradox:

> Retain faith that you will prevail in the end,
>> regardless of the difficulties.
> *AND at the same time*
>> confront the most brutal facts of your current reality,
>> whatever they might be.[2]

These twin expectations of faith and fact help us to believe we can prevail in the end but remind us that the process won't be easy.

I express these twin expectations to myself using different words. As I prepare to lead, I think of *hope* and *hard*. These words help me personally to handle the very different expectations needed for leadership. *Hope* empowers me to believe that I can make the climb. It fuels me with energy to continue when I get tired. And it enables me to speak hope into the lives of the people who are journeying with me. I cannot give hope to others if I do not possess it myself.

It must come from a place of authenticity because you can't fake hope. As you encourage yourself, your people feel that encouragement too. As you encourage them, you also become encouraged. It creates a positive cycle that keeps everyone moving forward.

While I love the encouragement of *hope*, I also value the level-setting word *hard*. It balances my expectations and prevents me from being naively optimistic. I remind myself that the leadership journey is often difficult. Much of success lies in possessing right expectations.

I confess that during the early years of my leadership, I possessed an excess of hope but had very little knowledge or expectation for how hard leading would be. As a result, I set myself and those I led up for disappointment. We expected the best, and that's the only thing we prepared ourselves for. When things got hard and didn't go perfectly, we weren't ready for it. When you don't prepare for the worst, the worst wins!

WHEN YOU DON'T PREPARE FOR THE WORST, THE WORST WINS.

Management consultant and business visionary Peter Drucker said, "A time of turbulence is a dangerous time, but its greatest danger is the temptation to deny reality." As leaders we can't deny reality, nor should we try to sugarcoat it when communicating with our people. We need to bring reality into the conversation as soon as possible. In other words, we should strive to be up-front with the hard part of any journey we plan to take others on.

I used to wait for a good time to share hard realities with others, and then I realized that there's never a good time to share hard news, and the longer I waited, the harder it was to talk about it. Since then I've made it a regular practice to look for and mention any downside to a process I'm trying to communicate. I want people to know there is a price to pay for progress.

No matter what you want to do in life, you have to face reality, and you have to be willing to pay the price required to go uphill. The sooner you start climbing and the more you're willing to pay, the higher you can go.

CONSIDER

There are leadership goals you have abandoned and important tasks you avoid because you have told yourself you can't achieve them. What if those tasks aren't really *can'ts*? What if they are actually *won'ts*? Make a list of leadership hopes, dreams, and aspirations you once possessed that have fallen to the wayside.

_____

_____

_____

_____

_____

_____

_____

_____

Now do some serious soul-searching. Which of those one-time desires is really something you are not pursuing because you don't want to pay the price? Sometimes that decision is good and right. Sometimes it isn't. Which of the items on your list should you pick back up and pursue again? Mark them.

2. Example—Leaders Acknowledge They Must Climb the Hill First

All people with leadership ability have one perspective in common: before and more. They see things *before* other people do, and they see *more* than other people do. However, what sets great leaders apart from all other leaders is this: they *act before* others and they *do more* than others. Great leaders face their uncertainty and doubt, and they move through it to pave the way for others. And because they are willing to pay the price first and often pay more than others do, they can say with moral authority, "Follow me."

When times are tough and challenges are difficult, being first isn't a perk. It's a cost that has to be paid. In the uphill climb to achieving something worthwhile, leaders have to pay that price by climbing first and leading the way. There is no elevator to the top. Someone has to find the path and set the example.

WHAT SETS GREAT LEADERS APART FROM ALL OTHER LEADERS IS THIS: THEY *ACT BEFORE* OTHERS AND THEY *DO MORE* THAN OTHERS.

A person's title or position doesn't help here. The climb isn't enhanced by college degrees. Or material possessions. No one is inspired by any of those things. It's the actions leaders take that inspire others to follow and to rally to the vision. Great leaders take action. They move out front, staying ahead but within sight of their people, and they say, "follow me." The example of a good leader continually inspires people.

Follow-me leaders know it's their responsibility to set the example. Over the years, I've observed that they share three common before-and-more characteristics:

Follow-Me Leaders Believe in Themselves Before and More Than Others Do

I've observed a lot of successful people whom others have not believed in, but I've yet to meet a successful person who did not believe in him- or herself. Self-belief comes first. As leaders, we cannot give to others what we do not possess ourselves.

Self-belief is more than saying positive words to myself or receiving them from others. As radio broadcaster Paul Harvey said, "If you don't live it, you don't believe it." Words of affirmation without the work of accomplishment are hollow. Even if others believe in you, their borrowed belief must be activated by success and become self-belief if it is to be sustained. Borrowed belief without results soon loses its power. A leader's self-belief must be authentic, and it must be backed up with successful action.

Follow-Me Leaders Set Expectations for Themselves Before and More Than Others Do

Leaders are in trouble when they need someone else to set the level of expectations. If that continues, they will cease to lead others. Sadly, there are a lot of people who go in the opposite direction, trying to do as little as they can to stay afloat in their careers. It's like they're treading water in the pool during an Olympic swimming race.

If you want to be a good leader, you must have high expectations for yourself. I like the advice given by Dianne Snedaker, executive vice president and chief marketing officer of First Republic Bank, who said:

> Set your standards high and keep them high. If you are interested in success, it's easy to set your standards in terms of other people's accomplishments. And then let other people measure you by those standards. But the standards you set for yourself are always the more important. They should be higher than the standards anyone else would set for you, because in the end you have to live with yourself, and judge yourself, and feel good about yourself. And the best way to do that is to live up to your highest potential. So set your standards high and keep them high, even if you think no one else is looking. Somebody out there will always notice, even if it's just you.[3]

You can't set a low standard of performance for yourself and expect to lead others effectively.

FOLLOW-ME LEADERS MAKE COMMITMENTS TO THEMSELVES BEFORE AND MORE THAN TO OTHERS

To be successful, leaders must continually make commitments. Commitment is key. But the first and most important commitment that any leader makes is to him- or herself: a commitment to integrity, responsibility, and selflessness. Good leaders promise themselves they will pay the price and follow through regardless of the circumstances.

One of the leaders I most admire is Abraham Lincoln. Before Lincoln became president, few people expected him to be one of the nation's greatest leaders. In fact, the *New York Times* said he was unqualified for the presidency of the United States. But Lincoln was committed to helping the nation. He later revealed his mind-set of commitment: "I have never done an official act with a view to promote my own personal aggrandizement, and I don't like to begin now."[4]

* * *

If you're a leader, or you desire to become one, you must always be ready, willing, and committed to climbing the hill first. Climb first, setting the example, and call out "follow me." If you're willing to do that, there's still one more quality you must display as you pay the price of leadership.

CONSIDER

Think about the leadership example you set for others by answering these three questions:

Do you believe in yourself before and more than others do? (If so, what examples of belief can you list as evidence? If not, how must you change?)

_____

_____

_____

_____

Do you set expectations for yourself before and more than others do? (If so, what examples of expectations for yourself can you list as evidence? If not, how must you change?)

_____

_____

_____

_____

Do you make commitments to yourself before and more than to others? (If so, what examples of commitment can you list as evidence? If not, how must you change?)

_____

_____

_____

_____

3. CONSISTENCY—LEADERS UNDERSTAND THEY NEVER GET TO STOP CLIMBING

I have another confession to make. Early in my leadership, I thought that if I led well for a season, I could earn the right to take shortcuts and quit making sacrifices. I thought I could pay the price for a little while, be done paying, and then enjoy the good life—the perks that came with having paid a price. That created a blind spot in my leadership and led to "destination disease." I thought I could arrive at a time, place, and situation that would give me the greatest of all perks—recognition without responsibility.

There is no such place—unless you get out of the game. But I don't want out of the game. I'm more than seventy years old, and I still like the game. What I've discovered is that I had to give up to go up, and I have to give up even more if I want to stay up!

There is a reason that sports teams seldom have back-to-back championships. The perks that come with the first championship often become a hindrance to achieving the next one. When a team earns the first championship, they don't get the next one free. Dwight D. Eisenhower, whose leadership experience included serving as both a general and the president of the United States, said, "There is no victory at bargain basement prices."

If you desire to go to higher levels of leadership, you need to keep paying the price. That price will be higher than you think, and it will have to be paid continually and consistently. Jim Collins said, "The signature of mediocrity is chronic inconsistency." A corollary to that would be that the signature of excellence is relentless consistency. But excellence doesn't show up quickly. And you have to work at it to sustain it. Here are some of the ways consistency will help you as a leader.

CONSISTENCY PROVIDES SECURITY FOR OTHERS

Anthropologist Margaret Mead observed, "What people say, what they do, and what they say they do are entirely different things." If you're consistent as a leader, that should not be true of you. Your words, intentions, and actions should all line up. People know where you stand and how you deliver. Others can depend on you, which is perhaps the highest compliment you can receive as a leader.

CONSISTENCY ESTABLISHES YOUR REPUTATION

Just about everyone can be good every once in a while. It's more difficult to be good every time. Consistency lifts people above the crowd and sets them apart.

It can make you someone that others notice. And that's important in leadership because the people you lead are always watching you. When you deliver time after time, you develop a reputation for coming through when needed. Not only does that help you to influence people, it also sets the tone for your team. People do what people continually see. The more consistent you are, the more consistent they will want to be.

CONSISTENCY KEEPS YOU IN THE LEADERSHIP GAME

When you're consistent, it means never having to restart or get back "into the swing of things." You're already swinging. Your constant progress keeps morale high, keeps enthusiasm brimming, and increases your investment in whatever goal you're pursuing. Author and speaker Michael Angier said, "If you develop the habits of success, you'll make success a habit." If you consistently stay on top of your game, you never have to gear up to get back into the game.

CONSISTENCY COMPOUNDS

What did genius Albert Einstein call the greatest mathematical discovery of all time? Not Arabic numerals. Not calculus. Not the theory of relativity. Compound interest—wealth that grows based on continual reinvestment. And what's the secret to compound interest? Consistency! It never stops growing.

One of my favorite examples of the compounding power of consistency occurred in the world of professional baseball in the 1980s and '90s with Cal Ripken Jr. He is in the Hall of Fame, but he isn't there because he was the best hitter, best fielder, or best base stealer. He's there because of consistency.

Ripken played in 2,632 consecutive games, the major league baseball record by a long shot. Only one other player passed the 2,000 mark: Lou Gehrig, with 2,160. For more than forty years, baseball fans believed Gehrig's record would never be broken. The rarity of that kind of consistency becomes clearer when you recognize that only five other players in major league history have ever played in more than a thousand consecutive games. Maybe that's why the game in which Ripken passed Gehrig's record was voted the most memorable in MLB history, ahead of Gehrig's farewell speech in 1939, ahead of Hank Aaron's home run record, and ahead of Jackie Robinson breaking the color barrier in 1947.[5]

Ripken was quick to say that his success didn't come from being more talented than everyone else. When asked if he was a superstar, he responded, "Superstar?

Oh, no. . . . I don't think I stack up with the great talents in the league. I have talent, no doubt. My advantage is that I know the game well." Years later, Ripken said of his record:

> The streak was really born out of a very simple and honest approach. Dad always taught me to show up at the ballpark each and every day ready to play, and if the manager believes you are one of the nine guys who can help the team win that day, he knows he can count on you and will put you in the lineup. That's simply how the streak started and grew over the years.[6]

In other words, he showed up, worked hard, played hurt, and gave his best—every day for sixteen years straight. He was the definition of consistency.

ASSESS

In what area of your leadership are you highly consistent? What has made that consistency possible?

_____

_____

_____

_____

In what area of your leadership would you receive the greatest benefit if you became more consistent? How would it help you? What can you change immediately to pay the price of greater consistency in this area?

_____

_____

_____

_____

_____

_____

_____

_____

*   *   *

Recently I was backstage before a speaking engagement, waiting to be introduced to the audience. The host described me as "an amazing leader." I mention this only because I know I'm not amazing. Rather, I'm experienced as a leader, and I've stayed consistent. I'm just experiencing the compounding effect of having paid the price to improve as a leader for a really long time. So at this point in my career, I look better than I actually am.

If you want to have an amazing impact as a leader, you need to make the shift from perks to price and do many unamazing things as you make the difficult uphill climb of leadership and set the example for your team. The reality is that:

- Practicing is not amazing.
- Studying is not amazing.
- Showing up is not amazing.
- Working hard is not amazing.
- Asking questions is not amazing.
- Changing is not amazing.
- Trying is not amazing.
- Failing is not amazing.
- Trying again is not amazing.

But every one of these things is necessary. They are the price you must pay every day to reach your potential. If you pay that price and do it consistently, the final result can be amazing.

PERKS TO
PRICE

THE COST SHIFT

DISCUSSION QUESTIONS

1. What is your earliest memory of wanting to become a leader? What motivated you?

2. What motivates your leadership now? Would you assess that motivation as positive, negative, or mixed? Explain.

3. How do you respond to the expectation that you must always set the example for your team and go first in the unpleasant tasks? How do you handle that responsibility?

4. How well do you balance faith that you will prevail with willingness to confront the brutal facts? Which is easier for you? How do you keep doing the other?

5. How well have you embraced the idea that leaders should never stop climbing? Explain. What are the results of your perspective? What must you do to change?

PLEASING PEOPLE TO
CHALLENGING PEOPLE

THE RELATIONAL SHIFT

You cannot lead people if you need people.

Pleasing people is not the same as leading people. That was one of the first important lessons I had to learn in leadership. It defined a new reality for me, and it was very difficult for me to learn. Early in my life I realized that most people liked me. My relational connections with others were strong. My teachers liked me. Kids wanted to hang out with me and be around me in the classroom and on the playground. Intuitively, I knew what mattered to people and was able to please them. So naturally, I worked hard at developing my people-pleasing skills. I felt like my leadership mojo was making everyone happy. And doing it made *me* happy.

During those early years, I might have defined leadership as, "Make people happy and they will follow you." I was continually asking myself one question: "Is everybody happy?" But if you're a leader, the answer is no. You can never make *everyone* happy. And wanting to do so is a setup for disappointment or failure.

WHO NEEDS A WAKE-UP CALL?

I started my professional leadership career at the age of twenty-two. As already mentioned, I was the leader of a small congregation in Indiana. For the first six months, I felt that everybody was happy. The people there liked me, and I liked them. It was all kum-ba-ya.

Then one day I created trouble in paradise. There was an ugly painting in the small lobby of the church. I had noticed it before and thought about how it needed to go, but it hadn't been a priority. I didn't say anything about it to anyone, but I got around to removing it. I considered it a small improvement that I was glad to make.

The reaction was immediate and negative. You'd have thought that I called somebody's baby ugly. Right away I learned that two members of the congregation had given that painting as a gift to the church and had placed it in a prominent spot themselves. When they learned that I had removed it, to say they were not happy is a gross understatement.

I quickly apologized and put the painting back. Whew! That was close. I had dodged the bullet and gone from bad leader to good leader because everyone was happy again.

But a few weeks later, I faced another problem. The youth of our church were playing in a basketball game, and I had promised to attend. But then a member of the church called me with an emergency situation, and I missed the game. The coach of our team and a few of the parents were not happy about it. Uh-oh. I needed do something. So I explained the situation, and the parents got happy again.

But the coach still wasn't happy.

I went to work pleasing him. I visited him twice to smooth things over. And attended the next two games, even though I hadn't promised to. Finally, I had won him back over to the happy side. Yay. I'd succeeded. But boy was this happy stuff beginning to wear me out. How could I possibly keep up with making everybody happy?

For two years I did everything I could to try to make everyone I led happy. I sincerely believed that if my leadership was good, everybody would like me and everything I did. And if someone—anyone—didn't like me or something I did, then it must mean there was something wrong with my leadership and I needed to fix it. That thinking motivated every action I took and every decision I made.

What a mistake! No leader can please everyone all the time. Even history's greatest leaders had their opponents. But back then, I hadn't yet realized that. When the reality struck me that *everyone* wasn't happy *all* the time, I hit an emotional wall. I believed that I was a bad leader, and I even wondered if I should resign from my position and try to lead somewhere else.

But then I got wise counsel from leaders with more experience. They helped me to understand that it's impossible to please everyone. Then they taught me an even more important insight about myself. I was doing things backward. My goal had been to get people to like me enough so that I could gain the confidence to ask them for commitment. If they declined, I simply worked harder to try to get them to like me more, thinking that would solve the problem. Worse still, I gave the most time and energy to the unhappiest and least-committed people, even though they were not contributing to the vision or helping to move the organization forward. I was letting the tail wag the dog.

I finally realized that I wasn't leading people. I was trying to make them and myself feel good. I wasn't moving the organization forward. I was in the friendship business, not the leadership business. I wasn't taking people anywhere or helping them to do better and get better. I was trying to live in Happyville.

To get the best out of people, leaders must ask for the best from people. I wasn't doing that at all. Once I realized this, I wish I could say that I shifted from pleasing people to challenging people quickly and easily, but I can't. The process of change for me was very slow. My desire to be liked by others was deeply rooted within me to the point where my best days in leadership were the ones when people affirmed me. I craved that affirmation every day. But I recognized that affirmation doesn't equal leadership accomplishment, so I vowed to change. Step by step, I talked myself out of the idealistic thoughts and feelings I had as a young leader and coached myself to try to become the leader that the people really needed, not just the one they wanted. I made the leadershift from pleasing people to challenging them.

How to Shift from Pleaser to Leader

I don't know whether you have the people-pleasing tendencies I once had. If so, you need to make the same leadershift I did, because you can never really lead your organization, serve your people, or reach your leadership potential if you're always trying to make others happy. You have to put *doing* what's right for your people and organization ahead of what *feels* right for you. To make that shift, you need to do these seven things:

1. CHANGE YOUR EXPECTATIONS TOWARD LEADERSHIP

I had to change the way I thought about leadership and the way I interacted with others to become a good leader. I had to stop seeking affirmation. I had to stop trying to be everyone's buddy. One of the people who helped me improve in this area was my mentor, Fred Smith (the consultant, not the founder of FedEx). Once while we were discussing how to handle difficult situations with people, he said, "Always separate what's best for you from what's best for the organization." That statement felt like a smack in the face, because too often I had put myself first. I had always thought about what was best for me. Fred gave me a new perspective and suggested that I think about things in a different order:

1. What's best for the organization?
2. What's best for other people within the organization?
3. What's best for me?

By learning to ask myself these three questions in this order, I was able to clarify my motives for leadership decisions.

CONSIDER

When you have to make leadership decisions, what is the order of your thinking? How does it impact your effectiveness as a leader? What, if anything, needs to change for you to better serve your organization and team?

_____

_____

_____

_____

_____

_____

I must say that during this relational leadershift from pleasing people to challenging people, I felt great loneliness as a leader. The affirmation that had been such a wonderful sound to my ears went silent during this season. The people who used to seek me out for consensus avoided me when they were unhappy. Some of the people who used to "toast" me now wanted to "roast" me. But as I stepped back from the crowd, I started to find myself. I discovered that if I *needed* people, I probably couldn't lead them well. That gave me determination to shift from making them happy to helping them get better.

Eventually I began to desire what was best for the people, I felt released to do the right thing as a leader. I shared the vision, raised the bar, challenged others, showed the way, asked for commitment, and stopped waiting for consensus. The organization was able to take ground, and I was able to help people start reaching their God-given potential. Those who didn't want to go with me, I allowed to go their own way without expending all my energy trying to win them back.

One of the greatest lessons I learned in this season was that you never know if people are really with you until you ask them for commitment. When you ask others for commitment, you lose the uncommitted people and you gain the committed ones. When you don't ask for commitment, you keep the uncommitted and lose the committed. You choose who you lose.

> **YOU NEVER KNOW IF PEOPLE ARE REALLY WITH YOU
> UNTIL YOU ASK THEM FOR COMMITMENT.**

If your leadership is motivated by pleasing others or receiving approval, you need to change your expectations. Shift your focus from what you gain to how you can help people, improve your organization, and achieve your vision. Otherwise, your leadership will always be limited.

2. VALUE PEOPLE AS MUCH AS YOU VALUE YOURSELF

Valuing people is a high priority in my life; every day I intentionally add value to others. For me, this always starts with valuing myself. We see others as we see ourselves, and if we value ourselves, we are able to value others.

Your value assessment of yourself determines your personal investment in others. If you feel that you are worthy of opportunity, you will give others opportunities. If you feel that you are worthy of being developed, you will be willing to develop others. If you see yourself as a 9 (out of 10), you will be more likely to value others highly. If you devalue yourself, you will probably devalue others too. And that's critical because you can't devalue others and be a good leader. To get the best out of people, you need to *believe* the best about people. Only then will you give them your best—and ask them to give you their best.

3. WORK TO ESTABLISH EXPECTATIONS UP FRONT

In my people-pleasing years, I never established expectations up front. I'd tell myself that sometime, somewhere, somehow, I'd broach the topic of expectations *when the time was right*. But the time was never right, and I never initiated those conversations. Instead, I would work hard to win people over relationally, hoping that they would guess what I wanted from them and that when the tough times came, they would hang with me. But assumptions are never a good method of operation in the leadership world. They always lead to unfulfilled expectations and disappointment.

As a leader, you can either set expectations on the front end and set up the working relationships for success, or you can leave expectations unstated and deal with disappointment on the back end for both you and the people you're leading.

Today, I see the sharing and setting of expectations on the front end as the litmus test for a leader. I go out of my way to be up-front with people.

- Up-front *appreciation* places value on the person and increases the value of our time together.
- Up-front *expectations* increase the value of any meeting. (The sooner I set expectations, the quicker and easier the meeting.)
- Up-front *questions* are the quickest way for people to understand one another and increase the value of our time together.
- Up-front *discussion* influences the way and direction we lead others.
- Up-front *decisions* increase the value of our time together.

Being up-front means you're out in front.

When I am preparing to have an up-front conversation with someone, I work to level-set the interaction with one question and seven statements. First, the question:

WHAT ARE YOUR EXPECTATIONS FOR OUR INTERACTION?

When I have a conversation with someone, I always invite the other person to go first. It's not only polite but it's smart. Asking a good question without a slanted preamble is good because you can find out what the other person is really thinking, and that's more important than what I want them to think. In addition, if I listen first, the odds increase for the other person to listen to me, because he or she has already been heard.

When I start a professional relationship with someone, the most important thing to establish up-front is our expectations for each other. What does the other person expect of me? What do I expect of him or her? That way we can find out if our desires are compatible. We may need to adjust our expectations to bring them into alignment so that we can both sign off on them. And if I'm the leader in this relationship, the better I know the person, the better I'll know how to lead them.

Once I've learned the other person's expectations up front by asking questions, I set expectations for the other person by communicating these statements:

IT'S NOT ABOUT ME—IT'S NOT ABOUT YOU—IT'S ABOUT THE BIG PICTURE

A mature person has the ability to see and respect different perspectives. However, when you're leading a team, department, or organization, you must always keep your eye on the big picture. To fulfill the bigger picture, no individuals—not any team member and not the leader—can lose sight of the goal and get consumed by themselves.

YOU MUST VALUE OTHER PEOPLE

All leaders are in the people business. If we want to work well with people, we need to value them and add value to them. And here's the good news: adding value to people is also good for business.

Anyone who works with me needs to value people. That's the core of who I am and it's the core of all my companies. We must be willing to serve others, and servant leadership isn't difficult if we value people. When we value people, they feel valued. And we are able to succeed in our mission.

YOU ARE EXPECTED TO KEEP GROWING

How do you grow an organization? Through the growth of its individual members. The future of any organization can be found in the growth of the people who are a part of it, and especially the people who lead it. As the Law of the Lid says, leadership ability determines a person's level of effectiveness.

I am a lifelong learner who is intentional about learning something every day of my life. And I expect anyone who joins my team to be intentional about personal and professional growth. Growing together is even better than growing alone. Teams either grow together or they grow apart. Making a commitment to grow every day and then developing relationships with growing people will keep us on the growth track.

YOU MUST BE PREPARED TO CHANGE

There is a vast difference between conceding that change is inevitable and believing change is essential. The person who concedes that change is inevitable becomes resigned to it and is reactive, thinking, *Change is going to happen, so what can I do?* The individual who believes change is essential is proactive and thinks, *I will make change happen so that our team can improve.*

> **THERE IS A VAST DIFFERENCE BETWEEN CONCEDING THAT CHANGE IS INEVITABLE AND BELIEVING CHANGE IS ESSENTIAL.**

EVERYONE HAS TO EARN MY TIME

There are a lot of things I freely give to everyone in my organizations: vision, belief, resources, support, and leadership. One thing that must always be earned is my time. That is the most limited of my personal resources, so it must be earned before I give it. How does someone do that? By being a productive member on the team. In this, I practice the 80-20 principle. I give 80 percent of my time to the 20 percent of the team that produces 80 percent of the results.

ALWAYS TAKE RESPONSIBILITY

Most people want empowerment when what they need first are responsibility and accountability. As Kevin Turner, who is vice chairman of the board of managers of Albertsons and senior advisor to the company's chairman and CEO, said, "People want to be judged by their intentions not by their actions." But results are what make a difference, not good intentions. And results come only when people take responsibility for themselves.

I like what business executive Seth Godin said about this:

> Employees wait to be picked for promotion, or to lead a meeting or to speak up at a meeting.
>
> "Pick me, pick me" acknowledges the power of the system and passes responsibility to someone to initiate. Even better, "pick me, pick me" moves the blame from you to them.
>
> If you don't get picked, it's their fault, not yours.
>
> If you do get picked, well, they said you were good, right? Not your fault anymore.
>
> Reject the tyranny of picked. Pick yourself."[1]

That's what taking responsibility is. It's picking yourself. It's motivating yourself. It's bringing intentionality and energy to everything you do.

WE WILL NOT AVOID TOUGH CONVERSATIONS

Leadership demands that we tackle the problems. That includes tough conversations. And their difficulty increases when the issue is not easy and it involves people on our team. But we should never delay tough conversations. The more you wait, the more difficult they become. Why?

- Silence to most people means approval.
- When people have to fill in the blanks themselves, they do so negatively.
- Problems left unaddressed have a snowball effect: they become larger and gain momentum.
- Problems left unaddressed cause inner erosion: we lose respect for ourselves internally.

- The Law of Diminishing Intent is in effect: The longer you wait to do something you should do now, the greater the odds that you will never do it. One of these days becomes none of these days.

You've probably heard the saying that all's well that ends well. I also believe that all's well that begins well. That's what establishing up-front expectations does for you as a leader. It helps you begin well so that you can challenge people to become their best.

CONSIDER

What expectations should you be establishing with the people you lead? Write out the questions and statements you need to use with your team members to establish a better working relationship with them so that you can lead them well and challenge them to become their best.

_____

_____

_____

_____

_____

_____

_____

_____

Use this list whenever a new person joins your team. You may also want to sit down individually with current team members, apologize for not having done this sooner, and go over your list with them.

4. ASK YOURSELF THE HARD QUESTIONS BEFORE ANY POTENTIALLY DIFFICULT CONVERSATION

As I grew in my leadershift from pleasing people to challenging people, I had to work hard at becoming better at difficult conversations. One of the questions I began asking myself was, *What is the source of the problem prompting the need for this challenging conversation? Is it an external issue, is it a problem within the other person, or is it me?* If the issue was external, like poor communication, a bad system, or an external problem, it would be easy to solve. If it was a problem related to the person's attitude or actions, it would be more difficult. If the fault was mine, then I might not need to meet with the other person at all. I just needed to own up to it and fix myself! If it was any combination of the three, then the conversation would be very difficult because of the complexity.

As you think about any difficult conversation you are getting ready to have, I want to give you some help. Here is a checklist I've used *before* having difficult conversations to help me prepare:

Questions to Consider:	Yes	No
Have I invested in the relationship enough to be candid with them?		
Do I demonstrate that I value them as individuals?		
Am I sure this is their issue and not mine?		
Am I sure I'm not speaking up because I feel threatened?		
Is the issue more important than the relationship?		
Does this conversation clearly serve their interests and not just mine?		
Am I willing to invest time and energy to help them change?		
Am I willing to show them how to do something and not just say what's wrong?		
Am I willing and able to set clear, specific expectations?		
Have I previously addressed the issue or problem in a less formal setting?		
Total:		

Take a look at the tally of *yes* or *no* responses. If you have one or more *no* responses to any of these questions, consider what steps you need to take to make that *no* become a *yes* before you conduct that crucial conversation.

TAKE ACTION

The next time you need to address a problem you're having with a team member, use the list above to make sure you're prepared for the conversation.

5. WHEN A TOUGH CONVERSATION IS NEEDED, DO IT RIGHT

Because it was once so difficult for me, I want to give you some advice about how to make a tough conversation less tough. First, remember why you are having the conversation. It's because you care about the other person; you care enough to confront them. Your goal is to help that person.

Having the right attitude is essential because your actions often carry more weight than your words, and a negative attitude can cause more damage. People remember how they felt long after they have forgotten what you said. You can communicate the right attitude by seeking to understand. Here is a road map for the conversation:

- State the issue clearly at the beginning. Use the phrase, "Are you aware that . . . ?"
- Ask them to tell you their perspective. Start with the phrase, "I need you to help me understand your situation."
- Ask questions. Say, "Am I hearing you correctly?"
- Repeat back what you heard.
- Allow them to respond.
- Try to find common ground.
- Arrive at an agreement on what's best for both of you.
- If you cannot come to an agreement on the issue and solution, agree to meet again.
- See the growth opportunity that lies within the tough conversation.
- Seek to maintain a positive relationship.

Following this pattern and arriving at a positive outcome is not always possible, but it's worth trying to attain. You're always better off having the tough conversation and finding out where you stand rather than avoiding it and hoping the problem will resolve itself, because it never does.

TAKE ACTION

Use the previous bullet list to guide you the next time you need to have a difficult conversation with a team member.

6. UNDERSTAND THE 25-50-25 PRINCIPLE

Good leadership always challenges people to rise to the occasion, become their best, and achieve more. Some people accept the challenge and help the team to win. Others don't. As a leader, you have to manage the process that people go through. You can use the 25-50-25 principle to help you. I learned about it years ago when I attended a leadership roundtable in Los Angeles.

Here's how it goes: Whenever you cast vision and challenge people to become part of achieving an endeavor, they tend to fall into one of three groups. Typically, 25 percent of the people will support your efforts, 50 percent will be undecided, and 25 percent will resist change. Your job is to help the middle 50 percent join the first 25 percent. Here are tips for doing that and working with all three groups:

- Understand that the resistant bottom 25 percent are not going to join you, no matter what you try to do. The greatest leader in the world could be leading them, and they would still resist change. Accept that.
- Don't waste your effort trying to make this bottom 25 percent happy. They are not going to get happy. Trying to placate them will only encourage their resistance.
- Don't give the bottom 25 percent a platform or credibility. If you believe you're doing the right thing, why would you help them undermine that?

- Try to keep the bottom 25 percent away from the 50 percent who have not yet made up their minds. As baseball manager Casey Stengel said, "The secret of managing is to keep the guys who hate your guts away from the guys who haven't made up their minds yet."
- Ask the 25 percent who support you to help positively influence the middle 50 percent who are undecided.
- Give the supportive 25 percent credibility and a platform to speak. They will help you help the organization move forward.

Any movement you can create in the middle 50 percent toward your leadership and the vision is a win because it takes the organization in the right direction. Celebrate that and keep moving forward.

CONSIDER

How can you apply the 25-50-25 Principle in your organization? Is there an initiative or project where this dynamic is in play? What specific actions can you take to minimize the damage done by the bottom 25 percent?

_____

_____

_____

_____

_____

_____

_____

_____

_____

7. BALANCE CARE WITH CANDOR

I want to give you one more piece of advice related to challenging people, and it's an important one. As a leader, you need to bring both caring and candor into the relationship. I mention this because most people naturally default to one or the other. But here's why it's important for you to practice both:

- Care without candor creates dysfunctional relationships.
- Candor without care creates distant relationships.
- Care balanced with candor creates developing relationships.

Care and candor are like the two wings of a plane; you can't fly with only one. They must work together.

Care	Candor
Values the Person	Values the Person's Potential
Establishes the Relationship	Expands the Relationship
Shores Up Weaknesses	Brings Out Strengths
Offers Comfort	Offers a Challenge
Makes the Team Pleasant	Makes the Team Productive

Caring should never suppress candor, while candor should never displace caring. When I have the responsibility for leading people, I must care for them, but I must also challenge them by initiating honest conversations to help them improve. My mind-set should be, "I love you too much to let you stay where you are."

CONSIDER

Which is most natural for you: caring for others or speaking with candor? How can you improve in the area that comes less naturally to you?

_____

_____

_____

_____

_____

_____

_____

_____

It's been almost fifty years since I made the leadershift from pleasing people to challenging them. It's been one of the most difficult changes I've had to make in my leadership, but it has also been one of the most rewarding. If I hadn't been willing to face up to the need to change, I'd have gotten stuck in my leadership.

I don't know how much difficulty people pleasing has given you. Maybe it's not an issue at all. I hope that's the case. But no matter what, you need to learn how to positively challenge people if you desire to become the best leader you can be. If you can help people to positively reach their potential, you help them, your team, and yourself.

PLEASING PEOPLE TO
CHALLENGING PEOPLE

THE RELATIONAL SHIFT

DISCUSSION QUESTIONS

1. The quote at the beginning of the chapter says, "You cannot lead people if you need people." What is your interpretation of that? Do you agree or disagree? Explain.

2. What is the value of challenging people? Can you share an example of when you were challenged by a leader, and it helped you?

3. Can you share an example of when you challenged someone on your team and the outcome was positive? What strategy did you use with the person and why?

4. When having to make a decision, especially a decision related to people, how do you go about analyzing what's best for the organization, for the people, and for yourself? What criteria do you use for each area?

5. Is there a tough conversation you need to have that you've been putting off? How can you use care and candor to help you have that conversation? When will you initiate it?

NOTES

LESSON SIX

MAINTAINING TO
CREATING

THE ABUNDANCE SHIFT

The joy is in creating—not maintaining.

VINCE LOMBARDI

Have you ever thought about the expectations your profession or industry places on you? Are people in your leadership position expected to hold the line? Maintain the course? Change direction? Get out of the box? Blow up the box?

When I started my career, it never occurred to me to think about such things. I knew from a fairly early age that I was going to become a pastor. That determined my course of study in college, and after I graduated, I was happy to get my first job in rural Indiana. A few weeks after Margaret and I got married, we moved there and I started my career. That was back in 1969. In those days, the role of pastors was pretty set. We were expected to be shepherds, and our main job was to feed and care for the flock. The whole mind-set was *maintaining*. As much as I loved the people in my congregation and had looked forward to being a pastor, it wasn't long before I started to feel unsettled.

Each year the organization I belonged to held a meeting for the pastors and leaders of all the churches. Toward the end of my first year on the job, I went to my initial meeting as the leader of my own church. It was good to see some friends from college and to catch up with them. But what struck me most was how *traditional* everything was. The highlight of the meeting was when the pastor of the year was recognized. For the first time, it struck me. The people they honored were always the ones with the longest tenure, the leaders who were faithful—the maintainers, not the innovators.

I did not want to be a maintainer. Tenure wasn't my goal. I began to feel like a misfit among a group of people who valued tradition and conformity, and my sense of unsettledness only increased. And the way the organization worked was if you were a faithful shepherd at a small church and didn't rock the boat, you were eventually invited to pastor a larger church. If you were faithful there, you would get offered a denominational position. The recognized pastors maintained their way to the top. And on it went until you received recognition toward the end of your career as you approached retirement. I could see the whole path ahead of me. I was beginning to suspect that it wasn't a good fit for me. I wanted to innovate. I wanted to reach people. I wanted to build a great church.

Years later, someone in the ministry world pointed out that not all pastors are actually shepherds. He referred instead to another analogy: church leader as rancher. He described the difference this way: while shepherds are maintainers who care for the sheep they already have, ranchers are leaders who pioneer new ideas and build. Now, I'm not saying that people are livestock. But there's a difference in mind-set between these two types of people, and it was clear which type I was. I wanted to build.

There's an old saying: don't tear down a fence until you know why it's there. Within my organization, I wasn't someone who was itching to tear down fences, but I *was* a questioner. I was very quick to ask why a fence had been put up. And whether it still needed to be there. And if it could be replaced by something better. If the reason something was done was reasonable, then I'd leave it alone. If not, then I started asking, "Why not do it another way—a better way?"

Asking questions and exploring ignited my creativity. Although, within my organization, it seemed like I was the only one doing that. In fact, my questions annoyed them. They questioned my questions—they couldn't understand *why* I was asking them at all. It eventually became clear to me that I wasn't compatible with the culture, and I needed to make a change. So after several years, I left the organization.

RECOGNIZE WHAT ZONE YOU'RE IN

I don't want to put down the organization I was a part of or the people I grew up with. They were good people. However, I believe the culture they were part of was working against them. It's difficult overcoming a maintaining culture. And if you also happen to have an inherent tendency toward inactivity when it comes to innovation, you have even more to overcome.

I've observed that we all tend to fall into one of four different zones when it comes to innovation, which impacts how we live, how we lead, and what we achieve. Here are the zones, along with attitude statements that represent them:

1. *The Coasting Zone*—"I do as little as possible."
2. *The Comfort Zone*—"I do what I have always done."
3. *The Challenge Zone*—"I attempt to do what I haven't done before."
4. *The Creative Zone*—"I attempt to think what I have never thought before."

ASSESS

To which zone do you naturally gravitate? Do you tend to live in the coasting zone, casually—even passively—doing as little as possible? Do you tend to stay in the comfort zone, avoiding risks? Do you connect with the challenge zone, where you try new things and willingly risk failure? Or do you try to stretch yourself the furthest by living in the creative zone, where you explore new ideas, seek out other perspectives, and cross bridges in your imagination long before you physically reach them?

(continued)

Look at the four zones and indicate what percentage of the time you spend in each. Make sure your answers total 100 percent.

The Coasting Zone — "I do as little as possible."   _____

The Comfort Zone — "I do what I have always done."   _____

The Challenge Zone — "I attempt to do what I haven't done before."   _____

The Creative Zone — "I attempt to think what I have never thought before." _____

Total   100 %

The good news is that we have the ability to choose a zone different from our natural one. And I recommend the creative zone, because it is where we experience abundance and expand our potential. If you want to take your leadership to ever-higher levels, you need to make the leadershift from maintaining to creating and try to live in the creative zone.

UNLOCK THE MENTAL BLOCKS THAT KEEP YOU OUT OF THE CREATIVE ZONE

How can you make the shift from maintaining to creating? I believe you must start the process from the inside out. Begin by removing some of the mental blocks that cripple so many people's creative potential. Roger von Oech wrote extensively about many of them in his book *A Whack on the Side of the Head*.[1] I've included some of my favorites. Which of these phrases do you find yourself thinking or saying?

MENTAL BLOCK #1: "FIND THE RIGHT ANSWER"
It's wrong to believe there is only one right answer to any question. There are always other solutions. If we believe they are there and we're willing to look for them, we will find them.

Mental Block #2: "That's Not Logical"

Albert Einstein said, "Imagination is more important than knowledge. Knowledge is limited. Imagination encircles the world."[2] Imagination turns possibilities into reality. It's willing to take leaps that logic can't. While logic does have great value and you should keep it, you should intentionally add creativity.

Mental Block #3: "Follow the Rules"

I've always loved this quote from Thomas Edison: "There ain't no rules around here! We are tryin' to accomplish some[thing]!"[3] Most revolutionary ideas have been disruptive violations of set rules.

Mental Block #4: "Avoid Ambiguity"

Life is complex. It's messy. It's contradictory and paradoxical. Why in the world would we think that we should—or could—avoid ambiguity? There is never one fixed way to understand something—everything can be understood in more than one way.

Mental Block #5: "Failure Is Bad"

Creative people don't avoid failure. They see it as a friend. They know that if they are to experiment, innovate, and create, they will fail. They embrace risk.

Mental Block #6: "Don't Be Foolish"

To stand up is to stand out. You have to stick your neck out to put your head above the crowd. If others don't at first understand or accept you, so what? All the great dreamers looked foolish to someone. How you are perceived by others is less important than how effective you can be.

Mental Block #7: "I'm Not Creative"

The mental block that most keeps us from being creative is believing we don't possess creativity. This self-perception is a barrier to talent, opportunity, and intelligence. But the truth is that everyone can learn to be creative. The only real block to creativity is our disbelief.

I love what blogger Hugh MacLeod said about this: "Everyone is born creative; everyone is given a box of crayons in kindergarten. Then when you hit puberty they take the crayons away and replace them with dry, uninspiring books on algebra, history, etc. Being suddenly hit years later with the 'creative bug' is just a wee voice telling you, 'I'd like my crayons back, please.'"[4]

CONSIDER

Which of the seven mental blocks hold you back? Why? What can you do to remove them from your thinking?

_____

_____

_____

_____

_____

_____

_____

_____

CREATIVE PRINCIPLES TO LEARN AND LIVE BY

If you want to shift from maintaining to creating in your life and leadership, then you need to take your crayons back. Here's how:

1. BUILD A CREATIVE CULTURE

If you lead a team, department, or organization, take responsibility for promoting creativity and building a creative culture. Several years ago, I read an article in _Forbes_ that took tips from _Disciplined Dreaming_ by Josh Linkner, and they provide great insight in how to make your organization's culture more creative.[5] I've interpreted his ideas, plus added a few of my own.

FUEL PASSION

Creativity requires time, tenacity, testing, options, U-turns, imagination, questions, failure, and change. All these things require a lot of energy. Passion provides the fuel.

CELEBRATE IDEAS

What gets celebrated gets done. If you reward ideas with money, praise, and opportunity, people will come to value ideas and work toward generating and sharing them.

FOSTER AUTONOMY

George S. Patton said, "Never tell people *how* to do things. Tell them *what* to do and they will surprise you with their ingenuity." What he was really talking about was allowing people to have enough autonomy to be creative. Micromanagement undermines creativity while freedom and flexibility foster it.

ENCOURAGE COURAGE

Creativity requires risk, and taking risks requires courage. As a leader, you need to model it and encourage it. As Daniel R. Denison of IMD Business School said, "There is always a premium on being able to deal with the unknown. People will venture there if they feel they'll be secure in doing it. It's the leader's job to create that sense of security."

MINIMIZE HIERARCHY

In creative environments, decisions are made closest to the problems. For that to happen, leaders need to minimize the number of layers between the top and the bottom. A few years ago, I read an article by Robert Kaplan in which he interviewed now-retired General Stanley McChrystal, who said, "Any complex task is best approached by flattening hierarchies. It gets everybody feeling like they're in the inner circle, so that they develop a sense of ownership."[6]

REDUCE RULES

Author Henry David Thoreau wrote, "Any fool can make a rule and every fool will mind it." Creativity gets stifled when everyone expends too much energy worrying about following rules. Too many rules cause idea anemia. General Douglas MacArthur said, "You are remembered for the rules you break." I like that idea.

FAIL FORWARD

I once saw a sign that said, "Company Motto: We make *new* mistakes." I love that. I'm a huge supporter of the idea of failing forward. So much that I wrote an entire book on the subject. If you fall down, you should learn from it, get up, and step forward. Any time you learn what doesn't work, you're a step closer to what does work.

START SMALL

Too often we want huge breakthroughs and innovations when we should be looking for small ones. If you want one great idea, look for a lot of good ideas. If you want to create something significant, build it in small increments. Do that consistently, and you make creative progress.

TAKE ACTION

Create a plan to make these ideas part of how your team works. You may want to begin by reducing hierarchy and celebrating (and rewarding) ideas.

_____

_____

_____

_____

_____

_____

_____

_____

The more you foster creativity in the environment you influence, the more you instill an abundance mind-set. That's why I call this leadershift the abundance shift. It's like poet Maya Angelou said, "You can't use up creativity. The more you use, the more you have. Sadly, too often creativity is smothered rather than nurtured. There has to be a climate in which new ways of thinking, perceiving, questioning are encouraged."[7] As a leader, you have the influence and an obligation to try to create that climate.

2. MAKE EVERYTHING BETTER

You've probably heard the expression, "It doesn't get any better than this." Well, I have news for you. It _can_ get better. Everything can get better. And as leaders, we should be catalysts for improvement. We need to champion the idea expressed by poet James Russell Lowell, who said, "Creativity is not the finding of a thing, but making something out of it after it is found."

Ask these questions to help spur this process: Can we take an idea to the next level? Can we target a message even more sharply? Can we make a client's experience even better? Can we add something to an event to make it spectacular? Is there anything important that the rest of the team didn't see because they were too far into the weeds and didn't have perspective? What can we do to go the extra mile? This phase is where great innovation often occurs and we are able to maximize ideas.

ASSESS

What is your mindset when it comes to getting work done? On a scale of 1 ("That's close enough.") to 10 ("Nothing's ever good enough."), how do you usually think? Circle the number that applies.

1   2   3   4   5   6   7   8   9   10

How does your mindset impact your ability to be creative and make things better? How could you improve?

_____

_____

_____

_____

_____

_____

_____

_____

3. MAKE PLANS BUT LOOK FOR OPTIONS

No doubt good leaders use plans to get things done. But planning is not the end-all and be-all of leadership. Leaders who cling too inflexibly to a plan stifle creativity and miss opportunities. To be creative, leaders need to add options to their planning. I think of this as moving from Plan A to Option A.

More than two thousand years ago, Publilius Syrus wrote, "It is a bad plan that admits of no modifications." I believe what he really meant is that it's a bad *leader* whose plans don't allow modifications. Good leaders are flexible and their plans are fluid. They allow for creativity. They plan, but they look for options. And that's important. Options always present themselves soon after action is taken on a plan. If we don't open ourselves up to those options, we miss the chance to innovate, to create, and—sometimes—to win.

On his blog, author and speaker Steve Pavlina wrote about how good leaders look for options and make adjustments:

Stephen Covey often used the expression, "Integrity in the moment of choice." What that means is that you should not follow your plans blindly without conscious awareness of your goals. For instance, let's say you're following your plans nicely—so far so good—and then an unforeseen opportunity arises. Do you stick to your original plan, thereby missing the opportunity, or do you stop and go after the opportunity, thereby throwing yourself off schedule? This is where you have to stop and reconnect with your goals to decide which is the better course. No plan should be followed blindly.[8]

The best leaders are flexible. As leadership author Warren Bennis said, "Adaptive capacity allows leaders to respond quickly and intelligently to constant change. It is the ability to identify and seize opportunities. It allows leaders to act and then evaluate results instead of attempting to collect and analyze all the data before acting."[9]

ASSESS

Are you a planner or an improviser? On a scale of 1 ("I make my plan and never deviate.") to 10 ("Plan? What's a plan?"), how would you score yourself? Circle the number that applies.

(continued)

1	2	3	4	5	6	7	8	9	10

How does your attitude impact your ability to get things done while still being creative? In which area do you most need to improve? How can you do that?

_____

_____

_____

_____

_____

_____

_____

_____

4. PLACE HIGH VALUE ON IDEAS

Harvey Firestone, one of the most successful businessmen of the nineteenth and early twentieth centuries, said, "Capital isn't so important in business. Experience isn't so important. You can get both of these things. What is important is ideas. If you have ideas you have the main asset you need, and there isn't any limit to what you can do with your business and your life. They are any man's greatest asset—ideas." If you want to be creative, you must place high value on ideas and learn how to generate them.

CONSIDER

Where do you allow space for creativity in your team or department as you take on tasks? Review the steps below and write how you allow members of your team to inject creativity at each stage:

Task or Problem Identification: _____

_____

Information Gathering: _____

_____

Assessment: _____

_____

Process Development: _____

_____

Assignment of Responsibilities: _____

_____

Process Implementation: _____

_____

In-Process Problem Solving: _____

_____

Post Implementation Assessment:

_____

_____

_____

_____

5. SEEK OUT AND LISTEN TO DIFFERENT VOICES

Creativity thrives when one subject is approached from many different perspectives. It short-circuits the kind of one-way thinking that interferes with better solutions. If we get into single-perspective thinking, we find ourselves in ruts. If we see things from a new perspective, we can be like the mechanic who told his customer, "I couldn't repair your brakes, so I just made the horn louder."

CREATIVITY THRIVES WHEN ONE SUBJECT IS APPROACHED FROM MANY DIFFERENT PERSPECTIVES.

Norman Vincent Peale said, "Ask the God who made you to keep remaking you." I do that. I try to remain teachable, and I listen to many different voices and perspectives to try to improve myself. That's why I always try to surround myself with the best and the brightest people I can find. I like nothing more than to bring together a group of leaders, young and old, new and experienced, and ask them for their perspectives on a question, problem, or project. I'm a firm believer in the T-E-A-M principle: Together Everyone Accomplishes More. I want others' assessments. And I love that word: *assessment*. It comes from the Latin *assidere*, which means "to sit beside." I want people willing to sit beside me, share their perspectives, give their insights, add their ideas to mine, and make all of us better.

From about the age of forty, I have greatly valued the help of my inner circle, the people closest to me in life and in business. These individuals compensate for my weaknesses, focus on today, and implement much of the work in my organizations. Most of these people have worked with me for many years, some for more than two decades. But over the last few years, I have intentionally cultivated another group that I call my outer circle. These people have fresh eyes and can speak to me from a different perspective. They enhance my strengths, help me focus on tomorrow, and give me creative ideas. The people in this group change frequently, based on time and opportunities. Together, both circles complement or empower each other and complete me.

CONSIDER

Do you have an inner circle? An outer circle? Who you allow to give you creative or critical input into your life? List the people you invite and allow to speak into your life, along with the primary contribution they make.

---

6. LIVE ON THE OTHER SIDE OF "YES"

Recently I was casting vision to a large group of leaders. There was a great sense of anticipation as I shared the possibilities and opportunities that could be before us if we partnered together and joined hands to accomplish this vision. After that session, I met in the green room with the top leaders of that organization, continuing to discuss the possibilities of working together. One of those leaders, Larry Stockstill, interrupted the discussion and said, "John, the answer is yes. Count me in. Whatever this means, I am a 'yes.'" His response energized the room and everyone followed his positive lead.

After the meeting when Larry and I were together, I thanked him for his positive response. I was curious, so I asked what made him respond so boldly.

"I live on the other side of 'yes,'" Larry said, "That's where I find abundance and opportunity. It's where I become a better and bigger self. The opportunity of a lifetime must be seized within the lifetime of the opportunity. So I try to say 'yes' whenever I can."

How can you become more opportunistic and live on the other side of "yes"?

IMAGINE OPPORTUNITIES EVERYWHERE

Everything mankind has accomplished existed in someone's imagination before it became a reality. We create what we imagine, and imagination is one of the last remaining legal means you have to gain what feels like an unfair advantage over your competition. You can cultivate this imagination by:

- *Asking Questions:* Curious people are imaginative people, and questions are doorways to opportunity
- *Networking:* You are only a few people away from a wonderful opportunity. Right now, someone knows something you should know, and someone is doing something you should do.
- *Taking Action:* Action creates opportunities. The best opportunity is seldom behind the first door, but going through that first door will be essential to get to the other doors that present the better opportunities.

Opportunities are like rabbits. You get a couple and learn to handle them, and soon you have a dozen. An opportunity grasped and used produces another opportunity. The more successful you are, the more opportunities will be given to you.

PREPARE FOR OPPORTUNITIES

To be prepared for opportunity, you must produce results and make sure that you are the most qualified when the door opens. Are you working as hard as you can? Are you learning as much as you can? Are you connecting with others as often as you can? Are you building a team as well as you can? All these things make you ready and put you closer to the door when it opens.

ACTIVATE YOUR CURRENT OPPORTUNITIES

It's always easier to see opportunities we've missed, the ones behind us, than to see the ones in front of us now. To live on the other side of "yes," we need to focus on the current moment and activate whatever opportunity is presenting itself. We need to open the door before us, not lament the doors behind us that we missed. We must stay hungry, believe we will have opportunities, seize the small ones when we find them, and build upon them until we are ready for even bigger challenges.

Robert Lynch, president and CEO of Americans for the Arts, said, "Creativity is the most effective response to rapid change." Why? Because creativity always adds. Leadershifting from maintaining to creating allows you to lead people into the land of abundance and opportunity.

If you desire to be successful and to be the best leader you can possibly be, you cannot settle for the familiar. You cannot live in your comfort zone. Don't ever get comfortable. Make the shift to abundance. Get out on the edge. Break new ground. Seize opportunity. Get creative.

CONSIDER

What can you do to make the most of your opportunities and live on the other side of yes? Write how you will improve in the following areas:

Imagine and Identify Opportunities:

_____

_____

_____

_____

Prepare for Opportunities:

_____

_____

_____

_____

Activate Current Opportunities:

_____

_____

_____

_____

MAINTAINING TO
CREATING

THE ABUNDANCE SHIFT

DISCUSSION QUESTIONS

1. Which gives you the greatest inner satisfaction: executing a perfect plan, rethinking an old plan, or creating a new plan from scratch? Why?

2. Which of the mental blocks listed in the lesson is the most difficult for you to overcome?

   - "Find the right answer."
   - "That's not logical."
   - "Follow the rules."
   - "Avoid ambiguity."
   - "Failure is bad."
   - "Don't be foolish."
   - "I'm not creative."

   Why does it challenge you? What could you do to improve in that area?

3. How do you find your best ideas? How do you record them so that you don't lose them? How do you decide which to implement?

4. How do you think risk and creativity are connected?

5. What is the greatest challenge to creating a creative culture on a team? What can you do to make yourself and your team more creative and innovative?

NOTES

LADDER CLIMBING TO
LADDER BUILDING

THE REPRODUCTION SHIFT

If I have seen farther than others, it is by standing on the shoulders of giants.

ISAAC NEWTON

I've always been a talker, from the time I was a child, through high school, in college, and into my career as a pastor. That trait, coupled with a desire to improve as a communicator and a degree of success in leadership, landed me some big opportunities to speak at a relatively young age. Sometimes I got to speak before large crowds alongside some amazing speakers.

When I started getting these great opportunities for speaking gigs, my excitement was always mixed with fear. My eagerness to get out and speak was often tempered by worry because of my lack of experience. I was glad for the exposure and the chance to teach new audiences, but I was also aware that I was in over my head. Early in my speaking career, at most events, I was at the bottom of the class.

I dealt with this by becoming the chief cheerleader of all the other speakers whenever I got invited to speak. I sat in the front row. I laughed at their stories. I wrote down all their insights. I stood and cheered as they walked offstage. And I stood in line to thank them for helping me after the event.

After the thrill of being part of such wonderful speaking teams started to wear off, I began to analyze my communication and my impact on my audiences. Here's what I discovered: after I was done speaking, there was lots of inspiration but not a lot of application. People who heard me speak were glad they came, but they weren't sure what to do with anything I said when they got home. I was encouraging everybody, but I wasn't helping anybody.

TIME TO MAKE A CHANGE

It took me a while to figure out my problem, but after asking experienced communicators questions and listening to their responses, I realized what was wrong. My focus was totally on myself. The experience was more about me than the people I was there to help. My subject matter, my stories, my points, my thoughts, my delivery—it was all for me. After I spoke, the questions I was asking myself afterward were, *How did I do? Did they like me? Did they like what I said? Did they clap for me? Were they impressed by my talent? Do they admire me?*

When I realized what I had been doing, I felt exposed and saw the error of my ways. And I knew that I had to make a shift. My speaking had to change. So did my attitude. I needed to focus on others and on adding value to them when I spoke.

I took some time to reflect. I wondered how I could make the changes needed in this area. So I wrote something to help me. This is what I wrote:

- It's not about me—it's about them.
- Success is not a standing ovation—it's people walking out with a game plan.
- My talk is not to help me look good—it's to help them get good.
- If they can't relate to what I want to say—I shouldn't say it.
- If they can't apply what I say to their lives—I shouldn't say it.
- When I'm done, don't expect them to give me a hand—invite them to come shake my hand.
- When they walk away, hope that they say, "His name is John and he's my friend."

Eventually, this shift started to bleed into my leadership, where it wasn't ever supposed to be about me. Leadership should always be about others.

Before this, I was a ladder climber. Nearly everything I did was motivated by the question, "How high can I go?" But making this shift helped me to realize that there was more to life than getting to the top. Instead of just trying to be successful personally, I could help others. And over the years, I realized that there were a series of shifts I could make, and they came in stages.

1. *Ladder Climbing*—"How high can I go?"
2. *Ladder Holding*—"How high will others go with a little help?"
3. *Ladder Extending*—"How high will others go with a lot of help?"
4. *Ladder Building*—"Can I help them build their own ladder?"

This leadershift is about changing from being a personal producer to an equipper of others. It's a shift that takes your leadership math from addition to multiplication. It takes you from the solitary climb to the top of your ladder, where you might enjoy the view and wave to the people down below, to watching many people climb to the top of their own ladders, and you all enjoy the view from the top together.

LADDER STAGES

I want to explain the four stages that I went through to help you make this shift in your leadership:

1. LADDER CLIMBING—"HOW HIGH CAN I GO?"
Wanting to climb the ladder yourself isn't a bad thing, because credibility in leadership is often built on personal success. No one wants to follow a leader who cannot succeed. People want to be on a team only if they know they have a chance to win. So the first step in leadership is not leading others. It's leading yourself; it's showing you are capable of climbing the ladder yourself.

Speaker Glen Turner once told me, "The hardest challenge of getting to the top of the ladder was getting through the crowd at the bottom." Being able to climb the ladder yourself is the first step in separating yourself from the rest of the crowd. If you need help in figuring out how to do that, ask yourself these three questions:

> THE HARDEST CHALLENGE OF GETTING TO THE TOP OF THE LADDER
> WAS GETTING THROUGH THE CROWD AT THE BOTTOM.
>
> GLEN TURNER

WHAT ARE MY STRENGTHS?

Success comes from building upon your strengths and making the most of them, not from bringing your weaknesses up to par. For example, three of my top strengths are strategy, activation, and Woo (from StrengthsFinder).[1] Where am I weak? I don't do well with tasks related to administration or maintenance. And I'm absolutely terrible when it comes to anything technical. Any time or energy spent in these areas would be a total waste. Know what your strengths are and start developing them.

CONSIDER

What are your top three to five strengths?

_____

_____

_____

_____

_____

_____

WHAT ARE MY OPPORTUNITIES?

I believe everyone has opportunities. I do, and I'm convinced you do. The opportunities you receive may not be as big as you want. They may not be the kind that you want. But they are opportunities. What should you do with them? Apply your strengths to them and make the most of them. The meeting of your strengths with an opportunity is where you get the chance to start climbing the ladder. Make the most of it. Even if it's not the perfect opportunity—and trust me, it won't be, because there is no such thing—you can start the climb. Once you climb up out of the crowd, you'll discover other, better opportunities.

CONSIDER

What are your best opportunities that fit your strengths?

_____

_____

_____

_____

_____

_____

AM I TAKING STEPS EVERY DAY?

When you seize an opportunity and apply your strengths to it, you still have to do the work. If you can't answer yes to the question of whether you're taking steps every day, you won't succeed, and you'll have to forget about taking the next step toward becoming a ladder builder.

CONSIDER

What steps are you taking every day to maximize at least one of those opportunities? If you're not currently taking steps, what steps _could_ you be taking? Write them down, and commit yourself to following through with them consistently.

_____

_____

_____

_____

_____

How high do you need to climb? My answer is that you need to get to the top 10 percent. That's the magic number. That's where you become set apart from all the rest in the areas of money, influence, opportunity, and relationships. That's where the quality of people who want to be on your team changes drastically. So as you work to climb the ladder yourself, one of the things you need to ask yourself is whether you can get to that top 10 percent. If you can, then you will be able to start holding the ladder for others.

As you climb the ladder of success, here's some advice for making sure you're doing it as effectively as possible:

- Make sure your ladder is on a firm foundation of integrity and strong character.
- Make sure your ladder is leaning against the right "building" for your purpose.
- Never step on other people while climbing up.
- Don't skip any rungs of the ladder.
- Step back down occasionally to rest, reflect, and gain perspective.
- Don't step on anyone while descending either.
- Each time you start to climb back up, make sure you improve.
- Always value the people who are holding the ladder for you.

The better you are at climbing the ladder yourself, the more you will have to give others when you move on to the next phases.

2. LADDER HOLDING—"HOW HIGH WILL OTHERS GO WITH A LITTLE HELP?"

Kevin Myers, the leader of 12Stone Church, said, "Leaders should want far more *for* their people than *from* their people." I talked a little about that in Lesson 1 on shifting from soloist to conductor. When you want more for others and you're willing to give them some help, it's like holding the ladder for another person, giving them a secure base, empowering them to take moderate risks, and allowing them to climb higher.

I've benefited from many people who were willing to hold the ladder for me as I climbed, especially when I was younger. Their initial support was key to my success. They made me better. And their help inspired me to want to help others. If you've been successful, you're ready to begin helping others by holding the ladder for them. Here are the things you need to know to get started:

LADDER HOLDING BEGINS WITH A SERVING ATTITUDE

Ralph Waldo Emerson said, "Our chief want in life is somebody who shall make us do what we can." Adopting a serving attitude so that we will hold the ladder for others helps us to do what we can. Plus, living out an attitude of service sets a good example to the team and is a visual reminder of the importance of servanthood. When you show the people you work with that you are willing and able to serve, then they will be willing and able to serve.

LADDER HOLDING REQUIRES AVAILABILITY

To become a ladder holder, you must be open to people and willing to give of yourself. When someone asks a question, you must be willing to answer. If you're asked for an opinion, you need to be willing to talk. When people want your ideas, you need to jump in. If they want your endorsement, give it. Ladder holding is one leader helping another leader. When you engage with young leaders, value them, believe in them, encourage them, and give resources to them. Make yourself available to them.

LADDER HOLDING ATTRACTS PEOPLE WHO WANT TO CLIMB

The greatest way to raise up good leaders is to recruit people with good leadership potential. How do you attract those kinds of individuals? Develop a reputation for investing in others. Young, talented people who desire to achieve will begin seeking you out if you become known for giving others a leg up.

LADDER HOLDING IS A PRE-QUALIFIER FOR DISCOVERING A PERSON'S POTENTIAL

How do you gauge others' ability to grow? How do you determine whether they can become good or even great leaders? By watching how they perform when given opportunities. By holding the ladder and offering them the chance to climb, you find out whether they take the steps they can and how quickly and easily they perform. You get a sense of their ability and desire. And that gives you insight into their eventual potential.

LADDER HOLDING OVER TIME MULTIPLIES EFFECTIVENESS

Business magnate and philanthropist Andrew Carnegie said, "It marks a big step in your development when you come to realize that other people can help you do a better job than you could do alone." I've discovered that helping others helps me. Over the years, being a ladder holder has given me a huge ROI (return on investment).

* * *

My friend Chris Hodges said, "A dream is a compelling vision you see in your heart that is too big to accomplish without the help of others." When you start holding the ladder for others, you enlist their help. To take them to an even higher level, you need to do more.

CONSIDER

As you lead your team, do you want more *from* them or *for* them? Take a moment to write the names of each team member along with what you want from them and want for them. You will hold the ladder only for those you want to help.

Team Member	Want from Them	Want for Them

3. LADDER EXTENDING—"HOW HIGH WILL OTHERS GO WITH A LOT OF HELP?"
The next step in the process is to extend the ladder for others. When you do that, you empower them to climb higher and go to entirely new levels. How do you do that? By intentionally and strategically mentoring them.

Over the years I've sought out a lot of mentors who have extended the ladder for me. I've also been a mentor to many leaders, so I know this territory pretty well. Whether you're in the stage of your leadership to be extending the ladder to others, or you're looking for someone to help you develop, here are the criteria for being a good mentor:

LADDER EXTENDERS ARE SUCCESSFUL

Who you learn from is as important as what you learn. Good mentors are successful. Since the word *mentor* is both a verb, something you do, and a noun, something you are, a good mentor must exhibit ability in both areas. In the area of doing, this means they are productive. When it comes to being, good mentors possess strong character. If both components aren't there, don't consider asking them to mentor you.

> **SINCE THE WORD *MENTOR* IS BOTH A VERB, SOMETHING YOU DO, AND A NOUN, SOMETHING YOU ARE, A GOOD MENTOR MUST EXHIBIT ABILITY IN BOTH AREAS.**

LADDER EXTENDERS ARE SPECIALISTS

A mentor ought to be very skilled in just a few areas. Often, people seek out a mentor to help them in all areas of their lives. That's not realistic. No one can help you with everything. Instead of looking for one mentor, seek out several for each key area in your life that you're working on.

That said, when you're first starting out and learning the basics, one solid leader may be a sufficient help to you. As you advance and become more specialized in your growth, your mentors will need to be more specialized.

LADDER EXTENDERS ARE MATURE

The whole idea of working with a mentor implies that the person is ahead of you. He or she is bigger, faster, more knowledgeable, and more experienced. It means the person possesses maturity. Why is maturity essential in a mentor's life? Because we teach what we know, but we reproduce who we are.

LADDER EXTENDERS ARE PRACTICED IN THE ART OF ASKING GREAT QUESTIONS

Good mentors don't jump to conclusions. They ask questions and explore ideas to unlock doors that would otherwise remain locked. I emphasize this because I have not always been good at asking questions. I used to be very quick with answers and had to slow down to become a better listener.

A lot of leaders are too quick to give direction when what they need to do is ask questions. If you're in a place to start extending the ladder for others, develop the ability to ask questions and carefully listen. And if you are working with a mentor and the person isn't asking you any questions, be aware that he or she may not be able to take you very far in the process.

LADDER EXTENDERS ARE HUMBLE

The mentoring relationship is at its best when both people meet and interact on common ground. This is especially important since the mentor is usually working from the position of greater strength, position, and experience. How is this common ground maintained? Through the humility of the mentor. If he or she maintains an openness to sharing failures, disappointments, and losses, the person being mentored benefits tremendously.

ASSESS

Are you ready to mentor others? Mark your answer beside each statement.

YES   NO

❑   ❑   I am successful in my career.

❑   ❑   I have expertise as a specialist.

❑   ❑   I possess maturity, I see the big picture, and I can keep a confidence.

❑   ❑   I'm a good listener skilled at asking questions.

❑   ❑   I possess humility and will treat those I mentor as equals.

4. LADDER BUILDING—"CAN I HELP THEM BUILD THEIR OWN LADDER?"

Once you've climbed the ladder of success yourself, begun to hold it for others, and then learned how to extend it for emerging leaders by mentoring them, there's still another level you can go to as a developer of people. You can become a ladder builder. One of the best ladder-building leaders I know is Sam Chand. He has written several books that contain the word *ladder* in the title: *Who's*

Holding Your Ladder?, *What's Shaking Your Ladder?*, and *Who Moved Your Ladder?* Sam's license plate is LDDRMAN, and he was my inspiration for the title of this lesson.

Ladder building is all about giving another leader the permission, equipment, and empowerment to create their own ladder. As a leader, if you surround yourself with excellent people with high potential, there will be a time when you should allow them to build their own ladders. That's the time when you release them to lead on their own.

ASSESS

To lay the groundwork for becoming a ladder builder, start by asking yourself some questions:

YES	NO	
❏	❏	Do I develop leaders to benefit others, not just for myself and my team?
❏	❏	Do I relinquish control and give other leaders the freedom to be themselves and develop their own process?
❏	❏	Am I happy for a leader I help to move on without me or to enlist other mentors?
❏	❏	Am I willing to help other leaders build their own ladders and then genuinely root for them?
❏	❏	Am I willing to keep helping many leaders build their own ladders without expecting to receive any credit?

If you can answer yes to these questions, and you've climbed up the ladder enough yourself to have earned credibility, then you are ready to start your journey to becoming a ladder builder. If you're not ready, keep building your success and holding the ladder for others while working to shift your attitude to the place you can answer yes to these questions. Then start helping others and mentoring them. And when you see an opportunity to encourage others to build their own ladders, don't hesitate to give them a hand.

QUESTIONS TO ASK BEFORE YOU MENTOR SOMEONE

Andy Stanley often says, "Do for one what you wish you could do for many." That's great advice. And when it comes to investing in and helping someone by holding, extending, and building his or her ladder, it's important who you choose as that one. Your time is limited, and if you can spend time with only one person, it has to be the right one. With that in mind, ask the following questions about anyone you are considering helping:

1. Is This Person Hungry to Learn?

Author Napoleon Hill said, "Strong, deeply rooted desire is the starting point of all achievement."[2] Much of what people accomplish in their lives is based more on how much they want it than on how easy it was to get. Hope says, "There must be a way," while hunger says, "I will make a way." People with hope are many; people with hunger are few. I want to mentor one of the few. If you have to talk the person into being helped or convince him or her to follow through on your advice, that may not be someone you should be investing in. As poet Rudyard Kipling said, "If you don't get what you want it is either a sign that you did not seriously want it, or that you tried to bargain over the price."

2. What Is This Person's Capacity?

Hunger is easy to evaluate. Capacity is much more difficult. When I'm considering whether to mentor someone, I use the seven capacities that I wrote about in my book *No Limits* to evaluate him or her:

1. *Energy Capacity*—their ability to push on physically
2. *Emotional Capacity*—their ability to manage emotions
3. *Thinking Capacity*—their ability to think effectively
4. *People Capacity*—their ability to build relationships
5. *Creative Capacity*—their ability to see options and find answers
6. *Production Capacity*—their ability to accomplish results
7. *Leadership Capacity*—their ability to lift and lead others

I want anyone I mentor to show plenty of potential to grow in all seven areas. As David Salyers of Chick-fil-A said, "The mentor pours into the student knowing that as that person grows the return will be greater than the investment." People cannot show a great return if they don't have adequate capacity.

3. ARE THIS PERSON'S VALUES COMPATIBLE WITH MINE?

Shared values give you a track to run on with someone you intend to mentor. They provide a very important common ground and philosophical foundation. When I prepare to mentor people, I want to know that they . . .

- *Add Value to People*—They must be givers who want to help others, as I do.
- *Value Personal Growth*—They must demonstrate a lifestyle of learning.
- *Lead by Example*—They understand that follow me are the best words a leader can say to a follower.
- *Exceed Expectations*—They stand out and receive 80 percent of life's ROI.
- *Live Intentionally*—They know that everything worthwhile is uphill, and they climb intentionally every day.

Only if we share these common values will I invest time in them. Do you know what your values are? Identify them clearly so that you know whether or not you should invest in a potential candidate.

4. IS THIS INDIVIDUAL A LEADER?

Because my particular calling is to add value to leaders who multiply value to others, I will not invest in a person who is not a leader. I know that may sound very narrow, but it's focused and strategic. I discovered that when I mentor a leader, the ROI is much greater than if I pour myself into a follower. With a leader, I truly can do for one what I wish I could do for many, because that leader will influence many. With followers, that is not necessarily true.

CONSIDER

Before you mentor someone, be sure you can answer yes to these four questions:

YES	NO	
☐	☐	Is this person hungry to learn?
☐	☐	Does this person have the capacity to grow?
☐	☐	Are this person's values compatible with mine?
☐	☐	Is this individual a leader?

What do leaders need from a mentor? I like what Tim Elmore, the founder and president of Growing Leaders, says about this. Tim is one of the emerging leaders I helped more than thirty years ago. First I helped hold his ladder, then extend it. And more than twenty years ago, I helped him build his own ladder and cheered him on. He speaks extensively on mentoring and has written about it too. Some of the things Tim says a successful mentor gives to the person being mentored are: handles, laboratories, road maps, roots, and wings.[3] Let me explain:

HANDLES
Good mentors distill truths from complexity and divide the information into bite-sized principles that others can apply. All good mentors can put life lessons into a nutshell that is transferable. Are you willing to do the homework necessary to do that?

LABORATORIES
Good mentors provide a safe place where learners can practice the principles they're learning. Are you willing to create such a safe environment where people you're developing can take risks?

ROAD MAPS
Good mentors give learners direction for life and provide roadmaps of options for how to proceed to their destination. Are you willing to follow through with a good game plan for the people you mentor?

Roots

Good mentors provide learners with a solid relational foundation. Giving stability and security makes it possible for other people to grow and flourish. Are you willing to extend love and acceptance to the people you mentor and hang in there with them when they face difficulties?

Wings

Good mentors help people to see new horizons and fly to places beyond where they imagined they could go. This is true empowerment. Are you willing to celebrate when people you mentor fly higher or farther than you have?

Whys

I want to add one more quality to Tim's list. One of the most important things you can do for potential leaders is to help them see the big picture by teaching them the *why*s. This gives them context. It reveals to them the thinking and reasons behind your decisions. It teaches them decision-making. If you want learners to follow directions, you only need to provide the *what*. If you want them to lead others and give directions, they must also have the *why*. Are you willing to take the time and trouble to give them the *why* behind every *what*?

ACTION PLAN

Pick a leader with potential to mentor. Once you're sure he or she meets the four criteria above, write out an action plan for this person. Be sure to include handles, laboratories, road maps, roots, wings, and whys.

_____

_____

_____

_____

_____

_____

**IF YOU WANT LEARNERS TO FOLLOW DIRECTIONS,
YOU ONLY NEED TO PROVIDE THE *WHAT*. IF YOU WANT THEM TO LEAD OTHERS
AND GIVE DIRECTIONS, THEY MUST ALSO HAVE THE *WHY*.**

The bottom line is that leaders who shift from ladder climber to ladder builder help new leaders stretch to their potential. That's what I hope to do for the rest of my life and to leave as my legacy. And I invite you to do the same. You'll never regret investing in another leader who makes a positive difference in this world. It's the best way to extend your influence and achieve significance.

LADDER CLIMBING TO
LADDER BUILDING

THE REPRODUCTION SHIFT

DISCUSSION QUESTIONS

1. Where have you focused most of your time and energy in your career?

   - Climbing the Ladder of Success
   - Holding the Ladder for Others
   - Extending the Ladder for Others
   - Building Ladders for Others

2. Do you believe a leader needs to progress from holding to extending to building ladders? Or can a leader simply jump from climbing the ladder to building ladders for others? Explain your answer.

3. What experience do you have with being mentored? How was it? How did it benefit you? What didn't you like about it?

4. What experience do you have being a mentor to others? How did that go? What did you do well? What do you wish you would have done better? Was the time you put in worth the effort? Explain.

5. What impact would focusing on ladder building would have on you personally and professionally? What impact would it have on your leadership? What step in that direction would you be willing to commit to immediately?

NOTES

LESSON EIGHT

DIRECTING TO
CONNECTING

THE COMMUNICATION SHIFT

You don't lead by hitting people over the head—that's assault, not leadership.

DWIGHT D. EISENHOWER

All of the leadershifts in my life have not occurred in the same way or on the same timetable. Some have occurred gradually while others were almost instantaneous. Many were prompted by my leadership intuition, which has often been the catalyst for the changes I made. But some, like the communication shift from directing to connecting, went against my natural grain. This was a shift in the opposite direction of my experience, and it required time to develop.

I grew up in a home where directing was the practiced style of communication and leadership. My college theological training in communication and leadership reinforced this a methodology. In leadership, the authority in our ecclesiastical world was top-down. So I came from an upbringing and training that emphasized directing. On top of all this, my temperament is choleric, which means I love to be in charge and tell others what to do. I know where I want to go, and I'm not shy

8

125

about saying how we should get there. If you have a question, I've got an answer. If you're not sure about what you want to do, I can give you a plan for your life.

Directing others was a very natural leadership style for me. But what's natural for me is not necessarily what's best for others. Nobody wants to be bossed around. Many times I could sense that people were following me only because they had to, not because they wanted to. Even those who wanted to follow me didn't always buy into the vision and direction I was communicating as strongly as I had hoped. Intuitively, I began to understand that I needed to move away from directing. I no longer wanted to be a "leadership cop" standing at the intersection of my organization and directing traffic all the time. But at the same time, I didn't know what else to do. What better way was there to lead people?

WELCOME TO A NEW PARADIGM

Two experiences functioned as catalysts to help me reshape my communication and leadership style. The first occurred in 1988. That was the year I hired Bobb Biehl as a consultant. This was my first experience hiring a business consultant, and it was before I had developed much experience as a ladder builder, so the way Bobb started the process took me totally by surprise. We spent two days together and the entire first day Bobb asked me questions. The entire day! He'd ask a question, I'd answer, and he'd ask follow-up questions based on my answers. He worked with flip charts, writing the questions and the answers. At the end of the day, every wall in my office was covered with sheets of paper containing everything we had talked about. I was exhausted yet fulfilled. In those hours Bobb had drawn out my innermost thoughts, hopes, and aspirations in a way that never had been done before. With each question, he had peeled away another layer, revealing the depth of my thinking and feelings. It was exhilarating.

I learned an important lesson from that. Bobb had to *find* me—who I was, where I was, where I had been, where I hoped to go—before he could *lead* me. That opened my eyes to a better way of leading, and the discovery became the foundation of my practice of connecting with others. From then on, I started working to find people by asking questions before trying to lead them.

The second experience that impacted me greatly occurred in 2003. I was invited to attend a basketball game of the University of Tennessee Lady Volunteers coached by the great Pat Summitt. I attended their pregame and sat right behind the bench. At halftime, I was able to go into the locker room and observe how Pat coached the team.

When we got to the locker room, Pat and the other coaches huddled together away from the players, while the players immediately sat in a semicircle around a whiteboard that had three questions written on it: (1) What did we do right in the first half? (2) What did we do wrong? (3) What do we need to change?

For five minutes, the players discussed their answers to those three questions while one player wrote down their responses. I sat behind the players and watched. I was fascinated. Then Pat walked over to the marker board and looked at the answers. She made a couple of comments related to what they had written, and then she sent the players back out on the floor to warm up for the second half.

After the game I asked Pat about it, and her answer was stunning.

"John, too many leaders lead by assumption," she said. "They assume they know where their people are. That halftime exercise lets me find my players so I can lead them. That can only be done by asking questions and listening to their answers."

That was a huge "aha" moment for me and was the second bookend in my leadershift from directing to connecting. I was determined from that moment forward to use connecting as the basis for my leadership and communication style.

CONSIDER

Take a moment and look at the contrast between these two styles. On each line, mark the box that represents your natural style.

DIRECTING	CONNECTING
❑ Authoritative	❑ Collaborative
❑ Talking	❑ Listening
❑ Top Down	❑ Side by Side
❑ Enlisting	❑ Empowering
❑ Assuming	❑ Understanding
❑ Gives Answers	❑ Asks Questions
❑ My Agenda	❑ Your Agenda

The goal of connecting is to find common ground with the leader initiating. This is the place where . . .

- both people meet;
- both people are valued;
- both people share;
- both people listen and learn;
- both people adjust;
- both people settle on a game plan;
- both people take ownership of the game plan; and
- both people move together to higher ground.

Learning to connect is one of the most important things you can do in life.

MAKE THE LEADERSHIFT TO CONNECTING

If you want to become the best leader you're capable of being, you must learn to connect with people. To do that, you must find ways to overcome the challenges of connecting and finding common ground. This can often be a difficult process, especially with a varied team. Here are the seven things I have found to be most important to a leader who wants to connect with others:

1. HUMILITY—LET PEOPLE KNOW YOU NEED THEM

Humility is essential in connecting with people. It took me a while to learn this. In my younger years, I would ask God to help me be successful, but secretly I hoped that people would think I did it all myself. I possessed more human frailty than humility. To help me, God gave me a dream bigger than myself. It was so intimidating that I had only two choices: give up or get help. I chose to ask for help, which at first felt very humbling. But I quickly discovered how much I needed other people. And as a result, my leadership actually got better, not worse.

> GOD GAVE ME A DREAM BIGGER THAN MYSELF. IT WAS SO INTIMIDATING THAT I HAD ONLY TWO CHOICES: GIVE UP OR GET HELP.

Good leaders are aware that they need other people, and they let them know that. There really is no downside. It keeps the leader's ego in check, it connects the leader and the people on the team, it draws team members into the center, and it better enables them to fulfill the vison. So, if you want to be a connector, acknowledge your shortcomings and need for others and be willing to ask for help.

CONSIDER

How often do you tell the people on your team that you need them and are grateful for their contribution? How often do you admit where you lack ability and thank them for theirs?

_____

_____

_____

_____

_____

_____

_____

_____

2. CURIOSITY—ASK PEOPLE QUESTIONS

I'm known for asking questions. Whether I'm at dinner with friends, taking my grandchildren on a trip, or leading a business meeting, people know I'll be asking them questions. But I got my start as a questioner by asking myself questions. One of the things that stirred me to start asking myself better questions was Bob Buford's book *Halftime*. He had an important question for someone who is middle-aged, which I was at the time I first read the book more than twenty years ago. His question: "What kind of second half are you going to live?" Buford wrote:

> You will not get very far in your second half without knowing your life mission. Can yours be stated in a sentence or two? A good way to begin formulating one is with some questions (and nakedly honest answers).

What is your passion? What have you achieved? What have you done uncommonly well? How are you wired? Where do you belong? What are the "shoulds" that have trailed you during the first half? These and other questions like them will direct you toward the self your heart longs for; they will help you discover the task for which you were especially made.[1]

These questions helped me at mid-life to set myself up for potentially a good second half.

Today I'm in my seventies, and I haven't stopped asking questions. I'm still curious, and I want to remain that way. Why? Because without asking questions, I can easily become comfortable, stagnant. Entropy can easily set in. I would start to accept the status quo without asking if there were a better way. I would fail to recognize opportunities.

Too many leaders don't ask enough questions—of themselves or others. This happens for a variety of reasons:

- They assume they have the answers.
- They value what *they* think more than what *others* think.
- They prioritize directing others over understanding others.
- They don't recognize the need to find common ground.
- They don't understand that questions help to manage expectations.

I want to take a moment to address this final point. As leaders, we must manage expectations all the time. We have to deal with expectations we have for ourselves, expectations we have for others, and expectations others have for us. Any time our expectations or those of others don't align with what's actually happening, there are problems. In fact, I believe that disappointment is the gap between expectations and reality. How do we close that gap? By asking questions so that we can adjust our expectations. Knowing the expectations I have of myself makes me more self-aware, which paves the way for me to improve myself and become better. Knowing the expectations I have of others makes me better able to communicate with people and face reality. And knowing the expectations others have of me makes me better able to lead them. All of these connections are made when we use questions to build bridges with others.

CONSIDER

How often do you ask questions? Do you assume you have all the answers or have better answers than your team members? How can you become better at asking questions?

_____

_____

_____

_____

_____

_____

_____

_____

3. EFFORT—GO OUT OF YOUR WAY TO CONNECT WITH PEOPLE

Oprah Winfrey said, "The big secret in life is that there is no big secret. Whatever your goal, you can get there if you are willing to work." That is certainly true in connecting with people—you have to make the effort.

My grandson, John, started taking golf lessons when he was twelve. After months of lessons, it finally became time for him to play on a golf course, and I wanted to be the one to take him. Before we began I said, "John, I want you to try to get a par on one of the holes. If you are able to get on the green and putt for par, I'll take a video of you taking the shot and dropping the ball into the hole. That way we can show it to the family."

For two days, we played golf and worked on getting John his first par on a golf course. Every time he putted for a par, I pulled out my phone and videoed him. Four different times, he got on the green and had a chance to putt for par and missed it. But late on the second day on the sixteenth hole, John attempted his par putt and rolled the ball into the cup. And I had it on video! The first par he ever made.

We celebrated on the green, and then I immediately shared the video with the rest of the family right then and there. I also got a picture of John holding up his scorecard, proudly showing off his par, with his arm around me.

Now, why did I do that when it was so much work? Well, first of all, it was fun. But more importantly, I wanted to make a meaningful memory with my grandson. It's something both of us will always remember. And it created a special connection between us—one that will last well beyond our time on the golf course.

Every relational connection starts with the decision to make the effort to connect. It ends with what I call the mirror test: Can you look into the mirror and say to yourself that you did your best? If so, you have passed the test. As my friend Art Williams said, "All you can do is all you can do, but all you can do is enough."

ALL YOU CAN DO IS ALL YOU CAN DO, BUT ALL YOU CAN DO IS ENOUGH.

ART WILLIAMS

If you care about people, you will be capable of coming up with ways to create connecting experiences with others. But it will take effort. And it will take even *more* effort to follow through on those ideas. But if you don't, you're not really doing all you can to connect—or to become the best leader you can be.

CONSIDER

How can you go out of your way to connect with members of your team? Write the names of each team member along with an idea for a way to connect.

_____

_____

_____

_____

_____

_____

_____

4. TRUSTWORTHINESS—BE SOMEONE OTHERS CAN COUNT ON

People do not connect with someone they don't trust. They connect with someone they can count on. Author and speaker Simon Sinek addressed this issue when he said, "People don't buy what you do, they buy why you do it." The *why* deals with motives. Those motives come from the heart and play out as trustworthiness if the motives are good and right.

As a leader, I know I have to keep my motives right. If my primary motivation is to add value to people and help them, then all is good. If not, I'll get off track. And I'm continually aware that to remain trustworthy in the eyes of others, I have to work at being continually successful in three areas:

1. Integrity in my life
2. Consistency in my actions
3. Competence in my work

When I do these things well, I become more trustworthy and am able to connect with people—and build the relationship. When I fail in one or more of these, I lose trust and have to work to regain the trust I've lost. Because I'm only human, I do fail sometimes. How do I regain lost trust? By following this process:

- I fully acknowledge what I have done wrong.
- I explain exactly what I am going to do to try to make things right.
- I give them an opportunity to share their perspective and add anything to what I shared with them.
- I do the work to fix the problem.
- I follow up with them to confirm that the problem was fixed to their satisfaction.

The bottom line is that I do what I can to make it right. And trust me: I've had to do this too many times to count. But it works. And it's always amazing to me how forgiving people are when I follow this process with them. What's even more amazing is how often the relationship is strengthened and improved. It's often even better than it was before. I think there is a valuable lesson from this about trustworthiness. We often lose trust and connection with one another not because of an occasional failing, but because we neglect to take the right steps afterward to restore the relationship. Don't allow that to happen to you. Make the effort to be trustworthy, and when you fail, do what's in your power to make things right.

CONSIDER

Where have you broken trust with someone in your life? Commit to addressing the wrong you did. Prepare by making notes here:

What I did wrong: _____
_____
_____

How I'm going to try to make it right: _____
_____
_____

When I am going to talk to them and hear their side: _____
_____
_____

When I will work to fix the problem: _____
_____
_____

When I will follow up with them: _____
_____
_____

5. GENEROSITY—GIVE FIRST, GIVE CONTINUALLY

Albert Einstein said, "A person first starts to live when he can live outside of himself." It could also be said that a person starts to give when he lives outside himself. And giving is a good way to connect with others.

A PERSON FIRST STARTS TO LIVE WHEN HE CAN LIVE OUTSIDE OF HIMSELF.

ALBERT EINSTEIN

I have never known a stingy person with a scarcity mind-set who was able to connect well with other people. They are too often self-driven and make decisions based on self-preservation. As theologian Henri Nouwen said, "When we refrain from giving, with a scarcity mentality, the little we have will become less. When we give generously, with an abundance mentality, what we give away will multiply."

A few years ago I came across a transcript of the commencement address given by author Stephen King to the 2001 graduating class of Vassar College. As you might expect, it's written eloquently. In his address, he talked about money and generosity:

We come in naked and broke. We may be dressed when we go out, but we're just as broke. Warren Buffett? Going to go out broke. Bill Gates? Going to go out broke. President Ferguson? Going to go out broke. Steve King? Broke. You guys? Broke. Not a crying dime between you. And how long in between? How long have you got to be in the chips? . . . Just the blink of an eye. . . .

Should you give away what you have? Of course you should. I want you to consider making your lives one long gift to others, and why not? All the other stuff you have is just on loan. All you want to get at the getting place, from the Maserati you may dream about to the retirement fund some guy will try to sell you on sooner or later—none of that is real. All that lasts in this world is what you pass on. The rest is smoke and mirrors. . . .

Giving isn't about the receiver or the gift but the giver. It's for the giver. One doesn't open one's wallet to improve the world, although it's nice when that happens. One opens one's wallet to improve one's self. I give because it's the only concrete way I have of saying I'm glad to be alive and that I can earn my daily bread doing what I love. I hope you will be similarly grateful to be alive and that you will also be glad to do whatever it is you wind up doing. . . .

So I ask you to begin the next great phase of your life by giving, and to continue as you begin. I think you'll find that in the end you get far more than you ever had and do more good than you ever dreamed.[2]

Generosity makes you a better person, it helps you to become a better leader, and it paves the way for you to connect with other people. If you're not already someone who gives first and gives continually, then I encourage you to try it.

CONSIDER

In what areas of your life are you a giver? What do you give? How often do you give? What could you start doing now to become more generous?

_____

_____

_____

_____

_____

_____

6. LISTENING—OPEN THE BEST DOOR TO CONNECTING WITH PEOPLE

I once read a story about a tennis pro who was giving a lesson to a new student. After watching the student take several swings at the tennis ball, the instructor began to suggest ways the man might improve his stroke. But every time the instructor made a suggestion, the student interrupted him with his own diagnosis of the problem and how he might fix it.

After being interrupted yet again, the pro simply nodded in agreement and let the player continue on his own.

When the lesson was over, a woman—who observed the lesson, was familiar with the pro, and had seen the whole thing—asked, "Why did you go along with that arrogant man's stupid suggestions?"

The old pro smiled and answered, "I learned a long time ago that it's a sheer waste of time to try to sell answers to a person who only wants to buy echoes."

If you never listen, before long the people around you will stop talking to you, and you'll become isolated as a leader. If you *do* listen, not only will they tell you things you need to know but they will also connect with you because they see that you care and that you value what they have to say.

It took me a while to learn this myself. As a young leader I was like the tennis student who didn't listen. My highest priority was expressing my ideas and convincing others to buy into them, not listening to feedback or learning what others had to say. After a series of leadership misses, I recognized the problem in my unwillingness to make listening a priority, and I began shifting to do things differently. But it was hard fought. I struggled to change, but I eventually succeeded. Here's how I did it.

- I Made a List of the Negatives of Not Listening Well
- I Reminded Myself Daily to Listen Well
- I Stopped Interrupting
- I Started Asking Questions
- I Invited People to Hold Me Accountable for Listening

If you want to be a connecting leader, become a better listener. Invite others to hold you accountable. If you have the courage, meet with your team members, colleagues, friends, and family, and ask them how good a listener you are on a scale of one to ten. If your score is low, you might need to take the same steps I did.

CONSIDER

Talk to the three people on your team with whom you have the least smooth working relationship, and ask them these questions:

- Do you think it would improve our working relationship if I became a better listener?
- When should I listen more?
- How do you think that would help?

(continued)

Don't interrupt them or defend yourself. Take notes and thank them for their input. Then reflect on what that told you.

_____
_____
_____
_____
_____
_____
_____
_____
_____
_____
_____
_____
_____

7. ENCOURAGEMENT—GIVE PEOPLE OXYGEN FOR THEIR SOUL

As leaders, we must never underestimate the value of reminding others that we believe in them. If even the greatest of leaders need encouragement, then everyone does. That's why George M. Adams called encouragement oxygen for the soul.

When you interact with others as a leader, what is your mind-set? Is your intention to correct them or connect with them? Do you keep them down, or lift them up? You have that choice every day—with those you lead, with those who lead you, with your friends, family, and colleagues.

WHEN YOU INTERACT WITH OTHERS AS A LEADER, WHAT IS YOUR MIND-SET? IS YOUR INTENTION TO CORRECT THEM OR CONNECT WITH THEM?

If you're a fan of *The Lord of the Rings* books, and *The Hobbit*, you might be surprised that their author, J. R. R. Tolkien, required the encouragement of a friend and fellow writer to keep him going in the early stages of his work on those books. C. S. Lewis and Tolkien used to gather, along with a few other friends, in a group they called the Inklings. They met weekly to share what they were working on and to encourage one another. Tolkien credited Lewis as the person who kept him going when he felt discouraged. In an article about the two writers, Mark Moring said:

> Had it not been for Lewis, Tolkien wouldn't have written *The Lord of the Rings*. Tolkien wrote in a letter, "The unspeakable debt I owe him cannot be fathomed. For long, he was my only audience." Several times Tolkien really threw in the towel, and each time Lewis said, "Tollers, where's that next chapter? You can't give up now." Lewis was the only one who kept him going.[3]

Everyone in your life could use the encouragement that only you can give. At home, I've always tried to provide encouragement, first to my children and now also to my grandchildren. I also take the mind-set of an encourager onto the stage when I speak. As a communicator, I can either try to be a *sage on the stage* or a *guide by their side*. A sage looks down on others and tries to impress them with wisdom. A guide comes alongside, shares the journey, and encourages them to go the distance with him. I don't want to impress others; I want to connect with them and help them.

Billionaire investor and philanthropist Charles Schwab said, "I have yet to find the man, however great or exalted his station, who did not do better work and put forth greater effort under a spirit of approval than he would ever do under a spirit of criticism."[4] I believe most people are under-encouraged. You can correct that deficit by becoming an encouraging leader.

ACTION PLAN

Make a commitment to say one encouraging thing every day this week to each person on your team. Pay attention to how people respond and whether the work atmosphere changes.

Changing from directing to connecting is one of the most valuable shifts you will ever make as a leader. When you direct, it's like building a bridge to others, but the traffic only goes one way. When you connect, it's a two-way street. And because of that, everything improves. Not only are relationships better, but ideas improve because they're flowing in both directions. People work better together, and the team gets stronger. Problems get solved more quickly because communication is better, people know one another better, and they start pulling together. And the environment improves too.

Will it take time to build these connections? The answer is yes. But don't let that stop you. In the long run, you'll save time. Your team will get better. And so will you.

DIRECTING TO
CONNECTING

THE COMMUNICATION SHIFT

DISCUSSION QUESTIONS

1. Who is the best leader you ever worked for? How much directing and how much connecting did he or she do?

2. In what situations is directing more effective? In what situations is connecting more effective? Which is better for long-term team success?

3. How much does personality type affect whether a leader naturally directs or connects? What can someone who's not naturally a connector do to improve in this area?

4. How much of the ability to connect comes from internal factors, such as humility, attitude, and trustworthiness, and how much comes from practices, such as reaching out to people, asking questions, and listening? Explain your answer.

5. What is your greatest obstacle or hesitation about connecting with team members? What can you do to overcome it?

NOTES

LESSON NINE

TEAM UNIFORMITY TO
TEAM DIVERSITY

THE IMPROVEMENT SHIFT

Our differences can make a positive difference.

Of all the leadershifts I've made, this required the greatest leap. I say that because there is nothing diverse about my background. I grew up in Circleville, Ohio. It was in the middle of the country. The community was almost entirely white. And my family was lower middle class. There was nothing cutting-edge about the church I grew up in. We were conservative and old-fashioned. Even the theological and ministry training I received at the college in Circleville emphasized that Christians should separate themselves from the culture of society in some ways. We set ourselves apart and were comfortable spending all our time with people like ourselves.

My early days as a pastor were equally vanilla. The church I led was filled with farmers and their families. They were good-hearted, hardworking, salt-of-the-earth types of people. But they were not diverse or forward-looking. While I was at the church, NASA put the first man on the moon. The people in my church were not convinced that it had actually happened. Many believed it was a hoax that had been staged in the desert of the American West with trampolines placed underground and covered with sand. Really? Yes, really!

All the leaders in the church were old white men. They all seemed to be cut from the same cloth, adhering to the same rules, following the same model of leadership. They even looked like one another. As a pastor, I was expected to conform to the way other churches in our organization operated and follow all the same rules and guidelines everyone else did. As I already mentioned in Lesson 6 on the abundance shift, the emphasis was on tradition and conformity. When it was time for me to hire my first staff member, the advice I received was to try to find a "John Jr.": someone exactly like me. Their concept of progress was moving backward slowly, and their idea of innovation was *more of the same.*

GETTING OUTSIDE OF THE BUBBLE

The improvement shift from uniformity to diversity occurred slowly for me. The seeds were sown for it while I was still in college. It started because I was coaching a basketball team at a Catholic school. This was my first exposure to and long-term interaction with Catholics. At that time, I also met the first priest I ever got to know: Father Mike Elifritz. He was wonderful. After I was done coaching and I was getting ready to graduate from college, I had a lunch with Father Mike. I shared with him some of my apprehension about the next steps I would be taking in life. I'll never forget what he told me: "John, trust your future to God." Those words helped me to be more confident as I moved into the next phase of living.

Why were those words so significant? After all, I was a person of faith who was actually going into ministry! They resonated strongly with me because a Catholic was adding value to a Protestant. In my small sheltered world, that wasn't supposed to happen. Those two groups stayed on opposite sides of the line and were suspicious of one another. But his heart and support changed my thinking. It was catalytic for me and started to show me a bigger, more diverse world.

That occurred in 1969 and was the start of a long journey toward the appreciation of diversity that would take almost thirty years. Along the way, there were a lot of experiences that challenged my narrow, naïve thinking, and a lot of lessons that I learned. Hundreds of people different from me made a positive difference in my life. They . . .

- challenged my assumptions,
- changed my thinking,
- showed me better ways of doing things,

- helped me remove my prejudices,
- taught me to value everyone, and
- made me a better person.

Slowly I moved from valuing sameness to questioning its value. Diversity slowly marked me with this thought: people different from me could make a positive difference in me.

People different from me could make a positive difference in me.

This shift, which started subtly and grew over time, culminated when I relocated myself and my companies to Atlanta, Georgia, in 1997. Atlanta is a city rich in African-American influence and history. That was new to me. I'd lived in small-town Ohio, rural Indiana, and sunny San Diego. I knew there was a gap between me and the African-American community and their experiences, and I wanted to close that gap.

To help me, I enlisted the assistance of my friend Sam Chand, the president emeritus of Beulah Heights University, a predominantly African-American institution in Atlanta. Sam was born in India, but he was well-connected in our community. He arranged lunches every other month for two years where I got to meet more than three hundred local leaders. Overall, their journey was different from mine. I asked a lot of questions and requested that people tell me their stories. I'm happy to say that I was able to connect with most of the people I met. They reshaped my attitude, challenged my thinking, and touched my soul. I became a better person because of these experiences, and I made many new friends.

THE ADVANTAGES OF TEAM DIVERSITY

I saw a definition of *team* in the *Harvard Business Review* that I really like: "A team is a small number of people with complementary skills who are committed to a common purpose, set of performance goals, and approach for which they hold themselves mutually accountable."[1] This definition assumes that there is a variety of skills. That implies diversity.

Our differences really can make a difference in our teams, our organizations, and our individual lives. Once we find common ground and commit to bringing the best out of people who are diverse, good things will begin to happen. This is what I am discovering now.

1. DIVERSE TEAMS FILL IN THE KNOWLEDGE GAP

As a leader, it's important to know what you don't know. How? By engaging with diverse people on your team. If you include a variety of people, then *someone* on your team will be able to help you. That's why I frequently ask members of my team, "What am I missing?" I assume that I'm always missing something, and I believe someone can help me. When they do, then I'm freed up to focus on what I do know and what I do well.

2. DIVERSE TEAMS FILL IN THE PERSPECTIVE GAP

Malcolm Forbes said that diversity is the art of thinking independently together. I love that because getting good independent thinkers to work together is the leadership challenge I love tackling. When everyone thinks and says the same things, it's the end of creativity and death to an entrepreneurial environment.

As a leader, it is my responsibility to encourage and engage in conversations that draw out different perspectives. I don't need or want my team members to parrot back to me what I think or to try to guess what I want. I want to know what *they* think. I want my team to "take me on" when they see things differently. I want them to challenge me just like I challenge them. It is only then that we get the most out of one another. That's called win-win.

3. DIVERSE TEAMS FILL IN THE EXPERIENCE GAP

A little bit of experience outweighs a whole lot of theory as far as I'm concerned. The greater the differences in personal experiences, the greater the team's ability to achieve, and the greater number of "tools" the team has at its disposal. As the saying goes, if all you have is a hammer, everything looks like a nail. Diversity helps prevent us from hammering away at things that need a screwdriver approach.

CONSIDER

What knowledge, perspective, and experience do you lack that would benefit your team or organization? Does your current team have the potential to provide what's needed? If not, what kinds of different people could you recruit to fill these gaps?

_____

_____

_____

_____

BARRIERS TO DIVERSITY

The greatest of leaders seem to embrace diversity instinctively. Winston Churchill, who masterfully led the United Kingdom during the difficult years of World War II, brought political adversaries like Clement Attlee into his strategy meetings in the underground bunker in London. Churchill knew the crisis demanded extraordinary talent, not just the skills of the people he would be comfortable with. Yet, if inviting diversity is such a valuable practice, why don't more leaders embrace it? Because diversity is uncomfortable. Many leaders fail to deal with that discomfort and have a difficult time overcoming these common barriers to diversity:

1. FEAR OF CONFLICT

A diverse team will naturally possess differences of opinion, perspective, and worldview. That almost inevitably leads to conflict. Many people are afraid of that, yet it's a necessary part of life. Conflict can actually help us. Author and consultant Patrick Lencioni wrote about this in his book *The Five Dysfunctions of a Team*:

> All great relationships, the ones that last over time, require productive conflict in order to grow. This is true in marriage, parenthood, friendship, and certainly business.

Unfortunately, conflict is considered taboo in many situations, especially at work. The higher you go up the management chain, the more you find people spending inordinate amounts of time and energy trying to avoid the kind of passionate debates that are essential to any great team.[2]

Lencioni teaches that productive conflict has one purpose: "To produce the best possible solution in the shortest period of time."[3] When different people with different experiences sharing different opinions all sit at the table with the same objective, you can produce extraordinary results. But it requires people to set aside their titles and positions, personal agendas, and preferences. Everyone must want the best ideas to win, not just their own or their group's.

A marriage counselor once shared something with me about resolving the conflicts in marriage. People usually enter a marriage with different personalities, different experiences, different perspectives, and different expectations. Whatever differences existed before the wedding are intensified as the couple lives together for the first time. But happy marriages are based less on compatibility and more on how they deal with incompatibility. Rather than allowing the relationship to get tied up in knots, they need to learn to loosen the knot a bit—to face and resolve conflict.

CONSIDER

Examine these two approaches to conflict. Mark the phrase that best describes you on each line.

UNHEALTHY CONFLICT	HEALTHY CONFLICT
❑ Takes Differences Personally	❑ Sees Differences Impartially
❑ Dumps Personal Baggage	❑ Desires to Know the Person
❑ Searches for Retaliation	❑ Searches for Resolution
❑ Results in Hurt	❑ Results in Helpfulness
❑ Seeks Quick Conclusions	❑ Seeks Understanding
❑ Holds Back from the Conversation	❑ Becomes Part of the Conversation
❑ Values Self Above Solutions	❑ Values Solutions Above Self
❑ Defends Their Territory	❑ Opens Up New Territory
❑ Makes the Team Worse	❑ Makes the Team Better

What people often fear most are breakdowns and that irreparable harm may occur in relationships. But when you value diversity and are genuinely open to the ideas and insights of other people, you open up the possibility of discovering fresh ideas, building a better team, and taking new ground.

2. INSUFFICIENT PERSONAL NETWORK

Most people spend time with others like themselves. That often isn't out of prejudice. It's just how people act. When I was growing up, my mother used to tell me, "Birds of a feather flock together." She said it because she wanted me to spend time with other boys of high character, not kids who made bad choices and got into trouble. But the old adage she used to quote also is an indication that people naturally gravitate toward others of similar background, age, and race.

Take an honest look at your peers, friends, and colleagues. If most of the people you know look like you, vote like you, and listen to the same music as you, you probably need to put some work into expanding your network. If you need to expand your personal network, as I did, keep these things in mind:

EXPANDING YOUR NETWORK REQUIRES HUMILITY

When I started my leadership career, I thought I was always right. My greatest discovery as I started to meet people unlike myself was that they had so much to offer. Before making the improvement shift, I had shortchanged myself. Realizing that was humbling. When I recognized that others knew what I didn't, and that they had as much to contribute as I did, I could leave my world and enter new ones. Instead of fearing loss, I was anticipating what I would gain from our interaction.

EXPANDING YOUR NETWORK REQUIRES INTENTIONALITY

If you wait for connections with dissimilar people to happen on their own, they will never happen. You need to get out of your own natural "flock" and migrate to where other birds live and work. It will be uncomfortable, and anything uncomfortable or unusual must be done with high intentionality.

EXPANDING YOUR NETWORK REQUIRES ENERGY

Any time you try something new, it's going to take extra energy. That probably seems like common sense. However, people don't plan for it. If you want to make your team more diverse, gear up for it. Plan to keep going when you're too tired or don't feel like moving forward.

EXPANDING YOUR NETWORK REQUIRES TIME

The same can be said of time. It will take you time to build a diversified team. On top of that, it will take time (and energy) to see the benefits of diversity. You'll need to demonstrate patience as you start the "diversity dance," where you take two steps forward and one step back. It will take time for people to get to know one another. Everyone won't play nice at first. You'll encounter speed bumps and detours. That's true for any good team. But can you get there? Yes, if you give the time and energy required.

EXPANDING YOUR NETWORK REQUIRES LOVE

This one may be a surprise, especially in a business context, but I'm going to tell it like it is. Love makes all things work, and the foundation of love is being willing to value people—including people different from you and people you don't like. I've discovered that the more I value people, the more I add value to them. And the more I add value to them, the more value they return to the team. What gets appreciated, appreciates.

CONSIDER

What is keeping you from expanding your network? Lack of humility? Failure of intentionality? Unwillingness to expend energy or time? Indifference to people? What can you do to change?

_____

_____

_____

_____

_____

_____

_____

3. UNWILLINGNESS TO DEAL WITH PREJUDICE

I didn't grow up trying to isolate myself from people who were different from me—I just didn't know many. When I did eventually seek out relationships with people who were different, such as when I began connecting with the African-American business community in Atlanta, I discovered that I possessed a passive prejudice against people who were unlike me. Because of my ignorance, I had a blind spot. I assumed that people like me had good ideas that worked better than anyone else's. Exposure to different people from different backgrounds revealed my prejudice.

There's a saying I came across that really opened my eyes to what happens when you're prejudiced. I don't know who said it, but it's true: "The world is like a hand and all of the people its fingers. If you hate and destroy one group of people, you lose a finger, and the grasp of the world is less."

Embracing diversity has allowed me to have a better grasp of the world around me. My perspective has been changed. Does yours need to be? What prejudices, whether conscious or unknown, do you possess that are keeping you from connecting with people unlike you and diversifying your team? You need to identify whatever is holding you back and work to resolve it.

CONSIDER

The problem with prejudices is they often come from having blind spots, which means you can't see them. However, often there are clues you *can* see. Where do you suspect you may possess prejudices? Explore that. You can't deal with something you don't acknowledge.

4. ARROGANCE

Some leaders are so confident in their own genius that they can't imagine other people adding value to their work. They believe the less similar others are, the less they can contribute. And sadly, the farther down in the organization people are, the more they are ignored. But the reality is that no leaders are so good that they can afford to ignore the contributions of others. No one is indispensable.

If you dismiss the ideas and potential contributions of others, especially those offered by people different from you, you will never reach your potential and neither will your team. And, sadly, you will never even know it!

5. PERSONAL INSECURITIES

There's an old joke that the CEO of an organization met one day with the head of HR and said, "Search the organization for an alert, aggressive young leader who could step into my shoes, and when you find him, fire him." Just as the CEO in that joke felt threatened by strong young leaders, there are people who feel threatened or uncomfortable around those who are different. That personal insecurity is easily sensed by others and puts them off.

The topic of insecurity is a complex one, and if you're an insecure leader, you may need to get help dealing with it. But I will say this: the best antidote I've ever found for personal insecurity is to think about helping other people and putting them first. When you do that, you stop worrying about trying to look good, and you put your attention on making others look good.

THE BEST ANTIDOTE I'VE EVER FOUND FOR PERSONAL INSECURITY IS TO THINK ABOUT HELPING OTHER PEOPLE AND PUTTING THEM FIRST.

If you have insecurities, especially those driven by other's strengths or differences, start working on them. If you don't, your leadership will harm—not help—the team.

CONSIDER

What kinds of people intimidate you? Who brings out the worst in you? Who makes you nervous? Answers to these questions can give you clues about your insecurities. When you think about these people, what are you afraid of?

_____
_____
_____
_____
_____
_____
_____
_____

One of the ways to deal with insecurities is to admit your weaknesses and stop pretending they don't exist. Take some time to face your fears, acknowledge your weaknesses, and appreciate others who are skilled where you are not.

6. Failing to Be Inclusive

The final common barrier to promoting team diversity is the leader and team members' failure to be inclusive. When people are on your team but don't feel like they belong or contribute, they disconnect. And they don't bring their best gifts and talents to the table.

For many years I've taught people to seek common ground with others as the way to start the connection process and to further that process by valuing people and adding value to them. I still believe this is the way to start. But the whole idea of _inclusion_ and how it relates to diversity is changing because of millennials. I recently read a study about the approach millennials take to the workplace, and I thought, _No wonder the number one question I'm asked in the business community is how to interact with millennials._

The study was called "The Radical Transformation of Diversity and Inclusion: The Millennial Influence" and was published by Deloitte University. It said that my generation of baby boomers as well as Generation Xers see _inclusion_ as a function of morality—the right thing to do. We would define it in terms of representation, or ensuring fair inclusion of "gender, race, religion, ethnicity, and sexual orientation."[4] In contrast, millennials see diversity and inclusion as having intrinsic value. They allow voices to be heard that have a tangible and beneficial impact on business. The goal isn't just bringing together people of different races, religions, and genders; instead, they want to bring together people with differences in background, personal experience, style, and perspective.[5]

How those people are brought together is also important to millennials. As the study's authors, Christie Smith and Stephanie Turner, explained:

> When it comes to defining inclusion, millennials focus primarily and extensively on teaming, valuing a culture of connectivity, and using collaborative tools to drive business impact. Older generations instead defined inclusion in terms of equality, fairness, and the integration, acceptance, and tolerance of gender, racial, and ethnic diversity within the organization.[6]

Millennials are just happy to have people at the table. They want everyone to be seen as a contributor, and inclusion hasn't occurred until that's been empowered to happen.

Smith and Turner suggested that good leadership supporting inclusion and diversity will help millennials to become fully engaged. Leaders can do that by providing "a collaborative environment in which employees can see the impact of their work, understand the value they bring to the organization, and are recognized for their efforts. Leaders believe in openness and transparency and demonstrate that a cognitively diverse team is better for business."[7]

HOW TO LEADERSHIFT TO DIVERSITY AND INCLUSION

If you're a millennial, you're probably saying, "Amen." If you're a boomer or Gen Xer, you're likely supportive of creating an environment that's diverse and inclusive, but you aren't sure what to do with these different ways of thinking and alternate perspectives. I have three suggestions:

1. CREATE A CULTURE OF SHARING

No matter how diverse the workplace is, teams will not embrace creativity unless there is a culture conducive to interaction and sharing of knowledge. This requires de-emphasizing titles, positions, and roles. It means inviting everyone to speak up. It means giving people opportunities to lead before they have an official role—and sometimes even before you feel they are fully ready. And it means being more open to differences. When you share space, share responsibility, share ownership, and share rewards, everyone wants to contribute.

CONSIDER

How can you make your workplace more open to everyone's input, where you share responsibility, ownership, and rewards?

_____

_____

_____

_____

2. BROADEN YOUR PERSPECTIVE ON DIVERSITY

In an article in _Harvard Business Review_, business psychology professor Tomas Chamorro-Premuzic wrote, "Most discussions about diversity focus on demographic variables (e.g., gender, age, and race). However, the most interesting and influential aspects of diversity are psychological (e.g., personality, values, and abilities)."[8] This is also the way millennials see it.

Equality isn't just about giving everyone the same things; it's also about giving unique people what they need. Bernard Tyson, CEO of Kaiser Permanente, said, "We've evolved from equality to equity. Equality says everybody gets equal. Equity says no, everybody gets what they need. Part of building an inclusive environment is not how you're going to change the person. It's how you're going to change yourself and the environment in which the person is going to be successful."[9] That requires us to think differently and treat diversity differently.

3. PROVIDE SOLID LEADERSHIP FOR DIVERSITY TO BE EFFECTIVE

As much as diversity can help a team, it can also challenge a team. Bringing together a diverse group of people isn't easy. Chamorro-Premuzic pointed out, "The creativity gains produced by higher team diversity are disrupted by the inherent social conflict and decision-making deficits that less homogeneous teams create."[10] Good leadership can help bring strength to both ideation and implementation.

CONSIDER

What qualities and skills do you need in order to invite diverse input and creativity from people while effectively directing people so that the team achieves positive results?

_____

_____

_____

_____

_____

_____

_____

_____

I'm still on the journey when it comes to shifting from uniformity to diversity. Why? Because the way people think is still changing, and I have to keep changing to become a better leader. The greatest shift was from thinking I was right to realizing that people are different but they're not wrong. Once I was able to see from their perspective, I better saw their value, and I became open to it.

There's something of a paradox in all this. To embrace diversity, we must celebrate our differences. But I still believe the way we get there is to look for common ground. In the end, I think we all want the same things: to be heard, to value one another, to work together, to be successful, and to make a difference. If we can connect where we're similar and contribute using our differences, we can accomplish great things.

TEAM UNIFORMITY TO
TEAM DIVERSITY

THE IMPROVEMENT SHIFT

DISCUSSION QUESTIONS

1. What kind of community did you grow up in? Was it diverse or homogeneous? How did your community of origin impact your thinking about people different from you?

2. How much does fear of potential conflict affect your thinking when it comes to embracing diversity and including others who have strongly different perspectives from yours?

3. What challenges have you seen diversity bring to a team? What benefits?

4. How can a leader balance the pursuit of common ground with the promotion of diversity at the same time to obtain positive results on a team?

5. No one wants to think of himself as prejudiced, yet acknowledging prejudice is the first step toward overcoming it. What prejudices do you have toward others that you would like to eliminate? What steps can you take to make this leadershift?

NOTES

LESSON TEN

POSITIONAL AUTHORITY TO
MORAL AUTHORITY

THE INFLUENCE SHIFT

The true measure of leadership is influence—nothing more, nothing less.

THE LAW OF INFLUENCE

I've been known for my definition of leadership for more than forty-five years: leadership is influence. If you've led people for any length of time, you probably know instinctively that this is true. But have you ever wondered where the influence comes from?

NO AUTHORITY

I found myself asking that question in my first leadership job. Just a few weeks out of college, I became the pastor of a small rural church in the farming community of Hillham, Indiana. The word *community* almost makes it sound bigger than it really was: eleven houses, two gas stations, and a little country store.

It was a job I thought I could handle in an environment where I could learn the ropes. The church wasn't big, it wasn't in a city, and there were no titans of industry to deal with. I would be a medium fish in a small pond. The bylaws of the organization said that I was the leader of the congregation and the chairman of the organization's board. I thought that made me a leader.

The first time I met with the board, I prepared for it. I thought about the vision and how I would articulate it. I thought about how I wanted the meeting to go, and I wrote a detailed agenda.

I knew that, as the chairman, I was supposed to open the meeting and run it. So after the introductions and greetings were finished and we were sitting around the table, I prepared to start. But before I could say or do anything, Claude, one of the board members, said, "Pastor, why don't you open us in prayer?"

That's a good idea, I thought, so I prayed.

I opened up the file folder with copies of my agenda in it and was about to hand them out, when Claude said, "There are a couple of things I think we ought to talk about tonight."

Oh, I thought, *okay. We can take care of those things first. Then we can get to my agenda.*

Claude led the discussion and asked questions while the other men responded. I listened and tried to follow along. Most of the things they were dealing with were the kind of mundane, everyday items that need to be done in an organization, so there was nothing earth-shattering.

After about an hour, Claude said, "Well, that about does it. Pastor, why don't you close us in prayer?"

So I said a prayer, everybody got up, shook hands, said their good-byes, and went home. And I thought to myself, *What just happened?*

WHERE DOES AUTHORITY COME FROM?

That's the day I learned that a leadership position does not give someone leadership authority. And having a title is not the same as having influence. I had the title, but everyone followed Claude. His opinion was the one that mattered at the table. Everyone agreed with everything he said. And they were glad to do what he said.

A LEADERSHIP POSITION DOES NOT GIVE SOMEONE LEADERSHIP AUTHORITY.

Back then, I had not yet discovered my definition of leadership, but after that board meeting, I began thinking about the topic. And I started trying to figure out why all the board members followed Claude. He was a middle-aged farmer who also worked at the nearby power plant. He wasn't an especially impressive man. He wasn't educated. But he had influence.

I look back now, and I realize that in the small world of Hillham, Claude had a degree of moral authority. To the people in that church and on that board, his words carried great weight. Why? Because of the way he lived his life. He was a good man. He was honest, fair, and hardworking. His words and actions lined up, and that had been true for decades. He cared for the congregation and was always ready to help. Claude would not have recognized himself as a leader or called himself a leader, yet he had earned the right to be followed.

When it comes to leadership, I think there are all kinds of authority. Here are some examples:

- *Natural Authority:* Some people naturally lead better than others and therefore step into leadership roles.
- *Positional Authority:* This kind of authority comes with a title or a formal position in an organization and is the lowest level of leadership.
- *Knowledge Authority:* Knowing more than others do or having specific information can give people an influence edge.
- *Situational Authority:* A certain circumstance can arise that requires the most qualified person to lead in that situation.
- *Relational Authority:* When people have built relationships with others, that gives them influence to lead.
- *Proximity Authority:* When individuals are close to the real leader or authority figure, they can borrow from that leader's influence to lead others.

- *Success Authority:* Success gives people credibility, and others want to be on their team to be part of their success.
- *Mentoring Authority:* Developers of other people increase their influence with the people they mentor and gain a reputation for credibility.
- *Seniority Authority:* In some cultures, being an elder or having seniority in an organization gives authority.

My experience with Claude started me on a journey toward understanding different kinds of leadership authority and ultimately led me to the concept of moral authority, which is the highest level of influence. For fifty years I have been in the process of the influence shift, from positional authority to moral authority. It's a journey I'm still on, and a shift I'm still working to make.

What is moral authority? It can be difficult to define. Here's a perspective from Harvard Business School professor Kevin Sharer. He wrote:

> Moral authority is not easy to define precisely, but like many things, you know it when you see it, or especially when you do not. Lack of moral authority in leaders breeds distrust, creates cynicism and kills initiative throughout the organization. Over time, the lack of strong moral authority in the leadership is fatal to the enterprise or country.[1]

These perspectives make moral authority sound grandiose. It can be, but it doesn't have to be. Claude had moral authority and didn't even know it. But so did Nelson Mandela and Mother Teresa. So what is moral authority? Here's my definition:

> Moral authority is the recognition of a person's leadership influence based on who they are more than the position they hold. It is attained by authentic living that has built trust and it is sustained by successful leadership endeavors. It is earned by a lifetime of consistency. Leaders can strive to earn moral authority by the way they live, but only others can grant them moral authority.

Moral authority is truly the highest level of leadership influence, and many people recognize it. It comes from possessing good values. It adds value to others.

It inspires people. It helps the leader to make the right decisions for the right reasons. It marks a life of words and actions that line up. We know when we're in the presence of someone who has moral authority, and we want to follow them!

In an article titled "Four Ways to Build Moral Authority," Chuck Olson said,

> People follow people, not positions. Your business card may say you're a leader and in-charge, but if your bank account of moral authority is overdrawn, you will be forced to rely on extrinsic factors to rally your followers. No amount of skill, wealth, personality, education, or accomplishment can compensate for the absence of moral authority. Perks and paychecks are the currency required to enlist people in a project, but moral authority is the currency required to enlist people in a movement.[2]

Moral authority has the implicit power to transform what is into what can be. It takes people to higher levels of living and leading. It's inspirational, yet at the same time it is grounded and credible. It makes leaders better because they desire to do better. Moral authority brings out the best in teams because of the respect team members have for the leaders and the desire team members have to live up to and follow their example.

THE PATHWAY TO MORAL AUTHORITY

One of the dangers when anyone begins discussing moral authority is that it can sound mystical and out of reach. However, it is grounded in four things: competence, courage, consistency, and character. I believe anyone can pursue moral authority and develop greater influence by developing in all four of these areas. Let's take a look at each of them.

1. COMPETENCE—THE ABILITY TO LEAD WELL

Everything starts here. Competence is the core of moral authority. If you can't do your job, if you can't deliver the goods, if you can't lead the team well, why would anyone want to follow you? You can't cultivate moral authority unless people respect you. Author George L. Davis observed, "Authority is not something we buy, are born with, or even have delegated to us by our superiors. It is something we earn—and we earn it from our subordinates. No manager has any real authority over his people until he has proved himself worthy of it—in the eyes of his people—not his own, nor those of his superiors."[3]

COMPETENCE IS THE CORE OF MORAL AUTHORITY.

Doing your work with devotion to excellence and the will to follow through will give you a positive reputation for competence. That's true in any profession. But leaders need to also cultivate influence with others and demonstrate competence in their ability to engage with people and motivate and inspire them to work together. Forty years ago, I started teaching the 5 Levels of Leadership to help people understand how influence worked and to teach them a growth process they could follow to become better leaders. I write about this more fully in my book *Developing the Leader Within You 2.0*, but I want to summarize it here to help you get a feel for how you can develop your leadership competence.

LEVEL 1: POSITION—PEOPLE FOLLOW BECAUSE THEY HAVE TO
The authority someone receives at this level is very limited and is restricted to the leader's job description. A leader need not be competent to receive a leadership appointment. In some organizations, that person doesn't even have to be competent to *retain* a leadership position.

LEVEL 2: PERMISSION—PEOPLE FOLLOW BECAUSE THEY WANT TO
A leader begins to develop authority at this second level. When the leader builds relationships, people are willing to work with them because they like them and enjoy spending time with them. They are beginning to give permission for the person to lead them.

LEVEL 3: PRODUCTION—PEOPLE FOLLOW BECAUSE YOU DEMONSTRATE COMPETENCE
On this level a leader begins to demonstrate genuine competence. Being productive is a big step in gaining moral authority with others. People follow because the leader has produced results and is successful, and they want to be on a winning team.

LEVEL 4: PEOPLE DEVELOPMENT—PEOPLE FOLLOW BECAUSE YOU HELP THEM BECOME COMPETENT

When you start to invest in people and help them to become successful personally, your level of authority rises dramatically, the lives of the people you help improve, and this gives you a level of credibility you can gain no other way.

LEVEL 5: PINNACLE—PEOPLE FOLLOW BECAUSE YOU HAVE A REPUTATION FOR EXCELLENCE

When you live a life of competence, influence people at each of the first four levels, and develop leaders over a long period of time, you can approach the pinnacle of leadership. This is where true moral authority is established.

Moral authority is not based on position, but you must learn the skills of each level of leadership and master them to be seen as highly competent in leadership. However, competence alone is not enough to earn moral authority.

ASSESS

How do you rate your competence in your core work area? On a scale of 1 (poor) to 10 (excellent), how good are you at your job? Circle the number that applies.

1   2   3   4   5   6   7   8   9   10

What one thing could you do immediately to improve your score?

_____

_____

How do you rate your competence when it comes to influencing others on your team or in your organization? On a scale of 1 (positional influence) to 10 (pinnacle influence), how would you score your ability? Circle the number that applies.

1   2   3   4   5   6   7   8   9   10

(continued)

What could you start doing immediately to earn the next level of leadership with members of your team?

_____

_____

_____

_____

_____

_____

2. COURAGE—MOVING FORWARD IN THE FACE OF FEAR

Leadership authority shrinks or expands with a person's courage. Author and professor C. S. Lewis said, "Courage is not simply one of the virtues but the form of every virtue at the testing point." Without courage, you can't live any other virtue consistently. With courage, especially when facing great obstacles, you begin to gain moral authority.

I think everyone admires courage, and intuitively we understand that it carries weight. We can follow a leader who is courageous. More specifically, here's how courage relates to moral authority:

COURAGE ENCOURAGES PEOPLE DURING DIFFICULT AND UNCERTAIN TIMES

There is perhaps no greater need for courage from a leader than during difficult times. Poet Ralph Waldo Emerson is rumored to have said:

Whatever you do, you need courage. Whatever course you decide upon, there is always someone to tell you [that] you are wrong. There are always difficulties arising, which tempt you to believe that your critics are right. To map out a course of action and follow it to the end, requires some of the same courage which a soldier needs. Peace has its victories, but it takes brave men [and women] to win them.

The courage that people need to see and feel during difficult times does not have to be loud and dramatic, though many times it is. The difficulties of our everyday lives often require us to find and display courage.

COURAGE ENABLES PEOPLE TO MAXIMIZE THEIR POTENTIAL

In *Making the Courage Connection*, Doug Hall wrote, "Courage has a tangible quality. You can't touch it, but you can feel it. It feels like positive acceleration. Courage sends a rush of energy through your body. It makes you wake up in the morning with a feeling of wanting to wrap your hands around the day."[4] Being courageous not only fires you up but also fires up others and makes them more courageous. That's important, because nobody ever reached his or her potential by cowering in fear. Fortune favors the bold.

COURAGE HELPS LEADERS FIND THEIR VOICE

As leaders display courage in crisis, they often find their voices. During World War II, when England stood alone against Nazi Germany, Winston Churchill found his voice. In 1940 while addressing Parliament, he told his countrymen, "We shall never surrender." Martin Luther King Jr. found his voice during the civil rights struggle of the 1960s. His words still resound today: "Our lives begin to end the day we remain silent about things that matter."

Every leader who possesses moral authority has had to stand alone at some point in time. Such moments make leaders. Such stands are often very difficult, but when leaders look back afterward, they often see those as their proudest moments.

We don't choose the times or the circumstances we must face in life, but we do choose our responses. I love the prayer of the Special Olympics because I think it represents the mind-set we should embrace as leaders: "Let me win, but if I cannot win, let me be brave in the attempt."

ASSESS

How do you rate your courageousness? On a scale of 1 (meek) to 10 (bold), how willing are you to step up and do what's right when you're afraid? Circle the number that applies.

1   2   3   4   5   6   7   8   9   10

(continued)

> In what area of your life are you currently displaying too little courage? What one thing could you do immediately to improve your level of courage in that area?
>
> _____
>
> _____
>
> _____

3. CONSISTENCY—DOING WELL ALL THE TIME, NOT JUST SOMETIMES

In his fantastic book *Visioneering*, Andy Stanley described the value of consistency related to moral authority. He wrote:

It is the alignment between a person's convictions and his behavior that makes his life persuasive. Herein is the key to sustained influence. . . .

Moral authority is the credibility you earn by walking your talk . . . It is the relationship other people see between what you say and what you do, between what you claim to be and what you are. A person with moral authority is beyond reproach. That is, when you look for a discrepancy between what he says he believes and what he does, you come up empty. There is alignment between conviction and action, belief and behavior.

Nothing compensates for a lack of moral authority. No amount of communication skills, wealth, accomplishment, education, talent, or position can make up for a lack of moral authority. We all know plenty of people who have those qualities but who exercise no influence over us whatsoever. Why? Because there is a contradiction between what they claim to be and what we perceive them to be.[5]

What Stanley described is internal consistency between values and actions, which is essential to a leader's success if he or she desires to gain moral authority. Equally important is the ability to be consistent over time.

Consistency compounds over time. If you do the right things when you're young, it mostly goes unnoticed and unrecognized. But if you do the right things and lead well over decades, it becomes recognized, and you get more credit than you feel you deserve. That's the power of what I call layered living. If you embrace layered learning (as I described in Lesson 3 on shifting from goals to growth) and you practice layered leadership (by consistently living out your values and performing with excellence), then your reward can be layered living, where you reap the benefits of moral authority.

Consistency is so valuable to a leader that it's difficult to list all its benefits. Here are just a few:

- *Consistency establishes your reputation.* Nearly anyone can be good once. Being good continually is difficult. However, continued repetition leads to a positive reputation.
- *Consistency makes team members more secure.* Perhaps the greatest compliment a person can receive is, "I can depend on you." A consistent leader inspires team members to become more confident.
- *Consistency allows for accurate measurement of your growth.* It's difficult to gauge the progress of inconsistent people. The track record we establish shows what we have done and how far we have come.
- *Consistency makes you relevant.* People who bounce back and forth between engagement and disengagement always have to play catch-up. By staying consistently engaged, you don't fall behind.
- *Consistency models your expectations for others.* When you consistently model your values and work ethic, team members know what you expect of them because they've seen it every day. Consistency always reinforces expectations.
- *Consistency maintains your message.* When a leader communicates a vision but acts in ways that are inconsistent with that vision the result is confusion. It distracts from the message and makes it more difficult for everyone on the team.

ASSESS

How do you rate when it comes to consistency? On a scale of 1 (poor) to 10 (excellent), how would you score yourself? Circle the number that applies.

| 1 | 2 | 3 | 4 | 5 | 6 | 7 | 8 | 9 | 10 |

(continued)

What prevents you from scoring higher in this area? What one thing could you do immediately to improve your consistency?

_____

_____

_____

_____

_____

Consistency, along with competence and courage, is vital to a leader's ability to develop moral authority, but there's still one more component without which moral authority is impossible to earn.

4. CHARACTER—BEING BIGGER ON THE INSIDE THAN THE OUTSIDE

Moral authority is a result of right intentions, right values, right beliefs, right actions, right relationships, and right responses. There is a lot to do right to develop moral authority. That doesn't mean perfection. We are all human and make mistakes. But to have moral authority, our intentions must be right; the motives of the heart must be good.

While much of leadership is outward and public, the right motives and the good character traits we need to become leaders with moral authority are won in private. These two aspects of leadership, public and private, resemble the two parts of a tree. One part you see: our public leadership is like a tree's trunk and branches. That's the part that bears fruit. However, who leaders are in private is what can't be seen, like a tree's roots. If the roots are shallow, then the tree won't survive. Drought will dry it up. A storm will knock it down. But if the roots are deep, the tree can thrive in almost any circumstance.

What does it mean to develop deep roots as a leader? It means having strong character. What kind of character does a leader need to have? I believe good character demonstrates these four characteristics:

INTEGRITY

I define integrity two ways. First, it's the alignment of your values and actions. You know what's right and you do it. Leaders with moral authority hold themselves to a high standard of conduct. The second definition has to do with decision-making. Leaders of integrity do the right thing, even when it's hard, even when it's not best for them personally. They put the team, the organization, and the vision ahead of themselves.

> **LEADERS OF INTEGRITY DO THE RIGHT THING, EVEN WHEN IT'S HARD, EVEN WHEN IT'S NOT BEST FOR THEM PERSONALLY.**

AUTHENTICITY

Author and spiritual leader Mark Batterson said, "Authenticity is the new authority in leadership." I agree, because I believe that is an essential part of moral authority. People do not want to follow leaders who pretend to be what they're not. They don't expect perfection—just honesty.

This can be a real struggle for many leaders. They want to meet others' expectations and can be tempted to compromise their beliefs or standards. But to be the best leader you can be, you need to acknowledge who you really are and be willing to let people witness your authenticity.

HUMILITY

I believe humility is an essential quality for a leader who possesses moral authority. My friend Rick Warren said, "Humility is not denying your strengths. Humility is being honest about your weaknesses." No matter how you define *humility*, know that it means three things. First, you possess self-awareness and can criticize yourself. Second, you are confident and comfortable enough that you don't feel any need to draw attention to yourself. And third, you revel in the accomplishments of others and are eager to help them shine.

LOVE

The final character quality to embrace as a leader in order to have moral authority is love. You must care about people. You must respect them. You must value them. People can always tell when you don't, and that creates an instant disconnection that short-circuits moral authority.

What do you want to do with your leadership? I think every leader wants to make an impact, a difference. It's the reason we get up in the morning. It's why we work with people. It's why we create teams or build organizations. Do you have it in you to do something big? Do you want to change your organization, or your community, or your culture, or your country? How big are your dreams? The bigger they are, the more you need moral authority to accomplish them.

When I was in my early thirties, I started to get the sense that my leadership could be impactful and my life could make a difference. That prompted me to make some personal decisions. At the time, I simply thought they were the right things to do to be a better leader. Today, I can see that they helped me in the four areas I've written about in this lesson: competence, courage, consistency, and character. I decided to:

1. Always put people first.
2. Live to make a difference, not to make money.
3. Be myself, but be my best self possible.
4. Express gratitude—reject entitlement.
5. Be willing to be misunderstood and lonely for the right reasons.

I've worked hard to follow these guidelines for the last forty years.

In the end, you don't get to grant yourself moral authority. You can choose to strive for it, but only others can give it to you, and they must do so freely. But that should not stop you from doing everything right that you can to earn it. Because if you gain moral authority, it makes you worthy of respect, inspires trust and confidence, and enables you to lead at the highest standards of performance. This leadershift will increase your influence, giving you buy-in not only from the people on your team but from others who aren't under your formal leadership. And with that influence, there's no telling what you can help people accomplish.

POSITIONAL AUTHORITY TO
MORAL AUTHORITY

THE INFLUENCE SHIFT

DISCUSSION QUESTIONS

1. What value do you think moral authority has for a leader? What benefits do you think it would give you? What would you attempt to accomplish with it?

2. What kinds of authority do you most often rely upon to get things done? Why do you use them?

   - Natural Authority
   - Knowledge Authority
   - Relational Authority
   - Success Authority
   - Seniority Authority

   - Positional Authority
   - Situational Authority
   - Proximity Authority
   - Mentoring Authority

3. Which component of mortal authority have you found to be the easiest to achieve: competence, courage, consistency, or character? Which have you found to be the most difficult?

4. How would you prioritize the importance of the four components: competence, courage, consistency, or character? Explain your answer.

5. What one specific step are you willing to take in order to improve in the area that you believe to be the most important of the four? How and when will you do it?

NOTES

LESSON 11

TRAINED LEADERS TO
TRANSFORMATIONAL LEADERS

THE IMPACT SHIFT

If your actions inspire people to dream more, learn more, do more, and become more, then you are a transformational leader.

Of all the lessons in this book, this one is the most important. Why do I say that? Because if you make only one leadershift in your life, this is the one I would wish for you to choose. The impact shift from trained leaders to transformational leaders will bring the greatest change to your life and the lives of those around you.

If your actions inspire people to dream more, learn more, do more, and become more, then you are a transformational leader. You influence people to think, speak, and act in ways that make a positive difference in their lives and the lives of others. That kind of leadership can change the world!

MY CHANGE IN LEADERSHIP PERSPECTIVE

My leadershift from trained leader to transformational leader occurred early. This story is very personal to me, and it had a dramatic effect on my life. At the heart of this shift was my faith, which is at the foundation of who I am. However,

I value you whether or not you are a person of faith. No matter what your perspective is about faith, I don't want you to miss this, so I'll condense my story down to its essence.

At the beginning of my career, I cared mostly about myself and building my organization. Sadly, people were not my top priority. I regret to say that my selfishness sometimes kept me from doing the right thing. There was one particular incident that made me realize that my priorities were wrong. I failed to help a man because I was focused on myself. Then the man died. My selfish decision meant that he never got the help I should have given him, and there was nothing I could do to fix that.

I can't express the devastating impact this had on me. I felt terrible, and it caused me to spend several months reevaluating myself as a leader. For the first time in my life, I started to ask myself the hard questions about my motives and methods that every leader ought to ask. And I was not satisfied with my answers.

During the next few months, I spent a lot of time in prayer and reflection, and I resolved to become a different kind of leader—someone different from whom I had been up to that time. Thankfully my heart was changed, and my actions started following my heart. I became a person who valued other people and demonstrated that through my leadership decisions, which made others my top priority. The change within me was deep and made a difference that still influences me today. If I hadn't made this shift, my leadership would have been hollow and self-centered. I credit this with making possible whatever difference I've made with my leadership.

ESSENTIALS FOR TRANSFORMATIONAL LEADERSHIP

I'm a firm believer in training in leadership. I've done it myself for fifty years and helped others for more than forty years. But I also recognize there's a huge difference between trained leaders and leaders who are transformational.

For many years I have studied transformational movements and the people who led them. I've identified five actions common to all of them. If you desire to make the impact shift from trained leader to transformational leader, start doing these too.

CONSIDER

Take a look at the following comparison between trained leaders and transformational leaders. Mark the phrase on each line that best describes you.

TRAINED LEADERS	TRANSFORMATIONAL LEADERS
❑ Know How to Lead	❑ Know Why They Lead
❑ Are Liked	❑ Are Contagious
❑ Influence Today	❑ Influence Today and Tomorrow
❑ Ask People to Follow	❑ Ask People to Make a Difference
❑ Love to Lead	❑ Love the People They Lead
❑ Are Trained	❑ Are Trained and Transformed
❑ Help People	❑ Help People Change
❑ Have a Career	❑ Have a Calling
❑ Impact a Few	❑ Impact Many

1. POSSESS A CLEAR PICTURE OF WHAT TRANSFORMATIONAL LEADERS DO

On the surface, all transformational leaders look different from one another. They come in all sizes and shapes, from many races and nationalities, and with a variety of skills and talents. Their differences are many. However, there are a few characteristics that all of them share, and if you desire to become transformational, you must embrace them, too, so that you know what you're striving for:

TRANSFORMATIONAL LEADERS SEE THINGS OTHERS DO NOT SEE

Many people see problems and shake their heads. They experience adversity and throw up their hands. They look at challenges and ask "Why?"—not seeking a solution, just venting frustration. When they encounter problems, they see no possibilities. They become victims of negative circumstances and cannot help themselves or others.

Transformational leaders see things differently. They ask, "Why not?" because they're always thinking about trying to create a better future. They see more than others see. Of course, they see the problems. They may even be surrounded by them. But they also see potential in those problems. They believe there is always an answer, a solution, a better way, a brighter future. That belief creates anticipation, not desperation, during the darkest of hours.

How we view things determines how we do things. My friend Dave Ramsey said, "Organizations are not limited by their opportunity; they are limited by their leader." If we don't see the things others don't, how can we lead them to a better future?

> ### ORGANIZATIONS ARE NOT LIMITED BY THEIR OPPORTUNITY; THEY ARE LIMITED BY THEIR LEADER.
>
> DAVE RAMSEY

TRANSFORMATIONAL LEADERS SAY THINGS OTHERS DO NOT SAY

Transformational leaders speak up. They leverage their influence by speaking bold words about a better future. Their voice becomes a tool of transformation. Think of the bold words said by transformational leaders who were willing to describe a better future. Martin Luther King Jr. said, "I have a dream." It took courage for him to be the voice of change when others opposed him.

As I have become a better communicator, I've tried to use my voice to facilitate positive change. At times I was misunderstood. But I made decisions that I believed were right, such as when . . .

- I stood on the floor of a national meeting and promoted a policy of inclusiveness that I knew had no chance of passing.
- I said no to becoming the new host of a prestigious national radio show because I declined to sign a doctrinal statement I didn't agree with.
- I handed back a million-dollar gift given to my nonprofit organization because I proposed going in a direction that the donor did not like.
- I changed the nonprofit EQUIP from a training organization to a transformational one.

None of these decisions was popular when I shared it, and not everyone understood. But sometimes that's what a leader must do. Say things others won't.

TRANSFORMATIONAL LEADERS BELIEVE THINGS OTHERS DO NOT BELIEVE

Transformational leaders believe that they can make a difference. That becomes their passion. President John F. Kennedy said he believed that everyone had a change-the-world speech in them. I was thirteen years old when he said it, and I can still remember how I felt when I heard those words. Although I was only a young teenager, I felt that he was talking directly to me. I believed him—because he believed it.

EVERYONE HAS A CHANGE-THE-WORLD SPEECH IN THEM.

JOHN F. KENNEDY

Believing you can make a difference changes everything. When transformational leaders believe that their cause can make a difference, then they bring conviction to their leadership. Without this conviction, you may be able to get people to follow you, and you can be a good leader. But only when you understand that the higher calling of leadership is to get people to follow your cause can you become a great leader.

Transformational leaders believe in others. They are belief magnets. People are drawn to them because they believe in their message and believe it will help people. They rally people together to make a difference; they extend their hand and ask others to join them in their mission. Transformational leaders are belief-makers who help people to believe in themselves.

TRANSFORMATIONAL LEADERS FEEL THINGS OTHERS DO NOT FEEL

Peter Marshall said, "A different world cannot be built by indifferent people." Passion creates energy and tenacity in people. It fires up leaders and the people who join them for their cause. That fire helps them endure, the way Gandhi did in his fight for Indian independence. It was a process that took fifty-four years. During that time Gandhi fought through attacks, rejection, imprisonment, misrepresentation, and sickness with malaria. And then he was finally victorious. Passion carried him forward.

A DIFFERENT WORLD CANNOT BE BUILT BY INDIFFERENT PEOPLE.

PETER MARSHALL

I've seen passion emerge in the lives of people I lead, and it has changed their lives and the way they lead. This happens every time I invite a group of John Maxwell Team coaches to go with me to another country to train roundtable facilitators. Hundreds of coaches have volunteered to travel overseas, paid all their own expenses, trained twelve hours a day, then traveled in less-than-ideal circumstances to help others. They give up their time, their money, and their energy to do it. And they love it! They tirelessly give of themselves, and yet at the end I hear over and over that they feel they've received more than they gave. And they want to do it again. Paul Martinelli, president of the John Maxwell Team, said, "When the light goes on in your life, you want to turn everyone else's light on." I love that, and it's true. Transformational leaders have their lights on, and they want to help others turn theirs on.

TRANSFORMATIONAL LEADERS DO THINGS OTHERS DO NOT DO

While fear causes many people to shrink back from the unknown and avoid challenges that lie ahead, it causes transformational leaders to prepare and work harder. How do they overcome their fears? By tapping into their sense of purpose and by believing in a cause that is much bigger than themselves. They want to make a difference, and the only questions they need to answer are, "What kind of difference can I make?" and "How big of a difference can it be?" Their strong sense of purpose propels them to do what others aren't willing to do.

I've already mentioned that my greatest desire is to see a country transformed so much that the leaders and citizens acknowledge the positive change. That is a BHAG (Big Hairy Audacious Goal). And I may not live to see it happen. So why am I doing everything I can to be part of this? Because I would rather try something big that is almost impossible than something small that won't make a difference. If you want to make the leadershift from trained to transformational leadership, I encourage you to have a similarly audacious attitude.

CONSIDER

Do you have a clear vision of a way to help others and make a difference? If so, describe it. If not, dream a little. Look where your passion, your current opportunities, and people's needs come together.

_____

_____

_____

_____

_____

_____

2. FOCUS ON YOUR OWN TRANSFORMATION BEFORE LEADING OTHERS TO IT

In Lesson 3 I discussed how I developed the acronym R-E-A-L, with the *E* representing *equipping*. As soon as I understood how important equipping was, I studied the process and discovered the best way to train others. I came up with a five-step process that works no matter what task you're trying to equip another person to do.

1. I do it.
2. I do it, and you are with me.
3. You do it, and I am with you.
4. You do it.
5. You do it, and someone is with you.

Why do I mention this? Because I want you to notice that the process begins with *I do it*. If I want to help others be transformational, I must first be transformed. I cannot give what I do not have. Neither can you.

The first person you must lead will always be you. If you want to see positive changes in your world, the first person you must change is you. As leaders, you and I have to be changed to bring change. We teach what we know, but we reproduce who we are.

Before I personally experienced the transformation of shifting from a desire to make my life successful to a desire to help other people's lives improve, it never entered my mind that I could be a catalyst for positive change. It never entered my heart either. There was no passion within me to help others experience positive change. However, when I began to experience positive change in my life and became less selfish, I was eager to share what was happening with others. Knowing that I was changing got me excited about helping others change too.

If you want to lead any positive change, you need to realize this: transformation begins with you. If you are not willing to change, you are not going to be able to help anyone else.

Philosopher and author James Allen wrote, "Men are anxious to improve their circumstances, but are unwilling to improve themselves; they therefore remain bound." If you want to lead positive change, don't remain bound. Be willing to change within. Start with you. That's always the first step to making a difference.

CONSIDER

What needs to change in you before you will be able to help others make significant changes? Where do you need to be transformed? What steps can you take immediately to begin that transformation process?

_____

_____

_____

_____

_____

3. TAKE POSITIVE ACTION BASED ON YOUR INTERNAL CHANGES

An essential step in the leadershift from trained to transformational is a commitment to taking action. For real change to occur, we must go from knowing to doing. It's at this point that transformation becomes difficult, yet the results are so beautiful. It's difficult because saying is always easier than doing. It's beautiful because action is what brings transformation.

Everything worthwhile in life is uphill—all the way. Transformation requires us to walk uphill. Everyday. All the way. Most people are unwilling to commit to that. Instead of climbing, they would rather be . . .

- *Talking:* "Let's discuss uphill climbing."
- *Thinking:* "Let's contemplate uphill climbing."
- *Planning:* "Let's strategize about uphill climbing."
- *Surveying:* "Let's ask others what they think about uphill climbing."
- *Studying:* "Let's examine what uphill climbing looks like."
- *Resting:* "Let's conserve energy before we start climbing."

Transformation is a result of application, not education. That's why Gandhi said, "An ounce of practice is worth more than tons of preaching." To lead transformationally, you must first live transformed. That takes courage, the courage to let go of the familiar and set off on a better way.

ASSESS

How inclined are you to take action? On a scale of 1 (thinker) to 10 (doer), how would you score yourself? Circle the number that applies.

1   2   3   4   5   6   7   8   9   10

If you scored below 7, what holds you back? How can you become more proactive? If you scored 8 or higher, what one thing could you do to improve by one point?

_____

_____

_____

_____

_____

_____

4. CREATE AN ENVIRONMENT THAT PROMOTES POSITIVE CHANGE

For years I have encouraged people to embrace positive change. More recently my nonprofit organizations have dedicated themselves to promoting transformation. Our experience working with tens of thousands of people has helped us to understand what creates an ideal environment. These are the essentials:

LEADERS WHO ARE PASSIONATE ABOUT TRANSFORMATION

Jim Collins said, "Transformational movements require transformational leaders." Only transformational leaders can bring about transformation. What I've said for years is true: everything rises and falls on leadership.

This poem by Lawrence Tribble really says it all:

One man awake, awakens another.
The second awakens his next-door brother.
The three awake can rouse a town
By turning the whole place upside down.
The many awake can cause such a fuss
It finally awakens the rest of us.
One man up with dawn in his eyes
Surely then multiplies.[1]

Some man or woman has to start that process. The person who does is a transformational leader.

RESOURCES THAT TEACH GOOD VALUES

Many people are unaware that there is a better way to live. They are stuck in the life they have because they are not sure where to go, nor do they know how to move beyond their current situation. I'm convinced from personal experience and observation that good values are the road to a better life. And placing resources that teach good values in the hands of people turns the light on for them so that they can see a better way.

Good values are teachable and reachable. Just one good value in a person's life can bring great benefit. Here are some of the values my nonprofit organizations have helped people to understand and embrace over the years:

- *Attitude:* your attitude colors everything in your life
- *Commitment:* it separates doers from dreamers
- *Competence:* the shortest path to credibility is competence
- *Forgiveness:* forgiveness empowers you to live with a light heart
- *Initiative:* you cannot experience success unless you start
- *Integrity:* living with integrity leads to a life of wholeness
- *Personal Growth:* people who keep learning always have a future
- *Priorities:* clear priorities show you what to do and where to go
- *Relationships:* the quality of your relationships determines the quality of your life
- *Work Ethic:* working hard brings inner satisfaction every day

We've created resources to help people explore ideas, examine themselves, and decide how they will take action to embrace good values and change their lives. If you desire to shift from trained leader to transformational leader, you need to give people resources to help them. Most people cannot find the pathway to a better life without help.

Small Groups Where People Learn and Participate

Too often, training that begins in our heads stays in our heads. We learn something new, but we don't apply it to our lives or put it into practice. That's why transformation needs a living laboratory to be effective. That occurs best in a small group of people where all the members of the group share ideas, speak about themselves with candor and honesty, state their intentions, and hold one another accountable.

EQUIP and the John Maxwell Leadership Foundation, the two nonprofit organizations I founded, use roundtables in small groups to facilitate change. We've found that groups of four to ten can create the perfect environment for people to develop relationships, get to know themselves and others, and experience growth. Most people do not have a high level of self-awareness. They spend so much time and energy projecting a positive image that they don't examine themselves and their motives as much as they could. A safe small-group environment where people see the others as peers, everyone is asked to participate, and the leader of the group is open and authentic about his or her shortcomings encourages everyone to participate, ask questions, listen, share, reflect, and commit to taking action. And if members of the group report back the next time they meet to honestly share both failures and success, everyone is encouraged to grow and change.

I've experienced the positive power of participating in small groups in my own life. Some of the greatest changes that have determined my most important decisions occurred in small-group setting. I wasn't *expecting* these things to happen, but once I committed to a group and fully engaged in the process, good things began to occur. Small groups can bring big growth.

COMMITMENT TO REPRODUCE LEADERS

By definition, for someone to be a leader, he or she must have followers. If you think you're leading but no one is following you, then you're only taking a walk. However, it's not enough to gather followers. To be transformational, leaders must develop and reproduce leaders.

I started to learn this lesson more than thirty years ago when I was leading Skyline Church. We recognized the transformative power of small groups, so we started a small-group program. Naïvely, we thought we could simply put people together in groups and they would flourish. We quickly discovered that if we didn't train leaders, the groups didn't succeed. So we dismantled the program, started training leaders, and relaunched. We were successful this second go-round, but then we learned something else: trained leaders could sustain a group, but transformed leaders could gather, grow, and reproduce groups. They could train other leaders who reached other people and trained other leaders.

When this happens repeatedly, individual transformation leads to group transformation which leads to community transformation. It starts with transformed leaders who want to lead others to transformation.

5. COMMIT TO MAKING A DIFFERENCE WITH OTHERS IN YOUR COMMUNITY

Making positive changes requires commitment from leaders who want to make a difference. Civil rights leader Walter E. Fauntroy eloquently expressed this in an inspiring speech he delivered at Howard University. He said:

> The past is yours. Learn from it. The future is yours. Fulfill it. Knowledge is yours. Use it. Cancer is yours. Cure it. Racism is yours. End it. Injustice is yours. Correct it. Sickness is yours. Heal it. Ignorance is yours. Banish

it. War is yours. Stop it. Hope is yours. Confirm it. America is yours. Save it. The world is yours. Serve it. The dream is yours. Claim it.

Don't be blinded by prejudice, disheartened by the times, or discouraged by the system. Face the system. Challenge it. Change it. Confront it. Correct it. Don't let anything paralyze your mind, tie your hands, or defeat your spirit. Take the world—not to dominate it, but to deliver it. Not to exploit it, but to enrich it—take your dream and inherit the earth.[2]

Change does not happen unless transformational leaders commit themselves to making a difference in their community and invite others to join them in the process. All transformational movements follow a pattern. They occur:

- *Top-Down*—Leadership influence filters down, not up.
- *Small to Big*—Mass movements begin with a few people.
- *Inside Out*—Inner values determine outward behavior.

If you're willing to commit to changing yourself, inviting a small group of people to join you in the process, and preparing other leaders to become agents of transformation, you can change your world.

TAKE ACTION

If you're ready to make a difference and start changing the world, then take action.

Change Yourself: What transformation needs to occur within you (or has already occurred within you) to qualify you to help others experience transformation?

_____

_____

_____

_____

_____

_____

Invest in a Small Group of People: Who can you help? Who do you know who is open to growth and change that would benefit from being in a group you lead? What material or resources could you use that would help them to grow? When will you invite them? When will you start the group?

_____

_____

_____

_____

_____

Develop Other Leaders: Of the people you plan to invite into your group, who has leadership skills or leadership potential? Make additional investment into those people and prepare them to become transformational leaders.

_____

_____

_____

_____

AMAZING TRANSFORMATION

I want to close this lesson with a story told to me by my good friend Jerry Anderson. Jerry was a serial entrepreneur who kept failing until he met John Schrock, a successful businessman who lived his life in accordance with positive values he'd learned by reading Proverbs. Jerry was mentored by John, and it transformed his life. Jerry went on to become highly successful himself, and out of gratitude and a desire to make a difference, he started teaching the values he had learned from John to others. When his efforts started to gain momentum, Jerry founded the nonprofit organization La Red to multiply his efforts.

In the early 2000s, Jerry's organization was invited to Colombia. The reason? The prisons of Colombia were notoriously corrupt at that time. They were run by organized crime and the most powerful inmates. The prisoners were organized and often armed. Money flowed into the prisons. Some of the more powerful inmates had set up suites. A few were even equipped with doors to the outside so that associates and women could come and go at will, bringing money and drugs, among other things.

This criminal environment bred corruption among the guards. Since they could not beat the inmates, they simply joined them. They served the wealthiest criminals and treated the other inmates like slaves. The prison system was brutal. On average, there was a murder every day within the 143 prisons. Jerry said in one instance, a man's head had been cut off and used as a soccer ball in the prison yard.

The Colombian government desired change, but they weren't sure what to do or how to start. They knew they would not be able to change the prison with more guns or new buildings. What they needed to do was change the hearts and minds of the leaders. To do that, they invited Jerry's organization La Red into the prison system to work with the guards.

La Red introduced character development and values into 143 prisons, believing they could transform the culture of the prison by teaching the guards and other prison employees character-based values. They met regularly in small roundtable groups. Any employee who refused to participate in the weekly meeting lost his job.

Slowly, the culture of the prison began to transform. The eleven thousand guards in the prisons were changing. They no longer embraced corruption. They started treating people better. They asked others to forgive their previous behavior. They started to regain their dignity. The change was so dramatic that prisoners started writing letters to the director asking for the same training that the guards were receiving.

What happened next was remarkable. The guards started to allow one prisoner to become part of a roundtable group of guards. To participate, that inmate had to agree to lead his own group with other prisoners in his cell block. The process began with fifty-six prisoners. As these individuals were trained in values, their thinking changed. Their values changed. Their actions changed. They were transformed by the time they started their own groups in their cell blocks. As they led their groups, many of the inmates who were receiving training in the small roundtable groups started to change too. Over several years the entire prison system and its eighty thousand inmates were transformed. Many of the inmates expressed that if they had learned these values earlier in life, they probably would not have ended up in prison. Perhaps most remarkable of all, the murder rate in the prison went from an average of one per day down to one per year!

The success Jerry had in the prisons was so dramatic that the Colombian military invited La Red to train their military troops in character development. The governments of other countries contacted him too. The last time I asked Jerry, he said La Red has helped people in forty-four nations. He estimates that more than one million people have participated in the transformational small groups they offer. And they're still going strong. That's the power of the impact shift. If you leadershift from trained to transformational leadership, there's no telling what kind of impact you can make or how far your influence will go.

TRAINED LEADERS TO
TRANSFORMATIONAL LEADERS

THE IMPACT SHIFT

DISCUSSION QUESTIONS

1. Do you agree that transformation needs to occur in a leader before he or she can lead others to experience transformation? Explain. What difference does it make?

2. Which do you think usually occurs first: discovering of the need for transformation within the community or transformation within the leader prompting him or her to reach out to the community?

3. Do you believe you have the potential to lead positive change within a large or small community? Why?

4. What problem or injustice bothers you the most? Where do you see the greatest need for transformation in your community?

5. What are you willing to attempt to make a difference for people you care about?

NOTES

LESSON TWELVE

CAREER TO
CALLING

THE PASSION SHIFT

Some wake up to an alarm. Some wake up to a calling.

UNKNOWN

This last leadershift should be the most natural shift a person can make, yet many people miss it. They are so busy with their day-to-day existence and with making a living that they don't think about it. Or they've been told that life has no greater meaning—and they actually believed it. I'm here to tell you that this leadershift is available to you if you're willing to reach for it.

WHAT DO YOU DO?

I want to start by asking you a question: How do you currently think about what you do for a living? Yale professor Amy Wrzesniewski has done research with employees in the workplace and observed that people tend to fall into three groups.

What's remarkable is that individuals fall into these three categories regardless of the industry they work in, the social status of their profession, their pay, or their title. For example, in a study, roughly equal numbers of administrative assistants surveyed fell into these three categories. And employees who mopped floors in a hospital were equally likely to fall evenly into these three groups.[1] Think about which best describes you.

1. You Do a Job

When you have a job, your main goal is often to earn a living and support your family. You may not think about it beyond the time you spend on the clock. You may do your job with excellence or you may simply mark time, but either way, when you finish your day or your shift, you walk away and don't think about it. Satisfaction and fulfillment for people who have a job-only mind-set comes from activities outside of work. And while people in this group may hope to advance, they don't think in terms of a strategy of career building.

It's been said that if you choose a job you love, you will never have to work a day in your life. I think that's good advice, but it should be a starting point, not an ending goal. A job is not your calling, no matter how much money it will allow you to make or how it allows you to serve people. A job is merely a vehicle with the potential to take you toward your calling. That's the way you should think of it.

2. You Build a Career

Most people would acknowledge that it's a step forward to think in terms of developing a career rather than just holding a job. When you have a career, the implication is that you are headed in a direction. You're making progress attaining positive achievements. An upward trajectory of skill mastery, larger responsibilities, and greater earnings are all marks of a successful career.

3. You Fulfill Your Calling

Author Frederick Buechner said that our purpose is at "that place where your deep gladness meets the world's deep need." Your calling, when you find and embrace it, will result in the merging of your skills, your talents, your character traits, and yourexperiences. It will make use of your experience, your gifts, and the lessons you've learned. It will be represented by a deep desire to create, lead, inspire, and make a difference.

CONSIDER

Take a look at the difference between a career and a calling. Mark the box on each line that best describes you.

CAREER	CALLING
❑ Mainly About You	❑ Mainly About Others
❑ Something You Choose	❑ Something Chosen for You
❑ Separated from Your Best Life	❑ Integrated into Your Entire Life
❑ You Can Take or Leave It	❑ Never Leaves You
❑ Something You Can Do	❑ Something You Must Do
❑ Measured by Success	❑ Measured by Significance

Wouldn't you like to find and fulfill a calling that makes a difference and gets you excited every day for the rest of your life? Finding your calling is like finding your *why*—the reason you exist, your purpose for living. When you do, it changes everything:

- When you find your Why—you find your Way.
- When you find your Why—you find your Will.
- When you find your Why—you find your Wings.

Your life will never be the same once you know what you're called to do and are working to fulfill it every day.

WE ARE ALL SEARCHERS

I believe *everyone* has the potential to find and fulfill his or her purpose. Everyone has the ability to be called. In each of us there is a desire to know more and be more. There is something in us that calls to something bigger. Richard Leider, author, coach, and founder of Inventure, the Purpose Company, has written extensively on the subjects of purpose and calling. He said:

The search for callings is not a trend. It is something much deeper. If it needs a label, it is searcher. James Kavanaugh captured the essence of the drive when he wrote, "I am one of the searchers. There are, I believe, millions of us. We are not unhappy, but neither are we really content. We continue to explore life, hoping to uncover its ultimate secret."

We humans are searchers for meaning. . . . Work has meaning if it serves others. Calling joins self and service. As Aristotle said, "Where our talents and the needs of the world cross, there lies our vocation."[2]

WHERE OUR TALENTS AND THE NEEDS OF THE WORLD CROSS, THERE LIES OUR VOCATION.

ARISTOTLE

THE DAY I WAS CALLED

It's never too early, nor is it ever too late to find your purpose, your calling. I consider myself to be fortunate because I received my calling when I was twenty-nine years old. I was old enough to appreciate it and young enough to have plenty of time to make the most of it. I want to tell you about the experience. Because I'm a person of faith, my experience involves God. However, you do not need to be a person of faith to receive a calling. You just need to be open and watchful.

I experienced my unique calling on July 4, 1976. I was speaking in celebration of the United States' bicentennial, and suddenly I had a clear and compelling sense that God wanted me to invest my life in developing leaders and teaching leadership. It was perhaps the greatest moment of clarity I've ever had in my life.

On the drive home, I told Margaret about it. She listened, as she always does when I'm excited by an idea. She asked, "What are you going to do?"

"Nothing," I answered.

She was surprised, because back then I usually dove right into strategy mode and started creating my plans. But this was different from any other experience

I'd had. Yes, I was excited. I couldn't wait to train leaders for the rest of my life. At the same time, I was also patient, and I felt very settled—calm.

"If this is a calling," I told her, "then doors will open." And they did. Before the week was out, two different groups called to ask me to speak to their leaders.

In most areas of my life at that time, I was very ambitious. This was different. This was God's personal invitation for me to work on his agenda, using the talents he'd given me, doing work that I sensed would be eternally significant. I felt grateful to be called to something important, but I wasn't thinking in terms of goals or timelines. I just wanted to be my best and do my best. I can honestly say that today, more than forty years later, I'm just as excited as I was that first day. I'm still thrilled to have been called to teach leadership and develop leaders. I want to add value to leaders who multiply value to others. That's my calling and purpose in life.

THE CHARACTERISTICS OF A CALLING

You have a purpose in life, too, and you can receive a sense of calling. I don't want you to miss this just because I'm telling you about my calling in the context of my faith. You can be of a different faith than me or have no faith at all, and you can still be called. Your calling can give you a fruitful and fulfilling life, one that fills you with passion and motivates you to make a difference. When it is your calling, you won't have to chase it. You will be *captivated* by it.

WHEN IT IS YOUR CALLING, YOU WON'T HAVE TO CHASE IT. YOU WILL BE *CAPTIVATED* BY IT.

I want to help you to understand calling so that you can find yours if you haven't already done so. I want you to be ready when it comes.

1. YOUR CALLING MATCHES WHO YOU ARE

No one has ever been called to do something he or she wasn't suited for. Calling always matches who you are. For that reason, it's important for you to be self-aware as you stay attentive to finding your calling.

CONSIDER

Here are some questions that can help you think about calling:

If you could do one thing for the rest of your life, even if you never got paid for it, what would you do?

_____

_____

_____

What experiences have you had that you desire to help others with?

_____

_____

_____

What do people often ask for your help with?

_____

_____

_____

What lights you up?

_____

_____

_____

What do you love learning about?

_____

_____

_____

What could you talk about for hours and hours?

_____

_____

_____

What activities are you always self-motivated to do?

_____

_____

_____

What can you do that makes a positive difference in the lives of others?

_____

_____

_____

What would you like to do that would live beyond you?

_____

_____

_____

The calling you receive often taps into not just one or two of these things but *all* of them. Look at your answers to those questions. What is the common thread?

_____

_____

_____

_____

_____

2. Your Calling Taps into Your Passion

Impacting the world is hard. If you lack passion for the call, your energy will fizzle out. You should use the sleepless night test for this one. Is there a cause you want to pursue that is consuming you so much that you can't sleep at night? That's a sign that you might be called to it. I like the advice of author, philosopher, and civil rights leader Howard Thurman, who said, "Don't ask what the world needs. Ask what makes you come alive and go do it. Because what the world needs is people who have come alive." Passion is a great driver toward calling.

CONSIDER

What is your answer to Thurman's question? What makes you come alive?

_____

_____

_____

_____

_____

Talent, skills, experience, and opportunities all align with calling, but passion provides the fuel to pursue your calling.

3. YOUR CALLING IS IMPORTANT TO YOU, BUT IT'S NOT ABOUT YOU

A true calling is never about the person being called. It's about helping others. A calling moves us from the center of everything in our world to becoming the channel through which good things come to others. As Nelson Mandela said, "What counts in life is not the mere fact that we have lived. It is what difference we have made to the lives of others that will determine the significance of the life we lead." When you're called, you have an important role to play, but it's never about you.

CONSIDER

If you could do only one thing to help others in this world, what would it be?

_____

_____

_____

_____

4. YOUR CALLING IS BIGGER THAN YOU

A calling always involves something that feels big, something that's bigger than you are. It may intimidate you. It may even seem impossible. Yet you feel compelled to get out of your comfort zone to fulfill it. You are willing to stretch to complete it. You keep moving forward despite the odds.

5. YOUR CALLING CHANGES YOUR PERSPECTIVE

Having a calling makes you see your world differently. Where you once saw only obligations and responsibilities, you will begin to see options and opportunities. No longer will you be focused on the tasks you are required to do. A whole new world will open up to you of things you *want* to do.

CONSIDER

Take a look at the difference between the two perspectives of responsibility and opportunity. As you think about the one thing you might aspire to do in order to help others and improve the world, which phrase on each line best describes your perspective?

RESPONSIBILITY PERSPECTIVE	OPPORTUNITY PERSPECTIVE
❑ Feels Heavy	❑ Feels Light and Exciting
❑ Is a Burden	❑ Is a Privilege
❑ Consumes Energy	❑ Creates Energy
❑ Can Seem Meaningless and Rote	❑ Feels Purposeful and Meaningful
❑ Is Driven by a Sense of Duty	❑ Is Driven by a Sense of Optimism
❑ Is Something We Have to Do	❑ Is Something We Want to Do
❑ Leads to Routine and Repetition	❑ Inspires Creativity
❑ Discourages Efficiency	❑ Inspires Efficiency
❑ Tends to Drag Out Tasks	❑ Desires Bang for Our Buck
❑ Repels Others with Negativity	❑ Attracts Others with Positivity
❑ Gives a Sense of Completion	❑ Gives a Sense of Possibility
❑ Is Associated with Pushing	❑ Is Associated with Inspiring
❑ Leads to Success in 10 percent of Our Lives	❑ Leads to Success That Opens Up the Hidden 90 percent

A calling lifts our hearts and expands our options. It can make even the mundane meaningful. It drastically changes our perspective for the better.

6. YOUR CALLING GIVES YOU PURPOSE

Sheri Riley is a John Maxwell Team coach who has worked for many years with professional athletes and celebrity entertainers. She recently published her first book, called *Exponential Living*. In it she wrote about how many people get so caught up in the grind of life that they lose track of why they do it. She said:

> Many high achievers are so focused on working that work becomes an end in itself. They become addicted to the demands, the stress, and the sense of accomplishment they get from working hard, even if their hard work isn't leading them anywhere they want to go. Often, high achievers don't even realize they have achieved what they are working for and that it's time to move on to something else.
>
> Work is labor, folks. That's all it is. It has value only to the extent that it accomplishes something you truly desire. Many of us high achievers operate under some version of the Puritan work ethic. That is, we believe that work has value in and of itself. So therefore, if we do a lot of it, *we* must be valuable. So we take on lots of work, and keep ourselves very busy, but not necessarily as productive as we could. We exhaust ourselves because we confuse work with value. At the end of a tiring workweek, we look back and say, "Well, at least I did *that*." We may not be any closer to our dreams, but we sure did work.[3]

At one end of the spectrum are people like the ones Sheri described, the high achievers who work for the sake of work. On the other end are people who work because they have to but find no fulfillment in what they do. Author Seth Godin was talking to these people when he said, "Instead of wondering what your next vacation is, maybe you should set up a life you don't need to escape from." The answer for both types of people is the sense of purpose that comes with a calling.

7. YOUR CALLING HELPS YOU TO OVERCOME OBSTACLES

What do you draw upon when you hit a wall in your life or your leadership? Do you rely on grit? Do you draw upon discipline? Do you work harder? All of these things are good, but they can't compare to the power of calling to keep you going.

My friend Dave Ramsey said, "Higher calling matters. When you care so deeply about the why—why you're doing what you're doing—then and only then are you operating in a way that allows you to overcome the obstacles."

8. YOUR CALLING BRINGS FULFILLMENT

Nothing in life is as rewarding as fulfilling your calling—nothing. Wealth, fame, achievement, recognition: all of them fall short. Why do you think so many celebrities and athletes champion causes? They're looking for the fulfillment that comes only from pursuing a calling.

I've observed and known many who lived without a calling. As the years pass, their deepest needs and desires go unexplored. They are busy, but they develop a vague anxiety that their life has not achieved its ultimate meaning and significance. They live with a restlessness because they are not firmly attached to the moral purposes that give life its worth. Because they don't follow a calling, they lack the internal compass to make unshakable commitments. They never develop the inner consistency that they long for. Every day they come up short in obtaining the fulfillment they crave, and it frustrates them.

Calling changes everything. It's the missing piece in the puzzle. The plot in a good story. The musical note that completes the piece. Every day I experience the euphoric feeling of fulfillment as I write, speak, and lead. When I'm engaged in my calling, the sense that I experience is, "I was born for this!"

FINDING YOUR CALLING

So, what is your calling? Have you already discovered it? Are you finding clues as you answer the questions in this lesson? Or do you need some extra help finding your way? Fred Swaniker, the founder of the African Leadership Group, said, "Every now and then, we come to a fork in the road that requires us to either stay on our current life path, or change course and do something radically different." If you have not already found your calling, then you are at the fork in the road. I hope you will take the bold way, the radically different path that represents your calling. It may be frightening. It may be uncomfortable. It may feel uncertain. But I can assure you, if you find your calling, you will never regret the difficult journey taken to pursue it, because there's nothing else like it.

When I was in a class in college, a professor asked three questions to help us understand ourselves and find the pathway for our lives. Since I first heard them, I have asked them of myself repeatedly. Those three questions are:

1. What do I sing about? What fills my heart?
2. What do I cry about? What breaks my heart?
3. What do I dream about? What lifts my heart?

These questions set me on the journey that enabled me to discover my calling. As time went by, I experienced moments that spoke to me at a deep level of purpose:

- *Singing Moments*—Times when I knew that my leadership was making a positive difference for people.
- *Crying Moments*—Times when I wept because I saw that bad leadership misused or abused people.
- *Dreaming Moments*—Times when I dreamed of training leaders who would make a significant impact on people.

You'll notice that all these moments related to leadership because that's where my calling is.

CONSIDER

To find your calling, find what touches your heart. Answer the three questions:

What do you sing about? What fills your heart?

_____

_____

_____

_____

_____

_____

What do you cry about? What breaks your heart?

_____

_____

_____

What do you dream about? What lifts your heart?

_____

_____

_____

You may find your calling in a moment as I did, but I don't think you can force it to appear immediately if you haven't already discovered it. It usually takes time to unfold. I can look back at years of leadership moments, good and bad experiences, feelings of both discontent and contentment that set me up for my calling and prepared me for it. My best advice is to be attentive. Pay attention to your feelings. Take time to reflect. Learn from your experiences. Never dismiss your dreams. And when your moment comes, embrace it.

REVIEW AND RESPOND

Spend some time reviewing all of your responses in this lesson. Do you see a pattern that reveals or points in the direction of your calling? How do your answers line up? What is the common theme? What do you believe your purpose and calling might be? Describe it and date it here.

_____

_____

_____

_____

_____

_____

_____

HOW TO MAXIMIZE YOUR CALLING

I don't know what phase of life you're in as you read this book. Maybe you're simply doing a job and hoping for more. Perhaps you've developed a career yet still long for something more. If either of these is true, keep working your way toward your calling. However, you might be in the season of life where you know your calling and you're working out what to do with it. If that describes you, then I want to give you some advice. And if this does not yet describe you, then mark these words for when you do enter your calling season:

1. INTEGRATE A DAILY FOCUS WITH A LONG-TERM PERSPECTIVE

In his book *The Life Cycle Completed*, Erik Erikson told a joke about a man who is on his deathbed. As he lay there with his eyes closed, his wife whispered to him, naming every member of the family who was there to wish him shalom. "And who," he suddenly asked, sitting up abruptly, "who is minding the store?"[4]

People who have a sense of calling need to maintain a daily focus without losing their long-term perspective. I think of this as using both the clock and the compass. The clock helps me to stay on track with what I'm doing today. It encourages me to invest in my daily activities and to keep appointments. It allows me to fulfill the mission of the moment.

The compass helps me to stay on track with my destiny. It allows me to focus on the vision. It helps me know where I'm going. I maintain my overall values. I keep the vision before me. It allows me to fulfill the mission of my calling.

CONSIDER

How can you use the idea of the clock and the compass to help keep you on track?

_____

_____

_____

_____

_____

2. SET A CLEAR PATH IN A WORTHWHILE DIRECTION

One of the paradoxes of life is that you must follow your calling with clarity and purpose while living with uncertainty. So go forward in a direction that is worthy of the expenditure of your life, and go with confidence, but expect to write your story in pencil—one that has an eraser! I say that because as you pursue your calling, your life will be written and rewritten. Some experiences will end in a period—a full stop. Others will need the pause of a comma. You will have exclamation mark moments of victory and contentment. And of course, there will be many question marks.

Where will you end up if you follow your calling? Only time will tell. But the journey will be worth it, and the story will be amazing.

3. ASK OTHERS TO JOIN WITH YOU AND YOUR CALLING

Because every person's true calling is bigger than the one who has been called, it always requires the aid of others to fulfill it. If you've found your calling and not yet asked others to join you in it, you have neglected a crucial step, and it's time to start enlisting help. People who are successful often leave an inheritance for others. People who fulfill a calling leave a legacy *in* others.

CONSIDER

Have you invited others to join you in the effort you are making to improve the world? If not, why not? Who can you invite now? If so, who are they, and are you doing all you can to empower and release them to make a difference?

I hope you will do whatever you can to search for your calling, and then work with everything you have to fulfill it. And I hope that you will embrace not only this leadershift but all the other ones I've discussed in this book. Remember, every advance you make as a leader will require a leadershift that changes the way you think, act, and lead. You can only reach your potential if you embrace these leadershifts:

- Soloist to Conductor—The Focus Shift
- Goals to Growth—The Personal Development Shift
- Perks to Price—The Cost Shift
- Pleasing People to Challenging People—The Relational Shift
- Maintaining to Creating—The Abundance Shift
- Ladder Climbing to Ladder Building—The Reproduction Shift
- Directing to Connecting—The Communication Shift
- Team Uniformity to Team Diversity—The Improvement Shift
- Positional Authority to Moral Authority—The Influence Shift
- Trained Leaders to Transformational Leaders—The Impact Shift
- Career to Calling—The Passion Shift

Are there other leadershifts that you'll have an opportunity to make? Probably. I haven't yet discovered them, but if they're out there, I intend to. Why? Because long ago I made the personal development shift from goals to growth, and I'm still growing as a leader. If you're growing, you will discover them too. When you do, let me and others know about them. The better we can lead and help others to lead, the greater and more fulfilling our impact will be.

CAREER TO
CALLING

THE PASSION SHIFT

DISCUSSION QUESTIONS

1. Do you find it easy or difficult to believe that all people have a calling and can identify and embrace it if they're willing to try? Explain.

2. How would you describe your current work situation? You do a job, you are building a career, or you are fulfilling a calling. How content are you there?

3. How difficult do you think it is to find a purpose that makes the most of your talents, taps into your passion, fuels your passion, benefits others, is bigger than you, gives you purpose and perseverance, fulfills you, and draws you forward? Explain your answer.

4. How do you answer the questions about what makes you sing, cry, and dream?

5. Based upon what you know about yourself today, how would you describe your calling or purpose as you understand it so far? What action are you willing to take to pursue or fulfill it?

NOTES

ABOUT THE AUTHOR

John C. Maxwell is a #1 *New York Times* bestselling author, coach, and speaker who has sold more than 31 million books in fifty languages. He has been identified as the #1 leader in business by the American Management Association and the most influential leadership expert in the world by *Business Insider* and *Inc.* magazine. He is the founder of The John Maxwell Company, The John Maxwell Team, EQUIP, and the John Maxwell Leadership Foundation, organizations that have trained millions of leaders from every country of the world. A recipient of the Horatio Alger Award, as well as the Mother Teresa Prize for Global Peace and Leadership from the Luminary Leadership Network, Dr. Maxwell speaks each year to Fortune 500 companies, presidents of nations, and many of the world's top business leaders. He can be followed at Twitter.com/JohnCMaxwell. For more information about him visit JohnMaxwell.com.

ENDNOTES

Lesson One: Why Every Leader Needs to Leadershift

1. Eric J. McNulty, "Thinking Like a Leader: Three Big Shifts," Strategy and Business, July 28, 2015, https://www.strategy-business.com/blog/Thinking-Like-a-Leader-Three-Big-Shifts.
2. Bruna Martinuzzi, "The Agile Leader: Adaptability," Mindtools, accessed October 6, 2017, https://www.mindtools.com/pages/article/newLDR_49.htm.
3. *The Flux Report: Building a Resilient Workforce in the Face of Flux* (London: Right Management, 2014), p. 6, https://www.rightmanagement.co.uk/wps/wcm/connect/350a18c6-6b19-470d-adba-88c9e0394d0b/Right+Management+Flux+Report+Spread.pdf?MOD=AJPERES.
4. Paul Karofsky, quoted in Eric Yaverbaum, *Leadership Secrets of the World's Most Successful CEOs: 100 Top Executives Reveal the Management Strategies That Made Their Companies Great* (Chicago: Dearborn Trade, 2004), p. 161.
5. Maria Popova, "Malcolm Gladwell on Criticism, Tolerance, and Changing Your Mind," Brain Pickings, June 24, 2014, https://www.brainpickings.org/2014/06/24/malcolm-gladwell-nypl-interview/ (emphasis original).
6. C. Vijayakumar, "Three Key Steps to Making Sure Your Skills Stay Relevant," World Economic Forum, May 24, 2017, https://www.weforum.org/agenda/2017/05/3-key-steps-to-making-sure-your-skills-stay-relevant/.
7. Brad Lomenick, *The Catalyst Leader: 8 Essentials for Becoming a Change Maker* (Nashville: Thomas Nelson, 2013), pp. 111–112.

Lesson Two: Soloist to Conductor

1. Laurence Vittes, "Four Soloists Talk About Stepping Up to the Conductor's Podium," *Strings*, March 11, 2016, http://stringsmagazine.com/4-soloists-talk-about-stepping-up-to-the-conductors-podium/.
2. Matthew 25:40.
3. Matthew Kelly, *The Four Signs of a Dynamic Catholic: How Engaging 1% of Catholics Could Change the World* (Hebron, KY: Beacon Publishing, 2012), Kindle location 2382 of 2488.

Lesson Three: Goals to Growth

1. Adlai E. Stevenson, "The Educated Citizen," speech at Princeton University, March 22, 1954, transcript accessed January 10, 2018, http://infoshare1.princeton.edu/libraries/firestone/rbsc/mudd/online_ex/stevenson/adlai1954.html.
2. C. S. Lewis, *Of Other Worlds: Essays and Stories* (1966, New York: Houghton Mifflin Harcourt, 2002), p. 26.

Lesson Four: Perks to Price

1. Jim Collins, *Good to Great: Why Some Companies Make the Leap . . . and Others Don't* (New York: Harper Business, 2001), p. 85.
2. Ibid, p. 86.
3. Original source unknown.
4. Douglas L. Wilson and Rodney O. Davis, eds., *Herndon's Informants: Letters, Interviews, and Statements About Abraham Lincoln* (Champaign, IL: University of Illinois Press, 1998), p. 164.
5. "Cal Ripken's 2,131st Consecutive Game Is Major League Baseball's Most Memorable Moment," mlb.com, accessed December 11, 2017, http://www.mlb.com/mlb/events/memorable_moments/mlb_memorable_moments.jsp.
6. Bucky Fox, "Cal Ripken Wields an Iron Will While Winning in Baseball," *Investor's Business Daily*, August 26, 2017, https://www.investors.com/news/management/leaders-and-success/cal-ripken-wields-an-iron-will-while-winning-in-baseball/.

Lesson Five: Pleasing People to Challenging People

1. Seth Godin, *Poke the Box* (New York: Penguin, 2015), p. 25.

Lesson Six: Maintaining to Creating

1. Roger von Oech, *A Whack on the Side of the Head: How You Can Be More Creative*, 3rd ed. (New York: Warner Books, 1998).
2. Albert Einstein, quoted in Jeff Nilsson, "Albert Einstein: 'Imagination Is More Important Than Knowledge,'" *Saturday Evening Post*, March 20, 2010, http://www.saturdayeveningpost.com/2010/03/20/history/post-perspective/imagination-important-knowledge.html.
3. Thomas Edison, quoted in M. A. Rosanoff, "Edison in His Laboratory," *Harper's Magazine,* 135 (September 1932), p. 403, col. 2.
4. Hugh MacLeod, *Ignore Everybody: And 39 Other Keys to Creativity* (New York: Portfolio, 2009), p. 26.
5. As summarized in Martin Zwilling, "Follow Seven Rules for a Creative Startup Culture," *Forbes*, April 10, 2011, https://www.forbes.com/sites/martinzwilling/2011/04/10/follow-seven-rules-for-a-creative-startup-culture/.
6. Robert D. Kaplan, "Man Versus Afghanistan," *The Atlantic*, April 2010, https://www.theatlantic.com/magazine/archive/2010/04/man-versus-afghanistan/307983/.
7. Mary Ardito, "Creativity: It's the Thought That Counts," *Bell Telephone Magazine*, 61 (1), p. 33, https://quoteinvestigator.com/2014/03/03/creative-maya/.
8. Steve Pavlina, "Do It Now," StevePavlina.com (blog), November 28, 2005, https://www.stevepavlina.com/blog/2005/11/do-it-now/.
9. Warren Bennis, quoted in Max Cates, *Seven Steps to Success for Sales Managers: A Strategic Guide to Creating a Winning Sales Team Through Collaboration*, 1st ed. (Indianapolis: Pearson FT Press, 2015), p. 26.

Lesson Seven: Ladder Climbing to Ladder Building

1. Lead Through Strengths, "Explore the Clifton Strengthfinder Talent Theme—Woo," Strengthsfinder, accessed May 16, 2018, http://leadthroughstrengths.com/woo/.
2. Napoleon Hill, *The Law of Success* (New York: Penguin, 2008), p. 420.
3. Tim Elmore, "Becoming a Life Giving Mentor," October 19, 2012, *Growing Leaders: Ready for Real Life*, https://growingleaders.com/blog/life-giving-mentor/.

Lesson Eight: Directing to Connecting

1. Bob Buford, *Halftime: Moving From Success to Significance* (Grand Rapids: Zondervan, 2008), p. 118.
2. Stephen King, commencement address, Poughkeepsie, NY, Vassar College, May 20, 2001. Transcribed from "Vassar College Commencement," video, C-SPAN, May 20, 2001, https://www.c-span.org/video/?164360-1/vassar-college-commencement.
3. Mark Moring, "Chronicling Caspian," Christianity.com, May 1, 2008, https://www.christianity.com/11622775/.
4. Charles M. Schwab, "Mr. Carnegie Understood This Great Thing," *System* (June 1922), 679, accessed May 17, 2018, https://books.google.com/books?id=rQRKAQAAMAAJ&dq=System%20Charles%20Schwab%20exalted&pg=PA679.

Lesson Nine: Team Uniformity to Team Diversity

1. Jon R. Katzenbach and Douglas K. Smith, "The Discipline of Teams," *Harvard Business Review*, March–April 1993, https://hbr.org/1993/03/the-discipline-of-teams-2.
2. Patrick Lencioni, *The Five Dysfunctions of a Team: A Leadership Fable* (San Francisco: Josey-Bass, 2002), p. 202.
3. Ibid, pp. 202–203.
4. Christie Smith and Stephanie Turner, *The Radical Transformation of Diversity and Inclusion: The Millennial Influence* (Westlake, TX: Deloitte University, 2015), p. 7, https://www2.deloitte.com/content/dam/Deloitte/us/Documents/about-deloitte/us-inclus-millennial-influence-120215.pdf.
5. Ibid., p. 5.
6. Ibid., p. 11.
7. Ibid., p. 13.

8. Tomas Chamorro-Premuzic, "Does Diversity Actually Increase Creativity?" *Harvard Business Review*, June 28, 2017, https://hbr.org/2017/06/does-diversity-actually-increase-creativity.

9. Stefanie K. Johnson, "What 11 CEOs Have Learned About Championing Diversity," *Harvard Business Review*, updated August 29, 2017, https://hbr.org/2017/08/what-11-ceos-have-learned-about-championing-diversity.

10. 1Chamorro-Premuzic, "Does Diversity Actually Increase Creativity?"

Lesson Ten: Positional Authority to Moral Authority

1. Kevin Sharer, "How Moral Authority Manifests in Truly Impactful Leaders," *The Harbus*, March 17, 2017, http://www.beatthegmat.com/mba/2017/03/17/moral-authority-in-truly-impactful-leader.

2. Chuck Olson, "Four Ways to Build Moral Authority," Lead with Your Life (website), January 5, 2016, https://leadwithyourlife.com/4-ways-to-build-moral-authority/.

3. George Lewis Davis, *Magic Shortcuts to Executive Success: 37 Ways and Timely Moves That Can Smooth the Path and Lead to More Rapid Promotion and More Important Jobs* (Upper Saddle River, NJ: Prentice Hall, 1962), p. 110.

4. Doug Hall with David Wecker, *Making the Courage Connection: How People Get from Fear to Freedom—and How You Can Too* (New York: Fireside, 1997), p. 47.

5. Andy Stanley, *Visioneering: God's Blueprint for Developing and Maintaining Vision* (Colorado Springs: Multnomah, 1999), p. 179.

Lesson Eleven: Trained Leaders to Transformational Leaders

1. Lawrence Tribble, "Awaken" (c. 1780), Push Back Now (website), October 31, 2011, http://pushbacknow.org/2011/10/31/awaken-a-1700s-poem-by-lawrence-tribble/comment-page-1/.

2. Walter E. Fauntroy, quoted in Pat Williams with Jim Denney, *The Pursuit: Wisdom for the Adventure of Your Life* (Ventura, CA: Regal, 2008), p. 196.

Lesson Twelve: Career to Calling

1. Amy Wrzesniewski et al., "Jobs, Careers, and Callings: People's Relations to Their Work," *Journal of Research in Personality* 31 (1997), pp. 21–33, http://faculty.som.yale.edu/amywrzesniewski/documents/Jobscareersandcallings.pdf.

2. Richard Leider, "Is Leading Your Calling?" *Leader to Leader*, Winter 2004, http://www.geneva.edu/graduate/assets/msol_writing_sample_article.pdf, p. 2.

3. Sheri Riley, *Exponential Living: Stop Spending 100% of Your Time on 10% of Who You Are* (New York: New American Library, 2017), p. 191.

4. Erik Erikson, quoted in Emily Esfahani Smith, "Psychology Shows It's a Big Mistake to Base Our Self-Worth on Our Professional Achievements," Quartz, May 24, 2017, https://qz.com/990163/psychology-shows-its-a-big-mistake-to-base-our-self-worth-on-our-professional-achievements/.

LEADERSHIP
FOUNDATION

transforming
LEADERS

transforming
COUNTRIES

Together,
WE CAN CHANGE THE WORLD.
jmlf.org

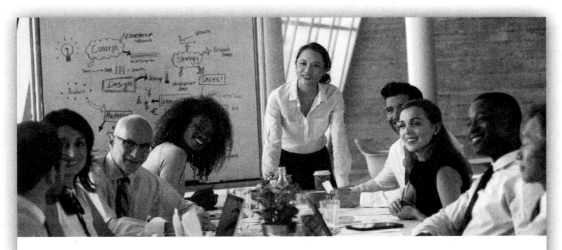

LEADERSHIP IS TAUGHT.
DEVELOP THE LEADERS WITHIN
YOUR COMPANY.

When you begin to invest in your human capital, watch what happens. Your workforce becomes aligned with your corporate initiatives. They begin supporting critical business priorities and change efforts, AND your business success begins to accelerate.

LEADERSHIP DEVELOPMENT   **EMPLOYEE ENGAGEMENT**   **CHANGE MANAGEMENT**